Sunlight and Shadow

Sunlight and Shadow

SUE BOGGIO MARE PEARL

University of New Mexico Press
Albuquerque

To Our Beloved Parents:

Joe and De Overturf
and
Dave and Fredia Pearl

First UNM Press edition 2012 published by arrangement with the authors.

Printed in the United States of America

17 16 15 14 13 12 1 2 3 4 5 6

Library of Congress Cataloging-in-Publication Data
Boggio, Sue.
Sunlight and shadow / Sue Boggio and Mare Pearl. — 1st UNM Press ed.
p. cm.
ISBN 978-0-8263-5276-7 (pbk. : alk. paper) — ISBN 978-0-8263-5277-4 (electronic)
1. Pregnant women—Fiction. 2. Missing persons—Fiction.
3. San Diego (Calif.)—Fiction. 4. New Mexico—Fiction. 5. Domestic fiction.
6. Conflict of generations—Fiction. I. Pearl, Mare. II. Title.
PS3602.A395S86 2012
813'.6—dc23

2012013014

Composition by Maya Allen-Gallegos
Composed in Palatino LT Std 10.25/13.5
Display type is Nueva Std

Acknowledgments

We are thrilled UNM Press is bringing new life to *Sunlight and Shadow*. Thanks to our intrepid editor in chief Clark Whitehorn and John Byram, director of UNM Press, for their vision. We appreciate all of the knowledgable professionals at UNM Press for their help every step of the way.

Sunlight and Shadow reached so many readers in its 2004 NAL/Penguin edition, and so many readers reached out to us to let us know how much they connected with the good folks of Esperanza and that they hoped that their story would continue. At the same time, we began to experience a deepening drought in New Mexico with serious ramifications to the environment, devastating fires, and hardship for the local farmers.

We began to imagine how this would impact the Vigil's chile farm, Sol y Sombra. Those issues, plus a few lingering ramifications from *Sunlight and Shadow*, sowed the seeds for our new novel, *A Growing Season*. And now, *Sunlight and Shadow* is reborn to join *A Growing Season* as its companion piece.

We are so grateful for the love and support of our parents and husbands. Our children and grandchildren enrich our lives beyond measure. We treasure our lifelong friendship and writing collaboration and feel so fortunate to be able to share our work with you, the reader.

Chapter 1

Abby dreamed differently now that she was pregnant. Her dreams pulled her into complex worlds that felt like an alternate universe populated with fascinating characters and illustrated with vivid colors never before seen or named.

Lying in bed, drifting between one of those compelling worlds and her real world, Abby felt her baby move for the first time. At first she thought it was some sensory trick of the dream. But as the dream dissolved, the quick insistent flutter just above her pubic bone told her this was real. She kept still, held her breath, and hoped it would happen again.

Abby wished her husband were there. Though it would be impossible to feel, Bobby would place his strong brown hand over the small tight mound of her belly and swear he felt his first child dance. He would grin and excited Spanish words would tumble out, too fast for her to translate. His impeccable English was for routine communication. Anything springing from passion came out in Spanish, whether it was when making love, watching his precious San Diego Padres baseball team, or tasting one of her new creations at her restaurant.

Two more days and he'll be here, she told her baby in the silent language that crosses through the placenta and whispers gently into tiny ear buds. She looked down to the gap between her short gray cotton tank top and bikini bottoms and peered in the early morning light at her white, faintly freckled abdomen. She was only in her fourth month, so Bobby would be with her for the most important part of her pregnancy. He was finishing the last three-month rotation of Navy submarine duty he would ever do. After twelve years, ten of them as a married man, Bobby Silva was finally coming home for good.

She loved to call him by his full name. Bobby Silva rolled off her tongue in a faintly erotic way. She learned she was pregnant the day before he shipped out. He hadn't missed much. Aside from her long hours at Abigail's, her successful restaurant in the Gaslamp District of her native San Diego, all she did was sleep. The very bed she lounged in was directly over her restaurant's kitchen. Thank God she didn't have morning sickness since her entire life revolved around food.

The phone rang and she knew before picking it up it would be Edward, her chef. Edward was the closest friend she had. Despite her very public life, sharing her public self with an entire city, only Bobby got to see behind the veil. Emotionally, he was her entire world, the world that mattered. Edward was her friend because he understood that.

"Good morning, Edward," she said.

"Do I have to come up there and throw you in the shower myself?" Edward asked.

"I'm pregnant, Edward. The baby just moved and I felt it."

"You're what?"

"Don't panic, it won't affect the restaurant. I'm just tired of keeping it to myself."

"How dare you keep it to yourself anyway! Is it mine?"

"Edward, we've never had sex. And without a doubt, you are the most gay man I know."

"Really? Thanks! But that's the only reason or I'd be jumping your bones every night your gorgeous husband's away."

"See, Edward, you'd rather jump Bobby's bones."

Before Bobby could set down his duffel bag, Abby had him in bed. No one told her pregnancy would cause such intense arousal. She was constantly finding the rub of her own clothing so stimulating, the increasing tightness of her bra against her ever-erect nipples, the hot dampness of her panties between her legs. It was a kind of physical hunger she had never known and even after pressing her own hand to her insistent flesh, the relief was marginal and short-lived. These were animalistic, primitive urges vastly different from her usual enthusiastic but more cerebral sexual feelings. Hormones, she realized with newfound appreciation for biology.

She came so violently she couldn't breathe, her strangled cries turning to sobs in Bobby's arms. She laughed and cried as the shudders finally subsided and she could hear Bobby's worried voice asking her what was wrong.

"Never leave me again," was all she could say.

They napped together then. Abby woke to the scent of roses and thought she was having olfactory hallucinations until she saw the bouquet Bobby had brought her scattered around the bed with them. The red roses seemed perfectly placed around their heads and in the folds of the white sheets, as if some interior designer had arranged them while they slept. She wanted to get them into some water but didn't want to disturb Bobby. They were entwined, his arm around her middle, his head on her breasts, her legs over his. The contrast of their skin tones reminded her of vanilla fudge swirl ice cream. A strand of her auburn hair wound over his dark thick locks. This was the moment she would keep in some inner pocket. A moment so complete and imbued with a clarity missing from the countless other moments lives are comprised of, when like insects, people go about their busy tasks failing to notice the perfection that surrounds them. Her baby stirred, her breaths matched Bobby's in tempo. Inhalation, exhalation. Rhythmic waves lapping the beach of this private shore, this sacred place.

Later, as they were dressing for the restaurant, Abby caught Bobby staring at her. She let her black slip slide over her head and settle over her like a second silken skin. She shook her collar length hair, finally growing out after that too short bob. What had she been thinking? A couple of passes through her auburn strands with her fingers and her hair curved naturally to rest against the base of her neck. Still, Bobby sat on the edge of the bed, his socks in his hand, burning holes into her with his charcoal gaze.

"What?" She blurted and then softened it with a smile.

He sighed, shook his head. "I look at you and I'm so happy it hurts." His hand still holding a sock went to his heart. "I can't feel this much happiness without feeling pain."

Abby came over to him, cradled his head against her abdomen. "Pain?"

"You are my heart. *Mi corazón.* You and the baby. I could never lose you—"

She wove her fingers through the black denseness of his close-cropped hair. She was used to the intensity of his feelings by now. In the beginning, his extreme passions were startling and foreign. Whether it was his culture's influence or just Bobby's own nature, she loved his capacity to experience everything so fully. "We aren't going anywhere. And finally, you won't have to go anywhere, either. It's over, babe. No more waiting months to be together, dreading you having to go again—it's over. We can be together all the time. You'll probably get sick of me!" She tousled his hair.

But when his eyes looked up at her, the shadows remained. "If anything ever happened to you . . ."

She knew then he was thinking about his mother, Magdalena. She had been pregnant with her second child and four-year-old Bobby had just been told he would be getting a new baby brother or sister when a drunk driver took them both away. Abby realized her own pregnancy must be stirring up the long buried trauma. "Hon, you didn't lose your mom because she was pregnant, it was an accident, a tragic, unpreventable accident. Think of the odds. Women have babies all the time, and everything goes perfectly. I'm healthy and strong. This is a happy thing, you don't have to be so worried."

He put his hands on her small waist and backed her up a step so he could stand to his full six feet two inches, and look down into her eyes. Abby could feel him summoning his strength, his adult male power.

"I don't think it's good for you to work so hard. On your feet for hours—"

"I'm not doing as much. Besides the doctor said to keep doing all my normal activities—"

"Normal is taking a walk, not lifting heavy hot trays from the oven, working nonstop for twelve, fourteen hours a day!"

"I hired two more sous chefs for Edward. I'm doing less actual work and more supervising. Edward is taking on more. I'm not much more than a glorified hostess!" She knew he wouldn't buy that last one. She was compulsively hands-on. "And now you're here to help."

"What about all the stress? There's a crisis every five minutes—"

"It isn't stress when you love it as much as I do. Look, we'll have to fight about this later. We need to get down there." She could feel the energy throbbing beneath her feet in the restaurant below. The pace had picked up in the kitchen. Only she could ever discern such a thing. No one could love it more.

"Great night," Paul said, snapping shut his laptop. Edward's brother had been Abigail's accountant and bartender since opening six years earlier. The Jimenez brothers couldn't have been more different from each other or more important to Abby. Paul took a gulp of his scotch, knocking the rocks together for emphasis. "We keep making money like this, we're going to have to get some of it sheltered or the taxes are going to break our balls."

"You're such a poet, Pauly," Abby said, stifling her yawn. It had been a great night. Incredibly smooth. Just the kind of night she prayed for to show Bobby this place practically ran itself. Edward had choreographed the kitchen into an up-tempo dance of fire and knives. Edward, Jamie, Christoff, and the new guy, Peter, turned out stunning plates in record time. Abby had started out the night checking every entree before her three seasoned servers whisked them to each of the twenty tables. Seeing it was hardly necessary, she spent her time circulating in the dining area, visiting with her guests, keeping an eye on the busboy. Paul had tried to convince her to put another six or eight tables into the room. There was space for it. But she liked the airy feeling, the privacy only twenty tables afforded and the number seemed right for the size of the kitchen, keeping the pace manageable.

Edward and Bobby emerged from the kitchen, laughing and goofing around. Good. Bobby looked relaxed. He'd stuffed himself on at least four courses that Abby had seen.

"God, the food is amazing! My God, that crab dish! I need to come here more often." He sat on the bar stool next to her and poured himself another glass of wine. He clinked her glass of sparkling water in toast.

"How's the new guy?" Abby asked Edward as he poured himself some tequila.

"Skilled. A little intense, though. He gets a very naughty look in his eye when he torches the crème brulée."

Abby felt a contentment that at last was complete. Her recently refinished wood floors reflected the warm glow of the candlelight; an eclectic collection of art from local artists graced the walls she and Edward had replastered and sponge-painted themselves. Everywhere she looked she saw the materialization of her lifelong dream. She half-closed her eyes and listened to her precious husband's lightly accented cadence as he and Edward continued their banter . . . the words didn't matter, the lilt of their voices and laughter was music composed just for her. The scent of her various culinary creations still hung in the air, an olfactory accompaniment. Her baby moved, stirring her to an even deeper, soul-expanding epiphany of perfection, of gratitude.

Paul put his empty glass in the tub under the bar and gathered up his briefcase and laptop. "Don't leave my bar a mess. I'm outta here. Sandy'll cut me off if I'm any later. Here's your loot." He laid the bulging cash bag on the bar in front of Abby.

"'Night, Paul. Have a great day off, say hi to Sandy for me." Abby squeezed his hand. "Thanks for everything." As emotionally ebullient as Edward was, his brother was only marginally tolerant of such affection, though she suspected he enjoyed it more than he let on.

Edward tossed back the last of his tequila. "I need a ride, Bro, my car's in the shop—"

"I told you that car would be nothing but trouble—"

"But it's a guy magnet, I swear."

"Yeah, it attracts big burly mechanics who screw you—"

"I should be so lucky."

As the door swung shut behind them, Paul pointed to the keys in the lock and motioned for Abby to lock up after them. What a sweetie. So gruff, but always looking out for everyone.

"Finally, I have you alone!" Bobby leaned over and planted a wet, merlot-flavored kiss on her mouth. "Let's go upstairs."

"I'm going to snag a snack to take up, I'm hungry already. Your baby has one hell of an appetite."

"I'll just tidy the bar and lock up—"

The door burst open, the keys jangling uselessly in the lock. Two men in ski masks thrust guns in their faces. It happened so fast, Abby could only be disoriented. "What are you—?"

"Give us your cash, bitch!"

Bobby hesitated, the cash bag next his elbow. The man who spoke suddenly struck Bobby on his temple with his gun, knocking him from the bar stool onto the floor. Abby jumped down to him so quickly, both men cocked their guns.

Bobby sat dazed, a line of blood trailing down from his scalp to the side of his face. As Abby cried and cursed and tried to shelter him, one of the men pulled her away by her arm. His gun prodded her back, forcing her to stand.

"Leave her alone!" Bobby managed to moan. "Take the damn money and get out!"

One of the men laughed. "What a tough motherfucker! I'm scared!"

The other man ran his hand along Abby's shoulder. "She's even hotter than she looks on TV. Let's take her to the back—"

The first man grabbed up the cash bag. "Naw, we gotta go. We'll be sure to come back for a little taste of Abigail!"

"Specialty of the house, man!"

Abby nearly retched when the man who held her squeezed her breast before shoving her to the floor next to Bobby.

As soon as they rushed out, Bobby scrambled to his feet. "Call the cops—"

"Wait, are you all right?" Abby tried to stop him but he tore away from her, running to the stairs in the kitchen.

By the time Abby finished calling the police, her emotions had caught up to her. She had always been like that. So mechanical in a crisis. Numb and robotic until in the aftermath she dissolved into a quivering heap.

"I'm going to kill those punks!" Bobby said, taking the stairs two at a time. He'd retrieved his service revolver.

Abby blocked his way. "Stop, they're long gone. Let the police—"

She pressed herself to him, her tears starting to erupt.

He stood stiffly. "I couldn't do a damn thing. They were going to rape you—"

She looked into his face. The blood encrusting his left temple and eye was like garish Halloween makeup. His dilated pupils and widely opened eyes created an expression she had never seen before. "We're okay, honey. It's going to be all right." She felt him go slack and reached down to take the gun from his hand and place it on the bar. Their arms tightened around each other and they held on for dear life.

Neither of them slept much. The phone rang at eighty-thirty, a few short hours after they finished with the police and paramedics. Bobby picked it up. It was Paul, who had just heard about the robbery on the news.

"No, we're okay. Hit me on the head, but you know how hardheaded I am—probably broke his gun. Yeah, it's only money."

Abby sat up, feeling the strain in her neck and shoulder. The paramedics warned her she'd be stiff and sore. Bobby hadn't needed stitches, but he was supposed to take it easy today and follow up with his doctor the next day.

"What?" Bobby was saying in a tone that made Abby pay attention. He listened for another minute. "Holy mother of God!"

"What?" Abby asked.

"Thanks, Paul. Yeah, talk to Edward for us. At least it's Sunday and we can all get some rest. See you tomorrow." He put down the phone and faced Abby.

"After those punks left us they went to Nunzio's. Left two bodies in the walk-in freezer."

"Oh my God!" Abby said. "Was it Antonio and his wife?"

"They haven't released the names yet. Paul said they must have put up a struggle, the place was trashed."

"We were lucky."

Bobby looked at her as if she'd lost her mind. "That could have been us! Those punks are still out there! They said they'd come back for you, remember?"

"They wouldn't be so stupid! They're on the run, probably in Mexico by now."

Bobby got out of bed and grabbed his jeans. "This is no place to have a baby. We should move out of the city. We have the money for a nice house somewhere—"

"Bobby, I need to be close to the restaurant. I can't be some two-hour commute away."

He sighed and reached up to feel the bump on the side of his head as if only just remembering it.

Abby reached up to him and he took her hand and tenderly kissed it. He dropped the jeans he held and climbed back into bed.

The phone rang again sometime after they had fallen back to sleep. Abby found it in bed with them as Bobby continued his soft snores.

"Hello," she whispered.

A man with a slight accent asked for Roberto Silva.

"This is his wife, may I help you?"

"This is Miguel Vigil, Roberto's old friend and neighbor. I'm afraid I have some terrible news. His father has passed away, very suddenly, a short time ago. They think it was a heart attack."

Abby held the phone, feeling the pain her husband would have spread through her own chest. She looked at him sleeping and didn't want to wake him. Protectively she watched him breath in and out, preserving his peace, what little he was finding after their nightmare.

"Are you there?" The man was asking.

"Yes, I'm sorry. I'll break it to him and he could call you back, Mr. Vigil. Would that be all right?"

"Yes, of course. I'll give you my number."

Bobby stirred when she got up to find a pen and paper. He was awake when she hung up the phone.

"Was that Edward?" He looked at the clock. "God it's after noon!" He got out of bed and actually smiled. "I just had the nicest dream of us taking our baby to the zoo. We should go there today, get our minds off this shit." He opened the shades to another perfect California day. When she didn't say anything, he came over to her. "You're right Abby. I'm sorry. We should feel lucky, we're alive. It's an insult to God's mercy if we—"

"Oh, Bobby, sit down, I have to tell you something," she said and began to cry.

He cried for his dead father. Ricardo had raised him alone after Magdalena's death. Abby had never met him, though she had suggested trips back to New Mexico many times. Ricardo stubbornly refused to leave his small farm to visit them. Bobby had returned home once every few years and the visits always took their toll.

She knew he was sparing her from what to him had become an ordeal, a painful penance due for loving a life so far away from home with no respect for his father's wishes. Ricardo had never been the same after losing Magdalena, and had held on to his son all the tighter. Bobby told her how terrible he had felt breaking his father's heart a second time when he left home at eighteen to join the Navy. He had gone back on the unspoken agreement that he would stay and work the land beside his father. Bobby ripped his life from his father's loving grasp and set out with it to distant shores, foreign waters.

After his last visit home, Bobby said his father was polite but distant and treated him like an honored guest, the worst punishment he could imagine.

Now he was dead and as she watched her husband cry, she felt guilty. Guilty for loving her life here with him, guilty over their happiness that now seemed somehow at Ricardo's expense. Guilty because if the phone call had been about either one of her parents, her eyes would be as dry as stones.

But if she felt guilt, she knew Bobby's was immeasurable.

After calling Miguel Vigil, Bobby sat at their table and stared out the window. Since it was Sunday, the streets were fairly quiet. Neighbors and some tourists strolled the block. Willoughby's Antiques and Coffee Shop across the street was doing a brisk business. Good, Abby thought. The robberies and murders in the neighborhood weren't keeping people away. At least not in broad daylight.

Abby sat next to him, but it felt like she was in another universe. As much as she wanted to be close to him right now, it felt like his grief had taken him where she couldn't follow. She felt hopelessly inadequate. Everything she said felt hollow and wrong. Her tea grew cold in front of her as she hoped being here with him afforded at least some measure of comfort.

"I need to get out of here," Bobby announced. "We need to get out of here."

"We could go for a walk on the beach," Abby suggested.

"No, that's not what I meant. When we go to New Mexico to bury my father, let's stay."

"Stay? Like a visit?"

"Live there, Abby! It would be perfect! It's so beautiful and peaceful there you don't even have to lock your doors. Miles away from the city, everything so green by the river. The incredible mountains in the distance. I can see our child playing there on acres of his own land, just like I did."

Abby gaped at him in horror. He must be losing it. The ordeal of their robbery, head trauma, maybe he had a mild concussion. The shock of his father's death. He just wasn't thinking clearly. She tried to be calm. "Bobby, I understand, I do, why that would appeal to you right now, but, let's be realistic—"

"I know I'm asking a lot and it's coming from left field, but, think about it! It really is the answer to everything. It's like my dad is giving us this gift, his death is like a sacrifice so that we'll move there and live in the house I grew up in and provide a better environment, a community for our child, around people who look like him. His culture."

Luckily, Abby was too stunned to speak for a moment. What was she? The incubator for his offspring? What about her life, her culture? Around people who look like her baby? Wouldn't her baby look like both of them? "My life is here," she said.

"You and your family don't even speak! You have a restaurant here—so what? You're a chef. You can open a restaurant anywhere. Albuquerque is a big city and it's only twenty minutes away. Or Santa Fe—where all the movie stars go—it's a little more than an hour. I inherit my family's home and land—it's not so fancy as where you grew up. No tennis courts or swimming pools. But it is beautiful and no one is trying to kill you or rape you!"

Now they were getting down to it. Abby knew he'd get to the estranged family part. And now he had last night to throw in her face. "There's brutality and crime in rural areas, and you know it. I've lived here my whole life and last night was the only time anything has happened. It's not fair, Bobby! You said we would live here after you got out of the Navy! I've built something here all these years you've been on a submarine half the time! I'm supposed to give it all up?"

Bobby fixed her with an unrelenting gaze. "I don't remember ever discussing it. I don't remember ever being asked what I wanted. Twelve years I had no say—the Navy owned me! I'm a thirty-year-old man! When do I get a say about my life? The life I want for my family?"

Abby wiped the silent tears that blurred her vision and annoyed the hell out of her. She hated to cry in an argument. It made her feel weak and manipulative. She wanted strength and respect and a level head. She could see why he wanted to leave but couldn't believe he was asking this of her. He was everything to her. She would never leave him or end their marriage over geography or a business. It pissed her off that he knew it. "What choice are you giving me? What happens to us if you can't be happy here and I can't be happy there?"

He visibly softened; his own eyes were moist and full of sadness instead of anger. "I love you more than my life, Abigail. I swear to you, this isn't some selfish wish to be happy with no thought of your feelings. I never would want to hurt you; it kills me to push this so damn hard. We have a baby to think about now. A baby who will be growing so fast we have to think about his future now. You've never been to my home, how do you know you couldn't be happy there? I have close friends there that are family to me—the Vigils, CeCe and Miguel, are like second parents to me. Their daughter Rachel was . . . my closest friend. I hurt them all when I left. I miss them and I want my child to know them and love them, too, it's all I have left to give him. I want to go home."

"This is our home! I love this city! I love my restaurant! I love the shopping and the movies and the museums and the ocean. You always have, too. What about our trips to San Francisco, Napa Valley?"

"I never said we couldn't ever come back. We could vacation here."

She rolled her eyes. "We could vacation in New Mexico. We're talking about where to make our lives."

He was silent, his fingers drummed the table. She watched him trying to come up with the magic words. A win-win solution. She folded her arms across her heavy, sore breasts. As if she needed to be reminded they were having a baby!

"What about a compromise? It's the third week in May, no? The baby's due in October. We could sublet this place. Edward and Paul could run Abigail's. We could give it twelve months. One year to see how it goes. If you still want to come back after one year then I agree, no argument. That's how sure I am that once you are there you will fall in love with the place, the people and you will know our baby is better off there, too."

Abby tried to imagine it. Thinking of New Mexico conjured up nothing but old 1950s movies about the Old West and Mexico. Saloons and Poncho Villa.

"Think of it as some time off. Just to be together, slow down and enjoy the simple things in life. The last five months of your pregnancy you could sleep as much as you want. Garden, take walks. Read books. Gaze at the stars. Then we have our baby and we can, how do they say?—cocoon together. No pressures, just time to be together. We have plenty of money, savings, our investments. The house is free and clear. We can generate some income from alfalfa and chile crops if we want. One year out of our lives, it's all I'm asking."

She could argue that a year away could kill her restaurant. She was Abigail's. Once she was gone for any length of time, her regulars might drift away. If it did survive, even thrive, it would no longer be hers in any meaningful way. And forget about being a regular contributor to the local TV show, those appearances were tied to her presence at her restaurant. There was a long line behind her of talented, charismatic chefs from up-and-coming restaurants waiting to fill her shoes.

Trying to straddle two worlds by commuting several hours on a plane would be stressful and exhausting, especially since she hated to fly even when she wasn't pregnant. Leaving either world for the other on a regular basis would hurt everyone concerned and take all the pleasure out it.

She realized, their marriage, with ten years of Bobby's long absences and being stationed in San Diego, had postponed any real discussion or decision that other couples have to resolve all the time. She'd never had to face that a marriage is two people, two individual careers, backgrounds and dreams. But a marriage is nothing if not about how to make a union from two separate entities that will travel through time and that demand sacrifices on both parts for the good of the whole.

She'd had it her way so long and without question, she'd forgotten there was anyone else to consider. Her heart tore when she realized she would be wrong to refuse him this. One year to live his dream and then right of first refusal.

"Do you trust me, Abby?"

"Completely."

"Then, you know I would never trick you into going there and then go back on my word. I can't be happy if you aren't."

A tear slid down her cheek as the sad irony nearly made her smile. "And I can't be happy if you aren't. Do you trust me, Bobby?"

"Absolutely."

"Then you know I'll go there and I will honestly try to be happy. That's all I can do, is try."

"And if you can't be. We'll move back here. I promise." He reached for her hand and she gave it to him.

"What's the name of this place, again? My new home?"

"Esperanza. It means hope."

In typical fashion, Abby focused on what needed to be done and pushed her emotions into that storage compartment that served her so well. She met with Paul and Edward, redirected Paul's stunned argument and Edward's emotional outburst and obtained their cooperation to run

Abigail's in her absence. Her attorney drew up papers securing her position as absentee co-owner, giving autonomous management to Paul, with profit sharing and an option to buy her out in one year if she chose to remain in Esperanza. She filmed her last TV segment with Edward who delighted the station manager and producers with his flamboyant humor and spectacular culinary skills. They agreed to let him transition into her spot. She managed all of this in four days.

Each night when she wearily climbed the steps to their condo, she found Bobby had packed more of their lives into boxes. They would leave their towering potted palms and other plants for Paul and Sandy, who were subletting the place.

Abby had tried to send Bobby on ahead to Esperanza.

"No, I'd never stick you with all of this," he said, stacking another box by the door.

"But the arrangements . . . aren't you needed there?" She sank down into a corner of the sofa that wasn't covered with ski equipment or scuba gear. Even as she asked, she realized Bobby would need her at his side when he confronted the physical reality of his father's death.

"Miguel and CeCe are handling it. The Rosary isn't until Friday and the funeral mass is Saturday afternoon. I can drive while you sleep. The movers will be here to put it into storage until we call from Esperanza to have it transported out to us. Gives us some time to get the house ready. We'll just take a couple of suitcases, anything we need right away. I keep thinking he'll be there—isn't that crazy?" He smiled and shrugged while some tears spilled down his unshaven face.

She stood and he pulled her into his embrace. She felt his sandpaper jaw rest carefully against her temple, his hot tears traced a path down her cheek mingling with her own. Maybe it was crazy. All of it. But in his arms crazy somehow made sense.

Chapter 2

The crisp early-morning wind blew against Rachel, penetrating the denim shirt she threw over her undershirt to do her milking. She shuffled through the weeds along the well-worn path to the barn. The tightfisted buds of young dandelions hit against her boots like piano hammers, accompanying the bird songs all around her. She loved this land. She'd lived in Esperanza all of her thirty years, and the world beyond didn't hold any interest. She had her small goat dairy. Not a huge enterprise, but as much as she could handle on her own. She sold cheese, milk, and goat soap at village farmers' markets. But she didn't do it for the profits. Compared to the amount of work she put into it, it really wasn't cost-effective. But this was her life. She couldn't imagine working a job where you couldn't wear jeans and have a pair of work gloves sticking out of your back pocket or a good pocket knife on your belt. The chile fields, the goats, Ma and Papa. She could no sooner live without all of this than without her own heart.

"That all the milk you got today, Millie?" she asked her highest producing goat, patting its bony head while it tasted her shirt. Barely six pounds of milk today. All the goats had dropped in production. And she hadn't changed their routine in any way. But the bruja had told her they were picking up on something—even if we couldn't sense it. Sometimes just the scent of the devil as he passed by.

"Meh!" they all screamed with exposed tongues as she walked out of the barn. The pink and red hollyhocks stretched to the sun outside its adobe walls. The goat barn was the remains of an adobe house that had once stood on their property a century ago.

"Meh, yourselves!" she said, smiling as they continued their cries like abandoned babies.

She pulled her kerchief over her nose and mouth bandito-style as the winds embedded dirt in her teeth. Empty metal buckets rattled and clanked around her as the wind played them. She put down her pail and swooped into the horse barn to throw a couple of blocks of hay over their stalls. Phew! Charlie was behind on stall duty. She had wanted it written in their divorce decree that, by law, he would continue to tend to the stalls. Instead she settled for one of his scruffy broad-grinned promises. Half the time he acted like he never signed the divorce papers at all. Her parents either for that matter. He still worked the farm, kept the horses, and fixed all the farm equipment that was old broken-down farm equipment to begin with. He still ate two meals a day at the table with Ma and Papa, while she usually fixed a plate and sat on the porch or stood at the kitchen counter to eat. He now slept in one of those silver humpbacked trailers on her parent's land close to the river and not in her bed.

So she wasn't surprised to see him there as her mother made huevos rancheros for him, her father and two Mexican nationals he said he'd met at the coffee shop willing to put in a good day's work mending fences. Miguel, her father, spoke fluently to them in Spanish as they chased red chile around on their plates with the fresh flour tortillas her mother made every morning. One of the things Ma did to try to pass herself off as a good Mexican wife.

Rachel nodded a hello at the workers as they flashed jack-o'-lantern smiles back at her. They were telling Papa about their families. Charlie tended the chorizo in a cast-iron skillet while Ma answered the phone. He hadn't bothered to button his shirt. That was just like him. Food before decency. Like everyone wanted to see his rippled stomach with dark hair running down the center like trees along the river. Please.

"And how are you this fine morning, Miss Vigil?" he asked, like not being Mrs. Charlie Hood anymore was some sort of a crime. She was an idiot for still putting up with him, but her parents needed him. He could do a lot better for himself if he'd have shaved more than a couple of times a month. Some women found his scruffy good looks appealing, but not her. Look at Papa. Always kept himself up for Ma. Always had his dashing Zorro moustache trimmed and his face smelling like a woodsy breeze. Every day he showered and combed his hair after a long hot day on the farm to spend the evening with Ma. Like every night was date night. Charlie wanted sex the minute he'd come in from the fields and her fresh out of the barns cleaning and trimming hooves. Maybe he'd wipe himself down with his undershirt while clomping up the porch steps. Say he'd been thinking about her all day.

Ma pushed at the dark wisp of hair escaping from her favorite silver and turquoise combs. The patina of the silver grew more beautiful with age, just like Ma. Her brow crinkled as she listened to the black receiver, her tan hand turning white against it. It took a few blank seconds before she hung up the receiver.

"Ricardo Silva is dead," she said.

"I just helped him unload a flatbed of alfalfa. He's not dead," Charlie said, scooping a spatula full of chorizo dripping with deep orange grease and dumping it on his plate.

"He died of a heart attack. Didn't make it to"—her voice choked—"the hospital."

"What? No! That's impossible!" Rachel blurted. "You heard Charlie!"

"Miguel. Call Roberto—he'll need you," Ma said.

Their families had once been inseparable. Ma, Papa, Ricardo Silva, and his long-deceased wife, Magdalena, who Ma always called Maggie. Rachel hadn't known life back then without Roberto. By the time they were teenagers, she hadn't known if she could ever live without him. She imagined each parent would give them, as a wedding present, equal acreage and have them snuggled between them. *Familia.* When Roberto's and her hormones kicked in, they began having sex. Like people do when they love each other. He was her life. He made it all perfect. Roberto.

It was snowing the day he told her he had enlisted in the Navy. A freak early-autumn snow that made you want to dance in it like goats. She loved the look of him as it speckled his dark hair while he told her. It was hard to focus on his words. The Navy was his ticket out of there. Something about submarines. She hadn't even known he loved submarines. But that was what he wanted more than anything. More than her.

He promised to write. Said he loved her, too.

She wrote. Sometimes twice a day. Wrote long and hard into the night as she cried. Poured out her love in poetic letters. He was all she could think about. Roberto and her empty mailbox. The waiting became more excruciating as his letters waned. He didn't make it home for Christmas. Came back at Easter. She couldn't wait to see him. To be with him.

She planned a picnic. The early spring was still gentle and the sun had begun to warm the earth. They sat on an old Mexican blanket as she unpacked lunch. He was quiet as they ate, staring far away, as far away as his precious San Diego.

She deliberately had not worn underwear. Just a skirt and cotton sweater. No bra. He had been so beautiful the time he took his first taste of her breast. His first taste ever. It felt holy. She rubbed the outside of his pants as he tried to tell her about his new life. He grew hard fast. She had known all along he still wanted her, loved her. She got on her knees on the blanket and guided his fingers up under her skirt. He pushed her back on the blanket and took her hard and fast. A lot faster than she wanted. She watched as he stood facing away from her as he zipped up his jeans, framed by the purpling mountains in the distance.

His exact words escaped her now. What she remembered was they were like a sickle ripping out her intestines. He'd met someone else. He loved her and they were engaged, some white college girl named Abby in San Diego. He was going to marry someone else . . .

Charlie had been watching her expression as her father and mother spoke back and forth. The workers took mouthfuls of strong coffee after finishing up their breakfast. They swished it around in their cheeks like mouthwash.

It wasn't fair to Charlie. He could have had any woman he wanted. He was undeniably handsome in an Anglo way. Every woman at Midnight Rodeo asked him to dance. Especially during the slow and sloppy songs. She'd seen them reach down him, arms like serpents, and whisper chile-hot things into his ear. But she never got jealous, not with Charlie. All of her jealousy was reserved for the woman who had Roberto. Feeling like that, it was a merciful act to divorce Charlie, set him free.

And now he watched her as she relived the intensity of her loss and love for Roberto. She didn't know why he even stayed around. As long as Roberto was in this world, she could never have room in her heart for Charlie.

"I saw Ricardo a couple of days ago, but you know him, doesn't say much. He looked okay to me," her father said. He smoothed his moustache and coughed into his fist the way he did when emotional. "We drifted so far apart. I should have been a better friend."

"We all tried to reach him. You can't blame yourself," her mother said. "Call Roberto. He needs to hear he still has family here."

The men pushed away from the table as Miguel explained to them what had happened. Her mother looked her dead in the eye. "He'll be coming home."

Suddenly Abby was beside Bobby in their Camry as he drove her away from the life she had built, the life she had fully imagined and might never complete. For most of the time in their ten years of marriage, she was either anticipating his return from submarine tour or dreading his departure for another three months away. When he was home, he fit neatly into her established routines. His leaving the Navy was supposed to have been no different. He was going to slip into her life, do a little bar tending at Abigail's, help with the baby, pursue some hobbies like deep-sea fishing and sailing. The speed with which it all happened made her know what it was to lose everything in a flash flood or tornado or some other heinous act of God. And yet, she felt strangely calm. The details of her cherished business had fallen neatly into place. Abigail's couldn't be in better hands. It was a great opportunity for Edward and he deserved it. Paul would manage the restaurant into even greater success and it would all be there for her in one year if she wanted.

Meanwhile, with the love of her life next to her, it almost felt like they were embarking on an adventure. Maybe he was right. Maybe it would feel wonderful to slow down, be together, explore his homeland and his heritage and bring their firstborn child into a tranquil and nurturing atmosphere. Newborns were all-consuming little miracles and at least this way her baby wouldn't have to share her attention with the nonstop demands of a restaurant. In the meantime, if she started feeling bored, she could begin putting together ideas for a cookbook or see about landing a food column for syndication. A year from now, their baby would be seven months old, and she could resume her career in San Diego. If she wanted. She tried hard to hang on to this fledgling feeling of hope and used it to hold back her persistent doubts.

She slept through most of California and part of Arizona. She would wake briefly to Bobby singing softly along to some Spanish song on the radio, see flashes of barren, withered landscape and lapse back into the safe amnesia of sleep.

"Look at that sky," Bobby said. "Beautiful."

She had never seen a place where the sky overpowered everything under it, making even the sprawling city of Albuquerque appear to have a miniature downtown skyline. The flat-roofed homes and buildings visible from the freeway seemed squashed by the weight of its dark immensity. Wind whipped what trees there were, a gritty wind that Abby imagined was scarring the perfect pearl finish of their car.

"See, over to the southwest, that's the storm moving in. See the rain, those dark streaks? It'll be here in the next hour, watch." He hunched eagerly over the steering wheel, watching the sky more than the road. Insane drivers swerved around them like more debris carried by the wind.

They headed south. The distant green band that surrounded the Rio Grande River led the way into the verdant valley to their right.

"Esperanza's just past Isleta Indian Pueblo, about twenty minutes south of Albuquerque." Bobby had told her this several times already, like he was trying to reassure an anxious child. Or perhaps he was the anxious child.

Abby looked out of her window and realized she felt nothing and knew it was a good thing. Trash danced in circles on the highway shoulder. Scrubby brown vegetation dotted the dirt slopes. Nothing had any real color, everything had been painted with the same dirty brush. Monochromatic grays and browns of the earth blended into the oppressive sky.

Her baby fluttered, turning her thoughts gratefully inward.

They exited the freeway and passed the Isleta gaming casino. Late afternoon on a Friday and the parking lot was overflowing with cars and semitrucks. Feeling her fragile optimism flag, she doubted very many would leave as winners and wondered how anyone could feel lucky here.

The exit ramp descended quickly as they made their way into the river valley. While the valley was not exactly lush, especially by coastal California standards, at least now there were trees and green vegetation along the two-lane highway. As the dirt storm gusted the car with unnerving jolts, Abby saw a small trailer off to the side of the road with a hand-printed sign: FRY BREAD AND OVEN BREAD. Two little brown-skinned kids about four or five played near it with a large yellow dog. Their wind-whipped black hair flew in all directions but did not obscure their wide, white-toothed grins. They chased in happy circles, yet had to feel the sharp sting of blown grit on tender flesh and unprotected eyes.

A few small adobe homes were visible, but primarily she saw field after field of farmland, outbuildings, stacks of alfalfa. Dirt drifted across the road in mesmerizing patterns. The dark hulk of mountains was ghostly through the clouds that fell like a curtain across the valley to the east.

"Here's Esperanza. The coffee shop there, two gas stations, the feed store. That's new, the Chavez house is an antique and junk shop." He slowed the car as his large dark eyes scanned over the sites. "It's usually prettier . . . the weather makes it look ugly, but wait, you'll see, it's really very nice."

He sounded so apologetic, so hopeful. She reached through her fears and misgivings to grasp his hand and squeeze it. It was warm and sweaty despite the air-conditioning. His skin against hers was all it took, all it ever took. Her love for him flooded through her, washing away anything else. His kiss was so grateful her heart hurt.

"Right up here, there will be a fork in the road. To the right leads to the Vigils,' to the left our place. We'll go check in with CeCe and Miguel first—I think they're having a dinner before the Rosary." Bobby trailed off as they reached the fork in the road. He slowed to a near stop as if he were suddenly reconsidering which way to go.

Straight ahead, a smaller lane led to some other house where she could barely make out a few broken-down vehicles behind a ramshackle gate. This is what held her husband's angry stare.

"Who lives there?" she asked as she watched his hands grip and squeeze the leather steering-wheel cover.

"Nobody," he said abruptly and gunned the car to the right.

It was a short ways to the Vigil house. Bobby explained that his great-grandfather originally had twenty acres but as time went on and family dispersed, chunks of land were sold off to finance moves to the city. Six acres remained, four were still tilled for chile and alfalfa. The farm animals had been sold along the way. Ricardo had no interest in them. But the Vigils still had a good sixty acres, most of it producing some of the state's best chile.

"Wow, this is huge," Abby said as they pulled up next to a couple of cars in front of a low adobe wall. A large courtyard paved with flagstone was bordered on three sides by the house. Flowers of every color and description exploded from planters and beds. The flagstone paving meandered around the towering shade trees. Little benches and chairs provided inviting places to relax and enjoy the lush surroundings. Even the wind died down to a pleasant breeze that ruffled the flowers and rustled the canopy of green leaves on the tree branches overhead.

Bobby stretched and came around to her side of the car. She could feel his eyes on her face as she surveyed the lovely scene before her. She met his gaze. "It's beautiful, Bobby."

"We can do this. Our courtyard is a lot smaller and my dad never did anything with it after my mom died . . ." It was as if he suddenly remembered why they were here. His shoulders slumped and he looked down.

She reached for his hand, "I'll help you get through this, honey."

"There you two are!" A woman called as she ran toward them from the open front door. "Miguel! Rachel! They're here!" She had the kind of voice Abby was sure they could hear inside the house.

The woman was suddenly in front of her, tall, early fifties, fit and quite striking with long dark hair, vibrant smile. "You must be Roberto's wife! I'm CeCe—short for Celia. Ah, honey, what a way to have to meet, huh?"

Abby was quickly enveloped into CeCe's ample bosom for a quick hug.

"It's wonderful to meet you. I'm Abigail . . . Abby." Bobby had filled her in on the Vigils during their drive from San Diego. CeCe was just as he'd described her, right down to her accent—New Mexico by way of Brooklyn, New York. Bobby had said that neither CeCe's traditional Jewish family nor Miguel's traditional Hispanic family had embraced their marriage thirty-some odd years before, but that CeCe and Miguel were the best example of la familia that he knew.

A man about CeCe's age, with a handsome, rugged face and trimmed moustache, joined them, quickly embracing Bobby. "Roberto," he said and held Bobby with unashamed emotion.

"Miguel, this is my wife, Abby."

His calloused hands gently took both of hers, "It is a pleasure to finally meet the woman who stole Roberto's heart."

CeCe led her over to a young woman, late twenties, maybe thirty like Abby herself. Her long dark hair was a mass of heavy curls, her skin unexpectedly light, with pale blue eyes that contrasted sharply with her hair. She was beautiful in an exotic way. "My daughter. Rachel, say hello to Abby, Roberto's wife."

"I know who she is, Ma," Rachel said and seemed to appraise Abby with coolness. Or perhaps it was the icy blue of her eyes that made it seem that way. "Hi, how was your trip?"

"Quick, actually. Bobby did all of the driving so I was able to sleep most of the way."

Rachel looked away. CeCe stepped in, "That's our Roberto, such a good man. I'm sure he's crazy about you—look at you, you're gorgeous!" She laughed good-naturedly. Rachel gave CeCe the drop-dead look that Abby recognized from her moments of humiliation with her own mother. When they were still speaking.

"Oh, come here, Charlie, and meet Abby." CeCe waved at a tall Anglo man in his early thirties. He smiled and his eyes twinkled the way a man's do when he knows he's extremely good looking but trying to be modest about it. "Charlie's my son-in-law."

"Ex, Ma, ex!" Rachel corrected.

"He can be your ex, I never divorced him." CeCe obviously enjoyed this needling.

Charlie shrugged and smiled. "Welcome, Abby, I hope you have as good a visit here in Esperanza as possible, under the circumstances."

"How long are you here for?" CeCe asked.

"We're going to live here," Bobby answered, leaving off the part about a one-year trial period.

"That's wonderful!" Rachel said as she hugged Bobby with sudden enthusiasm.

Abby noticed it was Bobby who broke the embrace to say, "These people are my second family. I spent more time at the Vigils' than my own house growing up."

"You were just hiding from your chores," Rachel laughed. "Your papa would get so mad!"

"I thought my cooking was the attraction," CeCe said.

"Yeah, you caught me. I've never been able to resist a good meal. Abby's an amazing cook, she ran her own restaurant in San Diego."

"Well, I tried to give you everything Magdalena would have wanted. She was my best friend so I probably smothered you. At least Ricardo's with her now. But what a shock, his heart giving out like that. But who knew he had heart trouble—he was such a hermit these last years."

"He was never the same after you left," Rachel said with a gentle tone that did little to soften the impact of her meaning.

"CeCe has cooked up a spread in there," Miguel said. "So we better eat and then get to the Rosary."

"I thought I'd run over and air out the house," Bobby said.

Miguel put a fatherly arm around his shoulder and guided him to the front entrance. "There will be time for that later. You're staying with us tonight."

CeCe held Abby back as Rachel and Charlie followed Miguel and Bobby. "You need to help us keep Bobby from going over to his house for as long as possible. See, when Miguel and I went over to get your phone number and a suit for him to be buried in, my God! What a sight!"

"What?" Abby prompted.

"Ricardo had pulled away from us over the years. Away from everyone. He seemed fine from a distance, you know? He farmed his alfalfa, sold it, went about his business. I tried to get him to come over for dinner. Miguel would ask him out for a beer but he never would. Anyway, we found the house in a mess. It's like he started hoarding stuff and it's stacked up all over the place which drew bugs. Anyway, it's going to be a big job to clear it all out and you can stay with us in the meantime."

"This is going to kill Bobby that his dad—"

"Exactly. Bobby needs to deal with one hard thing at a time. The Rosary first. Tomorrow the funeral mass and burial. Then after he gets through that, we'll try to get him to stay here one more night and Miguel can take him over the next morning and they can start working on it. Charlie will help. Meanwhile we have lots of room to spare."

Abby smiled with relief. CeCe was going to make all of this more bearable.

After dinner, Abby and Bobby were changing clothes for the Rosary in the large guest room. Bobby was fighting with his tie. "Christ Almighty! This damn tie!"

Abby put down her hairbrush and came over to him and silently began to tie the perfect knot.

"How can I face him? He died alone in the dirt! I should have been throwing those alfalfa bales for him!"

Abby smoothed his tie, resting her hand over his heart. "I know this is hard."

He stepped away and grabbed his dark suit jacket. "We better get going."

Our Lady of Fatima was a mission-style adobe church with massive three-foot-thick walls. The interior felt cool in a soothing way, the adobe walls hand-plastered to a smooth satiny finish. Ricardo's open coffin was placed in a side room, off of the vestibule. Sprays of flowers were arranged and a large standing wrought iron candelabra provided the subdued lighting. There were folding chairs in a semicircle for the family to sit and receive the visitors in. Abby had been to very few wakes or funerals and never a Catholic one so she planned to take her cues from Bobby.

Miguel and CeCe entered first while Bobby hesitated at the doorway. Rachel reached for Bobby's arm but he moved to the side, so she joined her parents. Charlie trailed behind her, seemingly invisible to her.

Miguel seemed to pray a moment and after making the sign of the cross, he said quietly, "I think we should step out and give Roberto a moment of privacy."

Bobby nodded as they passed. He held Abby's hand so tightly she could feel the throbbing of her pulse. He stepped forward and stood looking down into the face of his dead father.

Even in the paralysis of death, it was evident Ricardo had been a handsome man. His dark hair was thick like his son's, only touched with gray at the temples. His eyebrows were a little wild with curly salt-and-pepper hairs. His youthful face was clean-shaven revealing smooth brown skin.

Bobby began to cry and speak to his father in Spanish in a rush of words. Abby did not need to know the language to hear he was apologizing, over and over. He let go of Abby's hand as his voice became louder and he seemed to be pleading with his father. Abby didn't know what to do, she expected his grief, but he seemed on the verge of hysteria.

Miguel returned and put his arm around Bobby, speaking to him gently but firmly in Spanish. Abby stepped back, her own tears flowing, feeling utterly helpless. Rachel quickly moved to his other side, the place Abby had vacated, and he accepted her next to him. She spoke to him in Spanish and he hugged her.

Abby felt CeCe draw her away and they retreated to the vestibule where other members of the community waited. "It's okay, Abby, Miguel will comfort him."

Abby tried to stop her tears as she whispered to CeCe, "I've just never felt so different from Bobby or so useless to him."

CeCe dabbed at Abby's cheek with a lavender-scented hankie and smiled. "Tell me about it!"

After the Rosary, Abby and Bobby returned to the Vigil's. Bobby never mentioned going to his boyhood house. Instead, he loosened his tie and joined Miguel in his study for some beer.

Exhausted, Abby kissed him goodnight and after a hot bath fell into a strangely dreamless sleep.

In the morning, she found Bobby in bed with her, his suit thrown onto a chair. From the smell of his breath, he must have stayed up drinking half the night. She would let him sleep it off. She got up carefully and found her watch. It was eleven-thirty! The funeral mass wasn't until five p.m. with the burial after that. CeCe was right, the house should wait. Bobby could only handle one thing at a time.

After the mass, the funeral procession followed a deeply rutted dirt road to the cemetery. With each sharp dip and bump, Abby's hand went protectively to her low abdomen as she felt the twinge of ligaments suspending her expanding uterus. Her pregnancy books had explained all of this, but irrationally it seemed that with the right jerk her womb's tethers could snap like the strap on a well-worn bag and spill its precious contents.

Through a stand of poplar trees that served as the cemetery gates, she could the see a makeshift parking lot. Charlie and five other men were carrying the casket away from the hearse.

As Bobby pulled their dusty Camry in next to Miguel's and CeCe's car, the wind seemed to sputter and die. There was an eerie quiet when he shut off the engine. He sat as if he couldn't get out. He blinked, as if confused, the car keys poised in his hand as if he might change his mind and reinsert the key into the ignition.

Abby ran her hand softly down his muscled forearm and over his frozen hand. He released the keys into her fingers. "I'll help you," she said in a whisper.

He nodded, not meeting her eyes, blew out his breath and like a good Navy man opened his door, got out, and stood tall.

His arm was around her as if helping her over the uneven ground, but she felt him lean on her slightly. The graves they walked over had modest headstones, hand-carved Hispanic names, dusty artificial flowers anchored with rocks. Thin strands of grass clung to the earth like hair to a balding man's pate.

She heard the repetitive slamming of car and pickup-truck doors as people fell into a procession behind them to the nearby grave site. Men in crisp going-to-town blue jeans with ornate buckles on their hand-tooled belts, Sunday Stetson hats instead of straw field hats or seed caps. Faces were Hispanic, rutted as the road from a life under the sun. The women at their sides were sturdy, with hands that seemed made for rolling out bread dough and scattering chicken scratch. Their dark dresses were timeless, as if retrieved from the back of cedar closets.

Bobby had finally gotten out of bed around one-thirty. He had cleaned up and gone to see the priest for confession so that he could partake of the Holy Communion during his father's mass. He returned seeming introspective but less troubled and for that Abby was grateful. He was uncommunicative as they dressed for the funeral, accepting his fresh shirt and pressed suit without comment. Abby tried not to worry. He needed to grieve. He would be his old self again when he was ready. She felt better with him leaning on her now, accepting her support as they made their way to the grave site.

The simple oak coffin held a wreath of white roses as it seemed to float over the gaping hole in the earth. Next to it, Magdalena's grave, where they came to a stop.

As the priest murmured his holy words and spoke of Ricardo's simple hard-working life in service to his Lord Jesus, Abby thought of Magdalena resting under her feet. She read the tombstone:

MAGDALENA ORTIZ SILVA
BORN SEPTEMBER 10, 1950
DIED JULY 25, 1975

She was younger than Abby. She was pregnant, like her, probably farther along. She was happy, probably singing to the radio as she drove to her doctor's appointment, thinking, *How could life get any better than this?*

The suddenness of death, the ruthlessness of taking one so young, a mother leaving a small boy behind, a baby's life taken before it could take a first breath, made the priest's words seem hollow and ironic. If God was loving, he was also impotent. Her terror the night of the robbery a full week before was only now impacting her. Seeing Bobby bleeding on the floor, Abby had felt fragile and vulnerable in a way she had never experienced. Her previous bravado, the way she strode confidently through her city, never afraid, always trusting that only good things would happen to her, now seemed illusory. Feeling safe seemed suddenly foolhardy and naïve. The loss of her life in San Diego no longer felt like the worst that could happen.

Bobby put his arm around her as the wind began to strengthen; she wrapped her arm tightly across his waist. The tears streaming down his face, the silent shudder she could feel through his suit coat, only heightened her sense that they were powerless.

"Come on, it's already seven o'clock and almost dark. Come back and stay with us one more night, we'll have some *cervezas*," Miguel said to Bobby as they left the burial.

"I had too many of those last night!" Bobby managed a smile. "No, our bags are in the car. It's time to go home."

"It might be kind of hard to face," Miguel tried again.

"I'm fine, really. I want to be there tonight."

CeCe joined the conversation. "I got food, people are bringing so much. Everyone is gathering at our place. Come on and relax, bond with your neighbors."

Bobby leaned over and gave her a big hug and kiss. "Thanks but no thanks, CeCe."

Abby looked back at them worriedly as he led her to the car.

In the short drive, Abby struggled with whether to warn him about his father's house. Keeping it secret had been Miguel and CeCe's idea, but he'd be angry with her if he thought she had kept something from him, even out of concern. She couldn't figure out how to prepare him without making it worse, so she kept silent.

He pulled the car up next to an ancient green pickup truck sporting a bumper sticker that read viva esperanza! Affixed to the radio antenna was a small clump of faded artificial roses that bobbed with the breeze. The driver's door had been replaced somewhere along the line and had never been repainted to match. It was red with faded chipped white script, quality plumbing since 1932.

"Papa's truck," Bobby said unnecessarily.

Abby looked at the house. She was suddenly curious to inspect the place where she would bring her baby home from the hospital. Home.

"Now don't expect much, we can fix it up, add on, whatever you like," he said.

She knew he always thought that because of her wealthy family and upbringing she wanted more than he ever had to give. The one and only time she had taken him to the Gibbs' family estate had been a disaster on many counts—not the least of which was the shift in how he saw her. She was no longer just Abby, the college-dorm girl, she was Abigail, owner of tennis courts, swimming pools, beach houses, and stock portfolios. Telling him these were her parents' things, their life not hers, never made a difference. He suddenly saw her marriage to him as a giant step down. Then, when they disowned her for it, he felt like a home wrecker. His misplaced guilt nearly ruined their young marriage. He stubbornly refused to believe her genuine feeling that he had rescued her from a life she hated. Escaping that kind of a life, heavy with expectation and falseness, was as liberating as escaping poverty in some ghetto. From an early age she had the insight to realize it was better to have an empty bank account than an empty soul.

She looked at the tan adobe plaster that was cracked in places and missing all together in other places, revealing the neat rows of adobe bricks underneath. Vining red roses clung to the waist high wall that encircled a flagstone patio where they would sit in the evening in the shade of the ancient cottonwood tree that leaned over and cradled the entire roof with its generous limbs. On the patio there were empty flowerpots she would fill.

The gate was lopsided in Bobby's grasp and had to be lifted over to one side rather than swung. "Dad never fixes anything. The biggest procrastinator," he said with not a little irritation. "All kinds of good intentions but never follows through."

Abby followed him across the smooth planes of the flagstones. With Bobby's natural full-speed-ahead approach to life, it was easy to imagine the kind of conflicts that must have erupted between them.

Bobby tried the door and found it locked. This, too, seemed to annoy him. "We never had to lock the doors." He jerked his keyring, which still held the key, from his suit pocket.

Abby felt an unexpected surge of curiosity as he fumbled with the lock. It was like opening some huge package with mysterious contents. And it was pure, whatever it contained, untouched by her parents' money or control. So what if it was a mess, they could fix it up together.

The door swung open with a movie-soundtrack creak. The dark, impending storm sky did not provide much natural light. As Bobby switched on lights, they both gasped at what they saw. Stacks of newspapers, magazines, and cardboard boxes filled the room. Long black cockroaches dashed toward cover as the light hit their shiny backs.

"Jesus," Bobby said, "what the hell happened?"

This must have been the living room at one time. It was a large room whose opposite end opened into what must have been the dining room. Furniture was all but obscured by piles of trash. Abby made her away through narrow aisles behind Bobby who toured in shocked silence.

She jumped as a bolt of lightning and crash of thunder seemed to land right behind her. And then the rain began. It was as if the sky itself had ripped open. The rain was deafening, now mixed with hail that pounded the windows and roof with angry fists.

Bobby grabbed her hand and pulled her to the kitchen which was relatively clear of debris. It was a large country-style kitchen with ancient appliances, including an old washing machine next to the gas stove. The square wood tabletop was surprisingly empty and clean. The double sinks were empty. A yellow draining rack neatly held one white coffee cup, one bowl and one spoon. The window over the sink revealed the white sheet of pea-sized hail popping against the ground.

Bobby had to yell to be heard over the din of the storm. Lightning strobed continually, reminding her of the gay dance club Edward liked to take her to. "I don't know what happened!" her husband was yelling. "It wasn't like this when I came home!"

"That was over four years ago!" Abby yelled. But the storm was suddenly down a notch and her voice sounded too loud, almost angry.

He looked at her as if she'd turned on him. "I just mean, this could be recent . . ." She trailed off as he left the kitchen via a hallway to the left.

She followed him as he quickly inspected the rest of the house. Two of the three big bedrooms were in similar shape to the living room, crowded with stacks of an odd assortment of items like fishing equipment, books, clothing, boxes of tools and unopened cans of coffee, tissues, and huge sacks of rice and beans. The bathroom was strangely uncluttered and clean like the kitchen. A well-worn toothbrush hung on the wall next to a framed picture of Jesus; a threadbare washcloth hung neatly over the side of the pedestal sink.

Bobby scowled, scratched his head, glared at the mess as if some imposter had come in and altered everything. He brushed past her and returned to the kitchen, sat down at the table, his hands clenched together against his forehead as if in prayer.

Abby sat down in the other chair and said nothing. She knew her husband. He would be angry at all of this and whatever she would say would make it worse.

"He must have lost his mind! On the phone he always sounded normal. How was I supposed to know?" Her silence only seemed to rebuke him. "Yeah, I should have been here. I should have come back more often. I could have helped him, the poor crazy son of a bitch."

Abby fought back her own irrational, exhausted, paranoid feeling that he was accusing her of having obstructed his ability to be a good son. In fact, she used to encourage him to take the time to go home and see his dad, spend more time with him. He would grow sullen and quiet and say she just didn't understand. His dad would spend the whole visit guilt-tripping him about moving back. Better to not put either one of them through the same old battle, the same old wounds.

"His heart may have finally killed him. But the stress of dealing with . . . the stress, that's what took him. He was alone, too proud to ask for help. He shouldn't have had to ask. I have to live with that."

"Sweetie," Abby tried to get him to look into her eyes, but he was staring at a burned place in the wood of the table, rubbing his thumb over it as if he might be able to erase it away. "It's not your fault, you couldn't—"

"He said my going away would kill him—he stood right there and said it. It took twelve years but he was right."

"Don't do this to yourself. You're a good man!" Abby felt her voice strangle with impending tears. "It's only natural to grow up, leave home."

"In your world. In your crazy white world, it's natural to defy your family. Disown your children if they should marry a filthy Mexican—what is that, disown? In my world, this world, you stand by your family! La familia! You show some respect! That's what's natural! He was right, he told me if I went out into the white world, I would get poisoned, my soul would forget what is right."

Then Abby knew she would lose it. She could taste how wrong her words were before they reached her lips. She didn't care. It was like needing to vomit. "I'm sorry, okay? Is that what you need to hear? I'm sorry you ever left this place! I'm sorry you fell in love with me and ruined your father's life! Me and the U.S. Navy! We poisoned you! I'm sorry my parents are assholes, that they think I give a shit if I see them or their money! I made my own money, I made my own life—"

"Yeah, and I make you give it all up to follow me to some roach-infested heap! Admit it—you want to go back to San Diego, to your restaurant! Your life!"

She said nothing. She could feel his eyes pull the truth from her and it was hopeless to try to conceal it. In that split second, in that terrible moment, she couldn't deny it. But it wasn't the whole truth. She was going to say, it's hard right now, but she'd get used to it. Give her some time. All that mattered was being with her husband, having their child together. It was all she wanted. It didn't matter where. That was her truth.

But before he could see it in her eyes and before those words could pass her lips, a corner square of patched ceiling plaster gave way and tumbled onto the floor behind them in a burst of water.

Sparks flew from the old fuse box as leaking water penetrated its switches. A hissing sound, smoldering smell, a puff of smoke and the lights went out.

By the light of distant flashes of lightning, Bobby scrambled for a bucket. Abby managed to find some stubs of candles and matches in a kitchen drawer.

Then they stood there, in the semidarkness, too far away to read the look in each other's eyes, too far away to reach for each other. The moment was lost.

Bobby went into his father's room, muttering to himself in Spanish, digging around through papers piled on his father's desk using a flashlight that seemed on its last ounce of juice. Abby held a candle and stood in the hallway watching.

"Bobby, you need to calm down, get hold of yourself. When you get this upset you get impulsive and do things you regret—"

"I regret not being here for my father when he needed my help! Maybe it's not too late to make things right for him! Maybe it's time I grow up and be a man!" He shoved piles of papers onto the floor, yanked open drawers to pull out more folders. Receipts, scraps of paper, remnants, minutia of a life. What was he looking for? He would never tell her, even if he did know. She suspected he was just pitching a fit, randomly acting out his rage and helplessness at his father's desk, once the repository of everything deemed important. Car maintenance records, bank statements from previous decades, store coupons. Everything that once seemed so vital to save, but after death becomes instantly and painfully trivial.

When the hot candle wax drooled and clung to her fingers, she returned to the kitchen, lay down her head and cried into the kitchen table. Grateful for the muffle of the thunder, she let her sobs wrack her. In her near hysteria, she almost began to laugh. The last thing that kitchen needed was more water.

She sat up when she heard Bobby coming, tried to wipe her eyes. He stopped at the doorway, stuffing some papers into his jacket pocket.

The storm rumbled away in the distance, the rain was still steady but not violent. The stream of water from the hole in the ceiling thinned to a melodious trickle as it hit the nearly full bucket.

"Bobby—"

"I have to go out. I have to take care of something. Get some supplies, food."

"I'll go. I'll make a list—"

"No, I have to do this on my own. I'll just get a few things for tonight. Make a list if you want. We'll do the real trip in the morning. I'll be right back."

"Bobby, we need to talk."

"When I get back."

She tried to get up. Her high heel caught the chair leg, sitting her back down. When she looked up he was gone. She heard the rumble of the old truck starting up and felt as if she were in one of those terrible dreams where if you could only move you might save yourself.

Chapter 3

"I wonder how Roberto is taking seeing the old place. Maybe we should have given him some kind of warning. He's been through so much in such a short time," CeCe said, picking up coffee cups and plates speckled with cake crumbs off of the dining room table. A clear crystal vase shaped like a pear held freshly cut spring flowers she had cut from her garden. Even here in the desert, her flower garden rivaled anything in Better Homes and Gardens. By summer, hummingbirds flitted over it like a swarm of Tinkerbells. She said flowers had these enlightened little souls that were as fated as saints. Not that Ma had known anything about saints before she married Papa. But they're very big with her now. Jewish mothers and martyrs. Pretty self-explanatory. "What? These people can't eat over a plate?" she said, brushing crumbs from the table into her hand and clapping them onto a plate.

"There was no talking him into staying here one more night," Miguel replied, folding the long aluminum table that had held the banquet put out by CeCe and her girlfriends.

"Maybe you should go over there, see if everything's all right. They might want to come back and stay here after seeing the inside of the house." Rachel could tell her mother was anxious by the way she obsessed over a stain on the tablecloth.

"I think we should let them be, have some privacy. Besides, the bedroom's neat as a pin, kept up as if Maggie were still there," Miguel reasoned. He plopped on his hat before braving the weather, taking the table out to the shed by the house.

The word "bedroom" made Rachel deflate after sailing all afternoon on the way Roberto had reached for her hug at the Rosary. It had felt so natural, so loaded with emotion. She recalled seeing Abby over his shoulder as they embraced, she soothing him in Spanish. The years between them had disintegrated. She had been right. Their love had never died.

Roberto's wife seemed so highfalutin for the likes of Esperanza. What could that *guera* know about la familia? She'd never last here. She'd whine about wanting one of those big, fancy houses in the foothills with the coyotes eyeballing her in the dark like she was just another dumb house pet.

Bonnie, short for Bonita, Carmen, and Hazel, CeCe's cabal, as she referred to them, had stayed to help clean up and gossip. They came walking in from the kitchen where they had been chatting nonstop like ducks, tin-foiling and zip-locking the leftovers as every once in a while Bonnie's cackle harpooned out like she was laughing at one of her own dirty jokes.

"Did you get a load of Blanca's dress? Is that appropriate for a funeral? *Híjole!* I felt people turning over in their graves right under my feet!" Bonnie said sucking cake crumbs out from under her long, red squared-off nails. She had closed her beauty shop that she ran out of an addition to her house so she could go to the funeral and help Ma afterward. Every couple of weeks Bonnie did something chemically different to her hair. Today it was a dark plum that matched her lipliner and lipstick. She was a little plump, but hourglass with an ample round butt that wiggled when she shot pool and got her a night of free beer from the leering men at the bar. She tore a corner off of a leftover piece of cake on a deserted plate. "I can't help myself. I'm addicted to carbs, but tomorrow I'm going to start a new diet," she said through another mouthful. She couldn't swallow fast when she said "Oh, guess what? I heard Blanca's new boyfriend drives a Lexus. So you know what he's into . . ." She pursed her forty-year-old lips together making them look like two prunes and charaded sniffing a pinch of something up her nose.

Hazel, a retired nurse in her late sixties, picked up four folded chairs and carried them to the door. She had lent them to Ma for the occasion. Rachel couldn't remember when she had last seen Hazel wearing something different than some type of exercise clothes. She wore a black suit that in her tall, bony frame reminded Rachel of Abe Lincoln in a dark, dyed Joan Baez haircut. For being in her late sixties, she was well toned and more youthful than her age. Her dyed hair certainly looked more believable than Bonnie's, which was starting to get that troll-doll texture. "Blanca's boyfriend is a podiatrist. He works out at my gym. He's into feet, I'm afraid." Her long arms propped the chairs against the wall.

"So is Bonnie. Her foot is in her mouth," Carmen said, removing the paper doilies between the cups and saucers. She smiled impishly. The silver cross around her neck swung as she leaned down to pick up the cups and saucers. She was never without it. She went to church more than once every Sunday, and would do anything for anyone in the community. Her husband had been killed on the job resurfacing I-25 South. Hit by a drunk driver who had three prior DWI arrests. People talked about how this petite lady went on like a saint after the tragedy. Some said—behind their hands, of course—that the fat settlement helped.

Hazel opened the screen door to begin loading the chairs and the wind took it. The rain had gotten worse, likely flooding out roads and arroyos.

"My God!" CeCe said with a start. It took Hazel some grappling to get control of the screen door. It yanked away from her like an angry child. "You all better head home. It looks pretty nasty."

"We can't leave you with all this mess," Carmen protested, but only a little. Hazel and Bonnie had already grabbed their bags and purses and whatever container they had brought some food in.

"Don't be silly. Rachel and I can manage," said her mother.

Rachel was always dutiful. She was a good daughter in that way, at least. Ma could complain about a lot of things, but never that she had a lazy daughter.

Carmen, Hazel, and Bonnie hugged and kissed CeCe good-bye in a group embrace under the slanted roof of the front door telling her if she needed anything at all not to hesitate. Bonnie flipped the hood of her raincoat up to protect her newly dyed hair, Carmen gave Ma a sweet pat on the cheek that lingered with affection. "We love you!" Hazel yelled waving and jogging to her truck way ahead of the other two.

Rachel followed her mother into the kitchen with a stack of plates and cups teetering dangerously.

"That dress was a little short for a funeral. I just hope God takes me before I lose my senses and end up doing something like that," said CeCe continuing to *tsk* and scrub the dishes clean before sticking them in the dishwasher Papa had gotten her for their thirtieth anniversary. Her silver earrings hung free from her pulled back and braided dark hair and dangled like wind chimes as she worked. Her mother's skin reminded Rachel of finely cracked porcelain, but light brown like an egg. With her eastern European background CeCe looked like a gypsy in her Mexican and Indian jewelry, and much like the beautiful flower child she was in the sixties.

Charlie made his usual entrance by shuffling in on his muscled legs like his feet were barely attached. He carried a glass baking dish in each hand with leftover cake in them. "What do you want me to do with these, Ma?" He still had some cream-cheese frosting on his upper lip along with maybe four or five days of stubble.

"Take that one home to your trailer. It's Rachel's carrot cake. You love her carrot cake."

"Ma! He doesn't get to have my carrot cake anymore! We're divorced."

Charlie shrugged sheepishly at CeCe. "Same deal with sex." He put both dishes on the counter.

"Well, I didn't sign any divorce papers. Here, *bubeleh*, take the other one," said her mother, handing him the chocolate cake Angel Martinez had made and brought with her. Angel had been an acquaintance of the Silvas, but she was also one of Charlie's dancing buddies. She claimed she was only forty. All that tequila aged a woman.

Rachel studied the murky contents in the bottom of a cup. The cream was starting to adhere to the sides. She tried to sound nonchalant. "Too bad Roberto didn't come over." When no one replied she continued, "I bet she didn't want to. She seemed pretty stuck up for the likes of us." Rachel glanced sideward for response.

"She seemed lovely. And beautiful. Roberto probably can't keep his hands off of her," her mother said, as if the words were blank bullets after all this time.

"Mother, he just left his father's funeral. Sex is probably the last thing on his mind."

"Maybe it'd be the last thing on your mind," she said, smiling at Charlie. They always acted like they knew something she didn't. "Honey, sex is the best comfort for grief. Next best thing to crawling back into the womb. Charlie knows what I'm talking about, am I right?" she asked as if confirming aspirin for a headache.

"It's as good a reason as any." He winked and popped a handful of mixed nuts into his mouth. Like he ever needed a reason. She had never wanted him in the ravenous way he had always wanted her. She couldn't. She tried, but just couldn't.

"You guys are terrible," Rachel scolded. She did not want to think of Roberto home with that other woman, making love to her. Him crying in her hair. His Anglo wife. How could he marry an Anglo after Rachel had tried so hard to be full-blooded? At least she was half, and having been born and raised in Esperanza, made her as good as whole. That was what she comforted herself with as a child when the most popular Hispanic kids would chide and not include her. At least Rachel knew how to be Hispanic. She knew the meaning of familia. Better yet, she embraced it. She was an only child, her father's son more than her mother's daughter. She had a great responsibility to their land, the farm, the house. Houses on farms were designed to absorb the old and new generations as they came into this world and left it. No matter what the relationships were like.

She caught a look from Charlie who, she suspected, knew she had been thinking about Roberto. He'd seen that look before, that was for sure. But what she felt for Roberto was hard to hide. Her mother recognized the look, too.

"I got some barn shoveling to do. Shit's getting pretty deep," he said directly to her and left without fetching his hat.

It was his own damn fault if he got huffy. He'd chosen not to move on after the divorce. He just hadn't let go the way she had. You would think he'd have gotten the picture after she divorced his ass. How do all the women who fell all over him tolerate him? Then again, they only wanted him for his movie-star good looks. They'd have to live with him to know how he really was. Treated life like some joy ride. Never worried about anything and always needed to touch and kiss all the damn time in malls, rodeos, a Duke's baseball game.

Charlie was Anglo. She couldn't help it if her father's Hispanic blood ran through her in a way her mother's Jewish blood didn't. She had tried as a little girl to be part Anglo when Ma clumsily did the Chanukah and Christmas thing till Rachel was about four or five. Rachel would light candles at Chanukah, but never understood or connected to any of it. She and CeCe both lost interest fast. She was Catholic. That's what her community was. That's what Papa was and wanted her to be. Papa and Ma managed to have that happy marriage despite their cultural gap. Good for them. But who paid the price on that one? She still felt the hot humiliation in her eyes when she was banned from certain lunch tables in middle school because she had her mother's fair skin and a pair of Anglo eyes. Her parents never saw her cry at night or heard her ask God why. But by high school being with Roberto, who was popular and beautifully dark, validated her in the eyes of her peers. With him she was whole. He devastated her when he left for the Navy. Devastated Ricardo. Left her floundering around inside and out. She could only imagine how Ricardo must have felt. A real slap in the face in front of his community that his only son did not think enough of him to stay and help. To marry in the family church and have Ricardo's grandchildren in Esperanza. She could have understood had Roberto married a full-blooded Hispanic over her. But a full-blooded Anglo?

She looked up to see her mother staring at her, holding the dishtowel at her waist. "I don't know why you go out of your way to drive Charlie off. The institution of marriage is sacred. Just because you didn't believe it in your marriage doesn't mean others don't believe it in theirs. I hope you keep that in mind."

Abby sat at the kitchen table waiting. She was afraid to move. If she stayed perfectly still, he would come right back. She would hear the rumble of the truck, the headlights would shine through the open door like spotlights and he would see she trusted he wouldn't really go without her. Her faith kept her rooted there as another wave of storms exploded overhead, lightning so close she felt the hair on her arms stand up. Thunder so loud it nearly obliterated her thoughts.

Her back hurt, her bladder was going to burst. She wouldn't think about how much time must have passed. She stripped off her watch and laid it face down on the table. Finally she picked up the candle and slowly made her way to the bathroom. She stared into the flame, not looking down to where she imagined streams of cockroaches on their nightly rounds.

When she made her way back from the bathroom, she glanced into the bedroom. The candlelight illuminated the neatly made bed with its worn chenille bedspread, the picture of the Virgin Mother Mary hanging over it.

The Virgin drew her near. Her eyes were turned heavenward as she cradled her baby to her, a look of peace and rapture on her face. Abby felt an exhaustion as powerful as anesthesia overtake her. She set the candle on the nightstand and let her body crumple onto the bed.

She woke with a jolt when a sharp angle of light hit her face. She jumped out of bed and stood weaving while her thoughts tried to catch up. The bedspread was smooth except where she had collapsed. Bobby had not come to bed.

She didn't bother with her shoes as she searched the house in her nylon-stockinged feet. In the light of day, the bugs had retreated. "Bobby?" she called, her voice dry and thin, as she made her way through the bizarre stacks of junk like someone caught in a maze.

It was very quiet. Some roosters crowed in the distance. She thought of their condo back in San Diego, how the sounds of the city were a constant backdrop, how her restaurant would hum, alive beneath her floorboards. Even when Bobby was on submarine tour, she had never felt so alone.

She stopped in front of the open kitchen door. Through the tattered screen, their Camry stood shiny and clean from the rain. Next to it, tire ruts held standing water. Insects circled over this sudden oasis. She looked all around, as far as she could see, down the gravel drive, across the fields, over the distance to the house on the far right, the one with all the roosters and junked cars in its yard that had made Bobby scowl. She shaded her eyes and squinted straight across the property to where the Vigils lived, even though the house was not visible behind a cluster of giant trees.

Bobby must be there. He must have come home late and saw that she was sleeping, so he went to the Vigils'. Maybe he wanted to talk to Miguel about the house.

She began to rush across the weedy, muddy field. Not knowing how to think in acres, she judged it looked like a little more than a couple of city blocks. Her stockings ripped and mud clung to her feet. Her stockings were thigh-highs, so she reached down and stripped them off, leaving them strewn over some daisies. She knew she must look like a wild woman, unwashed, rumpled blue silk dress, her red hair tangled around her neck. Her eyes must be puffy from crying. She didn't care. Once she saw Bobby, everything would be all right.

As she passed the rooster place, dogs rushed the fence. Ugly, vicious-looking things. Their barks and growls brought out a man who glared at her as she ran past.

She gave it all less than a passing glance. However disgusting that dump was with its earsplitting roosters, nasty-looking man and dogs, it had nothing to do with her. Just as in the city, sometimes you just had to tune out the creepy element.

She tried to run. Her sore breasts protested, and she couldn't catch her breath, her heart pounded in her throat. Usually she could run for miles on the beach. Maybe it was the altitude, or pregnancy, or the fact she hadn't eaten in almost twenty-four hours. As she caught her breath she looked around. The view of the mountains to the east was startlingly lovely. The sky was intensely blue, a few white clouds looked painted into the scene as they nestled around the peaks of the mountains. Bobby was a little boy here. He played where she stood, in this verdant valley below these mountains. It was beautiful.

She felt suddenly ridiculous. Just because she couldn't imagine why Bobby hadn't come home to her didn't mean anything was wrong. Maybe the truck had broken down. There had to be some simple explanation. Yet, here she stood, a total mess, about to embarrass herself in front of his friends, acting like some hysterical city chick. She should just turn around and go back, get her suitcase from the car, shower, get into some comfortable clothes and come back in a civilized manner.

She looked up to see it was too late. Across the narrow dirt lane that divided their properties, came CeCe.

CeCe's expression told her she must look even worse than she thought. As CeCe drew near, she began to run. Abby stood there, rooted helplessly in place, wishing she could disappear.

CeCe took the last few steps slowly, as if she didn't want to spook a wild animal. It gave Abby an absurd moment to notice again how good this woman looked for her age. In her shorts and sleeveless blouse, she looked like those forty-year-old women who worked out at the health club and could kick her ass.

"What's wrong? What's happened?" CeCe said.

Abby wanted to keep it together. This is the closest she would have to a mother-in-law. She wanted to be cool and dignified. But the sun blinded her, the sound of the insects humming deafened her, the ground kept rolling beneath her feet. She opened her mouth to speak, but was seized by sudden nausea.

CeCe's strong arms were around her waist as she leaned forward and dry heaved.

"Miguel! Charlie!" CeCe's voice rang in her ears.

Someone came. She was picked up and carried. She tried to say she was all right, really. Instead she looked at her feet as they swung up in the air. The drying mud encased them like little slippers, her toes like chocolate-dipped berries.

She had never been the fainting sort. She had never been fragile or sickly a day in her life. In her family, self-reliance was the unspoken rule and she was very good with rules. Until she selected whom to love. She'd broken all the rules then.

"Put her on the bed in the guest room." CeCe's voice was commanding, no one argued.

Abby's eyes opened and tried to focus. It was Charlie laying her like a broken doll onto the bright yellow floral print comforter. CeCe put a towel beneath her muddy feet and tucked extra pillows under her head. She sat down next to her and looked intently into Abby's bleary eyes.

"Where is Roberto?"

It took Abby a moment to remember that no one called him Bobby here. "I don't know. I came here to find him. He's not here?"

"No, honey. When did he go? Early?"

Abby felt her mouth quiver. She didn't want to say these words. She didn't want to hear them. "Last night . . . he was upset about the house . . . He went out in the storm. He didn't come back."

"Charlie," CeCe said, "go over to Ricardo's and look for Bobby. Get Miguel to help you."

"We're going to take care of you," CeCe said.

Abby didn't have the strength to protest as CeCe stripped off her clothes and bathed her in the old, deep bathtub. Her strong fingers shampooed her hair until her scalp tingled and rinsed her with repeated scoops with an oversized soup ladle. She rubbed her skin dry until it was pink and then slipped an embroidered white cotton gown over her head that smelled lightly of roses.

"Bobby always brings me roses when he comes back from sub tour," she whispered.

CeCe helped her back into bed. "There you go, he's off buying roses."

She must have dozed for a moment. She woke to see a circle of people around her bed and it made her think of *The Wizard of Oz*, when Dorothy wakes up after her trip to Oz. CeCe stood nearest. Then an unfamiliar elderly woman, short and round with a shock of black hair, heavily lined face, too much red lipstick and peering black eyes. Rachel stood next to her. Abby noticed again how beautiful she was, even in her work clothes. Rachel was snatching sneaky glances at her, as if she couldn't look at her head on.

Charlie was next, standing closer to Rachel than she obviously wanted. He smiled at her, the only one who did. It seemed kind.

"This is Maria Valenques, she's an old-time healer around here and Papa's great-aunt. Until you can see a doctor I thought she should check you over," Rachel said.

"But only if you want," CeCe said, giving her daughter a stern look. "Some people aren't comfortable with this sort of thing."

"The men should leave," Maria said in a tone that revealed she had little use for the species in general. She began to prod and stroke Abby's arms. She lifted her nightgown and with both hands, grabbed her belly and ran her fingers from below her breasts to the top of her pubic hair and then pulled the nightgown back in place. "Open your mouth."

She put a finger inside her cheek and examined her tongue and gums.

"This woman is pregnant and she's dry as a bone! Why don't you eat and drink for your baby? Huh? Don't you want it? Make her eat a fresh-killed chicken, including the liver! I want nothing left but its bones before dark, understand? And she must drink water, no? Until her teeth float!"

She muttered in Spanish, and hustled away. At the doorway she turned, "Do as I say if you want this baby!"

"I'll go prepare the chicken and get it in the oven. And make some tea, Ma," Rachel said.

CeCe sat back down next to Abby. Miguel came in as Rachel went out.

He held his hat in his hands and worked the brim of it nervously between his fingers. "I went over and checked the house and the fields. No sign of the truck or Roberto. I see the roof's been leaking. I should have gone with you last night, to help soften the blow. I'm sorry. Roberto can get himself all worked up, but he'll be back."

"His name is Bobby," Abby said in the strongest voice she could muster. "He doesn't like to be called Roberto."

Rachel reached into the chicken she was eviscerating and pulled out the heart and liver. Their warm, lifeless heaviness tried to ooze between her fingers as she held them. There was hardly any time to drain the blood. Usually this was considered unhealthy except when a bruja ordered it as a remedy. She pinched off the green gall bladder and contemplated its power of turning anything it touched bitter with its contents. Gently she rolled it in her fingers admiringly, like a poison pill. That woman in there was pregnant with Roberto's baby. She imagined his fingers hovering down in wonder to rest on his wife's abdomen, the look of adoration in his dark, fudgy eyes, and how he loved that woman all the more for what he imagined growing magically under his hand.

She cut the poultry into parts and slam-dunked them into a pail of ice water. And now her mother was doting on this Abby woman like she was the Virgin Mary arriving at the inn. But why should she have to slave over her, too? So Roberto walked out on her. Needed to cool off down at a bar. He'd probably passed out somewhere or run into some old acquaintances. Served Abby right. Bet it wasn't the first time.

There had been something in that hug at the Rosary that assured her it would all just tumble into place again like a combination to a locked safe. The way it used to be. He had just needed a wake-up call. Only matter of time now and maybe a potion or two from Maria.

Charlie burst into the kitchen obviously on a mission from CeCe. He rooted through cupboards, covered tins and the refrigerator like a hunting dog.

"What are you looking for," she asked, deciding to put him out of his misery. She may not have wanted him around anymore, but she hated to see the poor thing suffer.

"Ma said Maria wanted some *poleo* and sent me for it. What the hell is it anyway?" He bent down to check out a shelf under the counter. His butt strained through the stringy matrix of the threads of his worn jeans. She found herself staring and quickly looked away.

Maria had brought Rachel into this world because CeCe, Mother Earth incarnate, had wanted a home birth. Her mother had come out to New Mexico with a few college friends following the Grateful Dead around. As her mother told it, her first day in New Mexico she saw Miguel. They had just pulled the Volkswagen bus into a gas station. He sat at the end of his old Ford pickup, shirtless, sucking down a bottle of Mexican beer, sweat dripping down both their brown forms. The most gorgeous thing she'd ever laid eyes on.

"Poleo is a mint. She wants some tea made from it. Abby must be running a fever or something—helps her sweat it out." Rachel explained and produced a tin from the refrigerator, then put the kettle on. It all felt so strangely detached and dutiful as she went through the motions of helping a woman she despised.

"Hell, I just stopped in front of the bedroom door to bend down and pet the damn cat and Ma yelled at me to get it. Far as I knew she could have been making *posole*. Thanks, hon."

After she made Abby tea and shooed Charlie away like he was a rat that had gotten into the barn, she took the bowl of offal and headed out to the sight of her future vegetable garden to bury it just deep enough that nothing will find it.

Abby woke as if coming up for air after a high dive. She was hot and sweaty, the sheet clung to her legs as she tried to sit up. The room was light. How long had she slept? She fumbled for her watch next to the empty teacup on the nightstand: 3:45 p.m.

She looked up to see that their luggage had been moved back into the room. For the first time it bothered her that their luggage did not match. Hers was a blue floral print with brown leather trim and grips. Bobby's was standard Navy issue. Bobby.

He might be back. He might be downstairs visiting right now. She scrambled out of bed, jerked open one of her bags, pulled out some khaki shorts, a white T-shirt, underwear and got dressed like the house was on fire. She ran her fingers through her hair and ran out of the room.

As she quickly made her way down the long shiny brick-floored hallway, fragrant with the smell of baking chicken, she could hear voices. She felt a flood of relief as she imagined Bobby teasing her for her panic, his arms around her in that way that made her feel complete.

She rounded the corner to the living room, feeling herself smile in anticipation, a giddy little laugh escaped her lips. Everyone looked up.

She felt her eyes dart from one to the other. Miguel, Rachel, CeCe, Charlie, and a man in a uniform. She completed the circle again before she let it sink in that Bobby was not there. A flush of embarrassment replaced her smile. "I thought I heard Bobby."

CeCe was at her side. "Come and have a seat, honey. We're just talking with Sheriff Bowman. Sheriff, this is Rob—Bobby's wife, Abby."

The men stood as she let CeCe guide her over to a southwestern style sofa. CeCe sat next her and kept a reassuring hand on her shoulder.

The men sat back down. The sheriff was a rail-thin overly tan white man with thinning blond hair. She could smell the cigarette smoke on him from six feet away. His smile revealed too many large teeth for his mouth. Their yellow tobacco-stained tint did not improve matters.

"Mrs. Silva, I'm just here to help out if I can. It's too soon to issue a formal missing-persons report, but I can do some sniffing around. So if you could answer a few questions for me."

Abby nodded.

"The burial was over approximately seven p.m. The Vigils here hosted a supper afterward. Where were you and your husband at that time?"

"Bobby wanted to go to the house, we hadn't been there yet. He was anxious to get us settled in." She felt everyone's eyes on her. She looked up and Charlie gave her an encouraging smile. She looked at Rachel who quickly looked away.

Miguel shifted in his chair like someone unused to sitting at this time of day. "I told the sheriff about the mess in Ricardo's house. You and Roberto must have been shocked to see such a thing."

"Bobby was pretty upset," Abby admitted. She stared down at the tangle of her interlocking fingers.

"If you could break it down for me in details, ma'am, that would be helpful," the sheriff said.

"I don't know. We were both tired, we'd had just buried his father so Bobby was distraught and then he sees the house. And the storm started, the roof caved in."

"How did he express his upset?" The sheriff peered at her with watery blue eyes.

Flashes of the night before intruded Abby's thoughts. "He felt guilty . . . that he wasn't here when his dad needed him. He . . . we . . . you know, we were so tired. We said things. Or, didn't say them."

CeCe's arm was around her shoulder now and it was that simple empathetic gesture that pushed Abby over the top. When her genuine compassion and fear seemed so right, so appropriate, it struck Abby how horrifying this really was. She was sitting here, over a thousand miles from home, telling a sheriff in the presence of complete strangers about her missing husband. Her Bobby. Who she knew would be here if he could. She wept like a child.

"Now I know this is rough, Ma'am, but I need to know. Did you have some sort of disagreement?"

With that her tears turned to anger. "He blamed himself! He blamed me—that he loved me! It was his irrational guilt. He could see how confused and lost his dad must have been and so he lashed out—"

"Did he hit you, hurt you in any way? Did you have to defend yourself?" The sheriff's sour breath clung to his every sordid word.

"No! That's not what I'm saying! You're twisting my words! He was angry at himself, he felt like he'd let his father down by living so far away. He gave up his life here for the Navy, for me and then my family rejects him. Both of us. So that's what we talked about. It was painful, that's all. And then he left."

"So you had this fight and he storms out."

"No, it wasn't a fight! He went to get some food and some stuff to clean with or something. There was water from the roof flooding the kitchen—why are you making it sound like he left on purpose?"

"Ma'am, it's what you're saying, I'm just putting two and two together. You had a marital squabble and he went off to chill out. Think about it, happens every day. You should be relieved to think about it like this. Here's a man, a tired, grief-stricken man who gets into it with his wife, they fight about the house, your parents that don't want their pretty white daughter hooked up with some Mexican boy, his poor old Mexican father that he's been neglecting, it all comes to a head. He takes his daddy's truck, not your slick silver Camry, and takes off. That's what I think. And my advice to you, Mrs. Silva, is sit tight. When your husband is ready, he'll come on home."

"Bobby would never do that! I know my husband! Something has happened! You need to look for him before it's too late!" Her voice was strident as her heart throbbed painfully. She was right and he would never believe her.

The rest of that day, Abby felt stunned into some kind of trance. She would feel a sudden urge to get in her car and start her own search, canvas the entire county. But physically she felt weak and her mind seemed unable to bridge the gap between a thought and an action. She couldn't even think about the baby. For months now it had been practically all she could think about. Now, she would feel it move and be surprised. She would forget entirely. Remembering gave her no joy and then came the taste of guilt, a cold metallic taste that would coat her throat. What kind of mother was she? What kind of wife was she? She deserved this hell. When you thought about like that, it made sense.

She sat in the back garden. CeCe brought her out here for air. The vintage shiny green metal chair was cool against her thighs. She sipped ice tea with fresh mint. She watched Rachel with her goats. They bleated and danced around her like children. Kids. So that's why they call them that. Rachel looked happy. It was the only time she smiled and even laughed out loud. Charlie watched her, too. He wore his love for her like cheap cologne, with too much hope.

She wished the sheriff was right. That Bobby was some asshole who would punish his wife like this, show her who's boss, put her in her place. Or he's had a nervous breakdown. He's wandering the streets of Albuquerque mumbling nonsense, hearing voices, hallucinating, as nuts as his old man. Maybe he's filling up the back of the truck with more rubbish to cram into the house. Or he's wandering lost in the desert with stress-induced amnesia. The robbery, getting hit on the head caused some kind of delayed reaction. A brain hemorrhage or sudden neurological event. Or he just decided he doesn't love her anymore. Doesn't want to ever see her again, or her baby. Maybe he went back to San Diego and hopped a submarine. But it was ridiculous, all of it. There was no other logical explanation other than her beloved husband was in some kind of serious trouble.

Don't lose hope. *Esperanza!* They all said it over and over. *It's not even been twenty-four hours yet. Keep the faith.* What if your faith says, *he's a good man. He loves you. He'd have to be hurt or worse not to be here.* What do you hope for then?

CeCe sat down next to her. She handed her a plate with cottage cheese and sliced peaches for dessert. The peaches' golden, red-tinged flesh matched the hues of the setting sun. She took a bite and was surprised at how good food could taste, how much she could enjoy it. She hadn't really tasted the chicken earlier. Her fork struck the china plate as it chased the last slice of peach, sounding like wind chimes.

"Miguel just spoke with Sheriff Bowman, filled him in about the robbery and head injury. He's agreed to file the missing-persons report early. He put out an APB on the truck. Tomorrow I'm getting together volunteers to make up leaflets, posters to put up with his picture. We'll set up a reward fund at the bank. We'll get our own army together and find him!"

Abby felt such gratitude she reached for CeCe. The plate slid down her lap into the grass. She was careful not to put her foot on it as she leaned into CeCe's embrace. She inhaled CeCe's scent as she laid her head on her shoulder. She smelled of this morning's faint perfume, a long day of honest work, sweet perspiration evaporating into the night air. Cicadas hummed, crickets chirped. Her baby stirred and she felt thankful. Stars gathered against the ever-darkening sky. A moon, full and female lifted itself over the mountains. *Esperanza.*

The hard mud of the adobe wall felt cool as Rachel made her way around the dark house. She couldn't sleep. Her mind wouldn't stop. Images popped up and scared her like those cardboard creatures in a haunted house. She thought a little warm milk might help. It had to be at least three a.m. Milking was just a couple hours away.

She heard her mother giggle and followed the faint sounds as they grew stronger. In the sunken area of molded adobe in the back room off the kitchen were her parents lying in front of a very small fire in the kiva fireplace. Its glow barely illuminated them there on the floor. Her mother lay on her back, her head perched against pillows. Her father leaned on his elbows next to her, listening. Occasionally he would lean over and taste her chin and neck which caused her to giggle. They were clearly lovers after all these years. She felt naughty watching from the shadows. When she was little they'd always lock their door at night. Sometimes she'd listen against the thick wood. Her mother would laugh in a way she never did in the daytime. Once she heard her stifle a raspy scream that came out of her like Mrs. Sanchez's burro. She couldn't understand what could be happening to her mother and why Papa let it go on so long.

She and Roberto would have been aged lovers like them by now. As fine a vintage as her parents. For as much as her parents must have made love, it surprised her she remained an only child. It probably had more to do with something being wrong with her than with her parents. A punishment. Maybe a blessing. At the age of thirty, she hadn't figured it out yet.

Miguel threw a couple of small, dried cottonwood branches into the fire behind the half-circle mouth of the fireplace. He came back to lie next to CeCe like he had been gone an eternity. The fire crackled happily and blew more flames, their orange tips dancing up to the darkness.

"I can't imagine what could have happened to Roberto," her mother sighed. "I can't believe he could do something like leave his pregnant wife. The poor girl." Rachel thought she saw some glassiness in her mother's eyes hit by the fire glow. The memory of her mother feeding Abby chicken and making her sip poleo tea spun in her head until she felt nauseous. Years ago when Rachel lost Roberto, you never saw her mother hold her or make her drink tea. A woman with a baby inside was more important.

"We don't really know him anymore. We don't know about their marriage. He's someone called Bobby now," her father said. She noticed the grief in her father's voice. He had always loved Roberto. He had lost him, too.

"I'd like to think married people are like us." Her mother reached down his shirtfront and stroked the thick hair on his chest. "And if that's true, I know what she must be feeling. How terrified she must be. I'd be going insane if it were you." She sat up and crinkled her brow. "I wonder what's going through our daughter's head. She's never gotten over Roberto. She seems to be crouching in the shadows. I can't tell what she's up to."

Rachel backed up further into the darkness. How dare her mother accuse her of crouching in shadows. Indignantly, she strained to listen.

"No telling what she's got your Maria concocting," her mother went on. "Some kind of witchy bruja stew, no doubt, and I don't mean a good Jewish *tsimmes*."

"Maria's devoted to Rachel," her father reasoned, "she would never do something to shame or hurt mi'ja." He tried to kiss her neck again, but she stopped him with her hand against his unbuttoned shirt.

"That would be all well and good if I thought Maria had any judgment. The woman curses people as a profession. You couldn't have had some nun relative follow you in your exile from your family. No, it had to be one of the most renowned brujas of New Mexico. As if a Jewish mother doesn't have enough to worry about."

Since when had her mother ever worried about her? She had doted completely on Charlie the whole time during their divorce. Catered to his feelings. Made him his favorite meals. Saw her as the bad guy. And now the same shit with Abby. At least Maria understood and knew how to come up with potions and curses that could make things go away, or at the very least, less irritating. CeCe had never even tried.

"She's my beloved grandmother's sister—I was raised with Maria. She's a powerful bruja, but loves as deeply as the next person. Ultimately, she'd want what's best for Rachel," her father said.

"I know my daughter and what she thinks is best for herself, and how good she is at convincing Maria," said her mother, shaking her head in disapproval. "So headstrong."

"I wonder where she gets that," teased her father. He kissed CeCe deeply, refusing to be held back any longer. Her mother whimpered like a hungry puppy.

Rachel turned around and slithered along the wall back through the shadows.

Chapter 4

The next morning Abby woke early, scrambling to get showered and dressed. She threw on a comfortable beige linen sun dress—ignoring the suitcase wrinkles—and her brown leather sandals.

When she emerged from her room she could hear the sounds of activity from the living area. She found a room full of people gathered around some folding tables and chairs. CeCe rushed over to her.

"What I tell you! This is our army—the good people of Esperanza. We're getting organized. Here, I'll introduce you. Hey, everybody! Here's Abby, Bobby's wife."

The group of maybe twenty-five or thirty people stopped talking and all eyes were on her. She recognized most of the faces from the funeral. "Thank you for helping," she said as she smiled a little hesitantly.

CeCe motioned to the man standing next to her. "Abby, this is Ramone Lavato Jr. He's Miguel's lifelong buddy and the retired sheriff—the one before Bowman—so he has loads of good ideas. Tell her, Ramone."

Ramone was a big teddy bear of a man with graying wavy hair and a paunch large enough to rest his clipboard against. "Well, the sheriff and his men will do their thing. It's good they got the APB out last night instead of waiting another twenty-four hours. They'll be interviewing everyone from the funeral and the community. But we can do some of that ourselves. I already have three trucks full of guys searching the back roads, the river ditches—there's a lot of horse and jeep trails back in there. They all know Ricardo's truck. I'm going to go interview the businesses that were still open that night in the area, hardware stores, grocery stores, bars. CeCe gave me a fairly recent picture of him to show around."

Abby looked at it clipped to his clipboard. It was Bobby's Navy picture, so handsome in his dress uniform, with his bright white shining teeth in his proud smile.

CeCe added, "The rest of us are having a flyer made with that picture. Ramone helped us with the wording and description. We're going to get them printed up and start plastering them from Albuquerque to Belen. We've set up an answering machine on the phone for when people call us with information."

"I've called my friends at the Isleta tribal police and briefed them," Ramone continued, "and also the other county villages with their own police forces, like Bosque Farms, Los Lunas, and Belen. I talked to APD, that's the Albuquerque police, and gave them a heads up. Of course these law enforcement folks already have the APB on the vehicle, but I wanted to give them more to go on. And it helps if they know this community effort will be checking in with them."

Abby nodded, her eyes threatening to spill tears. This is what she needed to hear.

"Abby, I'm Hazel Diego, one of CeCe's close friends and I'm a retired registered nurse. I'm going to canvas all the area clinics and all the hospitals up in Albuquerque. Now don't think the worst—I'm just thinking some health-related problem might have him getting treatment somewhere." She was a tall, no-nonsense looking woman, probably not the kind of nurse you could argue with in her day.

"I'm Carmen Lujan," a petite dark-haired woman spoke quietly but intently. "Another one of CeCe's friends. I'm going to all the parish priests and nuns to see if Roberto has sought spiritual help." In her simple dress and large cross around her neck, she might have been a nun herself.

A third woman, flashy clothes and makeup, a little heavy in a very round way stepped up to Abby. "Hi, hon, I'm Bonita Alvarez of Bonita's Hair and Nail Salon right on Highway 47. I have connections to the media in Albuquerque. I do Carla Armenta on Channel Four's cousin's hair. So, I'm going to alert the TV stations and newspapers to get the word out."

"I think this is enough to hit the poor girl with when she hasn't even had her breakfast," CeCe interjected. "So everybody go get busy and Abby and I will catch up later."

The din in the room resumed as people began to clear out on their designated tasks, calling out their good-byes.

"Thanks, CeCe," Abby said. "After I eat something, let's go help put up flyers. I really need to do something productive."

"Yeah, we'll pitch in later, but they're off to a good start."

After the flyers were made, a team of people came back to the Vigils' and they divided up territory to cover. They put an enlarged map of Valencia

County on the wall and drew a big target around it with Esperanza as the bull's-eye.

CeCe and Abby spent the entire day plastering them in Isleta and Esperanza, stopping only for a quick lunch. By dinner time, Abby started to drag and CeCe noticed.

"That's enough for one day! Bobby will kill me if I let you overdo it."

"You're right. At least today I felt like we accomplished something."

CeCe glanced at her again as she drove her home, "We got the wheels turning, that's the main thing. Ramone is a smart man, much smarter than Bowman, he'll make sure everything is done right. And the rest of those good souls! See, when you have people like that, you can rest easier. Let them take on the legwork. They're the foot soldiers. We don't have to run you ragged."

Abby nodded. Delegation. Something that was always hard for her, but now she had no choice. Even back at the restaurant she was just learning to let go, give up some control and trust Edward and his assistants to do their jobs. Then, leaving Abigail's was the ultimate delegation. Her stomach churned with worries and curiosity about how it was going in her absence, questions she hadn't even had time to think about since all of this happened. She longed to call Edward to cry out her heartache and hear his reassurances. Except, Edward would be the one crying and she'd end up giving him support and then he'd be too much of a mess to do his job and Abigail's would be in trouble. Bobby and Edward, the two people she was close to, and neither of them could help her through this.

"Ramone seems great. Why did he retire as sheriff?" Abby asked.

"He's taking care of his dad, Ramone Senior. His brother and sisters all moved away and he's the one left at home. He considered becoming a priest before he went into law enforcement. His dad had a mild stroke two years ago that left him needing a walker and his eyesight was failing, so Ramone didn't want to be working so much. He can leave him for four or five hours, but then he needs to help him with his medications and with his meals and stuff. He's a good son, a real *mensch!*"

La familia, Abby thought. What Bobby would have done.

The next morning, after Abby finished her morning shower, she stood naked in front of the guest-bathroom mirror. It was a large mirror, framed with yellow and blue Mexican tile. Little birds. Even the sink beneath it was made of hand-painted Talavera tile.

She wiped the steam from the mirror and looked at her swollen breasts and the gentle swell of her lower abdomen. She wanted to look more pregnant. She couldn't wait to have a big round belly that no one would mistake was a baby. Right now, finishing her fourth month, it only resembled a modest beer gut.

Tuesday. She hadn't seen Bobby since Saturday night. When she woke, she knew without having to remember. She felt a strange numbness. Like all the pain and fear was hovering above her somewhere, encased in a tight, overfilled balloon threatening to pop.

She dressed in jean shorts and a striped blue tank top. After she towel dried her hair, she put on a little makeup like this was a routine day. If only that were true.

As soon as she emerged from her room she could smell food. She found CeCe in the kitchen, singing to the radio in the midst of some cooking project. It was such a sunny room. Everything in the Vigils' house seemed awash with yellow light.

"What is that wonderful smell?" Abby asked.

"Good morning! Did you get some sleep?" CeCe's smile and eyes were so warm, all the golden light seemed to emanate from her.

"Like the dead. Any news?"

"I called Ramone on his cell phone, he said 'nothing big.' He's meeting with some cop friends up in Albuquerque. He'll be over later to go over the details. Hazel, Carmen, and Bonnie will show up at some point. A few crackpot messages from some sicko was on the answering machine. Nothing helpful."

There was a big pot of something simmering on the stove. Abby looked into the soft billows of steam with curiosity.

"Green chile stew. I put in browned pork, a ton of garlic, onion, potatoes. I'm about to make some flour tortillas, want to help?"

"Sure," Abby said. It was exactly what her restless mind and powerless hands needed.

"I'll scramble you an egg to eat with the first hot tortilla, for your breakfast." CeCe laid out her long pastry board. "The first year of our marriage, Miguel taught me every family recipe he knew. His family wouldn't come near us. I felt terrible; no one should pay such a price for love. So I figured, I had to learn those recipes. I would cook all the foods he loved." She shrugged. "Seemed like the least I could do."

"What about your family?"

"All back in New York. They had a fit, of course. I brought home this beautiful boy, I mean I knew they'd be upset he wasn't Jewish. But I was eighteen, naïve; I didn't factor in the Mexican part. My *bubbe* promised to die before the wedding. She was so disappointed when she didn't. I think the whole family was, they wanted her death on my head. Instead of a wedding, they planned a funeral. But the wedding went on—at the courthouse. They all came so they could cry and show their disapproval. I didn't care. My bags were packed. I was crazy in love."

She dusted the board with flour and shoved it aside. In a big white bowl, she measured flour with the scoop of her hand, threw in salt and baking powder.

"Did they disown you?" Abby asked as young Frank Sinatra crooned in the background. CeCe listened to one of those stations that played music from fifty or sixty years ago.

"We stay in touch. Not like some of Miguel's family who live two miles from where we stand but never speak to us."

"My parents disowned me. We haven't spoken in ten years."

CeCe worked some lard into her flour mixture. "You miss them?"

"We were never close. It wasn't that kind of a family. That's why I became a chef. I spent all my time in the kitchen with our Mexican cook, Lupe. She wasn't allowed to cook Mexican food, so I didn't learn about that until later on. But I did watch her cook intricate nouveau California cuisine, French cuisine, all the dishes my parents served at their swank dinner parties."

"Miguel likes my Jewish dishes, too. I'll get to craving some matzo ball soup or noodle kugel. Rachel won't eat it. She won't cook either, except to make her goat cheese." CeCe added some warm water and kneaded the dough until it was elastic. She covered it with a slightly damp dishtowel, and shoved it aside to rest.

Abby stepped back as CeCe rummaged in her bottom cupboards, producing a huge cast iron griddle, lifting it to the stove top as if it were as light as a cookie sheet.

"What kind of food did you have at your restaurant?"

"Very eclectic. I like to learn about different ethnic foods and create something new. Unusual flavors, different vegetables. I do some Mexican seafood dishes, but California Mexican is really different from New Mexican, Bobby always tells me . . ." Her last few words came out as little more than a whisper. Her cloak of numbness threatened to unravel. She shifted her focus back to the cooking, a familiar therapy.

"Okay. We can shape our tortillas with our hands and then roll them out and cook them here on this dry griddle." CeCe put some flour on her hands and rubbed the excess onto Abby's palms. They pinched off egg-sized balls and rolled them in their hands.

Abby's hands were instantly at home in the dough. She rolled out perfect seven-inch circles and placed them on the griddle. They worked without conversation. Tony Bennet sang to them, Duke Ellington made them dance. The hot bready smell was intoxicating. The stack of lightly browned, supple tortillas grew and in far too short a time they had scraped the last of the dough from the bowl with their fingernails.

Abby's stomach growled in anticipation as CeCe scrambled her eggs, turned them out onto a tortilla, added a ladle of green chili from the pot, a handful of grated cheddar cheese and rolled it up. "Here you go, honey, enjoy."

Miguel came in the back door, stomping imaginary mud from his feet, taking off his gloves and mopping his brow. "Where's my dinner, woman?" He winked at Abby as he hugged and kissed CeCe.

"It's only eleven-thirty!" CeCe said.

"I've been walking the chile fields since six! Man, it's going to be great crop this year. That last rain we had, those plants are half a foot taller already." He got himself a bowl for his chile, a rolled tortilla hung from his mouth as he sat next to Abby. He bit off a mouthful and then dunked the remainder of the tortilla into the steaming bowl.

Rachel came in the back door. Her white T-shirt was streaked with dirt, her thick long hair was wound into an impromptu knot. She washed her hands and forearms at the sink, casting glances over her shoulder in Abby's direction.

Abby chewed the last bite of her burrito. The cheesy, eggy flavor juxtaposed with the indescribable fire of the green chile to produce a culinary experience she had never known. "I have to learn all of your recipes, CeCe, for Bobby."

Rachel filled her bowl and sat on Miguel's other side. "There you go, Ma, the daughter you've always wanted."

CeCe brought Abby another hot tortilla, this time slathered in butter and honey. "Magdalena, his mother, was my other teacher. Little Roberto would beg like a puppy for tastes. He spent more time getting under foot in the kitchen than Rachel. She was always outside catching bugs, getting dirty. Maggie and I would laugh that our kids had their personalities switched at birth."

"After she died, I don't know what he ate, Ricardo was no cook," Miguel said.

"I know what he ate! Don't you remember I made two batches of whatever I cooked and took it over to them? After a while Roberto spent all his time over here anyhow and Ricardo started to open cans or eat those godawful TV dinners. No wonder Roberto married the most beautiful cook he could find in all of California."

Abby smiled. She almost thought she saw Rachel roll her eyes. But then her aquamarine gaze fixed on Abby. "You seem a lot happier, did you finally hear from your wandering husband?"

Her tone was as sweet as the honey melting in Abby's mouth. It took a second for Abby to process the hostility behind those words, their deliberate invisible arrows shot so accurately, straight into her heart. It knocked her back into her chair.

CeCe rushed in to rescue her. "Rachel! You know we haven't heard, or it would have been the first thing we said—"

"It's okay, CeCe," Abby broke in. She looked at Rachel, who continued to eat as if all of this had nothing to do with her. She summoned all her nerve and used the voice she would use on smartass busboys or tardy restaurant suppliers. "Wherever Bobby is, he's trying like hell to get back to me and his baby."

"Of course he is!" Miguel said. "None of us doubts that for a second, do we Rachel?"

She looked at him with a brief flicker of anger and then calmly paused to lick some chile from the corner of her lips. "Sure, Papa, sure. He'll be back."

After lunch, Abby put on her running shoes and told CeCe she was going out for some exercise. Truth be told, she had to get out of there. It was either long, sad, sympathetic looks or whatever mind games Rachel was playing; either way she couldn't stand another minute of it.

She strode briskly, just short of a jog, propelled by the energy of her anger. She felt more alive than she had in days. She followed the road toward the main the highway and village.

It was warm but her perspiration evaporated so quickly in the dry air it kept her comfortable. She picked up the pace to a rhythmic jog, reassuring herself that her doctor had said there was no reason not to continue her already established exercise routines. Her industrial strength sports bra kept her breasts from hurting.

The oxygen she sucked in and pumped through her veins cleared her head. She reviewed the facts of her situation. Number One: Bobby would never stay away on his own accord. Number Two: She was of no use to him if she succumbed to her emotions and took to her bed. No, she had to hang tough, use her brain. She had to lead the efforts to find him. Bobby's life might depend on it and she wouldn't let him down.

She knew him better than anyone. He'd been with her these last twelve years. Ten years as her husband. Rachel didn't even know the man he had become. She only had distant memories of a little boy or a young teenager. She could think what she wanted. Her own intimate knowledge, her oneness with Bobby would be the key to solving this, but she thanked God there were so many people generously volunteering to help.

She reached the main highway and continued her jog through town. Her ponytail felt like a flag as it swung behind her. She managed to smile as she passed people in the small grocery store's parking lot. The parking lot to the junk shop was crammed, as was the feed store's. She slowed down when she saw Charlie loading bags of something into the back of his dusty white pickup. His light blue T-shirt was soaked through with sweat.

"Hey," she said.

"Hello," he said, squinting in the sun. "Come all this way to just to help?"

She looked at the fifty-pound bags of chicken scratch, dog and cat food he was loading. "Oh you look like you can handle it."

"These are the last three bags. I'll buy you something cold to drink."

"Sure," Abby said, tasting how dry she was. She must have sweat off a quart on her jog.

He tossed the last bag in and secured the tailgate. "Coffee shop is right over there."

"I'm pretty sweaty," she said.

"Well, there is a strict dress code and you might just make the sweat minimum but you're not nearly dusty enough. Lucky for you I got enough for both of us, so I'll get you in." He gave her that killer smile.

The coffee shop was in an old pink adobe structure with a wood-plank porch and overhang. Charlie opened the screen door that jangled with bells and a gust of swamp-cooled air gave Abby goose bumps. Her leg muscles twitched happily from her exercise.

The inside was darker and it took a moment for Abby's eyes to adjust from the intense afternoon sun. It was mostly empty: a couple of women shared a back table, sacks from the junk store at their feet. They had their heads together in girlfriend confidante mode.

Everything was wood. The floors, the mismatched tables and chairs, the long bar where customers placed their orders. There was even a small dance floor and tiny stage on the far end of the room.

"What can I get you?" A teenage girl with a tuft of magenta hair and a pierced eyebrow asked.

Abby smiled at her. She could be back in San Diego. "Do you have any iced herbal tea?"

"I can make whatever you like, here's the list."

"Lemon Zinger," Abby said.

"I'll take some regular iced tea," Charlie said.

They sat down. Charlie leaned back and appraised her. "You're holding up."

She nodded. "Everything that can be done is being done. I just have to have faith we're going to find him and he's all right."

"Yeah," Charlie said, "can't be easy."

Their drinks arrived and there was silence as they gulped as much as they could in one breath. Abby held the icy glass to her face.

"How did you and Bobby meet up?" Charlie asked.

"I was a freshman at San Diego State, he was in the Navy. We met at a party. He was totally unlike any guy I'd ever gone out with. Not just racially, I mean that's a given since up to then I'd only dated sons of my parents' friends, you know, the country-club scene. Which I hated. Anyway, it was just instant connection. We couldn't get enough of each other." Charlie leaned closer as he studied her face. She found herself blushing. "Corny, huh."

"No, no. So you got married when?"

"Spring break after my parents forbade the engagement. I got my MBA and went straight into the California Culinary Institute in San Diego for a year. Bobby started his first sub tour. I opened Abigail's the year after that. Got my own investors and everything. I was able to buy them out after the first year and own it free and clear." She cringed, hearing herself sound a little too proud. "Anyway, I'm sure my parents were pissed about that."

"They didn't want you to be successful?"

"Not after I married Bobby, not without needing their money. They thought cutting me off would make me fail, make me leave Bobby and come crawling back. They underestimated me." She felt her cocky smile.

He lifted his glass and toasted hers, "Something I'll never do."

"So what's your story?"

"I'm originally from Texas, a little place called Sweetwater. I did farm and ranch labor, took some classes at a community college in Austin for a couple of years. Realized the only stuff I liked was stuff I'd never make a living at. You know, art, literature, writing, philosophy. So, I packed up my truck and headed west. Texas may be big, but it was too much of the same thing. 'Good old boy' mentality."

"You're not a good old boy?"

He laughed. "Nope. Not that kind, anyway. Turned up in Esperanza, New Mexico. Met Miguel, he hired me on. That was six years ago. Rachel avoided me the first few months, but gradually I wore her down. She hated how much her parents liked me. Once I proved how hardworking

I was, how I didn't have any hidden agendas, she started letting her guard down."

"So, eventually she fell in love with you?"

There was a pause as he jiggled the ice in his glass. His hazel eyes searched the tin ceiling for words. Finally, he just shook his head as if bewildered. "I don't know if she ever did. I think she finally married me out of sheer fatigue. It was CeCe, me, and Miguel on one team. She couldn't beat us so she joined us."

"Why would you settle for that? Come on, look at you, there's got to be women all over you." There was something about him that emboldened her.

He shrugged, smiled, and even appeared a little embarrassed. "It's a sickness, what I have. Maybe 'cause she didn't want me. Maybe I like a challenge. Maybe I'm just a guy in love."

"So, what happened?"

"Sometimes it seemed like she was going to relax into it. We had some real good times." His eyes looked above her. Then, his smile faded. "But, there's always been the part of her I couldn't reach. A year ago she decided she had to get divorced. I couldn't stop her. I was going to leave."

"Why didn't you?"

"I never had much of a home growing up. I knew what I had here I'd never find anywhere else. Why should I give it up?"

"You still love her."

"If you find a cure, let me know."

Abby hesitated, not sure how she should frame this and then just said it. "Rachel seems to really resent me. In fact, she's a real bitch."

Charlie laughed. "Yeah, she can be like that. There's another side, she just isn't showing you yet. Part of it is, it hurt her real bad when Bobby left home and she blames you for him settling down so far away from here. Then there's you being white."

"So are you!"

"Yeah, and it was a real problem for us at times, especially at first, and then anytime after that when she wanted to push me away, it was a convenient weapon."

"But nobody else seems that way around here, at least I haven't picked up on it."

"Oh, it's around. Most people are real cool here and don't make race a big deal. I run into it once in a while. I think Rachel's more defensive, being mixed. When you're a kid, things are supposed to be black or white, you know? You choose teams. I think she caught some flak from the white kids for being Hispanic and from the Hispanic kids for being less than full-blooded. At least that's how it was in Texas."

"But her parents seem so happy, wouldn't she see that as a good example?"

Charlie chewed some ice. "Naw, see, in her mind, her dad screwed up for marrying a white Jewish New Yorker. But since she's a real daddy's girl, she doesn't blame him as much as she blames her mother. So CeCe gets the fallout. Of course, as much as I love CeCe, she does a fair amount of pushing Rachel's buttons, too. Miguel and I just try to stay out of the way when those two get going."

Abby nodded and then noticed Ramone was coming toward them.

"Que pasa?" Charlie greeted him. "Sit down, join us."

Ramone sat down with his giant glass of soda pop. "I've been on a wild goose chase all afternoon. I got a call from Albuquerque that Bobby was seen at some bars on Central, so I was checking it out. Nada!" He took a long drink from his glass. "But here's something and I know Bowman is hot to spring it on you. There are witnesses who put him at Pablo's Bar the night he went missing."

"Who?" Charlie and Abby asked simultaneously.

"Pablo, Pablo's nephew, and Sammy West so far. They're tracking down whoever else was there that night. Bowman has the details and he's headed out to the Vigils' place."

Abby rode back with Charlie. When they arrived, the sheriff's car was parked under the shade of a cottonwood tree. Abby felt her chest constrict, an involuntary surge of adrenalin doubled her pulse.

Charlie opened her door and took her hand. When he must have felt it shaking, he gripped it tight and looked into her eyes and gave a quick nod.

It was all she could do not to run into the house. Charlie kept a hand on her shoulder, very casually. It kept her at a normal pace. "Breathe," he whispered.

They were seated at the kitchen table, the heart and hearth of the Vigil home. Just as Abby and Charlie entered the room, he surreptitiously tickled her along her ribs and laughed a jolly little laugh as if they were finishing some private joke. She gave something close enough to a laugh so that when they faced Miguel, CeCe, Rachel, and Sheriff Bowman, she was smiling.

"Hello, what's all this about?" Charlie said with total nonchalance.

Abby looked at him with gratitude and managed to sit down with an air of confidence. "Hi, Sheriff, any news?"

"Yeah, I was just telling the Vigils here I got a little bit, not much, but it's a start."

"Good!" Abby said, perhaps a bit too enthusiastically.

"After Bobby left you, he showed up at Pablo's Bar around eight-thirty p.m. Pablo's nephew was at the bar. Says Bobby had three quick beers and looked upset. Sammy West was there, said the same thing. Bobby had his beers and then downed a shot of tequila that Pablo gave him on the house to welcome him home."

"Did he talk to him, what did he say?" Abby blurted.

"Sammy talked about what a shame it was about his dad. He said Bobby was polite but not too talkative. He did go over and speak to your crazy old aunt Maria, who was grabbing at his hand, trying to read his palm or some fool thing. He came in angry and he left drunk and still angry maybe an hour later. Sammy and Pablo agree on that."

"Bobby never drank like that. He never drank to get drunk," Abby insisted. Then she remembered his drinking the night before the funeral.

"I remember a time when Roberto could drink with the best of them," Rachel said with that infuriating smugness.

"What about the store? He was going to the store to get us some food." Abby could feel herself start to plead with him. Charlie reached over and patted her leg under the table.

"He never made it to the store. They were open until ten p.m. and Rosie was the only checker. She said she would have loved to seen Bobby, hadn't seen him since high school. But she would have known him."

"What do you make of this, Sheriff?" Miguel asked.

"It may not have been Bobby's pattern to go off and get drunk, but a man doesn't bury his father every day. And he was mad at his wife. Do I think he's come to some harm? Possible, but no sign of that. This is only Tuesday and he was last seen late Saturday night. Could be he drove himself out into the mountains and got lost, broke down, or picked up more liquor at some convenience store somewhere and is on some marathon bender. There's thousands a miles of back roads in this state. He could be anywhere. But this is where he ain't, he ain't in any hospital or on any slab in the morgue. No law enforcement has had any run-ins with him in the whole state. No warnings, no DWIs. No arrests to sleep it off in the drunk tank. The truck is still missing, so it's safe guess wherever it is, is where he is, and frankly," he paused to bite his dry cracked lips, "that could be anywhere."

It was late afternoon before Rachel finished the second milking and she could sneak away to see Maria.

The potion Maria was boiling on her old stove stunk up her kitchen. When Rachel was a little girl she used to believe the stinkier the potion the better it would work. Maria rattled through jars and bottles in her pantry until she found just the right ingredient and added a tight pinch to the brew. She looked just like the witches in cartoons, down to the lopsided toothless mouth. She was a powerful bruja and had a large following of Hispanic families from all the Rio Communities. Some came seeking the right job, some wanted to be irresistible to a new love interest. She spent a lot of time uncursing babies who had been given the evil eye. Hysterical mothers would practically prostrate themselves and beg her to save their child who had been doomed by having been admired by some Anglo. They came to Maria first, the priest second. A bruja was close to the devil. Had more bargaining power.

Maria stirred the liquid and took it off the heat, still stirring away in small aggressive circles.

Rachel could see Reyes out of the window over the old woman's shoulder. He was the closest thing she had for a sibling. She'd known him since he was thirteen, when he arrived on Maria's doorstep. Her old friend Señor Maricos from Mexico had rescued him after his parents were murdered for a pathetic few pesos crossing the border. Unable to palm him off on any of his relatives who already had too many mouths to feed and more on the way, he turned to Maria who could see the potential usefulness of a sturdy young back around the place.

Reyes struggled with English and was of borderline intelligence, so he took a lot of teasing and torment from their classmates. Rachel looked out for him, feeding the enormous crush he had on her. She tolerated his sad little love notes scrawled in phonetically spelled English until he became more of a social liability in high school, when she began to distance herself from him. Anyone could see how jealous Reyes was of Roberto, who was always good-natured about Reyes's feeble attempts to compete with him for Rachel. Reyes snubbed Roberto's hand of friendship, embarrassing Rachel with his obvious mad-dog dirty looks.

Watching how hard he worked, clearing the trash and weeds in the hot sun, she felt a pang of guilt thinking of how she treated him at times. He'd grown into a large man but kept the shape of a pudgy young boy. His already balding head glistened with sweat and she wanted to scold him for not wearing his cap. Big misshaped dark plastic bags encircled him like black boulders. He picked up a dead chicken and stuffed it into a bag as if it were just another piece of garbage.

"The sheriff said you were at Pablo's the night Roberto was there," Rachel said, turning her attention back to Maria. "Why didn't you tell me?" It wasn't like the old bruja to keep something from her. They shared everything. Good or evil.

Maria hacked up a phlegm ball, spit it into the brew and kept stirring. Must be an antidote to reverse another bruja's curse. Probably one on a man who couldn't keep it in his pants and his scorned girlfriend or wife had a curse put on him. Maria got a lot of those. Her dried apricot face peered into the pot, sniffed, and then looked at her with her beady eyes. "There is nothing to tell. I was at my table in the back reading tea leaves, mi'ja, like I always do." Maria lied better than she told the truth.

Locals believed Maria took the shape of animals and traveled unnoticed, listening, watching, cursing. Or that her soul entered a raven at night and flew the sky acrobatically peering into windows to learn the secrets that made them weak. Maria knew what made Rachel weak and she was glad her old aunt loved her beyond reason. Maria would never use her mi'ja's weaknesses against her.

"Someone said Roberto bought you a glass of sangria and you two were sitting at the back table together. That you were looking at his hands—his palms, tía."

"He was showing me how they have softened since he left us. That is all. He went and got drunk after that," Maria said, pouring the slimy solution into a small funnel sticking out of a green-glass beer bottle.

"You were reading Roberto's palms, tía! You saw into his future! Tell me what you saw!" Rachel begged. She would not let him slip away from her again. There was so much to tell him. Confess to him. And him to her.

"His palms were soft and impressionable. That is all I need to know. His future is what we make it," Maria said, taking her veiny brown hand and smacking the cork tight down into the bottle, "Sit, mi'ja, talk to your old tía."

After her hour-long confession to Maria, Rachel left, stopping on the front lawn to stretch and breathe in some air that was not saturated with that foul potion.

"*Buenas tardes, señorita,*" Reyes greeted her.

He appeared from nowhere and she jumped. "Oh, I didn't see you! You sure are working hard out here. Where's your hat?" she asked, her heart still thumping.

"I think I lost it. Did you find Roberto yet?"

Rachel realized he still saw Roberto as competition. She smiled at his sweet, immature attentions. She shouldn't have been such a bitch to him in high school. "You don't have to worry about Roberto, he'll be back soon. But you know you'll always be my buddy, Reyes, no matter what, right?"

Chapter 5

Wednesday morning, Abby woke crying. Her nightmares segued seamlessly into the hell of her waking life. She gave in to deep wracking sobs. How was she supposed to get up and function like a normal person? Showering, dressing, eating, all the stupid unavoidable tasks seemed an affront to the reality of her missing husband. Her Bobby! She cried, the sheets stuffed to her lips, needing his arms around her, remembering every time she may have taken him for granted. Cursing everyone and everything that led to the night he left, including herself. Why did she feel so much guilt? It was irrational, so why did it so easily penetrate her heart and spread through her like poisonous venom?

Her baby began to kick and turn, reminding her she didn't have a choice but to be strong and brave. She didn't have the luxury to writhe in bed, refuse food, not survive. Whatever happens or had already happened, she must go on.

After her shower, she gave up trying to conceal her red head complexion's evidence of crying, and after grabbing a carton of yogurt for her breakfast, found CeCe with her girlfriends in the living room. They were doing their crafts for the nuns at Our Lady of Fatima's Church. CeCe was working on a colorful lap quilt. Hazel had her woodcarving tools spread onto some newspapers and was whittling one of her folk-art animals. Carmen held a needlepoint ring and Bonita's hands rhythmically worked her crocheting needle in and out of the rainbow afghan on her lap.

Hazel saw her first. "I was just asking CeCe what obstetrician you're going to have."

Abby sat next to her on the huge sofa, stirring her yogurt and trying to think. "My doctor in San Diego gave me a number for New Mexico Women's Specialists and I called from there and made an appointment with a Dr. Lark. It's not for a few weeks yet."

Hazel smiled and nodded. "Oh, you'll like her, she's wonderful. She's with Presbyterian Hospital, so you'll deliver there and it's one of the best. How are you going to pay for it all?"

"Hazel!" CeCe admonished.

"Well, I'm a nurse, I think of these things!"

"It's okay," Abby said. "We've still got insurance through the restaurant's health plan."

"There, are you satisfied, Nurse Budinski?" CeCe teased.

Hazel made a quick jab with her knife in CeCe's general direction setting them all off into giggles.

"Don't mind us. We're crazy. We'd all be locked in the nut house but as long as we do our group therapy here, we're okay," Bonita laughed. "It's not really about doing charity for the nuns, we just like to dish some *mitote*, you know, girl talk."

"Speak for yourself, Bonita. For some of us it is about the nuns and serving the poor with our donations," Carmen said, threading her needle with blue yarn.

"I forgot you never were a girl, so how would you know about girl talk?" Bonita shot back. "Abby, I heard Ramone was following a lead up in Española and Chimayo. There's this drug cartel up there. It's a hotbed for heroin—"

"Bonnie, what could that have to do with Roberto?" CeCe interrupted.

"I'm just saying what I heard! Where there are drugs there's crime! Maybe Roberto stumbled into a crime scene and they took him hostage—"

"Put a sock in it, Bonnie! Abby doesn't need to hear rumors and gossip hot from the beauty shop. Jesus!" Hazel rolled her eyes.

"Excuse me, Hazel, but invoking our dear Lord's name in vain does not help matters, although I happen to agree with you about Bonita's sources," Carmen said in her quietly pointed way.

"You don't need to shelter me," Abby said. "If Ramone is checking it out, maybe there is something to it. What else are people saying?"

"This is a small town, Abby. When there is no news, they make it up," CeCe said. "Española and Chimayo are over two hours north of here. It's pretty unlikely Bobby could be mixed up in anything that far away. Ramone is checking it out just in case. No stone unturned, you know?"

Bonita began to stuff her afghan into a rhinestone-studded denim bag. "I have to do a perm in fifteen minutes, so I'm out of here." She stood and pointed a long magenta fingernail. "But I'll say one last thing, Abby is right. Don't protect her about what people are saying. Ninety-five percent might be total bullshit! But it only takes one person whispering the right clue and the whole thing is solved. Ramone is smart enough to know this and that is why he listens to me and my sources. Things are said in a beauty shop that they don't even tell to the priests."

Bonita turned to Abby. "Come over to the shop. I'll give you a facial and scalp massage, on me."

"Thanks," Abby said, accepting her perfumy, bosomy hug.

"Abby has an interview with KOB TV on the noon news," CeCe said. "So we better get moving, too."

"Do you want me to do your hair and makeup? I could squeeze you in," Bonita offered, running her hands through Abby's hair, her brow furrowing with the possibilities.

Abby's eyes wandered over Bonnie's kind but overly made-up face, her big hair and politely declined.

Over the next week, Abby was interviewed by every network TV affiliate and local station in Albuquerque and Santa Fe. It was just the kind of story people couldn't get enough of: pretty, devastated wife, local boy who had served his country and come home to bury his father and raise his unborn child, only to vanish without a trace on a dark and stormy night.

Increasingly, Abby didn't recognize herself. There was a part of her watching as she gave flawless interviews, balanced with just the right portions of wrenching grief, understandable fear, admirable strength, and unyielding faith. Who was this woman who could get dusted off for shine, sit professionally in front of cameras, and give articulate answers to invasive questions?

Abby didn't know. She could only let her take over, run the show. If it could help find Bobby, it was worth it. At night, writhing alone in bed, her pillowcase clamped between her teeth so she wouldn't scream out loud, tears and sweat drenching the sheets, she was herself again.

"What did your friends in San Diego say when you called?" CeCe asked.

Abby sat there, as they were riding into Albuquerque for a radio interview in CeCe's 1965 ice-blue Mustang convertible, trying to think of how to explain it. She slid slightly on the slick white leather bucket seat and looked out the window at the now too-familiar scenery as it whipped by. CeCe took full advantage of the seventy-five-mile-per-hour speed limit and then some.

She knew in a situation like this another woman would call her close friends, her family, to fly to her side, give her support, sustenance.

"I called Edward, but I didn't tell him. I love him and it was great to hear his voice and hear him go on about how wonderful Abigail's is going and all about his new boyfriend, but if I told him, he would totally freak out and try to lean on me for support, which I don't need. And then I'd have to worry about the restaurant while he's falling apart. No, I want Paul and Edward to have only positive thoughts of me and Bobby starting our new, wonderful life together."

There was only one person she could think of, whom she would give anything to call, and he was the one person she couldn't reach. The situation was like one of those mind-teasers that turned your thoughts into circles; she needed Bobby at her side to help her through his not being at her side. As for her parents, the last thing she needed would be their I-told-you-so's amid their racist comments.

Bobby had never understood how to Abby, the loss of her family was no big deal. She knew he was haunted by his father's disapproval. He had looked at her with a mixture of amazement and suspicion that her family could mean so little to her. That the people who brought her into this world could drop out of it like spoiled fruit.

At first she tried to compare it to a divorce. They were all better off without some imposed and implied relationship that didn't exist. But with divorce, usually there had been something to value in the beginning, something that had become lost or damaged. There was grief for what used to be or what might have been.

In her experience, a mother and a father were titles for jobs, like, say, the housekeeper, the pool man, the gardener, the driver, and so forth. She figured her parents were hired like the rest of the staff, she just didn't know by whom. Her nannies seemed to change with the season and had approached their posts with little enthusiasm or personal investment. She wondered now if that wasn't by design, a condition of hire. Or, were her parents merely drawn to women who mirrored their own emotional detachment?

In any case, Abby had tried to explain to Bobby, she came into consciousness with a particular reality she accepted without question or judgment, the way all children do. How could she miss what she never experienced? When she read storybooks with affectionate mommies and daddies, she figured they were in the same category as talking bunnies and duckies.

Adults, it seemed to Abby at the time, were like tall paper dolls. Two-dimensional and boring. Until Lupe came into her life, that is. She was six when her parents hired her to replace the cook caught stealing meat. Lupe was a revelation. Boisterous, all arms and bosom, as round and soft as the sweet-smelling rolls she made every morning. She sang songs in a language that stirred Abby as surely as if she'd used her big wooden spoon.

Abby spent every spare moment in Lupe's kitchen. Lupe, being both a loving and a practical woman, put Abby to work. Abby loved the feel of flour in her hands, the way lemons released their juice in her fists. The colors, scents, and textures made her dizzy with joy. It was way better than crayons or modeling clay, this was real art.

Abby's parents became aware of the situation when Nanny Clare, who seemed more miffed that her territory had been invaded than actually rebuffed when Abby preferred the Mexican cook, informed them. As the field-hockey champion at her former girls' school, a time of glory Nanny Clare was fond of retelling, Abby figured her competitive nature had become reawakened, not any sudden desire for Abby's company.

Abby's parent's informed her it was not appropriate for her to ensconce herself in the kitchen with Lupe. When she pressed them for a reason, they said, "She's not like us."

"I know," Abby remembered informing them. "She's better."

It occurred to Abby now, as CeCe continued to glance at her while driving, that her parent's had said pretty much the same thing when she brought Bobby home to meet them. Only this time their apathy didn't clear the way for her victory. This had ramifications. Their daughter marrying a Mexican would never be endorsed in their social circles. How could she do this to them? They pulled out their only weapon, a weapon they could not imagine would fail. They threatened to disown her. If she went through with this insanity, she would no longer be their daughter, their sole heiress. Abby shrugged and took them up on it.

"And my parents are the last people I want to talk to about it," Abby finally said, knowing CeCe would understand.

Ten days after they had arrived in Esperanza, a week since his disappearance, with no new leads and Ramone running in circles, it occurred to Abby they were supposed to have called the moving company in San Diego to arrange transport of the rest of their possessions. In the rush, Bobby thought it would be easier to put their things in temporary storage and just get themselves to Esperanza, to get settled before they had to deal with all the boxes of books, clothes, Abby's cooking paraphernalia, skis, camping equipment, two TVs, stereo, CDs, computer, linens, towels, artwork, and the myriad of other sundries that somehow became necessities.

As soon as she thought of it, she desperately wanted her stuff, their stuff. She wanted to smell it and touch it and know that it was real. She wanted to breathe in Bobby's DNA that was all over it.

But where would it go? Charlie and Miguel had started work on Ricardo's house a couple of days ago. She had been apathetic about it when they encouraged her to go over with them, discuss what needed to be done, pick out paint colors. Suddenly, this was the most important thing she could imagine. She could immerse herself in home decorating, lovingly placing their stuff all around her, create the place Bobby must have imagined when his eyes lit up, telling her how great it would be to live in the house he had grown up in. The home he would return to, any minute now.

First she would run over and inspect their progress. She hoped they hadn't started painting yet. She would estimate how long they needed to get things in order and then call the movers to arrange the date.

"I'm going over to the house," Abby called to CeCe as she ran past the kitchen. CeCe came after her, dishcloth still in her hand. "I'll come with you!"

It was hot under the midday sun. There hadn't been a drop of rain since the storm when Bobby disappeared and none was predicted. The ground was dusty where Abby's feet had once been stuck in the mud. The wide expanse of sky was a soothing shade of blue uninterrupted by a single cloud all the way to the mountains in the east.

"What's the deal with them?" Abby asked over the constant cacophony of roosters as they approached the fenced, ramshackle property.

"Baca family. Not the neighborly type. Real losers. They started out renting the place from Ricardo, it used to be a nice little place he and Bobby built for rental income about twelve years ago now. In fact, it was Bobby's idea before he joined the Navy. Bobby thought it was a waste of space and they might as well make some money and even get a tax break if they weren't going to farm it. The two of them built it over the summer after Bobby graduated high school. I guess it was Bobby's plan to leave Ricardo with something, since he'd already enlisted and not told anybody about it. But that's a whole other story. So, the Bacas moved in. At the time, they were just a young married couple with her mother. Her mother died of cancer a few years after that and the wife had a little boy. Then things started to change over there."

They stopped under the shade of a tree about thirty feet from the chain-link fencing on the Baca property line. CeCe squinted toward the Bacas' house, barely visible in the jumble of rooster cages, trash, and a large tin-roofed shed. "They fought all the time. You could hear them sometimes, terrible yelling and screaming. Miguel called the cops more than once. Then one day the wife left for good. But he wouldn't let her take the boy, little Santiago. His brother moved in after his wife left. Brought the gang life with him. There's cockfighting, drugs, you name it. Ricardo didn't like it, even tried to evict them once, but he got threatened. See, around here, it's blackmail. It's understood that people like the Bacas will retaliate by killing your animals, vandalizing your property or worse if you mess with them and they know that law enforcement won't do anything because they can't prove it. So anyway, then they pressured Ricardo to sell them the place. He tells Miguel, 'I don't know. I don't want to sell it to them but I could use the cash and be done with it.' Miguel tried to talk him out of it, said he would try to protect him if things got nasty but he goes ahead and sells it. In a way, I was relieved, I didn't want them coming after us. And they keep to themselves. Except for the roosters, it's been a lot quieter in the last few years. I worry about that little Santiago. At least with them still here, we can keep an eye on him . . ."

She trailed off as Baca seemed to materialize from the weeds and a junked car near the fence line. He was big, more than six feet tall, and might have been a boxer at one time, before all the beer had deposited around his gut. He was bare-chested, and his jeans rode low on his hips exposing the grungy band of his boxer shorts.

CeCe startled Abby by grabbing her hand and marching her right over to him. "Mr. Baca? I want you to meet your new neighbor."

He was silent, facing them. He wore a blue bandana tied around his forehead, just above his dark glasses. Abby tried to look into them, find his eyes, but could only see herself wildly distorted in their reflection. "I'm Abby Silva, Bobby's wife. He's missing. Maybe you noticed something—about ten days ago—the night of the bad storm?" Abby came as close to him as the chain-link would permit, reminding her of a prison yard.

"The sheriff came twice already," Baca said, as if it was her fault.

"But did you see anything, like Bobby driving away, anything?" Abby persisted.

"Nada. Like I tell the sheriff, I don't mix with neighbors. I leave them alone, they leave me alone. Live and let live, no?" He turned away then, his roosters screaming as he moved through them, their shiny heads rising in chorus, wings flapping, like hysterical fans mobbing a celebrity.

"What a charmer!" CeCe said as they resumed their walk.

They reached the Silva house. Her house. In the daylight, without a storm pelting her with hail, she liked the look of it. The curves of its genuine brown adobe walls and roofline, the front door painted turquoise. The patio in front encircled by the low wall and garden gate. The empty flowerpots she would fill.

Charlie's familiar white truck sat there, its bed a jumble of tools.

CeCe opened the door, "Hey, fellas, you got company!"

As Abby came over the threshold, she felt herself start to tremble. She clenched her hands into fists to control their shaking. It felt like only moments ago when she had entered this house for the first time, with Bobby at her side. It came back in excruciating detail. The sound of the storm, the stench of the garbage, the sight of the cockroaches scurrying about as if they owned the place. The tension in the air between them. She wanted that night back more than she had ever wanted anything apart from Bobby himself when they first met.

With effort she managed to shove aside the images and focus on the house as it was now. The junk had all been cleared away. The front room was larger than it had first seemed, with large windows. There was an old sofa and a well-worn brown leather chair. It was obvious Ricardo had not changed anything after his wife had died in 1975. There was nothing in the way of decoration. The room felt empty, vacant in a way that may have prompted Ricardo's original wish to fill it with something. A wish that became confused and out of control.

"We'll get the fireplace chimney cleaned, there's a lot of creosote built up in there," said Miguel as he appeared from one of the back rooms.

"Where did all the stuff go?" Abby asked, as if she might have imagined it all.

"Some of it's in the landfill. The salvageable stuff, Barbara bought for her junk shop. I just put the proceeds in the reward fund."

Charlie came in, wiping his hands on a rag. "If it isn't the lady of the house."

Abby smiled. He always knew what to say.

"Here's what we have so far. Now, remember you told us not to worry about the money, just do what was needed, right?" Charlie said.

Thanks to the ongoing income from her restaurant and years of careful saving and investing, Abby and Bobby were financially secure.

"Yeah, whatever it needs, it'll be fine. I trust you."

"Miguel, you can go ahead and order that gold-fixtured imported marble Jacuzzi tub," Charlie teased.

"Man, let's put in some tennis courts while we're at it!" Miguel smiled and pulled one of those tiny spiral notebooks from his jeans' back pocket. "The roofers say you need a whole new roof, patching ain't going to cut it. I walked it with them, that's true. I hired Juan Cisneros, he's the best.

He's starting tomorrow. The plumbing looks good except for a few faucet leaks that Charlie is working on. The electrician was here yesterday and rewired the kitchen, put in a new fuse box. He said the rest of the wiring is sound. The gas company is coming out this afternoon to check the furnace, stove, and water heater. You might need a new water heater—that one is ancient. The stove is nothing fancy but it looks to be in good shape. The windows need calking, little stuff like that Charlie and I can do. And we'll paint once the roofers are done."

Charlie toed the wood floor with his boot, "I think we should rent a buffer and do her wood floors while we're at it."

"Good idea," CeCe said. "When Maggie was here, these floors glowed."

"It's good wood, it'll come right back to life," Charlie assured her.

Abby started to walk through the other rooms. Without the clutter, it was easier to imagine Bobby running around as a little boy, scooting toy trucks over his mother's shiny wood floors. The first bedroom was nearly empty. There was only an old dark wooden dresser and an antique-looking trunk.

"This used to be Maggie's sewing room," CeCe said from behind her. "She made all her own clothes, she could sew anything. We used to sit in here and talk and drink coffee all afternoon while the kids played. God, we had fun."

"It must have been terrible when she died."

"It nearly killed me, too. I was so depressed for the first year after, Miguel was at his wits' end. But you get over it enough to move on. I've never had so close a friend since her, though, no way."

The hallway was so wide now, without the towering pillars of boxes. The next room was obviously Bobby's. A twin bed with a faded cowboy bedspread. A small desk he must have outgrown before high school. Model ships, carefully painted, sat in a row on the bookshelf. Abby ran her finger along the spines of his boyhood books, old volumes of the Hardy Boys, *Huckleberry Finn, The Call of the Wild,* and an entire shelf of paperback science fiction books. "He loves to read," Abby said. "He always has two or three books going at once. It's how he got through sub tours. We have a ton of books coming that he wouldn't part with."

"Which room do you think you'll fix up for the nursery?"

Abby considered. "This one is closest to our room. But I hate to disturb it," she said. And then met CeCe's eyes. "I'll leave it up to Bobby. He'll decide."

Rachel awoke to a blustery summer morning. The winds outside caused branches to scratch and creak against the house and she could hear dirt and sand spitting and hissing on her bedroom windows. Not what she wanted to hear at four-thirty in the morning when she had to go out to milk. But goats needed to be milked twice a day whether you wanted the milk or not. She liked to get the first round of it done early so her parents would not have to put up with bursting-at-the-seams goats screaming for relief.

She danced around the chilly brick floor pulling on her jeans, socks and boots. She had stopped making a fire in the wood-burning stove in her large bedroom back in March sometime. Since then, she acrobatically jumped from Mexican wool rug to Indian wool rug across her floor to get ready in the morning. She buttoned a wool shirt over a tattered long underwear top of Charlie's. Its frayed and stretched-out bottom hung down far beneath the end of her red plaid wool shirt. He would be mad as hell to know she had gotten away with one of his long underwear tops. Actually she had gotten away with three. He sure had enough of them. Cowboys always did. When they were married she used to have to steal them hot from the dryer so he wouldn't know. It took a lot to rile the likes of Charlie Hood, but taking one of his long underwear tops could do it. She smiled as she buttoned her shirt over it.

She heard the goats stirring and giving lazy closemouthed bleats as she approached the barn. She hoped they were feeling cooperative about going to the milkroom and getting on the stand. When she turned on the lights to the barn they started screaming their joy. Her heart reacted as it did every morning when they greeted her with tongues and gums showing. There was nothing cuter. Except maybe the way their bloodhound-long ears sometimes stood out straight like airplane wings as they pranced in the pen.

Over in the corner Maisie, one of her pregnant does, lay panting and bleating. When Maisie saw Rachel, she managed to wag her tail despite what was going on. Rachel didn't know how long she had been lying there straining. She hadn't thought Maisie was this close to kidding. She ushered the others into the milkroom and went back to check Maisie. She didn't see a nose peeking through yet. Maisie tried to crawl into Rachel's lap but she pushed her heaviness back into the straw in the corner. "Stay right there, baby goat," she cooed. Maisie snuffled her hair and nibbled the ends affectionately.

Maisie noticed him first. Rachel looked up to see what spooked her. At the barn door stood the little boy from the Baca place. There were deep purple pools under his eyes as if he had not slept for days. His brown hands were ashen at the knuckles. He looked like an apparition ready to disappear at any second.

She smiled at him. "Hola."

He nodded and looked down.

"My goat here is about to have her baby any second. Could you get me the iodine and those burlap bags over there?" She pointed to some shelving made out of barn wood. Maisie let out a wail. She tried hard not to yell in panic. "Hurry, please."

The boy shuffled through the straw to the shelves and brought her a quart container of iodine and a tight fistful of burlap bags. As soon as she took them he squatted to pet the goat. His uncut nails were black underneath with dirt as they sailed back and forth against the goat's black-and-white-speckled coat.

"She likes you. You just keep doing that. See how's she's more calm?"

He gave a quick dingy smile.

"What's your name?"

"Santiago." His voice was mostly air.

"Well, Santiago, you keep petting her while I check her and see what's going on up there." Maisie had never had trouble kidding before, but something in her gut told her there was a problem. After washing, she reached her hand and arm into the goat's warm, wet insides. "Not something you have to do to chickens, huh?" Her smile collapsed as her heart began to race. She felt two noses.

"You're going to have to do me a big favor, Santiago. Will you do that for me? There's a real nice man named Charlie at the horse barn. All I need you to do is run and tell him I need him right now. That it's urgent. Can you do that?" she said, her hand still up the goat.

The boy nodded and scurried off.

She pushed the overeager second kid back. "Well that's just plain rude," she told it. Shit, the first kid was tangled. She couldn't quite get the leg uncurled. They were braided together. Maisie screamed as Rachel pushed herself in further. "Damn," she hissed. She tried to remain calm so the goat would, but she was scared. She relaxed her frantic hands. She petted Maisie who licked and nuzzled the wetness off her hands and forearms. Better wait for Charlie.

"This little guy told me you wanted me pronto. What do we have here, babe?" Charlie said coming in and scooting next to her.

"I can't get the kids straightened out. She's been straining a long time. Do something!" Maisie pleaded along with her.

"Hold it down, girls. Let's just take a look." After washing his hands and arms, Charlie gently entered the goat. The scruffiness of his handsome profile focused on what he was feeling with his hands. He chewed at his lower lip and squinted. She could see the strong muscles in his arm twitch, working his nimble fingers up inside the goat. "There, the legs are free," he said as the first kid slid out. "Woohoo!" He assisted the head of the second as it came out. Maisie started cleaning them as Rachel lightly scrubbed them with the burlap. Charlie took care of the cords, dipping them in the iodine. He beamed like a proud papa as she cried from watching them take their first tentative breath. "Two girls, babe. You're one lucky goat-breeding woman," he said, his eyes twinkling.

"And don't call me babe," she said giddily from the high of the birth. "Hey, isn't that my underwear top?"

"What do you think, Santiago?" Rachel asked. The goats stood wobbling like they were on a rough sea. "Aren't they the cutest things you've ever seen?" She turned around and honestly didn't know at what point he had gone.

Chapter 6

Rachel jiggled along in the front seat of Charlie's old pickup. He insisted on taking some adventurous back road to Madrid, an old shut-down mining town taken over by artsy love children of the sixties—now gallery and funky shop owners, bikers who lined up their glistening Harleys in the parking lot of the Old Tavern restaurant, and transient blues bands that gave concerts down at the old, sandy baseball field. The whole town wasn't a mile long and they were having their street fair on the main street, the only blacktopped road.

She and Charlie were on their way to sell their modest wares of goat cheese, six peach pies, and ten zucchini breads CeCe had made. Miguel donated three retablos, the portraits of saints he liked to paint in his spare time. Like the Spaniards so many years ago, he painted them to stay in touch with his faith. Each one was swaddled in an old towel. Rachel's small dairy business was something she and Charlie had developed, and she could not afford it or do all the work it took without him. She'd take a huge loss in the sale of the equipment. But it wasn't the money. She didn't know what else she could do in this world and didn't want to have to find out. She made sure they never missed a farmers' market, village fair, or fiesta. At least if she brought in a little money, or looked like she was trying, Papa couldn't fault her.

As Charlie flew over bumps in the dirt roads and maneuvered around gaping holes, she felt one of those tiny stinging pulls deep in her breast, like a rubber band stretching and snapping back. Good. She'd remembered to put in a tampon before they left in case it started today. She hated when Charlie had called her breasts water balloons right before her period, but that's exactly what they felt like.

"Why the hell did you take this way!" she finally yelled, breaking her cool, steely silence. When they had been married he'd been extra gentle in his lovemaking when her breasts were this sore. He'd treated them like bubbles. And if she told him, at this moment, she was in total discomfort because of her sore boobs and his insane driving, he would slow down and take it easy. But she would never tell him. He couldn't have the inside scoop about her cycle anymore. That information was personal and way too powerful.

"I have to see a man about a horse," he said, pulling over to the side. She knew that if it were not for this obligation with her, he would be over at Abby's practically rebuilding her house. She noticed that some of the little extras he used to do around her parents' farm were not being done anymore because of Abby.

He slipped expertly through the barbed-wire fence and headed out into the pasture thick and brilliant with the wide-open eyes of small sunflowers. He walked into the radiance of them as if he were passing through to the other side, like one of Papa's saints, then stopped, unzipped his pants and peed.

They were twenty minutes outside of Madrid and still had to set up. They'd never get a good spot at this rate. "Will you hurry up!" she yelled from the rolled-down window. He stood, his back to her. Finally she saw him do his little shake, replace, and zip. About time.

When he climbed back into the front seat she glared at him.

"It only comes out as fast as it's gonna come out, darlin'. Sorry." He held back a smile like she was the stupid one and started up the truck.

"Get out! I'm driving!" she shouted, her jaws practically unhinging. She pushed him out when he opened the door because he did not move his ass fast enough, and made him run a bit to hop in as she took off, gravel and dirt in a flurry behind them.

"Besides ever marrying you, have I done something wrong?" he asked.

"We're late," she said back. She wanted to tell him that everything he was doing was wrong. That sometimes he was excruciating. She held back crying as he stared at her. At least the bumps and divots in the road didn't hurt so much now that she was behind the wheel.

"I always thought goats stank," said a woman examining the cheese Rachel had piled in an ice chest.

"Those are the bucks. I artificially inseminate," Rachel replied. Amazing how so many people were goat stupid. The woman's fancy-schmancy perfume stank.

"How nice for you," the tourist lady said, putting the cheese back in the chest and moving on. At this rate she would never sell anything. Normally she'd hop right up with one of the pamphlets she'd paid some college kid to design on his computer and expound on the advantages of goat cheese to anyone who would listen. She could sell out quickly if she put her mind to it. Usually tourists were the easiest to sell to. They always wanted products with pamphlets and stories attached. They'd laugh to see pictures of her floppy-eared baby Nubians. She knew she could do a lot better if she had a web page, or a computer, for that matter. She knew nothing about either one.

Charlie was over at the green chile–jelly table. The deal was that Charlie did all the heavy *schlepping* on these outings, and she sat and did the selling. It was way over the top to ask him to sit in one spot for more than ten or fifteen minutes, unless there was sex involved. She watched him chat and sample everything there was to offer, sometimes more than once. An attractive Anglo woman at the winery table wore a halter made out of a silk scarf, and Charlie hung there a long time along with her breasts which were quite active under the silk whenever she moved. Her faded jeans were cut low and it was easy to see her pierced navel. It was obvious to Rachel he was only trying to make her jealous. If he wanted to sample those goods, more power to him.

"How much are your pies?" she heard a voice say and her head snapped around.

"Roberto?" she asked, her heart already pounding hard.

"Sorry?" he asked. He had the same kind of eyes, as dark and glistening as chocolate syrup. He repeated in Spanish as if she could not understand English.

"Um, oh, they are gorgeous, aren't they? My mother made them. She's so good at this crust," she said, slowly rotating the pie on her finger tips, "and we grow our own organic peaches." He wasn't Roberto, but he stirred her. A handsome Hispanic man with manners from the old way. She could tell. *Bien educada.* Familiar, like Roberto. "They're eight dollars. See how they're deep-dish?" Her best-selling technique was to transform herself into her outgoing mother. A day of that took it out of her. He seemed interested. In the pies? In her?

"I'll take all six," he said, reaching back to pull out his wallet, not taking his eyes off of her.

"Really? That's great. You'll love them. Try them hot with some vanilla-bean ice cream."

"I will do that. Do you have a box or something?"

"Of course," she said, reaching under the table to get the box used to bring the pies and bonking her head on the table when she came back up. She could die. She bet Abby never did stupid shit like that. Miss Lois Lane. The woman who could freefall, and eventually be caught by a man from out of the blue before she hit bottom. Charlie was playing right into her game.

"Are you okay? That sounded like it hurt," the handsome man said, squinting in empathy.

"I'm fine. I have my mother's hard head. I've heard my father say it enough times." She rubbed the small bump forming under her dark curls.

He held two twenties and a ten in his fingers. His nails were well kept and clean. Like Roberto, he had probably been brought up by a mother who believed all that cleanliness and godliness stuff. Roberto grew up believing how clean he was stood in direct proportion to how happy he made Jesus. Everything was connected to either the Virgin Mary or Jesus. Girls were to be clean and virginal until they married. They had *quinceañeras,* special ceremonies when they turned fifteen, celebrating keeping it intact. She remembered changing Roberto's mind on that belief one lazy afternoon after her fifteenth birthday. And for three years after that.

"Do you have a card?" his well-defined lips asked.

She reached over and grabbed a pamphlet. "I take special orders, so if you ever need—"

"Yes, of course. That's why I asked. I'll definitely be calling," he said, looking for the phone number on the pamphlet.

"Hey, babe. They're roasting turkey legs over there. Want me to get you one?" Charlie said, suddenly behind her holding half an eaten one in his fist. "You're kinda cute when you're gnawing on a bone."

The Roberto man picked up his box of pies. "Have a nice afternoon," he said to both of them and walked off.

"Enjoy the pies!" she sang after him and looked down to see her pamphlet dumped on the table.

Abby paced nervously in the Vigils' front courtyard, despite its serene sun-dappled shade, sweet-scented flowerbeds, and comfortable lawn furniture.

CeCe carried a tray of fresh-squeezed lemonade. "Just because Ramone called and said he wanted to meet with you doesn't mean he has bad news."

"I know, but he usually just comes over to talk. This time he called first, on my cell phone instead of your line." Abby made herself sit down at the table in front of CeCe's tray. There was also a basket of tortilla chips and a bowl of salsa.

"He knows you're getting ready to move into your own house . . . Well, here he comes, now." CeCe smiled her encouragement but Abby caught a glimmer of concern in her eyes.

Ramone got out of his huge gleaming pickup truck, his pride and joy. He kept the red finish washed and waxed to a glow, which took constant effort in this climate.

"Ladies," he greeted them, touching the brim of his straw hat. He sat down and accepted the tall glass of lemonade CeCe handed him.

"How's your father?" CeCe asked, passing him a plate for chips and salsa.

"Bueno, he's having a good day. He said to thank you for the cookies." Ramone scooped as much salsa as his chip could hold and munched happily. "You make the best salsa! If Papa and I had a woman like you in the house, well, we'd be even fatter!"

"What is the news?" Abby blurted.

Ramone finished his chewing and took another gulp from his glass. "I just wanted to sit down and talk about where we're at in this. This is June twenty-fifth, so Bobby's been missing three weeks. To be honest, the more time that goes by in a missing-persons case, the harder it is. Trails go cold, leads fizzle out. But, this case is different than any I've ever seen. No one can find any evidence of foul play, so that's great. No signs of struggle, no motives, no suspects. The reward fund is over eighty grand, so I have to believe if someone knew anything, we'd hear about it. We've had a lot of publicity so that should help. But, the leads I've been chasing from the tip line have all been bogus so far. Bowman doesn't have anything and he's not working too hard given he believes Bobby ran off and no crime was committed. But the Bobby I knew wouldn't do that to his wife. He's was a good kid, I coached him in little league and he always played fair."

"So, what are you saying?" Abby asked, feeling tears of frustration tingle behind her eyes.

"That I'm not giving up and neither should you. Three weeks may feel like a lifetime to you and if we had any evidence of foul play I'd be less optimistic. Bobby climbed into that truck willingly and drove to God knows where. We don't know why he's been gone this long and in the absence of knowledge, we tend to speculate. I haven't seen or talked to the kid in twelve years. Besides you, is there anyone else, say out in San Diego, like his Navy friends, we could talk to that maybe could give us some insight?"

"Nobody knows him better than me. Because of him being gone so much on submarine tours, we didn't tend to socialize when he was home.

Our lives revolved around my restaurant. Or we took short trips together in Northern California, just the two of us. He mentioned his Navy buddies, but he never suggested we hang out with any of them since he was usually sick of them by the time they docked back in San Diego. I guess it sounds weird, but we were each other's whole worlds and that's why none of this makes any sense! Especially with the baby coming! Bobby couldn't wait, he wanted to be a father more than anything. He was so glad to leave the Navy and finally be home."

CeCe handed her a tissue for the tears she didn't even know she was shedding.

Ramone nodded. "Why move back here so suddenly with Ricardo's death if your lives revolved around your restaurant?"

"It nearly broke my heart to leave. But Bobby wanted it so desperately and he's never asked me for anything. We compromised. I agreed to try it for a year, I needed to slow down for my pregnancy anyway and take some time off after the baby is born. The restaurant would be there for me if I still wanted it after that and in some ways it's easier to be geographically removed than in the condo right upstairs. It was a sacrifice in some ways, but I started to get into the idea once I surrendered to it. I love him so much, I wanted to give him this gift, and I looked forward to finally being together all the time."

"And then he disappears." Ramone shook his head.

"He was so upset about Ricardo's death but he told me how happy he was to be home in Esperanza," CeCe offered. "It just doesn't make sense that he'd leave."

"You've told me everything you can about that night. Is there anything else you can think of, something he said or did right before he left?"

Abby held her throbbing head and tried to think. She saw little bursts of images from that awful night. "The junk in the house that his father had hoarded made him feel even more guilty for not visiting in years. He was angry, but not really at me, at himself. He was consumed with beating himself up for betraying his father."

Ramone took her hand. "Abby? This is a tough question but I have to ask. He was consumed with self-hatred that night, he was irrational in his grief, he added a large amount of alcohol to it which distorts judgment and decreases impulse control . . . Could he have harmed himself?"

Abby gasped as she felt his words like a knife twisting in her chest. "Suicide?"

"I have to ask," Ramone whispered, squeezing her hand.

She forced herself to consider it. "He loved life. He was so enthusiastic about everything and had so much to look forward to. I never saw him depressed, ever. He'd get frustrated with his dad's guilt trips and I knew he always wished they were on better terms. But his dad was part of that. Bobby always said his dad was real withdrawn after his mom died and if it weren't for the attention he got from the Vigils he would have had a miserable childhood. In some ways, joining the Navy might have been getting back at his dad, he was pretty angry with him when we first met. But we were eighteen, everybody is angry with their parents at that age. I guess the anger turned into guilt over the years, he came back here a few times and always came back quiet and sad. But he'd shake it off and go surfing or sailing or something." She tried to focus on that night again and heard his words, his pain, his rage. "He was more upset than I've ever seen him the night he left. And he can be real impulsive. With enough alcohol and enough pain could he hurt himself?" Abby began to cry harder, "I hope to hell not! And if he did, wouldn't we find him?"

"Not if he was trying to spare you. He might have gone off into the middle of nowhere, thinking he was saving you the trauma of finding him afterward. I'm not saying this is what I believe; I just have to consider all the possibilities. I'm going to keep following every lead we can scrape up. There are explanations for the unexplainable that we just can't think up yet, that's all. That's why we keep going. That's why we don't give up."

Abby was out for her morning exercise when she realized why it was difficult to focus on her baby after months of doing little else. Why she deliberately ignored its gentle gymnastics inside of her, the multiplying of its cells that caused it to expand a little each day until there was ever more of it and ever less of her.

And that was just the physical part of it. She knew she was also avoiding the sense of its spirit, the presence that had joined her from the moment she lay in Bobby's sweaty arms, her breasts sliding against his chest, feeling the essence of him travel inside of her. She knew the night of conception, every move they made, every breath, the way the full moon watched from the open window, bathing them in blue light. How something from them, but not them, entered her.

When she allowed herself to remember this, to acknowledge the reality of her baby, she had to know something was terribly wrong with Bobby. She couldn't pretend there was some other explanation. If it had just been her, she could have deluded herself with hope and joined the common lore that he was off on some angry trip somewhere and would be home when he cooled off. Or was binging in some bar, whoring around with no intention of ever returning to his soured marriage. Even that allowed for a twisted kind of hope.

If hope meant believing he could forsake her, she could do it. But when the price of hope was believing he could forsake his baby, hope evaporated faster than spit on a sidewalk in this arid place. He would die first.

And ever since Ramone had introduced the possibility of suicide as an alcohol- and grief-induced, impulsive act, her thoughts took her there. He would never have planned such a thing, it was against his nature. But in one terrible, painful, drunken moment, could he have done it?

Abby looked up to see she was in town already. The distance from the Vigil's seemed shorter every day, her speed fueled by her futile attempt to outrun her thoughts. The sweat poured off of her, sticking her tank top and running shorts to her like a second skin. She walked it off, breathing hard, checking her pulse out of habit, making circles in Barbara's junk-shop parking lot.

People watched her. They knew who she was, their local celebrity. In San Diego, people would recognize her from commercials she did for Abigail's or appearances she made on the local morning television show cooking with the hosts, sharing recipes, giving tips on home entertaining.

But this was much more personal. When people looked at her now with that expression of recognition, it was because they knew her most intimate pain. Like some gaping wound hanging out there for all to see.

In this small town, if people wanted to look at you, they stared right at you. It didn't matter if you caught them. Eye contact just made it all the more interesting for them. You might reveal something. There was none of that big-city etiquette where you glance at someone and then look quickly away.

CeCe assured her they didn't mean anything by it. It was a form of honesty, really. She pretended not to notice as she walked over to Barbara's shady overhang where she kept an old top-loading Coke machine filled with bottles of soda pop and water. She dipped her hand into the icy water and splashed some onto her neck before pulling out a bottle of water.

Barbara watched her from the window. CeCe said Barbara was divorced and in her sixties. She had the kind of blond hair that didn't exist in nature, lacquered up in an old-style bouffant hairdo. She cracked gum and chain-smoked. Too much sun and too many cigarettes had not been kind to her skin.

Abby pulled a wrinkled, sweaty dollar bill from her running shorts' zippered pocket and went inside.

"That will be on the house, dear," Barbara said, her voice the perfect audible accompaniment to her leathery face.

When Abby didn't put her dollar away, Barbara began to cough. "Your money's no good in here," she said after clearing her throat.

"Thanks," Abby said, and began to look around out of politeness and to enjoy the stiff breeze of the swamp cooler.

"We girls have to stick together," Barbara said, her voice full of implication.

Abby knew her man had done her wrong and felt the impulse to defend Bobby but refrained. Instead, she looked at the tables and shelves of old glass doorknobs, glass jars, mismatched plates, the myriad cast-off objects waiting to be claimed as treasures. She wondered which of this stuff had been Ricardo's.

The door jangled as someone entered. She looked up to see it was Maria, the woman who had come to the Vigils' to examine her the morning after Bobby left. She could still feel the power in the woman's gnarled hands when she had gripped her belly.

Barbara scowled at Maria. "What do you want?"

Maria kept her eyes on Abby. "It's a free country."

"Hello," Abby said, feeling she should.

Maria didn't answer, just eyed her up and down. One of her eyes squinted slightly—perhaps from the smoke Barbara blew in her direction.

Abby took a long drink from her water bottle, feeling the water's coldness trace a path down her throat, deep into her.

"It may be a free a country but this is my shop so you can get the hell out," Barbara said with casual hatred. "I don't want your business here."

Maria took a step closer to Abby.

"Don't let her touch you, Abby."

Abby looked at Barbara. Was this part of some kind of feud between the two of them or blatant racism?

Maria lunged forward when Abby's gaze was diverted. Her bony hand gripped her wrist tightly for a second, and before Abby could react, Maria let go and began to cackle. She laughed and shook her fist at Abby, bracelets rattling. Then she turned and walked out, skirt swishing. The slam and jangle of the door punctuated her exit.

Barbara quickly stubbed out her cigarette and strode over to where Abby examined the red marks on her wrist. "Come with me!"

She put her hand on Abby's back and shoved her toward a door at the back of the shop. It was a tiny restroom. Barbara guided her in and squeezed her large hips in with her next to the sink, turning on the cold-water faucet. "Get some soap on there and wash, come on now."

There was something in her voice that made Abby want to do as she said.

"She might have put something on you, you can't be too sure."

"Like what?" Abby asked, vigorously scrubbing with the green bubbly industrial soap from the dispenser.

"She's a witch! Who the hell knows?"

"But why would she want to hurt me?"

"Did she seem friendly to you? Huh? Was she here to be nice to you with that crazy stare and waving her fist? I don't think so. She's up to something."

Abby rinsed and dried her hands and forearms with paper towels that Barbara ripped off and handed to her. Her heart was beating faster than it had been when she was running.

Barbara leaned in even closer, some strong tropical flower perfume competed with the cigarette smell. "People hire her to settle scores. It's what she does. I never used to believe in that stuff, but you live here long enough . . . Well, you'll see."

Abby found CeCe in the kitchen, making a bowl of tuna salad for lunch. She helped herself to a stalk of celery. CeCe smiled and kept chopping. Abby loved how CeCe didn't wear her hair short, like so many women by age fifty. Her skin seemed immune to the ever-present sun. Her clothes were not much different than what Abby would wear, simple clean lines. She was the kind of a woman who inspired much younger women that there was hope. You didn't have to lose your figure, your face, your hair or your sense of style as the decades went by. There was an earthy sexiness to CeCe, a self-assurance that Abby vicariously thrived on in these days of feeling uncharacteristically powerless and afraid.

"Carmen, Hazel, and Bonnie are coming over after lunch if you want to join us. Bonnie is determined to teach you how to crochet, whether you want to learn or not. How was your run?"

"Good. Helps clear my head." Abby said, trying to decide whether to tell her about the incident with Maria.

"Funny how times change. When Maggie and I were pregnant with the kids, our doctor told us to not exert ourselves but God forbid you should gain too much weight. These days it's exercise and gain at least twenty-five or thirty pounds—I read it in some women's magazine. Go figure!"

"I stopped in to Barbara's, to get some water."

"And a dose of secondhand smoke!"

"While I was there Maria came in."

"To Barbara's? There's no love lost between those two. What was she doing there?"

"This will sound weird, but it was like she had followed me. She just stood there staring at me with this squinty expression. I said hello but she didn't respond, just stood there giving me the eye. Maybe it's some cultural thing and I'm just being ignorant."

"What did Barbara do? Did she see what Maria was doing?" CeCe stopped her stirring, her wooden spoon coated with mayonnaise suspended over her green mixing bowl.

"She was pretty rude to her, ordered her out. But the strangest part was she made me wash where Maria had touched me on the wrist, said she was a witch."

CeCe shook her head. "Well, they have bad blood from way back. Barbara's husband was spending time with Maria, who was rumored to be providing services to a lot of the married men around here in those days. Miguel always said men went to talk to her about their problems and their jealous wives had overactive imaginations, but who knows?"

Abby smiled. "So maybe when Maria was acting spooky, gripping my wrist, it was just to get to Barbara."

"What she do to your wrist?"

"She gripped, real tight for a few seconds. And then laughed and shook her fist at me. But this was while Barbara was harassing her."

"She was probably just yanking your chains, she's like that, especially with white people. I wouldn't worry about it," CeCe said.

The back door swung open and Rachel came in. She went directly to the refrigerator, standing in the coolness of the open door, swigging the last of the orange juice from the carton. She lifted the mass of dark curly hair and let the cool air hit her neck.

CeCe put the bowl of tuna salad and fixings on the table. Rachel washed her hands at the sink as CeCe was trying to rinse her utensils. Abby sensed the underlying tension between them, a stiffness, and remembered what Charlie had said about their relationship. But compared to her and her own mother's estrangement, it seemed hardly worth noticing.

"This is great, CeCe. After my stuff gets here in a few days and I get my kitchen set up, I'll have all of you over for lunch."

Rachel sat down and helped herself to the tuna salad, spreading a thick layer onto her mother's home-baked bread. "Your stuff?"

"Yeah, the movers are bringing our belongings. We have more than fits in two suitcases, you know." Abby smiled.

"No, I just thought you'd wait before you spent all that money to move everything out here."

"Wait for what?"

"See if there was any reason to stay."

"Of course, we're staying. Why wouldn't we?"

Rachel shrugged. "I didn't think you'd stay if Roberto doesn't show up soon. I figured you'd rather go back home to San Diego. I mean, we'd call you with any news."

"Rachel—" CeCe began but Abby cut her off.

"Esperanza is our home, not San Diego." Abby was surprised at her own sudden emphatic commitment to the place. But if Rachel wanted her gone, all the more reason to stay. As if she'd ever leave with Bobby missing. It already felt like a betrayal to enjoy tuna salad, to sleep even fitfully, to breathe one easy breath in his absence. "I'm sure I've been in your way here. I'll be moving into my home as soon as the paint dries." Abby stared her down as well as any witch. "So, get used to it."

Chapter 7

There was a hot morning breeze as Rachel walked to her mother's cucumber patch. Once in a while there would be a gust that felt like a nuclear blast against her. She imagined looking down at herself and seeing only skeleton. One of the hottest, driest summers she could remember in a long time. Several red chickens ran hopefully after them as she and her mother swung their empty red produce baskets by the wire handles.

"Don't pick them too small, Rache, you know about how I like them," her mother instructed. She was a stickler about the Kosher-style dills she made. She'd mail off a case or two a year to her relatives in Brooklyn, usually around some Jewish holiday. CeCe managed to always keep track of that stuff. Eating dill pickles or the tsmmis her mother made with the carrots and sweet potatoes she grew was about as Jewish as Rachel got. Her mother was dutiful and attentive to her Jewish Brooklyn family, even though they barely spoke to her after she ran off with a Mexican. What did that say about how they felt about their little half-breed, Rachel? They could just stay over two thousand miles away, as far as she was concerned.

"Ma, I've done this with you almost every year of my life. I know how you like them. And I know exactly what size you want when you say dice, and what thickness when you say slice," said Rachel, squatting in the patch of cucumbers.

"Boy, are you on the rag, or what? Take it out on those weeds there," her mother said, pointing to some mustard weed nearby. She was wearing soiled cloth gardening gloves with small purple pansies on them.

"All I'm saying is that sometimes you say things to me over and over again like you must think I'm stupid," Rachel said, hating the fact her mother knew she was menstruating. Did all mothers have that advantage over daughters? Having that connection down to a cellular level? Of course they must. It was created in the womb. It panicked her to wonder what her mother might intuitively know about her. Or things she had done.

"How can you say that? I don't think you're stupid." CeCe's gloved hands went to her hips. She had on her faded overalls rolled up a ways with a tank top. "I'm the one who nagged you to stay in college when you dropped out after acing all your classes. You could have been one hell of an attorney. The way you argue—you should get paid for it."

"Never mind." The ground still felt soft from last evening's watering. The weed pulled up easily, and she tossed it to the side of the patch.

"No, I won't never mind. You think I think you're stupid. That's what you just said." Her mother sounded like one of her whining old aunts in Brooklyn. She always did when she got defensive. "You're my child—my baby. I don't think any such thing."

Rachel wrapped her hand around a cucumber, but its prickly vine wasn't giving under her twisting and pulling. It almost brought her to tears. She knew her mother watched from beneath the rim of her straw garden hat tied on with an old silk scarf, and held the garden shears she wasn't stupid enough to forget to bring. Rachel knew what her mother was thinking. On a cellular level. She pulled her knife out of its leather holster and cut the vine.

"Okay, sometimes I wonder about your judgment, but I don't say anything because I don't want to interfere," her mother confessed, as if that were some big secret. She stooped down in the patch.

"Wonder about my judgment? You were the one pushing me to marry Charlie and look what happened! Like I'm going to trust yours." She went for another cucumber and hacked it free, quickly this time.

"You just don't know a good thing when you see it. Charlie's a gorgeous hunk of a man, if you ask me, who's nuts about you to boot. Of course I'm going to wonder about your judgment. All the women in the village do."

"Maybe I believe there's someone out there that suits me better," said Rachel. "Why am I even bothering to have this conversation? Now you're saying I'm the village idiot!"

Her mother plopped several pickling cucumbers into her basket. "You've been spending a lot of time with Maria lately."

"I go over there to help her, like I always have." She eyed a small tuft of crabgrass growing in the patch and pulled it, wondering why her mother even cared. A group of roly-poly bugs were left in its place. "She likes having me around."

"Her judgment is worse than yours. Maria was a *curandera* at one time, but come on, for the last several years that's only been a sideline. Her heart is into being a cantankerous old bruja who would sleep with the devil for the right payment. Especially when it comes to you." Her mother yanked several weeds at a time like ripping out hair.

"You're imagining things. You just don't understand the connection. You couldn't. It's not in your blood," said Rachel. "Besides, you're always busy cooking with Abby or catering to her. Yeah, I'm going to spend more time with my tía. We're friends." Her handful of weeds gave way by their roots and it was satisfying. More dark roly-polies rolled to the center of the hole like rabbit droppings.

CeCe stood up and pointed a cucumber at her as if it were loaded. "It has nothing to do with blood. If Maria were red, yellow, or blue she'd still have lousy judgment. And with friends like that . . ." She squatted back down to pick cucumbers. After a few seconds of silence she added, "Maria was one of the last people to talk to Roberto before he disappeared."

"And?"

"And what does she think happened to him?"

"She thinks he has transformed himself into a hawk and flies in high circles above us watching and waiting."

"Okay, I'll bite. And what's he waiting for?" Three bees hovered around her hat, taking turns swooping in and out.

"She says he's waiting to see how the dust will settle." She smiled without thinking.

"I hope she's right. I hope he is out there waiting, and he comes back. For Abby's sake," her mother said, throwing a couple of bad cukes way out to the chickens. The hovering ballet around her hat made a beeline to the sunflowers.

"What makes you think he'll come back to her?" Rachel asked, coolly picking and stacking cukes in her basket. "Maybe he has walked out on her."

"You know as well as I do how Roberto was brought up. He would never abandon a pregnant wife, a woman he married before God."

Rachel stood up defiantly with her full basket. Who knew Roberto's honor better than she? "Well, all I know, Ma, is he wasn't dragged out."

That evening after her bath, Rachel stood in front of the mirror and let the towel drop slowly around her shoulders and down around her hips to the floor. Her dark curly hair hung in thick bundles against her shoulders and back. She imagined Roberto's eyes behind her own, eyeing the curve of her waist, the puckering around the outside of her nipples. She picked up a bottle of body oil Maria had mixed for her, turned it upside down on her index finger, dabbed it on her neck and traced a line seductively around her breasts and down her flat peachy abdomen like imaginary war paint. The woman gazing back at her looked determined. Their blue eyes met. "Don't worry, Ma. None of us are losing hope. The dust just needs to settle."

After a frustrating morning of worming goats, Rachel grabbed a couple of large pails and headed to the cherry orchard, a green half-acre patch filled with mature cherry trees dense with little red ornaments. CeCe had been adamant about making cherry preserves for the Corrales fair the following weekend. Last year she had won a blue ribbon for them at the state fair and used her ribbon in her advertising, tacked to a placard it read: BEST PRESERVES IN THE STATE. She'd give people samples spread on a cracker as if she were handing out communion. And they bought up every jar. Things always seemed to just happen for her mother.

Normally Charlie helped her with things like worming, but he had been around even less. Yesterday she had seen him as she drove to the feed store, standing on Abby's roof fixing a gutter. His shirt was off and Abby stood on the ground looking up at him, hand to forehead blocking the sun. They were having a conversation. Rachel saw the definition of muscle in his arms and chest all the way from the road as she passed. Abby will not be able to resist that. Her mother and she were the only two capable of resisting in the whole village, and sometimes she wondered about her mother.

Rachel kicked open the legs of a rickety wooden stepladder and climbed through the green leaves, where she was instantly cooler. Looking up she saw the marble-blue sky and hot yellow sun behind thousands of leaves lit up like stained glass. A cherry dangled in front of her eyes, its deep red body cleft, resembling a tiny baby's butt begging to be bitten. She felt like a goddess biting into its sweetness and knew there must be nymphs nearby. She looked down to see Santiago standing at the bottom of the ladder. He startled her, causing her to almost choke on the stone. The lithe branches gently held her in place as she balanced herself on the ladder as if she were on a pair of stilts.

"Santiago, you scared the hell out of me," she said when she finally could speak, and climbed down the ladder. He stood dwarfed by the basketball jersey he wore. She could see his skinny brown body through the huge armholes. He jerked back from her. "I'm not going to hurt you," she said, sad that he would think such a thing. She smiled at him and she could tell he relaxed. "Want to help me pick cherries? I can pay you."

He smiled and took the pail from her and climbed monkey-like up the ladder.

"Eee! Now you be careful! Okay, Santi?" she warned, squinting upward.

"Okay!" he yelled back, leaving the ladder to climb up into the tree, pail on his bony shoulder.

She went up on the ladder with another pail and began to pick. He traveled to the higher realms above her. "Don't pick any that birds have gotten to."

"I know," he said, and kept pulling branches toward him, picking like some arboreal endangered species. He giggled as they tossed rejected cherries playfully back and forth at each other.

When his pail was as full as he could manage for a successful descent he started down, handing her the pail as she reached up from the ladder to get it. She helped steady his tennis shoe on the top of the ladder and spotted him with her hands until his other foot had hit the top rung. He jumped to the ground creating a thud and a small cloud of dust.

"Let's go get you paid," she said, her hand resting ever so lightly on the boy's shoulder. He looked at her in surprise at first, as if he had never experienced a gentle touch.

As they were making their way back toward the house, she stopped. "I need to check something in the barn first," she said and led him to a fenced-in stall thick with straw. In the corner was a plaid dog bed with a Golden Retriever panting happily as four puppies nursed, their back legs and puppy butts moving gluttonously. A lazy breeze whirred across the dogs from a small fan.

Santi looked wide-eyed through the fence, his dirty fingers and nails curled tightly through the metal mesh.

"You want to hold one?" Rachel asked, unfastening the gate.

"Are they yours?" he asked, his voice quiet and hoarse.

"Well, now, that's the problem. They are all mine." He cuddled one to him and it licked him as if he were covered with liver paste. He laughed. And the more he laughed, the more the blonde puppy went at him. "I don't suppose you would take one in payment for picking cherries?"

"Really?" He held the squirming fat bundle in the air.

"I mean if you think your dad won't mind," she added. She'd feel awful if she got him into some sort of trouble. "You have to ask him first."

"He won't care. As long as I take care of it," he said, still rubbing his face against the corn-silk fur. "And I promise I'll take real good care of her."

Abby took a long swig from her liter water bottle, her constant companion these days. Her new Albuquerque obstetrician had lectured her on the dangers of dehydration in this moisture-sucking climate. A petite woman with strawberry-blond hair and five children of her own, Mary Lark had instantly instilled in Abby a sense of pure trust and confidence. Her strong, sure hands promised to catch her baby in a little less than four months. Her penetrating gray eyes looked deep into Abby's, scouring all doubt and fear away. Abby could do this. She would live and thrive for her baby. It was her mission. She was a zealous recruit, drinking her two liters of water, taking her prenatal vitamins, eating her fruits and vegetables and iron-rich protein to build a healthy baby.

When she felt the hope leaching from her bones she thought of Dr. Lark. When she couldn't think about Bobby one more soul-tearing minute, she thought of Dr. Lark. How proud Dr. Lark would be when she checked her blood and saw her hemoglobin rising like a flag in her honor.

The movers were finally gone. She stood in her living room letting her eyes move slowly over the stacks of boxes, all labeled in the neat, all-capital print of Bobby Silva's hand.

After all of her anticipation for the movers finally getting there, to get their possessions into her empty hands, she felt herself become deflated.

CeCe had offered to help, of course, but Abby declined before she could name why. Afterward she realized that while CeCe only had good intentions, unpacking was somehow too personal to share with anyone. Anyone but Bobby.

If he were here, it would be different. She could imagine it being a group effort, a moving-in party with music and food. The men setting up their bed in place of Ricardo's, the women deciding on which side of the sink the silverware should go on. Laughing at their precious junk, admiring the stuff that somehow said so much about them.

Without him, other people opening their boxes, handling their possessions, would be an obscene invasion of their privacy. They would involuntarily form impressions about their marriage based on the contents of those boxes, the color of the sofa, the texture of the bath towels that rubbed their naked bodies, the hills and valleys of their naked mattress now leaning against the wall. What else would they have to go on?

She took another swig of water, feeling Dr. Lark pat her on the back. She sat down on a box. The skyline of boxes around her was overwhelming. It seemed now like so much, too much. She was suddenly bereft of the kind of energy it would take to do this. Bobby should be here. It pissed her off to be stuck with all of this, all alone and nearly six months pregnant at five o'clock in the afternoon with nothing to eat. Dr. Lark would be on her side in this.

She heard a loud rap at the back of the house, at the kitchen door that was propped open for the swamp cooler to draw better on this hot July afternoon. She didn't feel like company, maybe they would go away.

"Abby? It's Charlie," he announced as he let himself in.

"Shit." She wiped her tears and looked up to see he'd caught her.

He seemed to take a minute to decide if he should acknowledge her tears. When she quickly looked away, he didn't. "Rachel and I got into it so I made myself scarce."

"What's in the sack?" Abby motioned at a nearby box for him to sit down.

He sat and put the large crumpled brown grocery sack between his boots. "I made turkey sandwiches, carrot sticks, swiped some of CeCe's chocolate chip cookies and a half gallon of milk."

She felt her stomach gnaw in response. She felt a grateful smile come to her lips, an expression that felt foreign on her face these days. She put out her hand.

The sandwich was wrapped in old-fashioned wax paper. It was so heavy from CeCe's homemade bread and the stack of turkey leftover from the previous day's Sunday dinner that she had to grasp it with both hands. She peeled back some of the paper and took a big bite. Crisp lettuce and lots of mayonnaise, the yeasty softness of the bread filled her mouth with joy. It was God's most perfect sandwich.

Charlie unscrewed the top of the milk jug, gave her a wicked smile before taking a long jaw off it. He wiped the rim with his shirttail and passed it to her.

She took a drink from it, imagining Dr. Lark's proud face, more calcium for her baby's bones. Charlie handed her a bouquet of carrot sticks. "You don't get your cookies until you eat your vegetables," he said.

Their crunching echoed in the stillness of the room. She appreciated the quiet as they ate, the time away from words. Some strength returned to her weary flesh and spirit.

The light in the room began to soften as the sun began to angle down. She liked how the pale salmon color she picked for the walls complimented the warm tones of the wood floor. Their sofa and chair, nearly visible through the boxes, were forest green with a subtle geometric pattern of salmon and black. Her vintage oriental rug, which echoed those colors and brought in some more, was rolled and leaning against the wall like a fallen timber. Her mind began to wander over the walls imagining what she would hang and where.

The earlier overwhelming blur of boxes and tasks seemed to come into some kind of focus. Tomorrow she would start fresh and it would all make sense.

"What can I do?" Charlie said.

"Tonight I'd like to sleep in my own bed."

He nodded and got to work. While he took apart Ricardo's bed to put into the storage shed, she found the boxes marked BATHROOM. She would set up her bathroom and have a long soak in the bubble bath Bobby bought for her and then climb in between her own sheets.

They worked silently as the sun lowered. Lights were switched on, cicadas serenaded from open windows. The dry air lost its powerful heat quickly. Abby unpacked the last stack of towels into the linen cupboard and stood back to look at her bathroom. It was surprising the comfort that the sight of her own towels hanging on the towel bar, her collection of scented candles grouped on the top of the small bookcase that had miraculously fit against the wall, could bring. She would pick out a new shower curtain and rug in ocean colors. Her big blown-glass jug of shells sat next to the candles; its silver ball lid the size of a softball reflected her face.

Her baby began his nightly calisthenics and she gasped at the strength of his stretches and punches. She put her hand over her side and felt the sure ripple of a foot as it poked and slid outstretched against the confines of its home.

She ran to Charlie who was making her bed. "Here, you have to feel this, it's amazing." She grabbed his hand and placed it under her own and she knew he felt the insistent prodding as his hand responded under her fingertips. He laughed and met her eyes with an expression of wonderment.

She drank in his amazement, to have someone to share this with, to witness it was real. Then, suddenly, his eyes were not Bobby's, his words were not her husband's, his hands were not her baby's father's. She recoiled as if slapped. The acuity of Bobby's absence came at her with a breathtaking physical pain that seared through her like a bolt of lightning must feel charging through helpless flesh and blood.

Charlie looked at her and with that silent communication they somehow shared, he seemed to be weighing whether his presence made things worse or better. She responded by falling against him, welcoming his arms tightly around her.

He held her and she cried. His arms were not Bobby's and they were not her father's arms that had never in her memory held her, but they were male and they were strong so that she could be weak and they expected nothing in return.

Chapter 8

The green of her father's chile field and the incredible blueness of the sky totally surrounded Rachel as she cultivated the field on the old tractor Charlie managed to keep running. Her father hand-hoed and inspected plants. There was no breeze; just sunny and as hot as an oven. The green fruits hid under their canopy of leaves like lazy cabana boys.

Mostly her father grew New Mexican green chile the first several cuttings, and then it matured for a red harvest in the fall. But he also grew some jalapeños and habaneros that he canned himself. Fresh chiles he sold to organic co-op stores, independent grocers, and local chile emporiums. CeCe had her own yield of jalapeños she liked to dry over mesquite and use to make chipotle, which she sold to some local markets and Old Town shops. She had designed the labels for the jars of chipotle sauce herself on her computer and ran them off on the color laser printer Charlie had won in a card game. CeCe had admitted the one good thing that came of Rachel's and Charlie's divorce was that Charlie had since taken up playing poker with the boys down at Pablo's. He had also won CeCe a bread machine that she hadn't used yet.

Rachel pulled the tractor up to her father, turned off the engine, and hopped down. Her boots hit, cushioned in the sandy, soft soil. He was splitting a pod and inspecting the contents.

"What's up?" Rachel said walking up to join him. His cheeks were as brown-red as basted turkey breasts.

He pulled out the soft placental tissue of the chile and examined it closely. He crouched down and looked at several leaves, obviously looking for small feeding holes.

"Pepper weevils?" she asked, bending down to look for the small brown bugs with long snouts protruding from their heads. They had had them last summer and she spent much of her time away from her goats and dairy, scouting the fields for her father. Her father would help her birth a kid or put new roofing on the barn, and she scouted fields for him when he needed it. That was farm life. Families worked as teams. Papa needed to help her out a lot more since the divorce, and she felt guilty. She lost one good laborer when she divorced Charlie, that was for sure. Her poor father had to take up the slack. But, selfishly she was glad Charlie wasn't around so much. Especially now since Roberto was out there somewhere preparing to walk back into her life.

"No pepper weevils. I'm just trying to maybe be one step ahead this season. I look for the little bastards every morning now as soon as the sun comes up. That's when you catch them," he said, checking the ground under the leaves for dropped pods. "Just a little end rot. I'll have to irrigate a little more often, that's all. I pray to San Ysidro every night, mi'ja."

Rachel pictured the bearded saint behind his plow and oxen working the fields, a little angel at his knee. Her father's belief in the saints was almost as strong as her belief in Maria's magic. Other than that he never seemed particularly religious. She had grown up with his watered-down version of Catholicism, but what she knew mostly came from Maria, who made up her own interpretations along the way to suit her.

"It looks like he's answering you. The crop looks great."

The muscles in his brown forearms twitched as he stood, hands on hips, surveying the field, and beyond the field to all of his land, Sol y Sombra. Sunlight and Shadow. Named for its vital balance of sun and shade. Two distinct opposites that only in combination yield perfection. She knew he would rather have emptier pockets and tighter purse strings than ever sell this richness, which Rachel knew was worth a fortune.

Her father's dark skin glistened with sweat. She hated that she had her mother's fair skin. She loved summers when she could tan up and look more Hispanic. Her father connected her to Roberto. They were Hispanics. She could produce beautiful brown Hispanic babies.

"You know, mi'ja, I'm going to be able to handle this. Your mother could use a hand with something, I bet." She could tell he had had this planned despite the matter-of-factness in his voice.

"No, thanks. I'm not going to put myself through that. My helping hands aren't usually good enough for her. She has something to say about everything I do. Híjole! She's so controlling! How do you put up with it?" She couldn't remember a time when her mother didn't come up behind her and re-season, remake, or redo whatever it was she was doing. Never good enough. She just wasn't.

"She is not my mother, mi'ja. That's how." His eyes gleamed like they did whenever he spoke about her. "You're being pretty hard on her, don't you think?"

"Here we go. You always defend her. She doesn't do anything wrong. You've made her into one of your saints, Papa, and I've got news for you! Open your eyes. She cares more about strangers than her own daughter."

"You sound like Maria! She may have been the one family member who didn't disown me, but she never liked the fact that I married your mother, either. She's been stirring up this nonsense. Making your mother sound like the evil one," he said, defending CeCe like a disciple. "I've got news for you, mi'ja." His eyes darkened as he bore an angry look right into her, the look that took the place of spankings a couple of decades ago.

"You gave up everything for her! Your family, your culture! She came with a big price tag. How can you not be angry about that?"

"You are the angry one. You need to understand that years ago the rules for la familia made more sense than they do now. They forbid marrying outside our culture because they were afraid their ways would not be preserved. My love for your mother happily and willingly crossed the boundaries set up by my ancestors. We both understand culture. I am no less of a Hispanic for marrying your mother. In fact, I'm a far better one." He wiped the sweat off the back of his neck.

Birds cascaded down from treetops behind him at the freshly turned soil to feed. An expression of disappointment hung on his face. "The funny thing is, Rachel," he said, "what I love most in her is what I love most in you. You just can't see it." His sad eyes searched hers and made her feel, in that instant, they were strangers.

The smell of burning wax was the first thing to greet Rachel as she entered Maria's house. The enclosed front porch served as the altar. Various bultos of saints stood and Jesus hung from the wall on crosses of every conceivable size. Perpetually lit candles sat on an old black velvet shawl covering a low-legged table against the wall under all the crucified Jesuses suffering in various stages of death. A two-foot-tall ceramic Sacred Heart sculpture was the centerpiece of the table, Jesus's hands outstretched. His eyes glistened in a frozen look of forgiveness. Freaky how real they looked. How they made you believe he forgave you everything. Puppy dog brown eyes, like Roberto's. His exposed, bleeding heart caused Rachel to flinch with a fleeting thought of Roberto's body maybe shot dead on the streets somewhere. The thought was as hard to shake off. That was what hanging around with morbid, naïve Abby was doing to her. Roberto would come back, and come back to her. She will get pregnant right away, so Abby will no longer have that last bit of advantage over her.

The moan of Maria's patient came from the room off of the kitchen. Water boiled furiously in a big copper kettle with thick steam pouring out its spout on the kitchen stove and a pungent smell and ribbons of smoke from smoldering dried herbs wafted out like a stream of seductive dancing girls from where her great aunt and patient were. When she got to the doorway she saw Maria passing the burning bundle of herbs around the woman in the chair, mumbling her Spanish incantation. The woman had three rolls of stomach fat cascading down from her breasts, landing in her lap. Her hair was copper-blond from full-strength peroxide.

"You're late," Maria snapped at Rachel as she set the smoky herbs in a mud pot. The smoke continued to wind up and around them.

"After I helped Papa, I had to deliver some cheese samples to a shop in Old Town. I think they may end up giving me an order. Anyway, there was an accident on the interstate coming back," Rachel explained.

Maria shot her a look that clearly said she should have gotten out of the car and flown. "Eh! I got everything ready myself. What I couldn't do, Reyes did for me. Waiting on you is like waiting on dead chickens to lay! Why do you work so hard to make no money when you have a fortune right there in meat! *Caramba!* You are like your hippie mother in that way," she said. "As if CeCe wasn't bad enough being a Jew—she had to be a hippie!" Maria hated the hippies. They were novices in herbal cures and they brought marijuana to the forefront, getting law enforcement all riled up. Made it hard for Maria to grow her own after that. She had been shotgunning it to her dying patients to relieve their pain or those too nauseous to eat before any of those hippies or their parents were born. "All full of peace and love. Against war and revenge. They took away from my business!"

Reyes lumbered in and handed Maria a basket of herbs she'd had him cut. His hand shot up and waved at Rachel clumsily.

"Hey, Reyes, que pasa?" Rachel smiled in return. He produced a white rose she recognized from Mrs. Ortega's rose bushes up the road. It was limp and soft like a newly hatched bird blown out of its nest. It still had a sweet scent as she held it to her nose. "*Mmmm*, pretty, thanks," said Rachel. She felt so sorry for him at times.

"Nada, same always," he grinned. He stood and stared at her unabashedly before leaving. He passed by her so closely he brushed against her. It felt slimy, like an old, drunken *viejito* down at Pablo's trying to get a cheap thrill. For the first time he gave her the heebie-jeebies.

"Don't you think Reyes has gotten even stranger the last couple of years?" Rachel asked. She could still feel his brush against her arm like a snail trail.

Maria snorted, digging and sniffing the plants in the basket he had brought in. "All I know is that he's useful to me. An old woman needs someone useful. Especially since you are late all the time. Now, let's get back to work."

Maria prayed with broad gestures over the woman's head. The broken overprocessed hairs stuck up straight like a tiny *esplendora*. Her spindly, big-knuckled fingers rested on the woman's meaty shoulders and then slid down her spine three times. Her hands embraced the woman's cranium. She closed her eyes and prayed again, her translucent, veiny eyelids like small toad bellies. "We are done here."

The woman got up, thanked Maria and dug in her pocketbook. She pulled out a few bills and a silver bracelet as payment. *"Gracias, gracias."* The woman nodded, held Maria's hand for a second, then saw herself out.

Maria examined the bracelet. Bit it. Smelled it. Rubbed it against the nubby thick cotton of her broom skirt and held it out to Rachel. "Here, mi'ja. Such a beautiful thing is wasted on the arm of an old woman. You take it."

"No, tía, you could sell that. You need the money more than I need a bracelet." It was the oldest, most exquisite silver bracelet Rachel remembered Maria ever receiving for her services. It must have been one powerful cure.

"You will need something beautiful and borrowed to wear when Roberto returns. Take it, mi'ja." The smoke from the smoldering smudge hugged Maria like devoted ghosts. Rachel slipped the bracelet on her wrist as if it were Roberto's wedding ring. "I would need a dress . . ." she accidentally thought out loud.

"I will make you the most beautiful dress myself out of old Mexican lace. He will never take his eyes off of you again." Maria laughed until she dislodged phlegm.

A surge of excitement hit her. It was happening. Their words made it so. She allowed herself to feel complete. She wanted to dance with her dream round and round in circles and turns. It could be any day now she would feel Roberto against her, and Abby's real suffering would be just beginning. No wonder Abby wanted to think something happened to him. She didn't want to think about her baby only knowing its father through cards, air-mailed packages, and delinquent phone calls. Death was an easier blow to take than betrayal.

"Tía, what cure were you doing on that woman?" she asked, sniffing from the potion bottle. There was a rankness that stayed in her nostrils. She had seen Maria many times take a potion in her mouth and spray it on her patients while in one of her trances.

"Her husband doesn't find her attractive anymore," Maria said, shaking her head like she did when she thought about men. She worked her gums faster.

"But can you blame him?"

Maria exploded into laughter so big you could see every rotten or missing tooth in her mouth, until it was just a high-pitched wheeze. She smacked at Rachel's arm and laughed some more. "You're so bad," she scolded in Spanish. She cleared off the materials from the previous session, blowing various dried-weed crumbs from the table. She mixed a potion and chanted, going into a deep trance, adding each ingredient as if it were more powerful than the one before it. At the end she picked up a small silver dagger, stuck her finger and added three drops of blood. "Come, sit, mi'ja," she said as she swirled the liquid, "it is your turn now."

The days passed with few new leads, aside from dead ends which Ramone nonetheless pursued with unrelenting determination. Abby tried to stop asking what was new, pestering him with calls, knowing he would call her. The volunteers still brought her occasional casseroles, usually filled with labor-intensive homemade enchiladas. Something to offer her along with a few encouraging words. They replaced the weather-faded flyers with fresh ones, even as far as away as Albuquerque.

She called Edward about once a week and true to form he did all of the talking in his endearing if narcissistic way. She managed to talk about her friendship with CeCe and the craft ladies, dish about Rachel a bit and mention the goats. It seemed to satisfy him when she said everything was fine. And, it was a great comfort to hear the restaurant was thriving. He made her laugh, which had to be good medicine.

Bonnie taught her some simple crochet stitches and she started a baby blanket in shades of cream, pale yellow, and soft turquoise. It gave her restless hands something to do and a reason to hang out with CeCe's cabal. The ladies were a distraction, with their well-practiced fond bickering and gossip, mitote, as they called it.

Tonight, she had invited Ramone over for dinner after he had mentioned his father was staying with his sister in Socorro for a few days.

He arrived in a fresh blue shirt and black pants, carrying a carton of ice cream for their dessert. He was freshly shaved and smelled of men's cologne. It touched Abby that he had made such an effort.

He gave her a quick teddy bear hug, his routine greeting these days.

"The house is so quiet without Papa's Spanish TV blaring! I'm grateful to get away from it. He's only in Socorro and I miss him. I don't know what I'll do when he passes. Although the doctor said he's doing so well, he could outlive all of us."

Abby served him her red snapper Veracruz, a recipe from her restaurant, which he downed with gusto. *"Muy sobrosa! Gracias!"*

"Glad you liked it. Let's go sit in the living room for a bit before dessert."

"First, I will do the dishes. Go in and put your feet up, this will just take a moment." He gathered up their plates and began to sing as he ran water in the sink.

Abby knew better than to argue. She took her tea glass and went to her living room, turning on the old-music radio station, the one that played lots of Tony Bennet and Nat King Cole.

She closed her eyes, hearing Ramone sing along. Letting herself imagine it was Bobby in their kitchen and he was pampering her as usual. She always cooked, he always did the dishes. A female voice sang, "Embraceable You."

But it was Ramone who extended his damp hand and pulled her up for a dance, holding her at a respectable, fatherly distance, gliding her gracefully over the wood floor. There were no words between them, their mutual loneliness pulling them closer into each other's arms. Ramone might be thinking of the woman he never married or the daughter at whose wedding he would never dance. Abby thought of Bobby and prayed they would dance, just like that, to this very song, on their fiftieth wedding anniversary.

Chapter 9

Every morning for two or three seconds Abby would lie in bed and not remember Bobby's disappearance. That minute space between sleep and consciousness was her only peace. That fragile moment when, for all she knew, he was out for a morning run or making his famous huevos rancheros for breakfast, or in the bathroom shaving.

Back in San Diego she would run her hand over the bottom sheet to feel for the warmth his body would leave behind like a little gift for her that said *I'm not on sub tour, I'm here.* Those were her best days, the days when everything ordinary became extraordinary.

Now, she practiced breath control like tantric yoga to prolong those few seconds, disciplining her thoughts to dwell there and not come up for that bracing gasp of reality. He was reading the paper at the kitchen table, sipping peppermint tea so that his breath will be sweet when her lips found his. He's doing his sit-ups, feet hooked securely under the sofa, sweat spreading dew along his brow. She would place him in these highly specific and detailed scenes until some part of her began to reject them, pick them apart, argue against their plausibility. What was it about the human mind that sought truth no matter what?

The best two or three seconds of her day always preceded her worst. The contrast delivered its own special pain. The fact that she could get out of bed and continue to breathe told her she was surviving. The feel of her baby shifting within her told her she must.

Her baby turned to sit squarely on the pillow of her full bladder. She got up and padded to the bathroom, her bare feet appreciating the smoothness of the polished wood floors. Miguel and Charlie had done a beautiful job refinishing them. When Bobby came home they would dance wildly in their socks, slipping and laughing and holding each other up.

The dimness of the light filtering through the frosted glass above the tub told her the sun was just rising. She could hear the chorus of roosters from the Baca place.

It was still cool in the house, the miracle of adobe walls in the desert. It would take hours of high-intensity sunshine and highs in the nineties before she would need to switch on the swamp cooler. She couldn't believe that something as low-tech as a big fan blowing over dampened pads could cool down an entire house so effectively. Evaporation in this climate was a force to be reckoned with. At night even the swamp cooler was nonessential; the thin air cooled quickly all by itself. A couple of open windows and by midnight she had to reach for the covers.

She went into the kitchen next, feeling the dehydrating effect of breathing overnight. She reached for her glass next to the sink, filled it with crisp-tasting well water and gulped noisily. Some movement outside caught her eye as she lowered the empty glass.

She went to the back door to peer out the windowpanes that were conveniently eye level. A small figure darted behind the cottonwood tree. Her quick glimpse could only discern that the person, if there truly was one, was not an adult. Maybe she was just imagining it.

She opened the door to see the sunrise was in its most brilliant spectrum of crimson and golden hues. While she couldn't help but let her gaze linger there, she caught the barest movement from the tree trunk. From her peripheral vision she could see the shape of a head peek around its girth. Sensing it would disappear if looked at directly, she kept her gaze to the sky.

It was a boy, thin and solemn. He stepped out from his hiding place, baggy long shorts billowed over spindly legs. Shaggy dark hair couldn't hide the large brown eyes watching her. The Baca boy, Santiago. What was he doing here? He looked like a ghost child caught in the shadow of the tree.

As she began to step out she instinctively looked down. Right in front of her next step was a makeshift nest of straw holding three chicken eggs. She leaned down to touch them, to make sure they were real. She gathered one into her hand. It was still as warm as a smooth rock baked in the sun. She looked up to call out to him, to thank him for this strange offering, but he was gone.

She made an omelet with her fresh eggs and vegetables from CeCe's garden. CeCe brought baskets brimming with summer squash, onions, green beans, peppers, lettuce, spinach, tomatoes, and eggplant. Abby hadn't stepped foot in the produce section of the grocery store since moving into her new home.

As she ate, she wondered about Santiago. She had met him at the Vigils'. His face held too much sadness for someone on the planet a mere decade. He followed Rachel around, looking more skittish and shy of human contact than the animals he tended. He seemed to crave female attention, this little motherless child. Maybe that is what had sparked his sunrise visit. The last time she was visiting CeCe, she had noticed Santiago's eyes lingering on the growing evidence of her pregnancy. Devoid of women in his family, this was probably a highly exotic sight.

The eggs were so rich and flavorful she had no trouble finishing the entire golden mound that barely fit on the plate. She had paused to admire it before diving in with her eager fork. Bobby would always say that was one of the first things that attracted him to her, the fact that she thought food should be beautiful. He loved to watch her create culinary works of art, feasts for the eye as well as the palate. It became part of their sexual energy, lovemaking began in the kitchen with all of its scents and textures.

After checking in with Ramone and one of the volunteers, she had moving-in projects to occupy her nervous mind and hands. Today she would organize their closets and unpack the last of the boxes of clothes and shoes. The kitchen was now complete, her herb garden planted in the window box. The living room was transformed into a restful, cozy space with familiar objects and furniture but with added treasures from flea markets and unique shops she had discovered in Albuquerque's university district along Central Avenue. It was elegant yet harmonious with good honest southwestern touches, not pretentious Santa Fe chic. It was more rustic and primitive, old wood, sturdy Indian pots that somehow combined with delicate blown glass from her favorite gallery in San Diego. She couldn't wait for Bobby to see it, the way his eyes would widen when he took it all in, not missing any small detail. It was a game with them. After his long sub tours he would walk around their condo discovering little changes she had made out of restless boredom in his absence.

The few boxes marked NURSERY were stacked in Bobby's boyhood bedroom, the one room they would do together. The third bedroom she transformed into their library and music room. She bought big overstuffed chairs, a table for their tea, shelves for all of Bobby's precious books and her own collections of cookbooks. Their stereo and CDs were handy, along with their old vinyl collection of early jazz. She imagined lazy, rainy afternoons in that room, sharing the comfort of each other's presence without words.

What she had created in this home would astonish him. Charlie, Miguel, and CeCe were stunned when she unveiled it for them. It was like knowing you had found the perfect Christmas gift for someone you loved. Her excitement bordered on giddiness when she imagined presenting it to him.

She didn't dare guess what she would do when the last box was unpacked. Probably she would wander from room to room searching for some vase to move slightly to the left, a plant to turn a few degrees to catch the sun in the afternoon light. Waves of panic started to roil in her chest just thinking about having nothing to do but wait for some tip, some lead, some miracle that would bring Bobby back to her. Meanwhile, everything she, Ramone, and the tireless foot soldiers of Esperanza could think of was being done.

She was working up her nerve to tell Edward and Paul the truth and she had to do it fast. A network television news program had picked up the story and it may be expanded into a longer segment on one of those hour-long news shows. Only the long hours at the restaurant and Edward's general disinterest in the news had prevented them from knowing. Someone was bound to mention it to them. They would be upset with her for not telling them, yet under the circumstances, how could they stay mad?

There were national missing-persons web sites with Bobby's case listed. None of this had generated one helpful piece of information. It was as if he had driven his father's truck into another dimension.

Just as she finished rinsing her plate, she saw two more early morning visitors walking across her land. They were a ways off yet but if she squinted she could make out Sheriff Bowman's uniform and Rachel's determined stride. She ran into the bedroom to throw on some clothes, heart pounding, fingers fumbling to find something that would fit. She felt vulnerable enough around Rachel's bristly attitude without being caught in nothing but a nightgown. She pulled on a yellow rumpled linen shift that was baggy enough to go around her belly, ran her brush quickly through her hair, and when she saw the contradictory directions sleep had left, yanked it up into a ponytail. No makeup, a casual pair of glass bead earrings and sandals, she stood at the kitchen door as they approached.

The sheriff gave no hints about his business, sucked at his cigarette and then squashed it out under his boot heel on the flagstone path. Rachel looked bursting with news, her face a quick sequence of swallowed smiles and flashing icy-blue eyes. She wore a jean skirt and an embroidered Mexican blouse, not her usual work clothing.

"Come in, can I make you some coffee?" Abby tried to sound casual even as her throat threatened to constrict.

"Wouldn't mind a cup," Sheriff Bowman drawled, his nose seeming to pick up the scent of her omelet. He sniffed at the air like a hunting dog as he sat at her table.

Rachel remained standing, seeming not to know what to do with her hands.

"So what's this about?" Abby asked, filling the coffee maker with a less-than-steady hand.

"I got a call from the boys down at border patrol, El Paso. A vehicle matching Ricardo's, same license plate, was taped going over the border during the early-morning hours after the night he disappeared. Hispanic male, consistent with Bobby's description was driving, no passengers."

"Bobby went to Mexico?" Abby asked, trying to sit down before her legs collapsed beneath her.

"Yeah," Rachel said. "We used to go as soon as we were old enough to drive, you know, just for something to do."

"He wouldn't just run off down to Mexico without letting me know and be gone for seven weeks. This is crazy. And why are they just finding this tape now?" She got up to pour the sheriff his cup of coffee, grateful for the brief excuse to turn her back on their faces.

"Thanks," Bowman said as he took the steaming cup. He took a noisy sip. "They don't review tapes unless there is some reason to, they can't possibly keep up with every APB in the country. But one of them caught something on national television about Bobby a few days ago and decided to have a look at the tapes from that night he disappeared. The boys down there think he was leaving the country on his own volition."

"Where is this tape? I have to see it for myself. Are they going to investigate? Are you going down there, Sheriff?"

He let out a sigh that she recognized as a male response to having to deal with a difficult woman. "Ma'am, I'm closing my investigation. I'm real sorry, but it's clear to me your husband left you. There's no law against it and absolutely no indication of anything else. Maybe he'll come back after he gets it out of his system, maybe not. But I think it's best if you start to accept that fact. No sense in wasting my officers' time. I think you should call off your volunteers and decide about the reward money, maybe there's some charity you can donate it to."

"You're wrong!" Abby let loose her tears. "This is wrong! I'm calling Ramone—"

"You can call whomever you like, it won't change a thing." Sheriff Bowman took a calm gulp of the last of his coffee and dabbed at his lips with the napkin. "I'll be going, Ma'am. Thanks for the coffee. I wish you luck in coming to terms with this. I'm sorry you have to." He got up, averting his gaze to the tile floor and left.

"What are you doing here? Huh? Come to gloat? Think whatever you want, but you're wrong! And when Bobby comes back, I'm telling him what you thought, it'll piss him off, too, that his so-called best friend would think he was such a lowlife—"

"I don't know what to think!" Rachel interrupted. "But if you shut up for half a second I'll tell you what I think we should do."

Abby felt her words like a cold slap snapping her out of her rage. "We?"

"Yeah. I think we should go down there, see this tape for ourselves."

"Excuse me, but why should you go?"

"I know the area, our old hang outs. You need me." Rachel's chin tilted ever so slightly making Abby's fist twitch in her lap.

"I'm calling Ramone," she said, grabbing her cell phone.

After explaining what she had just learned, Ramone reluctantly explained he must accompany his father for some tests in Albuquerque that they'd waited months for, couldn't this wait a day? She put her finger over the phone. "He can't go until tomorrow."

"We don't need him and this shouldn't wait. I'm going today, so if you want to wait on Ramone, go ahead," Rachel said, starting to leave.

"Wait!" She quickly got off the phone with Ramone and felt Rachel's eyes on her as she grabbed her purse and walked around the house as if she had lost something. "Is this going to be an overnight trip?"

"No. It's only about a five-hour drive each way. We'll be back late tonight. I have milking to do in the morning."

"Should Charlie come with us?" Abby asked. "I mean, those law enforcement types take men more seriously and there could be trouble."

"Charlie is doing my evening milking. Why would there be trouble?" Rachel's tundra blue eyes were hard to look at directly.

"I don't think Bobby went willingly. I think there was a crime involved, so there could be people not wanting us to find him and besides, we'll be in Mexico, right?"

Rachel's face hardened. "Oh yeah, I see what you're saying. We'll be in Mexico. With all of those Mexicanos."

She said the word like it was dirty. Abby felt her face flush. "That was not what I was implying, I only meant, it's a foreign country, a border town where the crime rate is—"

"You don't have to go. You can wait on your buddy Ramone like some helpless female. I thought you'd demand to go to look for your own husband or I'd be just fine by myself. What's Charlie going to do? He's white and ignorant, he'll only piss them off. I speak Spanish fluently and I'm Hispanic."

"Half," Abby stared her down. "CeCe is your mother." She didn't know why, but she had to correct her.

Rachel ran her tongue over her perfect white teeth and took a minute to respond. "I am my father's daughter. Do you speak any Spanish?"

"Only a few words. I understand it better than I can speak it."

"You married Roberto and never bothered to learn his language?"

"Bobby's language is English."

Rachel smiled. "Oh yes, Bobby. Bobby is the man you married. Well, I think the man we're looking for is Roberto." She led Abby out of the back door to where the Camry was parked.

Abby followed her, a host of angry words crowding her brain, each one fighting to come out. Rachel stood on the driver's side of the car, her hand outstretched for the keys.

"I can drive," Abby said. "I'm pregnant, not an invalid."

"I know the way."

Abby threw the keys at her. This was not the battle worth fighting.

Rachel drove the luxury car as if it were a truck, bouncing too fast over the rutted road leading away from their properties. Abby wrapped her arms around her baby who became restless within her despite the natural shock absorption of the amniotic fluid inside her womb. She tried to ignore Rachel's irritating behavior and focus on what mattered. There was tape of Bobby going over the border. Why would he go there? She wracked her brain for some memory that would help explain it. Did he have friends there? Distant family?

Rachel drove south, through Esperanza, Bosque Farms, and into Los Lunas where she caught I-25 south. She switched on the radio, found a Spanish station and listened while the announcer spoke rapid-fire Spanish.

Abby guessed this was part of Rachel's earlier point. She had never met anyone who used race so much as a weapon. With Bobby, it was never an issue. He just didn't see the world like that. There were people he liked, people he didn't like, based on how they behaved, not what they looked like. They had friends of all races in San Diego. Nobody seemed to be running around keeping some kind of score, dividing up into race teams. Maybe this was a feature of rural life. In the city, there just wasn't time. There were tons of people all vying for the same job, the same parking spot. Like someone took a big spoon and stirred everyone up. Race soup. Out here, there was room to draw lines. And history probably came into it more, generations of land disputes, who invaded whom, who stole what. In the city, the present was what mattered and real estate was nothing more than an investment, not a reminder of old wounds.

The radio blared Spanish music and Rachel sang along, knowing every word. Abby felt tired, let her mind soften and become dreamy. She was back in her restaurant, in the stock room. The busboys were unloading an order, their little radio playing a Spanish station. It was a love song; they teased her by singing it with exaggerated expressions and gestures, as if they were competing for her love. Edward, also Hispanic, arrived to play the jealous husband, tearing her away from her suitors. But then, true to form, he mimed romancing them instead of her, causing the young men to laugh and be grossed out, their macho stance their shields. As she felt herself drift into a shallow sleep, she remembered how it felt to be happy.

She woke slowly, feeling the moist breath of the air conditioner, hearing only the sound of the tires meeting the road.

With her eyes closed, this could be the first week in June. Bobby is driving them to their new home in New Mexico. The bad dream is over. Like when she was a kid playing some game with her friends, if you messed up all you had to do was say "Do-overs!" and you had another chance.

Her eyelids fluttered open. No do-overs. Rachel sat in Bobby's seat, her strong hands on the wheel and glanced in Abby's direction.

Abby sat up, fought for mental alertness. "Sorry, I didn't mean to sleep so long." The dashboard clock said almost eleven. Over two hours since they'd left.

"You didn't miss anything." Rachel kept her eyes on the road.

The interstate cut a swath through the desert, all possible shades of brown interrupted only by scrubby vegetation until running into jagged mountains in the distance. The view was identical out of both sides of the car. But then, on the left, an expanse of blue water, shimmering like a mirage.

"Elephant Butte Reservoir," Rachel supplied. "Soon as we're past Truth or Consequences, you'll see Caballo Reservoir."

"Truth or Consequences?"

"Yeah, the stupid people won a game show to change the name of their town back in the fifties. Used to be called 'Hot Springs.' Doesn't really matter though, just white names anyway."

A pickup truck pulling a fishing boat passed them. Then another.

"Roberto and I and his dad used to come down here to fish. One time, we were maybe ten, he caught a five-pound bass and got his picture in the local paper."

Abby studied her expression as well as she could in profile. Rachel's smile was wide, pulling her cheek up into a delighted ball under her eye. So happy, so alive in a way she hadn't seen since her graveyard reunion with Roberto.

For a moment, Abby could feel such compassion for her and almost understand her resentment. Abby took away her childhood best friend. Like a brother, they had shared everything and then she was left behind to wait his return. It was easy to see how Bobby's father, all of them found it easier to blame his never coming back on his love for some woman. Her. He had forsaken all of their love and trust, broken his promises to return because of her. No wonder she was the enemy. She realized why Bobby had never brought her here on his rare visits. He was protecting her. If Rachel was resentful, she could only imagine how his father might have been.

"Bobby talks a lot about how much fun you guys had," Abby lied. Bobby rarely talked about his past.

Rachel glanced at her. "If you only knew."

Chapter 10

After grabbing some fast food in Las Cruces, Abby could feel their anticipation increase. She consumed her fish sandwich in a few quick ravenous bites. The vanilla shake she sipped cooled her throat but not her growing anxiety.

Rachel's fingers glistened with grease as she popped french fries in her mouth. Bobby never wanted them to eat in the new car. As Rachel's greasy fingers slid around the leather-covered steering wheel, Abby had to use great self-control to not say anything. Rachel was in a surprisingly good mood, no sense in threatening that.

The El Paso skyline at first shimmered like the Emerald City in the distance through the heated thin desert air. As they drew near, it resembled any large city with nondescript office buildings, crowded freeway system, and a blanket of brown air hovering over everything.

"We take Highway 54 to the free bridge—Bridge of the Americas. That's where the tape is. Do you want to stop and buy car insurance in case we go over into Mexico? You probably don't need it, but AAA sells it by the day, if you want."

"What did you and Bobby used to do about it?"

Rachel glanced at her before responding. A smile formed on her lips. "We usually dumped our vehicle on this side of the border and we'd walk over the Santa Fe Bridge because it comes out on Avenida Juarez where most of our hangouts were and it only cost like thirty-five cents to cross it. Since we were teenagers, AAA might not have sold us insurance, at least that's what we thought. Besides, usually our parents didn't know what we were up to. This was our big rebellion, leaving the country to party. There's some great after-hours dance clubs, all the cheap booze you can handle. It was a blast."

"Well, just in case, maybe we should get some. Bobby really babies this car. He'd probably think it was a good idea."

The law enforcement and border management division of Immigration and Naturalization had the El Paso sector headquarters at the base of the Bridge of the Americas. Abby felt her pulse rate double as Rachel parked the car in visitor parking. She got a tissue from her purse to have something to clutch in her shaking hand.

"There's an agent Kent Logan, that we're supposed to ask for. He's the guy I talked to," Rachel said as she fed the meter.

Abby looked down to try to gather her thoughts. The sunlight was so intense as it glanced off the white cement it felt like flashbulbs exploded in her retinas. With her eyes watering, she fumbled in her purse for her sunglasses. She caught Rachel looking at her like she was some kind of idiot.

The receptionist led them down a long hallway. Not a lot of money had been squandered by the government in the way of decor or furnishings, but they spared no expense on the air-conditioning. Abby felt like she had entered the walk-in freezer at the restaurant, goose bumps formed along her bare arms.

"You can wait here," the receptionist said, "I'll page him and let him know you're here."

They sat on the two available chairs in front of Agent Logan's cluttered desk. Abby let her eyes rest on the painting on the wall behind it. It was a large scene of a lake, in the foreground a man in waders was fly fishing. Bobby loved to fly fish, it was something he was looking forward to doing a lot more of when they got to New Mexico, in the renowned trout streams in the northern part of the state. Would she finally get some answers here? She felt her heart take a dangerous venture into hope.

"Good afternoon, ladies!" A voice boomed behind them. "Man, if I ain't one lucky cuss! Two beautiful ladies to brighten up my sorry day." Agent Logan thrust his meaty hands, one for each of them, for a quick shake. He exemplified what Abby imagined when she heard the term, Texas "good ol' boy." Well over six foot, sandy hair, reddish complexion, the hint of a beer belly pressing the front of his otherwise well-fitting uniform.

He sat at his desk, leaning toward them. "We get a million APBs down here as you might well imagine. We track them as well as we can, but frankly, our job is more to look at who's coming in more than who's going out. So, we film everybody and his brother, each and every license plate of who's entering the country. We keep databases; try to catch the bad guys. We don't always bother filming who's leaving. But on that particular night back on June the third, we'd had a bank robbery in El Paso so to help out we filmed the exiting vehicles. We give the tapes to the El Paso police to review. Yesterday, when they gave back this particular tape, I'd just seen the story about your guy on one of the networks. Since the date matched up, I popped the tape in, and hell if I didn't see the very vehicle crossing over. So I gave your sheriff a call and here we all are." He smiled broadly and nodded, looking from one to the other, like a puppy waiting for his pat on the head.

"I really appreciate your help in this. I've been frantic. This just isn't like my husband, especially with the baby." She caught her breath and willed herself to stop the blathering. "Anyway, whatever information you have is appreciated."

He nodded sympathetically and looked Rachel's direction. "Looks like you have a real good girlfriend here to help you out, one of those things you womenfolk are so much better at than us men."

Rachel looked like she was about to correct him but then didn't. "We're just so worried about Roberto, not hearing from him in all these weeks."

"Yeah, that's the real unfortunate thing about it. We got him crossing the border—what is it now—last week in July?—so, nearly two months ago. The trail may be stone cold. But at least it's a start."

He paused, watching them. When neither said anything else he got up and walked over to a TV and VCR that sat atop a wheeled cart. "Tape is still in here, I'll just get it cued up." He punched some buttons on the remote.

Abby and Rachel both got up and moved closer to the screen, one on each side of him. "Here we go, June fourth, oh-four-hundred hours." He sped it up until the truck came into view, "Here, it's this one."

It was dark, the lighting from the border station glared on the windshield as the truck approached. Abby could see a quick image of a man driving but it was impossible to make out specific features. Yet it was clearly the truck with its mismatched driver-side door. Abby's breath sounded loud in her ears, as when she was jogging. As the truck passed the camera, Agent Logan freeze-famed the rear where the license plate confirmed what she already knew.

"That was him!" Rachel said, "Thank God he's all right."

"How can you be so sure, I couldn't tell—you couldn't even see him through the glare on the glass—"

"Of course it's him, who else would it be? It's his size, Hispanic—it has to be him."

Agent Logan backed it up and started the tape again. This time he freeze framed the view of the driver. "It is hard to pick up anything specific about the guy. Looks alone. Going slow, not camera shy, not like he has anything to hide. Don't know that we can tell anything more than that."

"I don't think it's him. Something doesn't look right, the shape of his hair or something. Maybe this guy stole the truck and was going to sell it in Mexico for parts or something." Abby knew she sounded desperate and didn't know why she preferred this scenario to the idea that it was Bobby, leaving on his own.

"You know, if the vehicle in question was a brand new SUV or sports car that would make sense. But people don't normally go to all that trouble for an old patched-together truck. There's plenty of them south of the border." He looked at her and sucked on his lower lip. "I guess it doesn't help much to think it's him. And I got to say, it defies logic why a guy would leave as nice a gal as you. But I been in this business long enough to know men do some crazy things."

"It isn't my pride that makes me think it isn't him. We've been married ten years, I know how he looks, the shape of his head and hair—"

"And I knew him for eighteen years, was with him every day, closer than a brother and I say it is him. But either way, we've used up enough of Mr. Logan's time. Let's go into Juarez and talk to the police there."

"I'm not supposed to give these tapes to anyone but law enforcement. But I could make you all a copy to take back. You could take it on up to Albuquerque Police, maybe someone in forensics could take a look at it, play with it electronically to get a better image. Worth a shot, anyway."

"Thank you. That would be great," Abby said.

"I'll be back in a jiffy," he said, ejecting the video.

Abby and Rachel waited in silence. Abby wished she could feel as optimistic as Rachel seemed to be. Was it her pride that made her resist the possibility Bobby had run away from her into Mexico? Or was it that she knew him well enough to know this didn't fit the man she loved?

Agent Logan returned with the copy and held it out to Abby. "You keep the faith. My wife would do the same. Be careful over there in Mexico, you got a baby to think of. Don't do anything reckless."

As they crossed the bridge, Abby tried to imagine what had been going through Bobby's mind when he had crossed, if he had crossed. "Did he know anyone in Juarez? Old friends, family?"

Rachel kept her eyes on the throngs of pedestrians crowding close to their shiny new American car. Women and small children, some dressed in colorful native clothing, implored them to buy candies and trinkets.

"Tarahumara Indians," Rachel said nodding at them. "They come up from the Sierra Madre to try to make a few pesos."

"Bobby knew them?"

"No, I thought you might be interested, that's all." Rachel sighed. "Look, you keep trying to think of what Roberto was going toward. To me, that's backward. He was getting away from something, leaving."

"He wanted to move to New Mexico. He wanted to raise our baby where he grew up. Esperanza was a destination, not a place of departure."

"Well, sure, yeah, until he got there and reality set in. Believe me, it's not unlike Roberto to become overwhelmed and want to get away from things. This is exactly where we would go. It was always his idea. 'Rachel, I didn't study for my math test, let's ditch.' Or it would be a fight with his dad or being sick of the hard work in the chile fields. Roberto is a runner. When he's had it up to here—he splits."

Abby held back her arguments. She would only sound defensive. She looked out the window as they passed an elaborately domed building surrounded by a moat, connected by bridges to two other impressive buildings. MUSEA DE ART, the sign read.

"The art museum," Rachel translated unnecessarily. "There's also a museum of history and a museum of anthropology—Roberto and I had to do reports on them when we ditched. Oh, and Our Lady of Guadelupe Mission, we had to sketch it for art class. 'As long as you're down there, you might as well research Poncho Villa and the Mexican Revolution and give us an oral report.' We were such good students the rest of the time, we never got in too bad of trouble. I can't believe how big Juarez is getting, *mi Dios!*"

Without even trying, Abby could picture Rachel and Bobby as teenagers running those streets. The jumble of shops, open markets, people singing and selling their wares for a pittance in U.S. dollars. It would have been an adventure and Bobby did like adventures. When he was home on leave, he'd buzz from one activity to the next: surfing, hiking, fishing, parasailing, heading north to explore the wine country—she loved his enthusiasm and went with him whenever she could get away from the restaurant.

"There—*Policía de Municipal Cuidad Juárez.*" Rachel put on the breaks as an old man began to wave her into a parking place. His white cotton shirt was flattened with sweat against his skinny chest. His thin dark arms signaled as if he were guiding a jumbo jet into its gate. A straw hat rode low on his brow, he chewed the stub of a cigar between stained teeth.

"*Parquero.* Do you have a couple of bucks? He'll feed the meter and guard the car for us," Rachel said, unbuckling her seat belt. "Pretty good deal, considering."

Abby pulled out a five-dollar bill, the smallest she had. Rachel snatched it from her.

"For this, he won't even let his friends steal it."

She supposed as poor as these people were, someone would be brazen enough to steal it right in front of the police station. She smiled at the guy who smiled back and said something in a burst of Spanish.

As they walked up the sidewalk, Rachel said, "He said he would take care of the car for your very lucky baby. May God bless the two very beautiful angels before him."

The small waiting area in the old building was crowded with people who all seemed to be talking at once. Various ages and dress, some obviously urban, others in the plain sack cloth clothing of rural peasants. Arguments, weeping, even singing from one small group huddled around a guitar.

Rachel pushed past and led them to the counter that separated this melee from a front office, where a handful of workers typed and answered phones completely unaffected. Abby coughed on the thick stench of cigarette and cigar smoke that clouded the hot room.

Rachel shouted something in Spanish at the nearest employee, a young woman holding a stack of files, a pencil between her teeth. Thick dark bangs nearly obscured both eyes, she kept twitching her head to toss them off but they fell neatly back in place. She spit out the pencil and responded with something Abby couldn't hear, let alone translate.

"Come on, we're seeing Officer Armijo," Rachel said, opening a door and heading down a hallway to the left.

"Who?" Abby followed. At least the hallway was less congested. She looked longingly at an old drinking fountain but didn't dare.

"My brother, Officer Armijo. Saw his name on the roster." Rachel winked.

"Good thinking."

Officer Armijo was talking on the phone, one of those ancient big black dial phones that belonged in some old film noir movie. He was young, decked out in a black uniform that seemed right out of the box. His hair was neatly slicked back. He kept a protective hand on the gun holster that hugged his slim hip. From the tone of his voice, Abby guessed this was a personal call with a girlfriend.

The small room held six other desks, all vacated. Old phones, vintage typewriters, antique electric fans on almost every desk top rotated to blow the hot air toward the single open window at the back. Calendars with half-naked women adorned the cracked walls.

He hung up the phone and smiled at Abby. "How can I be of help?"

He gestured for them to sit and only after they sat in the metal folding chairs, did he sit.

"You speak English," Abby said.

"Yes, I speak English. I attended University of Texas, El Paso, for two years. I even know some French if that would help."

Abby couldn't resist. *"Ce n'est pas nécessaire."*

He laughed, "Good, that would be pretty bad."

"We're looking for someone," Rachel said, steering them back to business.

After they filled him in, he sat holding the flyer Abby provided, reading aloud. "'Six foot two inches, thirty years old, black hair, brown eyes. Roberto 'Bobby' Silva. Last seen driving a 1957 Chevy pickup, green with red driver's side door with script: quality plumbing since 1932.'" He looked up. "Juarez has changed a lot since you and Roberto were teenagers. There was probably half a million population back then, we have 1.2 million now. And still only ten police stations. If your guy doesn't want to be found, he's a needle in a haystack. He'll blend right in. And it's more likely, he didn't even stay here. He may have only passed through. My advice would be to go to the American consulate; it's on Avenue Lopez Mateos, number 924. You can fill out missing-person's documents—"

"Yeah and then they shuffle them for months. We don't have that kind of time. My husband is in some kind of danger, he'd have to be. What about the vehicle—it's distinctive, even if he's not." Abby urged with her eyes.

"Yeah, this truck with the odd door might have caught somebody's attention. I could do some checking around and give you a call if—"

"We would really appreciate it if you could do some checking while we're here," Rachel said. "You could go with us to some of his old hangouts on Avenue Juarez."

Armijo smiled flirtatiously to one and then the other. "I can think of far worse ways to spend an afternoon."

After giving the parquero another five dollars, they rode in the police car to Avenue Juarez. Abby sat in the back and sipped on some bottled water Armijo had provided and scanned the wave of pedestrians crowding the streets as if the next face she saw would be Bobby's.

Predominantly tourists strolled this early in the day and the locals vying for their American dollars. For some reason, it suddenly struck Abby as strange that in all the years they lived in San Diego, they never went to Tijuana together. She went with college friends a few times and even once while still in her private high school to have some illegal beers, dance, and then stagger back over the bridge. She never knew Bobby liked coming to Juarez.

"Here! That was our favorite bar—Pericos!" Rachel pointed across Armijo's chest, leaning into him.

He swung the car around to park in a loading zone and ran around to Abby's side of the car to help her get out. It was getting hard to be graceful with her protruding belly, her yellow linen shift wanting to ride up her sweaty legs, and manage her water bottle and purse. By the time she stood next to the car smoothing her dress, Rachel was already in the bar.

It was dark, smoky, and nearly vacant. An old man sat at the bar talking with the young bartender, drinking beer and smoking cigars. Rachel was conversing with him in Spanish.

The only light seemed to be the amber lights illuminating the tower of liquor bottles against the mirror of the bar behind them. Abby felt disembodied, as if she had floated into someone else's dream.

The Spanish flew between them and Abby tried to read their faces. Another guy emerged from the shadows to join the conversation. He was immensely obese and heavily tattooed with big-busted naked women on his arms and Jesus with a crown of thorns dripping blood onto his naked chest. "*Sí, sí!*" he kept repeating and pointed at the flyer.

"What, tell me!" Abby said.

"He knows the truck, he's telling us where to go," Rachel said in between rushes of Spanish.

The men began shaking hands. "*Gracias! Gracias!*"

"*De nada!*"

Abby found that she was gripping Armijo's arm; he smiled into her eyes. "Your luck is changing, señora."

Chapter 11

"How far is it?" Abby asked, wishing she had thought to use the bathroom in the bar. The bottled water was going right through her. And now her baby had chosen this moment to use her expanded bladder as a trampoline.

"Colonia Anapra is here on the western edge of Juarez, another few miles is all," Armijo said. "It's a very poor area, shantytown. The city has to truck water over to them. The houses are nothing more than hovels made from wooden shipping pallets and scrap wood. Most of the people are good people. They work hard just to exist, no? There's very little energy left over to cause trouble. We have almost a hundred thousand people without running water around Cuidad Juarez. We are a boomtown—ready to explode if we grow any faster. They come for work, our industry is legendary all over Chihuahua. Thirty thousand more come every year—at this rate we will all run out of water in another ten or twenty years."

Abby peered through the dust kicked up by the police car's tires on the unpaved road. Clusters of small dwellings, their roofs were sheets of plywood held down by old car tires. What would Bobby be doing here? This must be some mistake. Yet some small hope began to seep into her weary bones. Defying all logic. But maybe logic was the problem. Throw it out and you have faith. Bobby could be there, God knew why. But his truck had been seen repeatedly at Perico's Bar with a man named Hector Casteneda who lived in Colonia Anapra. And Hector had been seen with a man who fit Bobby's description.

"I could see Roberto here," Rachel said from the back seat. "He'd be more comfortable with good honest peasants than with obscene wealth and luxury." She caught Abby's eye in the rearview mirror.

"You're right," Abby said, knowing it would disarm her. "We just may find him here." She felt her heart flutter as fast as her baby was kicking.

After nearly two months, never mind how or why, to be safe in his arms again would make sense out of all that had been senseless. She looked in the mirror to see Rachel smile and smooth her hair, adjust her blouse. She believed it, too.

"Well, this is the main street, if you can call it that. The guy said to go about a mile and stop at a house with turquoise paint on the front and ask where to find Casteneda's place." Armijo slowed to a near crawl as little children formed a parade around his car. Several rode battered bicycles. Others danced in happy steps, waving and grinning. A long-haired lanky girl about ten strode next to Abby's window, making intense eye contact with her. Even through Abby's sunglasses, she felt the girl see straight into her.

Women gathered in front of metal tubs churning laundry through the soapy water, scrubbing it against washboards with strong hands. Their faces were smiling as they worked, talking to each other, laughing, pausing to call out to their children.

Armijo pulled the car up to the last house on the road. Turquoise paint covered the door and extended halfway up the front of its plastered wall. "Wait here while I get the directions."

A cloud of dust circled the car before wafting away on the breeze. The children stood patiently for the officer to conduct his business. He patted their dark heads as he walked by, sending them into fits of giggles.

"He could be in there," Abby breathed.

Rachel looked as antsy she felt. She squirmed in the back seat, not taking her eyes from the turquoise door. There was one window on the front of the house; a red-print curtain waved teasingly in the breeze.

Just as she felt both of them might spring from the car in unison, Armijo emerged. He repeated the head-patting ritual; this time the kids crowded up to him and tried to pat his head in return. He laughed and swung a few around by their skinny outstretched arms.

He opened the door and shook a few last kids off his back and climbed in. "Just around the corner, two streets over and he said we'd see the truck out front."

Abby felt tears sting her dry eyes. She blinked quickly and fought to remain calm. When they turned the corner and she saw the truck, a few tears escaped. She felt their hot trails through her dusty cheeks. Her finger twitched against the trigger of the door handle, ready to shoot herself from the car like a bullet.

Armijo was starting to say something as he pulled to a stop, but Abby was out of the car. The slam of Rachel's car door was only a beat after her own. He caught up to them at the door. "Let me," he said firmly, positioning himself in front of them. He knocked on the door. Spanish music drifted through the glassless window from behind its curtain.

The breeze had stopped. Time itself ceased. Abby stared at the thin white paint that clung to the door like a thin layer of chalk. It was something past hope, beyond a wish, surpassing prayer. She felt every cell in her body vibrate with sheer will that it be Bobby's face that appeared in the doorway, his eyes searching for hers, his presence obliterating everyone and everything else. Instead of a world without Bobby, there would be only Bobby and no more world.

Then, voices on the other side of the door, several talking at once. She felt Rachel's hand reach and grab her own. It gave her the absurd picture of a beauty pageant, the last two contestants holding hands, wishing each other luck when only one can win and the other must lose.

The door swung open, a man stood in the shadows. *"Qué pasa?"*

Officer Armijo began to inquire in Spanish. She could understand "Roberto Silva" and watch as he pointed at the truck. The man opened the door wider and invited them inside.

He was about Bobby's age and size. His hair was a little longer and his face could not be Bobby's no matter how hard Abby tried to make it so. "Where is he?" she asked.

Armijo turned and held her by her shoulders to look into her eyes. She tried not to see him. "You must let me do all of the talking right now. I must do my job. I will tell you everything, I promise."

"But she can understand, I can't." Abby heard her voice sound weak and high, and felt like a little girl jealous of her older sister.

Rachel was next to her, "Come on, I'll translate for you."

A little round woman with striped gray-and-black hair wound into a bun atop her head motioned for the women to sit at the small kitchen table on mismatched chairs. Armijo and the man who was not Bobby were joined by an older man with silver hair that stood on end like a curry brush. They stood in a small circle in the cramped space next to the table.

The younger man began to speak. His Spanish was musical, as if he were telling a story. Rachel whispered to Abby. "He says he first met Roberto a few months ago at Perico's. They drank beers. Roberto told him he was taking a vacation from his *la vida loca*—his crazy life. He was mourning his father, who had died after going crazy. His wife was pregnant. He made her leave her life in California and he feared she would never be happy in Esperanza. He was finally free of the Navy and now it seemed his troubles were only beginning."

Abby watched Rachel's lips move and heard her words like an echo to the drone of the male voice behind her. She wanted to think Rachel was making this up, but Armijo was standing next her and only nodded as he listened to both languages. Even as these words sickened and repelled her, she sat transfixed, as if this were Judgment Day and God himself were listing her transgressions.

"Roberto said he didn't know what to do but get away. He needed time to think. Hector invited him to stay here with his parents and himself. After about a week, Roberto and Hector went to a poker game, high stakes. Roberto won a great deal of money off some thug named Benicio. Benicio accused him of cheating and there was nearly a fight but Benicio's old lady showed up and made him come home. But Benicio told Roberto the money he won was owed to a drug dealer known as *El Grande Torro* and he was a dead man if he kept it."

Rachel paused as Armijo seemed to be clarifying something. "Armijo has heard of El Grande Torro and he's asking where he can find this Benicio to confirm the story. Hector says Benicio is hiding in the hills because the drug dealer's men are after him for gambling with the money. Roberto used some of the money to buy a purple motorcycle and said he was going to the Baja to ride down the coast, camp on the beach, maybe fish. The ocean air would cleanse his mind and help him know what to do. He gave them the truck for their generosity."

Rachel licked her dry lips and listened. Abby stared at her mouth, waiting for the next terrible words to emerge. "Armijo is asking when was the last time they saw Roberto. Hector and his parents say six weeks ago and they never expect to see him again. Armijo asks where did Roberto purchase the motorcycle. Hector says they had been drinking and they met some guy in the streets who was selling it. Never got his name. Roberto was excited because he always wanted this kind of motorcycle and wanted to be rid of the truck that had been his father's. He didn't want anything to remind him of his old life, especially if people were searching for him. With the bike, he would be free."

Abby felt she had been carved from stone. She couldn't move. Her flesh and blood had hardened, minerals had deposited, turning her into something that can't feel, react, or think. Something less than alive.

She looked down to see the old woman was weeping and holding her hand. All eyes were on her. Armijo was speaking to her perhaps in English, but her stone ears would not understand. The face of Hector and his father looked at her with pity. Rachel said one more thing: "I'm sorry, Abby."

There was something in her tone that cracked open the stone, that dissolved the minerals. Abby felt her blood begin to heat up, her baby thumped at her to come back to life. She yanked her hand from the calloused grasp of the old woman. "They are lying! Armijo, do something! Search the place. Check the truck for DNA evidence. Don't just take their word for it! They could have done something to Roberto or know who did and they got the truck to shut them up. Come on!"

But now they seemed made of stone. Armijo spoke to her like she was a little child. "Abby, I don't believe they are lying. There is no evidence. How would they know all those things about your husband if he himself had not told them?"

"Just look around! Please!" Abby cried.

Armijo humored her. A tour of the three-room shanty took all of ten seconds.

Abby felt her intestines churn, her bladder was hurting. *"Baño, por favor!"*

The old woman took her by the hand and led her out the back door to where a closet-sized structure with a blanket for a door stood. Abby lurched toward it, ready to vomit, urinate, and defecate simultaneously. A hole in the ground would do.

Armijo drove them back to their car. "You know, when I was in college in El Paso, people would call me 'Army-Joe' instead of Armijo. Even professors, even in a place where everyone should know basic Spanish pronunciation even if they can't speak the language. Hell, everything is named in Spanish—the streets, all the landmarks. Why do they suppose that is? Because we were here first—that's why."

Rachel nodded.

Abby was still furious with how this had gone. "The Spanish explorers were invaders and oppressors of indigenous people. They were not here first. Ask the Sumas and the Mansos Indians. Oops, can't, all gone."

"Point taken," Armijo said. "But, you can't deny what the white people did in all of this. They came out on top and made a world only their own kind is welcome in."

"Like the Spanish would have done it any differently. I'm not saying it's right or just, I'm saying it's reality. People can piss and moan about it or get over it and make something of themselves. That's what Bobby used to say."

"Exactly," Rachel said with that shit-eating grin. "That's what 'Bobby' used to say. I have a feeling Roberto would say something different about now."

It was after five p.m. when they started back to Esperanza in the Camry. This time, Abby was relieved when Rachel took the driver's seat. She needed to think.

She forced herself to consider the story that was told. Her Bobby would have to be one hell of an actor to live the way he did for over a decade and be hiding some deep racial conflict and resentment of the white world. He thrived in it. He loved it. He said he couldn't escape the narrow, small-minded community of his past fast enough. He had stayed in the Navy because he fit in and moved up the ranks. He was valued and he liked that. He was respected for his talents as a communications officer and he took his job seriously. He was quietly but strongly patriotic. He felt it was an honor to serve and defend his country. The only colors he saw were red, white, and blue.

Abby sighed and looked out the window. The sun was beginning to angle, though it wouldn't be dark for hours. It would be at least ten-thirty before she was home and soaking in a hot bath. Exhaustion settled into her. Her back ached. Despite downing another bottle of water, she felt dehydrated. She'd had shitty, nonnutritious food. She was left feeling toxic. Dr. Lark would not be happy.

"I really think you need to face up to some things," Rachel said, after a too-brief hour of silence.

"I really don't feel like discussing it. We'll never agree."

"It's not about agreeing. You will never get back your husband unless you figure some shit out. I knew Roberto for eighteen years. We were closer than you can imagine. He told me all his hopes and dreams, how he saw the world. Why do you so easily discount that?"

"I keep hearing about those eighteen years like you're keeping score. I'll put my twelve years over your eighteen. For one thing, the first six of yours shouldn't even count. You were babies fighting over toys. Pretty soon you were rebellious teenagers, so what? There's nothing special about that. Bobby came to San Diego as a man, to create a life of his choosing. I have twelve recent years of reality, naked in his arms where there is nothing to hide. He would talk all night sometimes. We had no secrets. There was nothing false going on."

"In the beginning, after he first left, he wrote to me. He talked about how much he had to deny about himself to fit in. How he was afraid of losing his identity. How people called him Bobby and he hated it. But what could he do? He didn't want to come home and prove his father right. Ricardo swore he wouldn't make it out there and Roberto was never going to give him the satisfaction of failing."

"He met me," Abby said. "He fell in love."

"Yes," Rachel said. "He became Bobby for you. Instead of it just being a name to feel separate from, it became an identity he grew into. He wasn't just fooling you—he fooled himself. And it worked for a long time. But, he never opted out of his submarine tours, did he? You were separated half of every year. You don't know for sure who he was half the time."

"He loved his work. I encouraged him to pursue his career just as I was pursuing mine. Our intimacy supported our individual freedom."

"Bullshit. You led separate lives half the time. It was easier that way—don't you see?"

Abby threw up her hands in frustration. "You think you have it all figured out, just tell me. Lay it out there instead of conducting this stupid debate."

"I will tell you what I believe. But first, you have to get out of your arrogant white mind-set. You have to be willing to think outside of that or there's no point."

Abby wanted to fire something back about her arrogant Hispanic mind-set, but her curiosity gave her self-control. "Go on."

"Because you are white, it is impossible for you to know how strong Hispanic blood is, how you feel it coursing through you. You are forever a visitor in the white world because the white world doesn't know who you are. It can't. You tell yourself you will never deny yourself, but you do. Not all at once, but gradually. A little of you goes each day you live in that world, breathe that air, do what you have to do to succeed. Roberto invented Bobby for that. Bobby could succeed, be accepted, live without conflict."

"You don't think he loved me."

"I think he fell hard for you. I think you became the biggest reason of all to stay Bobby. But what you fail to see is, it isn't that this man changed from the man I know to the man you married. I believe he split himself in two and let Bobby run things, hoping that Roberto would go away forever."

Abby watched the sun begin to skim the horizon. Car headlights were turned on. The immense sky glowed with the gaudy hues of a Mexican blanket. The craggy reddened landscape could be on Mars.

"But inside of him, probably outside of his own awareness the conflict simmered. Why do you think he never wanted to come home to visit?"

Abby shook her head. "I encouraged him to come home. It was bad enough my family didn't accept us. I didn't want him to lose his. But he hated the guilt trips his father gave him."

"He hated coming home because he was afraid. He couldn't be Bobby at home, he was Roberto. He was afraid he would never go back."

Abby found herself seeing Rachel's logic. Bobby's avoidance of Esperanza never really made complete sense until that moment. She had always sensed fear underneath his explanations and excuses. She felt her own fear as reality began to twist slightly, turn just a few degrees.

"The part of him that loved you was forever in conflict with everything else that is him. No matter how sensitive you were, open-minded, whatever, you could never really know that part of him because he held it back from you. By necessity, he buried it beyond reach, even from himself. So that he could do his job, live the life he had chosen and in many ways loved and wanted."

"You know, in your theory, there could be no successful interracial, cross-cultural marriages. But love transcends everything, crosses all barriers. Look at your own parents for Godsakes!"

"Exactly. My father sacrificed everything to be with my mother. His entire family stopped including him in all the family traditions. La familia is community, it's knowing who you are. I have seen the stress of that on their marriage. They love each other, but so what? My mother gave up who she is also. They are orphaned, isolated. A marriage shouldn't be like that, it should support who you are, there should be continuity between your childhood and your adult life, children should be born into a multigenerational, extended family. All of that got lost when my parents got married. It's selfish, when you think about it, to marry outside of your own kind."

"You married Charlie."

"It only proves my point. He's not a bad guy. It just can't work, and it ends up hurting everyone involved. Look at the pain you're going through." Rachel's voice was softer, less strident. As if she knew the power of the truth would suffice.

"So, in your theory, Roberto became Bobby, like a split personality. So why, after avoiding his past for so long, would he decide we had to move back to Esperanza?"

"He loved his father, but had to deny him to make the choices he made. He felt a lot of guilt about that, he wrote me about it. When his dad died, it was like a giant wake-up call; it broke through Bobby and reached into Roberto. Roberto was his father's son, not Bobby. The Navy was over, one of the other big props to keep Bobby going. Bobby was defined by these external worlds that were disappearing. Roberto had to come home to bury his father. Then, you add the biggest thing of all. His own impending fatherhood. He told you he had to raise his child in Esperanza, right?"

"Yes, but not at first. The violence of our robbery made him want to leave the city, find a house in the suburbs. Only after his father died, did he mention Esperanza."

"Sure. His father's death brought Roberto back to life. Roberto would never want to raise his child outside of his Hispanic roots. He couldn't do that to his child. And he could no longer deny his true self, his true destiny. He had to come home."

Abby let the sound of the tires on the road hum inside of her weary head. The silence in the car reflected the sudden silence in her mind; there was no more conflict. There were no more angry words elbowing each other to come out. There was only a strange calm, like the stillness of air after the turbulence of a wind storm. It was dark now. The dashboard's controls glowed like the tiny bridge in a miniature spaceship, hurtling them through space and time.

"Tell me about the words you and Roberto had just before he left."

Abby paused, not wanting to give Rachel any more ammunition. But then, as she saw the dreadful scene play in her mind like a home movie, she felt her voice rise involuntarily from her throat, his words claiming a life of their own. "He said his father had been right. That the white world would poison him and his soul would forget what is right," Abby quoted him word for word. Words she hadn't even remembered until this moment. Words she hadn't really heard until now.

Rachel took in a small breath that in the silence became a gasp. Abby kept her eyes on the road. The stripes of the highway pulsed, the asphalt flew beneath them. The headlights could only shine so far and beyond that was a vast darkness.

Chapter 12

Despite getting home late and not sleeping well, Abby woke early. She sat at her kitchen table waiting for the sunlight to reach her window. Sunrise here was a gradual thing, delayed by the jagged blockade of the Manzano Mountains in the east.

Her thoughts were sluggish and she knew to be grateful for that. There was no rush to be bombarded with the ruminations that would be triggered by yesterday's events in Juarez.

She heard a slight rustling outside her kitchen door. She crept over to it, careful to stay below the level of the window. Slowly she rose, peeking just her eyes over the glass. It was Santiago again, galloping like a young colt as he made his getaway across the field. Sunlight chose just that moment to break free of the mountain's shadow to illuminate everything below. Santiago serpentined like a prisoner trying to avoid the floodlights during a prison break.

Abby opened the door to find another makeshift nest of straw holding three perfect eggs. Next to that, a small white stuffed toy bunny missing one eye.

She cradled the eggs in her T-shirt and lifted the bunny to inspect it further. It was quite worn but clean, reminding her of *The Velveteen Rabbit*, her favorite childhood story.

As she scrambled her eggs, she thought about the story of the rabbit who was loved so much he became shabby. When she was a little girl, her mother had insisted everything be fastidious, especially her own impeccable clothing, carefully applied makeup and coiffed hair. Hugs and kisses were considered messy. "Not right now, Abigail." There was little danger of Abby becoming shabby from too much love. Although, the book did seem to say, it was the only way of becoming real. She never did feel real, either, in that too-perfect world. The book had been right about that. It wasn't until she met Bobby Silva and came alive with his relentless touch, real from his love. But had he been real?

She ate the eggs, their rich flavor quieting her thoughts, and for a few precious moments there was only pure enjoyment. She imagined them nourishing her baby as the toy bunny sat in front of her, appraising her with its one pink eye. One black whisker trailed from the side of its nose. Santiago seemed to have appointed himself her baby's guardian angel.

Tomorrow morning she would be prepared and try to talk with him without scaring him away.

After her breakfast, Abby showered and dug through boxes trying to find something that would fit around her pregnant belly. She ended up in a pair of Bobby's elastic-waisted black gym shorts and one of his U.S. Navy T-shirts. The thought of driving into Albuquerque to buy maternity clothes exhausted her so she lay down on her sofa, the bunny nestled against her chest, her pre-pregnancy bra pinching under the T-shirt. She thought about calling Ramone, telling him all about Juarez, but she didn't feel ready to rehash the painful details. The copy of the video was still in her purse. She would give it to Ramone, he would know where to take it. Her tiredness quelled her thoughts and she gratefully drifted into sleep.

A knock at her door woke her. She tried to ignore it but then became curious. She hoped it wasn't Rachel. Let it be anyone but Rachel. She had had enough of Rachel and her theories yesterday to last her a lifetime. It was CeCe. Her relief was so strong, she flung open the door and smiled.

CeCe was holding a large cardboard box. "You look better than I was expecting," she said as she breezed past Abby, plunking the box down on the kitchen table. "Miguel says I'm the world's worst pack rat and I guess he has a point. I packed this box over thirty years ago. I thought I was packing it for Rachel but I've about given up. Anyway, I thought some of this might be useful." Rotted tape from the top of the box fell off in her hands. She opened the flaps and began pulling out articles of clothing. "Maternity clothes. Retro, of course, but maybe be so 'out' they're back 'in.'"

"Anything to be more comfortable. Thanks, CeCe, you saved me from a trip into Albuquerque, and after yesterday I don't even want to look at a car."

"Ah, look at this! God this brings back memories. Just looking at these stretchy-front shorts and I remember how it feels."

It was easy to picture a young CeCe in these sleeveless blouses with tiny flowers and fruit, colorful clothing that expressed her enthusiasm for life in general.

"Oh, I forgot about these. Maggie loaned me this stuff after Roberto came first that long hot summer. I was so jealous that she got to deliver in July and I had to wait until the end of August. I never got the chance to give them back when she got pregnant again." CeCe quietly passed them to her, as if she were passing something holy.

Abby held the cotton-gauze embroidered blouses Bobby's mother had worn when carrying him. It was suddenly so overwhelming. She put their softness to her face and inhaled, as if somehow they might infuse her with strength or wisdom. As if she might somehow connect to Magdalena, whose floors she walked, whose son she loved. Her baby's grandmother, *abuela*. The tears that came were not for herself but for her baby. He or she would never know the loving arms of grandparents. Would there even be a father by the time it was born in three short months? The fact that she may be all her baby would ever have cast her into a whole new realm of loneliness.

CeCe's ever-ready arms gathered her close. "Ah, honey. I'm sorry. These just make it all worse and here I am trying to be—"

"No, that's not it. I love these! They're perfect, you're perfect."

"You sit. I'll make tea."

Abby welcomed the silence CeCe instinctively gave her. She refolded the clothes and emptied out the rest of the box. By the time her peppermint tea steamed in front of her, she knew she needed to talk. "Did Rachel tell you about Juarez?"

CeCe nodded and slowly stirred her tea.

"It's like going to a magic show, one of those really good ones. Where you see and hear what seems to be real, but it can't be real. It's an illusion. I mean, you know it isn't real, but you see it for yourself. What else can it be? There was the truck. Here were these people who claim to know Bobby, repeat all these personal things he supposedly told them. Everything fits like a perfect little jigsaw puzzle—only the picture it makes is all wrong."

CeCe only nodded, took a sip from her teacup.

"Rachel thinks she has it all figured out. I don't know, maybe she does."

CeCe sighed. "I love my daughter. But she told me her theory and I have to tell you, it sounds more like the world according to Rachel, not Roberto. Maybe it's because she is biracial, or a daddy's girl, who knows, but she has always waved the Hispanic banner and rejected anything from my side of her heritage. I've never made an issue of it. I figured, good for her, you know? She lives here in New Mexico, let her be. Even though Esperanza has a lot of great people, it struggles with the same conflicts other places have about race. I'm sure it would have been easier on Rachel sometimes if her mother wasn't white, never mind a Jewish New Yorker. And I certainly had to make an effort when I first got here to make friends and find my niche. That's why I loved Magdalena, my Maggie, so much. She embraced this loudmouth big-city *Yiddishe moid* and from there I was in like Flynn. But with Rachel, it's beyond Hispanic pride, there's always been a little paranoia, a chip on her shoulder about it that I know she didn't get from Miguel. Probably from her crazy aunt Maria, who, let's face it, hates me and anyone non-Hispanic in general."

She took another sip and played with the spoon and the tea bag and then continued. "But Roberto never drew lines like Rachel did. He used to make fun of her politics. His best buddy in school was Ronny White, and believe me, they don't come any whiter. They were inseparable. It used to make Rachel so mad. Ronny called him Bobby, too. If Ricardo hadn't thrown a fit, I think Roberto would have changed his name to Bobby even then."

Abby felt her head shake in confusion. "What Rachel said last night could be true. Maybe he did hold it all in. The more torn he was between wanting to fit in versus remaining loyal to his own culture, the more likely it could have reached some critical mass. I know the guilt about his father was real and the pull to come back here. I mean, it would easier to be like Rachel, make a choice, be a zealot, avoid any ambivalence."

"Okay. I see what you mean. So, let's say Bobby is having some kind of a crisis. Maybe that isn't so bad. 'Cause then, he can be getting it figured out. He can be getting it out of his system. And then he comes home to his wife he loves and lives happily ever after."

"I can think of more terrible explanations, believe me. So why does part of me say this is bullshit, Bobby would never do this to me. He'd stay here and make me crazy with his sulks and we'd argue, but he'd go through whatever it is with me. We'd go through it together."

"Unless he's had some kind of mental breakdown and can't help it. Temporary insanity." CeCe shrugged.

"What a thing to hope for."

After changing into one of CeCe's maternity outfits, Abby called Ramone and invited him over to discuss what had happened in Juarez. They sat outside in the shade of the enormous cottonwood tree, enjoying an afternoon breeze, watching thunderheads begin to stack up over the mountains for an evening shower.

"What do you think, Ramone?"

He exhaled a long breath, shaking his head. "It could be true I guess, but it fits almost too neatly. It's typical of Mexican police to take it at face value, they have so much else to contend with. If I could break away and go down there myself, I'd feel better."

Abby watched his face cloud and knew he was worrying about leaving his father. "I can't ask you to do that, Ramone. You've been so wonderful through all of this—"

"This case is personal to me. I worry that I've let you down, not thought of something, missed something. Bowman is useless. The volunteers are wondering what else they can do and I have no answers. I think it is time to call mi amigo, Javier Tapia."

"Who?"

"He's a private investigator I've known for years. I relied on him when I was sheriff sometimes and I think he's the best anywhere. I actually called him when Bobby first went missing, but he was working a long-term case up in Colorado. He might be free by now, I'll give him a call. But I'll warn you, he's expensive."

"Money doesn't matter. But please don't think you've let me down. You're my rock, my friend and nobody, not even your Javier, could have done any better. I'll be grateful to him if he can take the pressure off of you and go investigate in Mexico. You belong here with your father. And at my table for as many meals as I can bribe you with for your company." Abby felt her eyes well with tears, her heart expand with affection for this man.

They stood for a hug, Abby's pregnant belly connecting with Ramone's generous paunch. "You don't have to bribe me with your *muy delicioso* cooking, mi'ja. You are already in my heart, you don't have to go through my belly!"

Abby smiled. He called her his daughter.

Stars burst above Rachel's head as she cracked it on the low roof of a goat pen. "Shit," she cursed as she rubbed the spot that collided with the two-by-four. She felt like a total idiot every time. Two yearlings wandered up and sniffed at her loudly with searching nostrils. One tasted the pitchfork she held in her hand. But even the throbbing bump that was forming on her head and the dirty pens that awaited her could not dampen the mood she'd been in since their return from Juarez late last night.

Roberto was coming to his senses. She was certain of it now. Abby saw it as him losing his senses, but he'd said it himself before he left her. He had lost his culture. Rachel knew he was out there feeling lost, unsure. Probably the thought of the baby coming scared him into questioning what it was he really wanted. Of course he'd want to get away to think. Who wouldn't? Or maybe he was hiding out until Abby finally gave up and went back to her life in California. That would be easier on everyone involved.

She could still see the look of pain and horror on Abby's face in Juarez when she had translated what had happened to Roberto, and the sting in her own eyes as she watched Abby absorb the information. She found herself wanting to reach out to her, to help her in some way. She hated suffering and was beginning to hate that her victory would only cause even more pain for Abby. Hopefully, Abby would accept what Roberto had done, give up on her own and not torture herself by continuing the search. Under different circumstances, Abby could be someone Rachel could like.

She tried not to think about Abby anymore as she pitched at the straw rhythmically and instead imagined herself swollen with Roberto's baby. Working, cooking, and serving until she delivered like a good Hispanic wife. He would want a lot of babies with her. Her duty would also be her pleasure. Her groin twinged and throbbed as she remembered the thrusts of him warm inside her. The imagined baby within her moved with certainty. A pang of guilt came over her that was hard to shrug off.

When she had her last full wheelbarrow heading toward the garden, she heard the yapping of Santi's puppy chasing after him as he ran up to her. The puppy jumped excitedly all around them, its tongue hanging to the side like an unusable appendage.

"She's getting big, no?" said Rachel, kneeling and petting its golden silky fur. Its eyes grew wild with excitement and seemingly detached from any kind of brain activity.

Santi giggled and joined them crouched near the soil. The puppy jumped at him with great enthusiasm, licking him and wagging its tail as Santi rolled on the ground laughing and squealing for mercy as the puppy persisted.

"Well, you two seem pretty happy with each other," she said, pulling the puppy off him so he could get to his feet. "What have you named her?" She brushed at the debris on the back of his baggy jeans. His neck and elbows were black. She wondered how often he bathed. How often he ate. How he could bruise so easily. Her stomach became instantly sick as it had when she birthed that two-headed goat.

He smiled and laughed more now that he had a puppy. At least with her. His eyes beamed with reverence at her, the way people's do when they know you can answer prayers. "I call her Bésame, because she kisses me a lot all the time. Don't you, Bésame?" He put his hand down and she licked at it frantically. Her thick, blonde lashes hooded her creamy brown eyes. Her nose still held some baby pink with dark freckled continents encompassing it. "You can even say her name as 'Bessie May'—get it?"

"Perfect! There's even a song." She smiled and began to sing it for him, *"Bésame, bésame mucho!"* He giggled and tried to sing it, too.

She wanted to steal Santi, but she knew he got in enough trouble spending the time with her that he did. He never talked about home, only to say his father got pissed about this, or his uncle about that. She knew the people over at the Bacas' were drunk most of the time. God knew what else. Brawls and sloppy arguments came from there all the time. Strange cars pulled in and out at all hours. She'd held off calling the authorities. The state would probably take Santi and she'd never see him again. Or they wouldn't and she would have to put up with the retribution of the Bacas. Drug- and alcohol-infested neighbors could create hell if you tried to interfere. Here she could keep an eye on him. Snatch him and call the police if she thought things were really getting out of hand.

He grabbed her hand to show her the big rooster going after Bésame, who wanted it to play. Santi giggled as Bésame yapped and charged at the rooster flapping its wings. Honest, happy child sounds that must have felt so good for him to make.

After Ramone left, Abby held her cell phone and computed the time difference in San Diego. It would be just after 2 p.m., probably a good time to reach him.

"Edward? It's Abby." She blew out a nervous breath and paced around her living room.

"Hey, girlfriend! Long time no talk to!"

"Do you have a few minutes? I need to talk to you about something and it will take a while . . ." Abby's heartbeat pounded in her ears and it was suddenly hard to swallow. God how she hated telling him!

"Sure, I'm just kicking back listening to Madonna's new one which is frankly not that great. I think she's slipping. So what's up in Bumfuck, New Mexico?"

Abby began to cry, "I've been lying. It's horrible. I just couldn't tell you—"

"You're scaring me!"

"Bobby disappeared the night after his father's funeral. It's been almost two months; I'm surprised you didn't hear about it. The national news picked it up last week—"

"You mean he left you?"

"I don't know! He got into his father's truck to go get some food and there was a storm and we'd been arguing and he never came back. He might be in Mexico. They found the truck there. There have been searches, reward funds, investigations. The police think he just ran away and closed their investigation, but it isn't like Bobby to—"

"No, it isn't! That man is true blue! He loves you—oh my God! He must be dead or something!" Edward's voice cracked and now she could hear snuffling. "Why didn't you tell me and Paul?"

"I wanted you to take care of Abigail's for me and I knew how much this would upset you. Plus, I kept thinking he'd come back. If I just waited one more day, one more hour, he'd come bursting through the door with some amazing story to explain it all."

"Oh, honey! Are you coming back? Just get on a plane and come back here right now!"

"I'm hiring a private investigator to try to track him in Mexico. I need to stay here, how can I leave with him missing? It would be like giving up and I can't!" She sobbed. "Not yet!"

"If he doesn't turn up soon and the investigator can't find him, then he either doesn't want to be found or can't be found and then you should come back here. I'm going to call you every single day, you're not alone anymore. Oh God, how am I going to tell Paul? And Sandy is pregnant, they just found out. I see what you mean. It's hard to tell people you love something this terrible!"

"I need to go," Abby said, feeling even worse than before she had called, if that was possible. "Tell Paul and Sandy congratulations for me."

Over the next few days, Abby felt herself slow down. At first, it was nearly imperceptible. A slightly longer afternoon nap. Staying in bed an extra hour in the morning, not sleeping, just lying there. Time would slip by as she sat staring at a wall, not really focused on anything in particular. Ramone had not heard back from Javier. The volunteers had suspended their efforts. The reward fund was gathering dust and interest at the bank.

She felt the way her childhood tape player would sound when its batteries were losing juice. She found herself thinking about people in prison or the death camps in World War II. What did they think about? Where did their minds travel that their bodies could not? It struck her as miraculous that there was unlimited power and freedom in choosing what one thinks about. She didn't have to think about Bobby's absence.

She could remember every moment they ever shared, she could imagine every moment they would share. It was easy once she got the hang of it.

Entire days were going by as Abby lived in her thoughts. It was even possible to climb out of bed long enough to eat something, refill her water bottle, go to the bathroom, even soak in a hot bubble bath without losing the thread of her story.

It was like playing home movies in her mind, only so real she could taste his skin, smell his sweat, and feel his hair slip between her fingers like strands of black silk.

His voice was clear and strong, his hands animated as he told her dumb jokes he loved to torture her with, or related stories of his buddies aboard the submarine. Their lives were like a soap opera she heard in installments. Jerry who juggled two fiancées, Melvin who played jazz sax and wrote ten-page letters to his gay lover in New Orleans, Danny whose mother was sick back in Montana.

She found it easier to go backward through time instead of rewinding and starting at the very beginning. As if on an archeological dig, she painstakingly sifted through each layer of time for every artifact she could collect before moving on to the next.

Knocks at the door were easy to ignore. She put up a sign asking them to leave her alone for a while. She turned off her cell phone. She retrieved Santiago's eggs each morning to eat; a few more toys appeared. A tractor with a wheel missing, a baseball.

Even her dreams participated, assisting her waking mind with more images, fragments of truth and embellishment to weave into her fantasies. She staggered around like a drunk on a binge, keeping her thoughts saturated in this hopped-up high, playing their old music, wearing his old clothes. She was delirious and she knew it. It made her laugh to feel the power she had over so-called reality. This was her world, this crazy flight she was on, and she would ride it 'til the end.

After a while, it came to a point when she feared she was at the end of her memories. That she had exhausted the entire repertoire of their twelve years together. Rachel's words haunted her: "He was gone half the time on sub tours." If you counted it up, she had been without Bobby as much as she'd been with him. How could she have settled for that? Oh, she missed him, pined for him when he was away. But even that had its own kind of pleasure. To have someone to miss. What was there about her that accepted the idea of having him as much as actually having him?

It seemed insane to her now that she could glibly assure her friends that it was okay her husband was away so much, their love was so strong, their marriage so sound, that their time together more than made up for their time apart. What bullshit!

And why did she choose to fall in love with someone so foreign to her own world and culture? Someone she was sure her parents would never accept. How much of that went into her choice? How much of her love for Bobby had been a way to reject the parents she had long felt rejected her first? Possibly, their entire relationship was a complete sham. There was the whole invention of Bobby, Roberto's alter-ego who was obsessed with assimilating into mainstream white culture. As Bobby embraces surfing, baseball, and hot dogs, Roberto simmered just below the surface, angry and impotent. Bobby married a rich white girl whose parents had as much disdain for Hispanics as Bobby did. The girl, of course, was avoidant of all emotionally intimate relationships and loved her Bobby in direct proportion to how much he horrified her parents. They wedded. To both their silent relief, they were apart half the time, minimizing their need to actually live in the world they had created.

Only problem now was, they had created a baby, a flesh-and-blood product of that charade. Maybe that was what Rachel had seen all along. Maybe that was why she hated Abby. Maybe that was why she figured it all out so fast in Juarez. Before Abby herself had. As Roberto's best friend, how betrayed she must feel. How she must be rooting for Roberto now that he has shed his dead Bobby skin and was riding free down the Baja coast.

Abby got out of bed so fast she got dizzy. Then she realized she could not remember when she had last eaten or even refilled her water bottle. She couldn't say what day it was. She walked around her house, her hand to her face in stunned amazement at what she saw. Clothes strewn, dirty dishes here and there, record albums and CDs lying around. It was like she had hosted some drunken bash and this was the morning after.

As she stood in the kitchen with an armful of dirty dishes, wearing only her bikini underpants that rode beneath her pregnant belly and a thin white tank-style T-shirt of Bobby's, Charlie let himself in the back door.

"Don't you knock?" she asked angrily, dumping the dishes into the sink with a crash.

"I heard you weren't answering knocks. That's why I'm here. CeCe, everybody is worried." His eyes didn't seem to know where to land, but his glance kept coming back to her.

"I'd say I was sorry, I mean I don't want CeCe to worry, but you know what? I'm sort of unable to feel sorry about anything right now!"

Charlie sat down like he was here for the duration of whatever this was. "I heard about your trip to Juarez."

"I'm sure you did. Yeah, poor Bobby . . . he's decided to have himself a crisis." She paced in front of him, aware her braless breasts were out of control. But so the hell what. So was she. "Here's what I say, fuck his crisis! Fuck his fucking crisis. I'm the one entitled to a crisis, this is a crisis! I'm going on seven months pregnant, yanked from my home and career, and my Hispanic husband decides go play Mexican Easy Rider."

Charlie's mouth twitched as if he might smile.

"Go ahead, laugh! It's hilarious! *Rrrroberrrto* can't be with his knocked-up guera! What am I doing here? Huh? What the hell am I doing here? Two months ago I was happier than I've ever been! My restaurant, my baby, my husband finally leaving the Navy—a stupid robbery he over-reacted to and one phone call. That's all it took. One lousy phone call and my whole life goes to shit! How dare he do this to me!"

Charlie got up, dodging her pacing and filled a glass with cold filtered water from the refrigerator. He handed it to Abby. "Drink this and sit down."

She was breathing hard but could still drain the glass in a single chug. She sat down and looked at him like he were one of Bobby's coconspirators.

"I just have one question. Why on God's green earth would you ever take Rachel's word on this?" His beautiful hazel eyes bore into her.

"We're both a couple of schmucks. Do you realize that? Look at what they did to us, the two of them. Best friends, raised like twins. Evil twins! She treats you like shit and you keep loving her. He leaves me and I'm the slow-to-catch-on, loyal-til-the-end wife. We're total schmucks."

"I might be. But I don't believe you are for a minute."

"If this is the pep talk, forget it."

"No, I'm just being straight with you. Telling you what I really think. That's what friends do, right?"

She rolled her eyes and bit down a little too hard on her lip. "Okay. Go for it."

"Of course this is just a schmuck talking, and I don't know Bobby Roberto from the stuff my horse drops. But I do know the truth when I hear it and back in the coffee shop, right after he disappeared, when you told me about you and Bobby, I believed it."

"Well, so did I at the time. That's what makes us schmucks."

"No, it wasn't the words you were saying that made it true, it wasn't even that you believed what you were saying. It was a feeling I got. When you talked about your love for each other . . . it was just true, that's all."

"A man who loves a woman does not do this. Period."

"No, a man who would do what you were told is a shameless, self-centered asshole, incapable of real love. Does that describe who you fell for? Was Bobby some selfish prick for twelve years?"

She thought. She ran her hands through the wild tangles of her hair and then rubbed her hot palms into her closed eyelids. "No. But, he was gone half the time."

"Did you ever ask him to not do sub duty? I mean, after a while he had a choice, right?"

"It worked for us. I was so busy at the restaurant. I could work sixteen- to eighteen-hour days. When he was home I'd take some time off, meaning three days here or there. So I guess if he was selfish, so was I. And when he was there, it was high-intensity perfect. To be together was like this drug we shared, total exhilaration. I always thought we had something better than the continuous, day-in-day-out relationships our friends had. They always seemed bored. We never were. That's why I think the whole thing could have been built on fantasy."

He reached across the table. His hand was calloused from honest work, his flesh was warm on her fingers as he gently covered her hand. His hand over hers created a small sanctuary and she felt strangely protected.

"You're doing a lot of thinking, that's natural I guess. Trying to figure it all out. I'm not much for giving out advice, hell, look at my life. But there's one thing I believe with enough confidence to tell you. There's times when the brain will just plain get things wrong. It outsmarts itself with all kinds of elaborate inventions and is too ready to latch onto what other people say. That's when the heart is more trustworthy. Listen to your heart, Abby. It cuts through all the bullshit. What does your heart tell you about Bobby?"

Instinctively, she put her free hand to her heart. As if she might read its wisdom like braille through her fingertips. She looked into his earnest face and saw a loving man who lives with pain on a daily basis. His expression conveyed his complete dedication to her well-being. His heart she could trust, her own was suspect. "My heart is just . . . hurting, you know?" She felt unwelcome tears collect in her weary eyes. "Too wounded to speak."

He nodded. "Your heart's been battered around by your head. When it's recovered from that, it'll tell you. Throw a bucket of water on those fired-up thoughts. The heart speaks with something other than words. Softer. You got to be still and listen for it."

After Charlie left, she put her home back together, folded the last of the clothes and put them away. Her size eights, she put in the back of the closet. She cut down the last of the moving boxes. As her hands performed these tasks, she felt her mind begin to ease. Like a slow sink draining, eventually the backup of toxic thoughts emptied. She focused on housework in a Zen kind of way. Polishing furniture, dusting the floors. She showered, dressed. She unpacked the rest of the clothes CeCe had given her and hung them outside to air them. Clipped to the clothesline, they danced in the breeze, the pregnant ghosts of Maggie and CeCe.

That night, she sat outside on her front patio in a lawn chair she had found in the storage shed. Facing west, she watched the sun begin to set. The empty terra-cotta flowerpots caught her attention. Tomorrow she would go to a greenhouse and buy flowers.

Charlie was right about keeping her hands busy and her thoughts simple. She gazed over the tree line in the distance. Bright pastel hues spread themselves out in a wide band between the silhouette of the treetops and the darkening blue of the sky. Behind her, the mountains would become purple for a brief moment of celebration before darkening in the loss of light. Then, like a towering steel gray battleship they would stand guard under the stars.

The cicadas began to sing. She closed her eyes and felt the air begin to cool. Something near to peace lapped up around her like gentle ocean waters. Then her heart began to speak in pictures.

She and Bobby had been together about six months, she was still an undergrad. They were spending the day together on Silver Strand Beach on Coronado Island. It was a weekday, not high tourist season, so they had it pretty much to themselves. The sky was partly overcast with a strong breeze. The clouds parted and bursts of sunlight would shower down like unexpected gifts.

Bobby is chasing her along the beach, her bare feet slip and slog through the dry sand as she tries to keep ahead of him, giggling in her frantic ambivalence between not getting caught and the inevitable relief of being caught. His laughter behind her is maniacal, primitive, as if he were a caveman chasing down his prey or his female, and she will feel the conk of his club on her head any second.

Gulls scream overhead, waves crash sending spray over to her in a fine mist. She ends the chase, stops, turns and receives the blow of his body's momentum, tackling her to the sand. She is pinned, he is laughing inches from her nose, sand coats his skin turning him into a brown sugar donut.

"Abby," he says, his face serious now, his dark eyes penetrating her, "you have to marry me. I'll die if you don't. I love you more than my own life. I can't wait any longer, please, I've been waiting my whole life already."

"But, my family, your father—"

"They are our past. We are our future. The differences they would see—our bodies, our races—are just the wrapping, the part you wad up and throw away. We are what is immortal and infinite. We are the same soul begging to join and become whole once more. You can feel this truth, can't you?"

"Yes," she had answered, then. "Yes," she answered now.

She caught Santiago the next morning by standing behind the cottonwood tree. "Santiago," she whispered, trying not to startle him, as he passed within three feet of her.

He froze. The skin on the back of his neck tightened. Still, he didn't turn around. He just stood there like he was expecting a blow to the back of his head.

"I won't bite, I promise. I just want to thank you."

He turned slowly then, his hands full of eggs and some miniature cars. His eyes stayed down.

"Have you had breakfast?"

He shook his head no.

"Would you come inside and let me cook something? It would be nice to not have to eat alone."

He looked up at her then, his eyes widened with some kind of strong feeling she couldn't discern. "I can't stay very long."

He sat at the kitchen table, scooting the tiny painted metal cars around.

She made an omelet with mozzarella cheese, tomatoes, mushrooms and ribbons of basil she cut from her windowsill plant. She watched him from the corner of her eye. "I really think my baby will love the toys you brought."

"I don't have any girl toys," he said with an apologetic shrug.

"Well, I'll let you in on a secret. Girls sometimes like to play with cars and balls and stuff. So whether it's a girl or a boy, the toys will be just fine."

She didn't push conversation on him while they ate. He seemed so hungry, so used to silence. He dutifully brought his plate and fork to the sink to rinse it and scrub it with the soapy sponge. He finished his orange juice and then washed his glass, placing it carefully in the draining rack. Then he reached for her dishes. She nearly protested but seeing a familiar intensity with which he performed these tasks, she decided not to get in his way.

After he had polished the stovetop, he looked around the room with obvious interest and curiosity. She led him on a tour of the house. "It's so clean," he remarked.

He was most fascinated with Bobby's childhood room she had not yet converted into a nursery. He ran his hand along the spines of the books in the bookcase, looked longingly at the model ships and airplanes. "Whose room is this?" he asked.

"My husband's, when he was a little boy like you. This was his room until he grew up and joined the Navy. He's away right now, but he'll come back. We're going to make this room into the baby's room."

He pulled his hand back from the desk and quickly exited. "I have to go."

"You know, Santi, I would like it if you would come visit me. You seem to like to work, would you like do some things for me and I'd pay you?"

"Like what?" he asked, still making a beeline to the door.

"You know Charlie, right? Over at the Vigils'? He's been doing the mowing for me. Maybe you could help."

"He has a cool riding mower."

"I bet he'd teach you how to ride it. And there's always a million weeds to pull. I'd pay you five dollars an hour, how would that be?"

"I'll help you." He darted from the door and ran in the direction of his home.

Chapter 13

Rachel threw on her work gloves and headed for her pickup. She was down to her last bale of alfalfa in the barn and wanted to get fresh-baled hay from the field. Breeding season was in less than two months, and she fattened and pampered her does with grain and fresh leafy hay. It kept getting harder to work the dairy on her own, but Roberto would help her when he came back. She kept her sights on that. But more often now came a deep, nagging feeling. She wondered how Abby was doing. CeCe said she had withdrawn and taken to her bed and wouldn't see anyone. She probably needed some groceries by now.

Another sunny, roasting summer day. She walked along the ditch, an oasis amid the fresh green growth of weeds and Russian olive trees that were considered a bosque epidemic. Mulberries hung down overhead, fat and sweet. Sometimes she'd stop and eat them one right after the other until she was literally purple in the face. Her stained lips and hands always brought on her mother's scoldings since she was small about leaving enough mulberries out there to make the year's syrup.

Bales of hay sat in rows in the field. Green and fragrant. She loved the way it made her goats' breath sweet as they belched up cud. She drove not far off the pocked dirt road into the field alongside a row of bales, parked and got out. This was her most hated chore. It was hell trying to lift a hundred-pound bale onto her truck. She hated how the men could just swing them on up in. If it took brain power, she'd have them beat. No contest. But it was all about that upper-body strength they had. It took all the strength in her curled arms to carry it and get the end of it on the edge of the truck to push it in from there. The baling wire cut painfully into her hands despite her leather work gloves. It could be as simple as driving out to where Charlie and a couple of workers loaded up bales to be stored. He would gladly throw a few bales on her truck for her if she asked. But she would be damned.

After struggling with her third bale, she saw Charlie coming toward her. She wanted to check the soft under part of her forearm where the alfalfa scratched her through her cotton long-sleeved shirt. But not with him watching.

"You're looking like a damsel in distress." He grinned. Another reason she had divorced him. He grinned too damn much. Made her want to slap him into the next field.

"I hear that's what you're into nowadays," she said, not going for another bale in front of him. She refused to amuse him further. He could stand there as long as he wanted, she could wait him out.

"Do I hear a hint of jealousy?"

"You want jealousy, *chico*, you can go to the Midnight Rodeo and watch your dancing girls fight over you." She imagined kicking him right in his *huevos*. "So, did you walk over here to help or what?" She hopped in the truck to arrange the bales as he tossed them in.

He gave her that smile that worked on most people, wrapped his gloved fingers around the baling wire and heaved a bale, catching her off balance and landing her on her butt. He laughed.

"*Pendejo!*" She glared at him. "You did that on purpose!" She righted herself instantly. God, he made her so mad! A dried foxtail pricked her through her worn jeans, under her left butt cheek. But he was being the bigger pain in the ass.

"I'm just loadin' 'em, babe. You gotta pay attention. I don't have the time to wait until you're ready. Got other work to do."

Another bale came flying up. She grabbed the wires and heaved it on top of the others. It felt lighter this time. Just knowing her secret about Roberto crouched down, ready to jump and yell surprise to blank, astonished faces gave her strength. What a sweet last laugh then.

Charlie's jaw was set and she could tell he was determined not to say anything more. He had shaved for some reason, she noticed, as his jaw muscles twitched. His face hid and sweat under his hat, but she could still see he was amused.

"I know what you're thinking," she accused. She was not going to let him get away with his egotistical bullshit.

"For Christ sake, Rache—don't be crawlin' into my head and wantin' to control that, too."

She crossed her arms and aimed a mental hatchet at his head.

"Okay, what am I thinking?" He let go of the bale he was about to throw like he would play along.

"You're thinking what you always think. Smug shit, like I never should have divorced you, or that I'm having trouble working the dairy without you, or that I didn't know a good thing when I had one," she said, realizing she had become so loud that the workers looked and scratched their heads from where they were.

"Well, now, Rache. That was a mighty good guess, from your perspective, that is. 'Course you'd think what I'm thinking always has to do with you." He took his hat off and wiped his forehead. "But what I was really more or less thinking about was the big fat juicy roast beef sandwich I had waiting for me in my refrigerator." He put his hat back on, tipped it, and walked away taking off his shirt, signaling he was done for the day.

The secondary highway back from Albuquerque was Rachel's preference over the interstate. It was lined for miles by auto junkyards promising to have any and every part anyone could possibly need. Sand and gravel yards stood on hills behind other businesses near the road. From where she was the yellow bulldozers looked like toys in a sandbox.

Her old truck puttered a little hesitantly as if there were a fouled plug. She should have watched Charlie change the points and plugs so she'd be able to handle these annoyances. She just never had to worry when they were married about anything breaking down because Charlie could either fix it or take it apart and build it again like new. But now, if she broke down, she could go to one of the mechanic shops along old Highway 47. Because the gas gauge had stopped working, a full gas can rode in front on the passenger's side. The way people around there take whatever they want from the back of each other's truck, she didn't want to take the chance of putting it in the back. She never wanted to run out of gas again. She had been on her way back from the Valencia County courthouse in Belen after signing the divorce papers when the truck just expired under the gas pedal. One minute it had power and the next it was coasting silently to a stop. No death rattle. Nothing. She managed to pull over, while her now ex-husband waved and passed her standing stranded in front of the state correctional facility and a sign that warned drivers not to pick up hitchhikers. From that day on she kept a gas can on the floor next to her filled to the brim.

She pushed the pedal to the floor and raced three tumbleweeds that threatened to cut in front. One didn't make it and she felt the dried skeleton of it cracking and breaking into pieces under her bumper and wheels.

She averted her eyes from what lay at the side of the highway. More often than not, she found herself squirming and grieving over curled-up, dead retreads. But on the reservation strip of Highway 47, dead dogs and cats lay around for weeks along the road. She had seen it all her life but could never get used to it. Occasionally a cow lay stiff-legged in the middle of the road, but mostly it was dogs, cats, and coyotes day after day becoming highway jerky.

It was raining when she made the turn onto the back muddy road she took as a shortcut to Pablo's where Maria waited for her. Maria hung at Pablo's because that was where a lot of the debts people owed her for her services were paid. She also gave readings to sloppy-drunk women looking for love, or at least sex. Not that Maria couldn't really tell the future, she could quite accurately, but telling them what they wanted to hear kept them coming back.

Water-filled, muddy potholes were all over the back roads, which caused her to swerve back and forth, the movement of her arms and elbows exaggerated by the play in the old truck's steering. The mud hit loudly against the metal underside in cloddy thumps. As she crossed over irrigation ditches she noticed the creamy brown water, high against the edges and rushing quickly. She was already twenty minutes late and hoped Maria had not gotten pissed off and left Pablo's already. Just a couple more minutes and she'd be there. Maybe Maria had a line of women for readings and hadn't noticed the time. Rachel wasn't in the mood for one of her scoldings.

Maria was giving a reading at her usual table in the back corner, illuminated by one of those table cocktail candles enveloped in plastic fishnet. A crucifix lay on the table between the paying customer and her. The crucifix came out when she played the good witch. Truth was, Maria never even went to confession. She believed there were some things you just don't ask or expect forgiveness for, and there were a few of those under her belt. Whatever absolving the perpetual paraffin shrine to Jesus in her front foyer got her would have to do. She held the woman's hand near the candlelight, looking at her palm, touching the delicate lines and following them along, sometimes up to the wrist or around the mound under the pinky. Her tight lips moved as she gummed silent thoughts. The woman leaned close when finally Maria began to talk.

Rachel hung back for a while so the woman could hear about the dark, handsome stranger that was moments away from walking into her life. She had seen this woman before someplace, but not in a see-through blouse and a too-small black bra that carved trenches into her shoulders and back. She caught sight of Reyes at the bar staring at her with several empty bottles in front of him. She didn't want to appear too obvious that she saw him and accidentally invite him over.

Rachel approached Maria, noticing she was winding up by closing the hand of the woman whose long, curved fake nails almost touched her watchband. They also got in the way when the woman tried to get into her wallet and take out two fives. She had to hyperextend her fingers to do it. Her black eyeliner swooped up on the end like a ski slope. Their eyes met as the she got up and left, and Rachel realized she had been staring at her curiously, like she was one of those poorly put-together monsters in those 1950s movies. A couple of viejitos playing pool leaned on their pool cues and eyed her as she walked past. A frightening mess to have to wake up next to. Maybe she had been one of Charlie's dancing buddies.

"Sorry I'm late," Rachel said, sliding into the vinyl-covered chair. It was still warm. Maybe they had been more than dancing partners.

"I made ten dollars because of your lateness, so you are forgiven this time," Maria said, folding the two fives and tucking them into her left shoe. As old as she was, her hair had not turned to total gray, but had bold streaks of ghostly white swooping through it. Rachel took Maria's hands. Her knuckles were bony and her fingers crooked, and her skin felt thin and cool like that of garden toads' near dusk. The twinkle in her eyes faded in and out like stars about to fall.

"Tía, I know you can travel as a raven. Tell me, have you seen Roberto? Is he all right?"

"I took a powerful potion just last night and made a journey to him, mi'ja. He called to me in a dream, and I went to him. He is well. No harm will come to him," Maria soothed.

"But when is he coming back? Can't you make him come home faster? It's such prolonged agony," she pleaded like a child. She had always counted on tía to make things easier. Unlike CeCe who believed it was all about the struggle. Journey, *schmourney.* Mothers are supposed to kiss things and make them go away. Protect and eliminate. Tía could do that.

"I can do nothing until he finds his spirit, mi'ja. His soul has been split in two and he needs to have time to heal it. He told me his soul is awakening from a very long sleep, mi'ja. He asked if you were waiting."

Rachel smiled. "Prolonged agony."

"I've always taken care of you. It will be soon now." Maria spoke in Spanish when she added, "I would wrestle with el Diablo himself on the ground or in his bed for your happiness, mi'ja." The popped strands of yarn stuck out from the embroidered flowers on her shawl like broken *bandolin* strings. Everything about her seemed so fragile, and yet she was so powerful.

"I know your magic is strong, mi tía, but is it stronger than Roberto's will to do the right thing for his baby? I still wonder who he is coming back to." She didn't want to confess that she was starting to consider Abby a worthy opponent.

Maria's mouth exposed splinters of chewed osha root as she spoke. *"Sí, mi'ja, sí,"* Maria assured. Her hand now patted Rachel's. "There will be other babies in his life. They will come shooting out of you year after year. Her baby will lack for nothing. We need to go pick some wild asparagus root for you to eat to get your womb ready."

Rachel blushed as a dark Hispanic man came up to the table and held out a corked bottle to Maria. Probably his homemade tequila as payment toward a debt.

Maria took the bottle and flipped it upside down and back again to watch the fat curled worm float to the bottom like a pickled, bean-sized fetus. She nodded her head and gave an approving, not-quite-toothless smile. "You know what I like, Artemio. Your payment is as good as gold." Her laugh crackled and hissed.

"Gracias," he replied without expression and was reabsorbed back into the din of the bar.

Reyes was still there, a neon beer sign overhead reflecting red in the glassiness of his drunken eyes. He stuck out his tongue as if to show her the length, then licked his lips lasciviously. She could almost feel it against her bare skin and shuddered in disgust. She had that animal urge to dart away. She wanted to tell Maria, but what would she do? Probably tell her all drunken men behave that way. Definitely defend Reyes.

"What did he come to you about?" asked Rachel, nodding to the tequila bottle and trying to shake off the slimy feeling of Reyes's tongue and red devil eyes.

Maria put the bottle into a woven bag. "Trouble in the bed. He buys herbs from me that make him harder than a maraca." She put her hand up to her mouth and laughed. "Should I make some for Roberto?" she asked, peeking naughtily over her hand.

A flush rushed up Rachel's face. "Roberto won't be needing any such thing," she heard herself saying. Her sureness made her headier than the strong drink Maria had ordered for her. "And once he comes back, you will have a lot of time freed up, mi tía. Maybe you could take that trip to Mexico you always talk about. Roberto and I will help you with the money."

"You are the one who can relax now, mi'ja," Maria said and downed her drink. The liquid dribbled down her chin into some wiry hairs. She wiped it with the corner of her shawl. "I am just getting started."

CeCe's cabal gathered in her living room, their crafts in full swing. Abby sat in their circle, crocheting her baby blanket at about half the speed with which Bonnie's hands were whipping chain stitches across her king-sized afghan. But she was getting the hang of it and it was relaxing and mindless activity that produced tangible results.

Hazel was painting her folk animals, sitting cross-legged on the floor in front of the coffee table. Owing to her obsession with exercise, she demonstrated a woman in her sixties could still assume that position. She was wearing stretch black bicycle shorts with a T-shirt advertising Tito's Car Wash, her brother's place.

"Is that a horse or what?" Bonnie asked.

Hazel's paintbrush paused in midair as she looked at Bonnie with disbelief. "A burro. Can't you see his big ears and blanket on his back?"

Bonnie squinted and leaned forward, her cleavage spilling from her lime-green spandex tank top. One of her gold chains had disappeared into its depths completely. "It could be a great big dog, one of those Great Danes like Scooby-Doo."

Hazel rolled her eyes. "Yeah, Bon, I'm over here making dogs that are bigger than my pigs and ponies."

"*Sobre los gustos no hay disputa*," Bonnie declared and then turned to Abby to translate, "In the matter of taste there is no argument."

"I heard Mr. Espinoza had his gallbladder taken out and they found stones as big as lemons!" Carmen exclaimed, making the sign of the cross for some inexplicable reason.

"I'm surprised to hear Mr. Espinoza has any stones at all the way he lets his wife run around behind his back!" Bonnie smirked.

"You would say such crass things about a poor suffering man who had the misfortune of marrying a *puta*?" Carmen's eyebrows rose.

"Carmen? Do I hear a little crush here on Leo Espinoza? I know he's been helping you with your plumbing problems," CeCe said, sending them into fits of laughter.

"My sink was clogged! I don't have a husband anymore, so Mr. Espinoza is kind enough to help me out from time to time!" Carmen said, her blush giving her away.

"I never have had a husband and I take care of my own plumbing thank you very much!" Hazel chuckled. "Men are more trouble than they are worth, except Miguel Vigil. CeCe nabbed the best one in the county."

"I won't argue with that." CeCe smiled. "My daughter had a good man and still could if she weren't so stubborn!"

"She never got over her crush on Roberto! God, I can still see her lovesick mooning over that poor boy—" Hazel trailed off, looking at the doorway where Rachel stood. "Oops."

Rachel flushed and stood speechless, her eyes darting around the ceiling, biting her lip.

Abby felt moved to rescue her. "Well, who wouldn't have had an eye for Bobby back then? He had to have been the cutest guy in town."

Carmen nodded vigorously. "Oh my yes! He was the heartthrob for all the girls, wasn't he CeCe?"

"My daughter has always had good taste in men. Come on, Rachel, join us. There's iced tea and cookies."

"Here, I have a few goats that need painting, help me out. You're the expert," Hazel said.

Rachel managed a smile of apparent relief. "Sure, Hazel, I'll try. I don't know how good I'll be."

"It's folk art!" Bonnie said. "It's supposed to look all sloppy like some kid did it."

Hazel turned and smacked Bonnie on her freshly waxed leg. *"Híjole!"* she shrieked.

"You deserved it, Bonita," Carmen decreed.

Abby watched as Rachel held the carved goat in her hand like a sacred object, carefully and lovingly caressing its side with gentle strokes of her paintbrush. So, Rachel had romantic feelings for Bobby as a teenager. That explained a lot.

Chapter 14

The early August morning was cool and saturated with the sweet smell of the petite yellow blossoms of the Spanish broom bushes growing around the house. It would make such a perfect bottled scent, if it were not too elusive to be captured. Rachel headed out to the barn to saddle up her horse for a ride along the irrigation ditch. Lately she had been wrestling with her thoughts, mostly about Abby, and her rides along the ditch became prayers that everyone win somehow.

She heard her horse whinny in a way that was not the greeting for her, and hurried to check.

Her horse danced a little in its stall, happy to see her, and looking okay. She opened the stall to check its legs, ankles, and hooves. When she was turned around checking the back hooves, her horse whinnied and backed up. She heard a guttural, "*Buenos días,*" and then jumped around. Her heart beat against her chest so hard her shirt moved.

"Reyes!" she said as he stood blocking the opening to the stall, his arm slung lazily over the gate. "What are you doing here?"

"I have been watching the way you look at me."

"What do you mean?"

"I mean I am a man now, you are a single woman, and you are noticing me, no?"

"No! I mean, I don't know what's been happening to you, Reyes, but you're wrong! We've always been buddies, you know?" she said, inching around toward the front of the stall. He lunged and tried to kiss her, but she pushed him back like a defensive football player. "Reyes, no!"

Reyes kicked a pail of water against the stall, spooking her and the horses.

"I am not your retarded little cousin! I am a grown man!" he yelled.

Just then, with the sun behind him and illuminated like Our Lady of Guadalupe, Charlie walked in. "Is there a problem here?" he asked, coming right up to Reyes.

She had never so glad to see anyone. "No, Reyes was just telling me what Maria has been screaming at him about this time, isn't that right, Reyes?" said Rachel, hoping he would take this plea bargain. Rachel looked at Charlie. She fought the urge to jump into his protecting arms. "And he was just leaving, right, Reyes?"

Reyes, whose head hung looking at the straw, grumbled inaudibly, turned and shuffled out.

Abby ripped open the large manila envelope containing the mail Edward had forwarded from San Diego. Their credit card bills, bank statements, some junk mail and a card from Edward tumbled onto the kitchen table. She opened the card from Edward first.

Hey girlfriend,

How are you? Any news from your private eye? Paul and Sandy freaked out about Bobby. We forgive you for not telling us but we think you should come back. The restaurant is no fun without you but it's still packing in the crowds, Thank God! Paul and Sandy send their love and said to tell you that you can take back the condo if you need to, or stay with them while you look for a new place. There was a blurb on the news the other night about Bobby's disappearance. They showed some old tape of you and you looked fabulous. You had on that to-die-for slinky teal dress we found at Neimann Marcus for New Year's Eve, remember? This year you can wear it for Bobby. We're all thinking of you.

Love you,
Edward

Abby put the card to her nose and could swear she could pick up the scent of one of Edward's culinary wonders. She could get on a plane and be there in two hours. Back in Abigail's dancing with Edward after they tasted one of their latest creations. Except, because of all that had happened, that world didn't really exist anymore. Seeing that now, from this distance, how life was going on and even flourishing without her, even as her life was completely altered, brought that reality in a slam to her solar plexus. There was no going back without going back in time. San Diego meant nothing without Bobby. She could ask Paul and Sandy to leave the condo and she could move back in, but without Bobby, it would be just another circle of hell. Even her beloved restaurant couldn't begin to counterbalance the pain she felt. There was no escaping this nightmare and until she knew something definitive about her husband, she must stay and keep this vigil.

She looked around the kitchen, so quiet except for the sharp ticking of the old wall clock over the stove. The pull to escape was great. San Diego, even the altered one Edward described, called to her. Maybe, eventually, she would go back. If Bobby had truly run away and had the guts to set her free, she could go back and resume her life. She could raise her baby, get back into her restaurant and television. Abby shook off the vision. She was not ready to feel what that would mean. She would not consider a future without Bobby in it. Not until she absolutely must.

She ripped open the credit card statements. Ramone had her monitoring them for any signs of financial activity on Bobby's part. No new charges on either one since their trip out there, which she had paid last month. She never used credit cards, Bobby was the charge freak. The bank statement contained a few canceled checks she had written and listed the few times she had used the ATM card. Bobby had taken his checkbook with him that night. And, he always carried his credit cards, his ATM cards. What the hell was he living on? He made some cash gambling but how far could that take him after he bought a motorcycle?

Was he so paranoid about being traced he wouldn't use them? You could live cheaply in Mexico, but he'd need to spend something, and if the credit cards and checks had been stolen, someone would be having a field day. A cold dread spread through her. Over two months away and no living expenses—how could this be? Unless . . . he wasn't living.

A sharp knock at the door made her jump. "Are you ready? We better get going!" CeCe's smiling face peeked around the door as she swung it open.

Abby was blank.

"Your appointment with Dr. Lark—we were going to do lunch and shop—"

"Oh God, is it Friday already?" Abby jumped up. Luckily she had already showered and was wearing one of CeCe's donations, a pale blue cotton sundress with white embroidered flowers across the bodice. She grabbed her purse and sunglasses and left the mess on table. She would deal with it later.

They sat in the waiting room amid a circle of women in various stages of pregnancy. A curly blond toddler smeared his nasal secretions all over the front of the tropical-fish tank while his oblivious mother read a magazine.

"Hurry up and wait, huh." CeCe stretched in her chair. "You're sure quiet."

"I was looking at bank and credit card statements. Edward forwards my mail."

"Your chef friend?"

"Yeah, well, I still haven't mailed in the change-of-address stuff. Ramone has me watching for any activity on the credit cards and checking account. Anyway, Bobby hasn't used any of his cards, written any checks. He's got them, why wouldn't he use them?"

"Maybe it's guilt. He doesn't want to use money you might need."

"He knows I have plenty of money, and if he felt guilty at all, wouldn't he come back? He's supposedly doing this very selfish thing, this trip down the Baja coast, wouldn't he be living it up?"

"Maybe he doesn't want to be traced. No paper trail."

"I thought of that. But how long could his money hold out? It's been months. I guess he could have found work somewhere."

"What does your friend Edward think? He knows Bobby—"

"I love Edward, but he's pretty useless unless the topic is clothes or food. He can't picture the Bobby he knew doing this to me, but as gay guy, he knows what louses men can be so he doesn't put it past him."

CeCe sighed. "The longer this goes on I don't know what to think. When is Ramone's P.I. going to be available?"

"He's getting back next week and said he could start on our case right away. I can't wait for him to go to Juarez."

Flashes of Juarez returned to her. The dusty dark bar where they learned of Hector Casteneda. The trip to Colonia Anapra, the things the Castenedas said about Bobby. Maybe it was all lies. Maybe there was some other explanation for their detailed personal knowledge of Bobby. Officer Armijo and Rachel were so confident they were telling the truth that in her pain and fear she tried to believe it herself. In her gut she didn't believe it then or now. Even if it meant the truth was even worse, she owed it to Bobby to find out. From what Ramone had said, with Javier on the case, the truth would be found.

"Abigail Silva!" The nurse's voice rang out like a call to arms.

"Here," she said and stood up.

"Great," Mary Lark said, as she slid the doppler over Abby's belly. "What a wonderful sound! A strong, perfect heartbeat! Here, you can sit up."

Abby wrapped the gown around her and sat up. Mary's smile was beatific and pure. "Here we are on August tenth. I still think we're shooting for the last week in October, so I think we're at about twenty-nine weeks. You're urine is perfect, no sugar or protein. Your blood pressure is still in the normal range, but it has been creeping up and your weight gain is a bit behind what I like. So I want you to get more rest and eat more healthy protein and vegetables. We've put off that sonogram long enough. I'd really feel better if we could do that right away, like Monday."

"I was hoping my husband could be there."

"That's why I've been willing to wait, but his schedule just hasn't worked out, so we have to go ahead. I checked, we can do it at ten a.m. The other thing is Lamaze classes. You only have eleven weeks and the classes are six weeks long. Then you and hubby have to practice, so I want you to start next week on those, too. Connie, our nurse, does a great job, you'll have fun. There's about five other couples for this next session so that's perfect! It starts Wednesday at seven, goes to about eight-fifteen."

Mary's words and numbers came at her like chirpy little arrows. The holes they made let the truth escape. "My husband is missing. He's not away on business, like I said. He's been missing for over two months. They think he's in Mexico, they think he left me on purpose. But he didn't—something has happened to him and I'm going to hire a private detective and find out."

Mary stepped up to her and put her large hands over hers. Abby looked down at them, unable to look into the clear blue of her eyes. These hands would be the first to touch her baby. They were strong capable hands with miniscule strawberry-blond hairs and freckles sprinkled over them.

"Oh my God, you're that woman? I heard about that, but with my schedule I never really followed . . . Why didn't you tell me, Abby? I should have known you were under so much stress. That explains your blood pressure and slow weight gain."

"I wanted this to be one place where it wasn't true."

Mary nodded. "I'm so sorry about your husband. I hope he's found and he's all right. But, is there anyone else who can help you through your labor and delivery? I know it's hard, but if there's someone else you trust and feel comfortable with, it's time to choose. Time is dragging us forward. Your baby won't wait. It'll be here, ready or not, and we have to be ready. And you're going to have to take better care of yourself, especially with everything you're going through. Your baby's health depends on it."

Abby looked up and met Mary's eyes. Her life was moving forward without Bobby.

It had been a restless night. Abby stretched in her bed, blinking in the too bright sunlight feeling battered by her battle with sleep instead of renewed. Her back ached all night and she hadn't been able to find a comfortable position. She felt too cold with the swamp cooler on but when she turned it off, her skin throbbed heat like stones in the sun. Her baby was so active her stomach and bladder felt bruised. Before she was pregnant, when she saw a pregnant woman she had always assumed the fetus was neatly curled in a nice little ball in its own compartment. Reality was, a baby pretty much owns every part of you as it grows, kicking and shoving, like some manic interior designer rearranging furniture and moving walls, asserting its superiority over such mundane species as intestines, livers, stomachs, lungs, and anything else that happens to get into its way.

She couldn't imagine her own mother going through this. The lack of control, the surrendering to such a powerfully primitive process, so physically invasive in the most personal part of you. Like sex, which she couldn't imagine her mother ever tolerating either. Maybe that's why her mother never seemed to like her, the product of such indignities.

She had dreamed about her mother, in one of those sparse moments of sleep during the night. Whatever the dream had been, its details had vaporized, it unearthed some memories that clung to her psyche like a foul odor.

She must have been about five. Her parents were hosting someone's wedding on their estate. There was a carnival atmosphere as all these people erected tents and flowered trellises, a dance floor with stage, white tables floating on the lawns like an armada of boats. When everything was perfect and the guests were due to arrive, her mother dressed her in a pink satin dress with white lace tights and told her between gritted teeth, "Stay out of trouble and don't get dirty!"

At first, it was sort of fun, wandering around, looking at the all the pretty dresses and flowers everywhere. As part of the wedding glitz, the wedding planner had arranged to have two beautiful white swans adorn their pond. Abby was mesmerized. She stood on the edge of the pond, the sun glinted slightly on the surface of the water, the swans glided in lazy circles, as if they were moved by a magnet from beneath instead of by their own paddling.

Abby picked some grass and held it in her outstretched hand. "Here swans," she cooed at them ever so gently, "Here's some nice fresh grass for you!"

They glided over, closer and closer until she could look right into the jet-black marbles of their eyes. They were huge. One craned his long neck to inspect what she held out in her now-trembling hand. She held her breath, as his beak was only an inch from the small wad of grass, his black eye fixed on it. As he made a grab for it, his beak caught hold of two of her fingers. She shrieked as the beak's razor edges ground against her fingers; the swan reacted by charging up out of the water and Abby knew she would be killed and eaten. She kicked and thrashed as the swan attacked, pulling at her dress, taking little nips on her arms. Somehow she ran, screaming and crying, her throbbing fingers wrapped in her skirt. People's heads turned, the men looking like giant penguins in their tuxedos, the women in ball gowns, concerned eyes peering from under the brims of opulent hats. She tripped on the drive, scrambled up to find her tights were shredded and spots of blood welled up in the torn places.

Her mother appeared. "What did you do?"

"The swan, he bit me and chased me!"

The look on her mother's face was devoid of any concern for her, fully disapproving, the expression Abby always involuntarily pictured when she thought of her mother. The same expression Bobby saw the one and only time they met.

"Look! You got blood all over your beautiful dress! Why do you do these things to me, Abigail! Honestly!"

She was handed off to one of the help to clean up and spent the wedding in her room, watching from the window. As the string quartet played below and the bride made her long walk through the flower gardens, Abby dressed one of her Barbies in her bridal gown and held her own wedding. The best part of Abby's Barbie wedding was when she took her little snub nose scissors and cut off two of Barbie's fingers.

Ramone called to check in with her and after hearing what her doctor had said, insisted he would come over and make dinner for her that night. She also told him about her most recent credit cards and bank statements. "It's a good thing Javier will be here soon," he replied.

Still feeling hung over from her lousy night and painful memory, she made herself get dressed and go to the patio where her flowerpot project awaited.

She stood in the doorway, surveying the six huge round terra-cotta pots, the stacks of potting-soil bags, and the twelve red geranium plants in full bloom. Probably why her back had been hurting, lifting and carrying those huge heavy bags in some sudden zeal to beautify the front flagstone patio, a welcome-home gesture for Bobby. He had kept geraniums on the balcony of their condo in San Diego. She wanted pots overflowing with them when he came back.

She got to work. Luckily it was still early, the cool of the night had not yet been stolen by the sun. There was still a slant of shade from the house she could work in, sitting cross-legged on the stone, ripping open one of the big bags of potting soil. She inhaled the musky earthen scent that somehow seemed the scent of life itself. It felt good to thrust her fingers into the vaguely moist softness and make a bed for her crimson flowers. Bobby's flowers.

Bobby loved red. The color of passion and life. Red chile, the red glints of her auburn hair, red wine, and her red bikini.

Abby packed the soil down around the last geranium plant and looked up to see Santiago watching her. He was over nearly every day now, pulling weeds, mowing with Charlie. "Hi, Abby."

"Good morning, Santi. How are you?" She squinted in the sun to see him where he stood by the low wall's gate. "Come on in."

He came over to her. "I already put the eggs in the kitchen."

"Have you had breakfast, 'cause I haven't and I'm starving."

He smiled. "I'll cook today."

She had taught him to make scrambled eggs and he was fast becoming a pro. They sat at her table, finishing their toast with CeCe's strawberry jam. The quieter Abby was, the more Santi began to talk.

"Are you sad that your husband went away?" he asked, out of the blue.

She swallowed her bite and took a drink of milk. "I'm very sad. I miss him every minute and wish he'd come back."

Santi nodded. "Did you know my mom went away when I was four?"

"CeCe told me. Are you sad?"

He nodded. "I ask my dad why can't she come back and he says she wanted to leave us and we should be happy because she was a bitch and she's dead to us now so forget about her."

"But, you can't forget can you?" Abby leaned closer.

He glanced at her, little rapid glances as if looking directly hurt his eyes. "That's not it. I'm already forgetting and I don't want to." He got up, grabbed their dishes and scrubbed them clean.

Before Ramone came over, Abby ran a few errands, including picking up some of his favorite vanilla ice cream to go with the raspberries CeCe had given her. Since Dr. Lark wanted her to put on weight and ice cream was calcium-rich, it was perfect. She put off filling her car with gas, her least-liked chore, until the last. It was a chore Bobby always did for her when he was home, another reason to miss him when he was away.

She stood at the pump, trying not to breathe the fumy air and listening to the gas gurgle into the tank, when a voice spoke behind her.

"Mrs. Silva?"

She turned to see Santiago's father standing there, his arms full of two cases of beer and a box of donuts. He weaved slightly and from the look of his bloodshot eyes was probably already quite drunk.

"Hello, Mr. Baca," Abby said.

"I don't go butting my nose in where it don't belong, but I have some advice for you. Go back to California," he said too loudly. He waved his free hand westward, his bleary red eyes flashed in anger.

"What?"

"It's one thing for a man to leave a woman, but a man who would leave his child—I have no respect for such a man—he is beneath a worm!"

"He didn't—" Abby began her usual defense.

"I'm just telling you this for your own good. Don't be so damn pitiful, wasting your life waiting on such a loser. Go back to California where you came from." Still muttering, he turned and walked away, leaving Abby to stare after him as gas spilled over, flowing down the side of her freshly washed car.

Chapter 15

"Ramone is a good man and is very fond of you, so I want to be straight with you, Mrs. Silva. You could throw a lot of money at this and still have no answers." Javier Tapia squinted through his cigarette smoke. His speech was heavily accented and different from the subtler cadence one heard in Esperanza. As if Mexico was his first home. He was a man of perhaps forty but Abby guessed the lines on his face could be from something other than years. His dark hair was free of gray or any discernible style, unless he was going for early British Invasion. But, judging from his thrift-store shirt and tattered jeans, style wasn't high on his list of priorities.

"Money isn't an issue. Ramone has done everything he can think of and isn't free to go to Mexico. He said you're the best. I need you to find out what has happened to my husband. Please."

He threw the cigarette into the dirt of her driveway and ground it with the heel of his boot. "Then let's sit down and talk."

She led him inside and watched as he did everything but sit. He paced around, scrutinizing the place. He nodded to himself, as he seemed to be ascertaining God knew what from the pictures on the wall and the texture of the fabric on the sofa.

"You told me about Bobby, his leaving, your trip to Juarez on the phone. Ramone has filled me in on the investigation up to now. What I want to know is, what do you feel is going on here?" He had picked up a framed photograph of her and Bobby taken at Edward's thirtieth-birthday bash at Abigail's. They were a little drunk and disheveled, hanging on each other with ridiculous grins. But it was Abby's favorite picture of them because they were beyond any ability to pose.

"I feel those people in Juarez are lying. I feel my husband would never be away from me by choice. I feel something terrible is preventing him from being here."

"Nobody keeps somebody tied up for going on three months without making demands. You're saying your husband is dead." He replaced the photograph. His words came in a hoarse, heavily accented whisper and casual cadence, yet intensely pronounced.

"I'm not saying I'd rather he be a dead good husband than a live lousy one. Believe me, I'd much rather have to divorce his ass than bury it."

There was a pause. He took in a slow deep breath and then faced her.

"I want his military records including his separation papers, medical reports, blood type, fingerprints, pictures of him from every angle, scars, tattoos, financial statements, income tax returns, dental records, and phone records going back a full year in San Diego. I want a list of everyone on his last submarine tour. I want the names of everyone who saw him at his father's funeral, at the bar, every step of the way. I want to know anyone who claims to be a friend, casual acquaintance, enemy, or pen pal. I want a ten thousand dollar retainer for expenses and because working in Mexico is risky business—cash up front, and two hundred dollars a day to get up in the morning. If you can afford it, another five grand to wave under people's noses for information would make my job easier. Oh, and I want a list of all your past or present lovers, men or women you slept with or who wanted to sleep with you and you told them to fuck off. This could be as much about you as him. What better way to punish you? Anybody you pissed off through your restaurant or cut off on the freeway and you got their license plate number and I want all of this five minutes ago. I will start in San Diego and work from the Mexican Baja eastward to Juarez and then back here, as if I am retracing his steps. I will work on this twenty-four hours a day for at least four weeks. If we don't have any answers or solid reasons to keep going, then we are finished."

Abby nodded and felt the unfamiliar sensation of a smile work its way across her lips. "I've been waiting to hear someone talk like this."

"Talk is, well, not exactly cheap in my case, but how is it you cooks say: 'The proof is in the pudding,' no?"

Abby closed her eyes and deeply inhaled the sharply sweet scent of freshly mown grass. The rumble of the mower drew near and she opened her eyes to see Santiago flash a big grin and wave as he made his first solo trip on the riding mower.

"Keep your eyes on your path or you'll miss spots!" Charlie yelled over the engine noise as he jogged along beside him.

His jeans were covered in dust and stray clumps of grass thrown up by the mower. The breeze caught his hair. He pulled at the belly of his white T-shirt that was slicked down by sweat. Abby felt a brief pang of something like jealousy that Rachel could have this good and decent man who was alive and well right under her nose every day. And yet she scorned his every attempt to reconcile. It must be some kind of sin to waste love like that. What Abby wouldn't give to have that be Bobby running along next to their child. How playful he would be, how patient. Her hand absentmindedly rubbed the front of her protruding belly, as if to comfort her fatherless child.

The rumble stopped. The sudden quiet brought Abby back. Charlie was helping Santi dismount the mower. It was nearly five p.m., the time when no matter what Santi was doing he had to run for home. The time when his face began to harden, his brow to furrow. The transformation into a carefree nine-year-old he underwent whenever he was there began to reverse itself. Dark circles seemed to reappear beneath his eyes, his shoulders sagged. It was as if being with her or the Vigils was a short-acting potion that wore off as soon as the clock struck five, and in a pinched-face panic he would run for home, like Cinderella from the ball.

She held out the five-dollar bill for him to grab as he darted past. "Good night—see you tomorrow!" she called.

"Yeah!" he replied, not turning around.

Charlie stood next to her, watching the boy as his wiry legs sprinted over the freshly mown field.

She could feel Charlie's worry next to her own, their twin wish that he could stay with them and soak up the affection they ladled over him like a rich gravy. From the little he had revealed, his father and uncle, if they were home at all, were normally drunk. If they were passed out, Santi made every attempt to be very quiet and not wake them. Those were the good times at the Baca house. He didn't like to talk about what happened when they were awake. Except for drinking and whatever else they did to maintain their angry stupor, their only other interest seemed to be cockfighting, which thankfully took them away from home for long hours and sometimes days, liberating Santi for longer visits with Abby or the Vigils, where he was becoming a regular fixture.

At Abby's they played old board games from Bobby's room. He loved Monopoly and Chinese checkers, doing jigsaw puzzles they kept set up on a card table for days. They read books together, taking turns on chapters; Santi's sleepy head would sag against her shoulder as they nestled on the sofa. Each of them so grateful for the slightest brush with a human body, their shared loneliness somehow smaller when put together.

"I have steaks marinating for the grill," Charlie said finally, as Santi disappeared into the Baca property. "Let's eat over at my place tonight."

Abby smiled. "Got anything green to put with that?"

"The potatoes are getting a little green around the edges, does that count?"

"I'll make a salad." Abby laughed and couldn't resist giving him a swat on his biceps.

As they walked to Charlie's trailer, they cut a wide swath past the Vigils', taking the long way around to avoid the fences and livestock. They also avoided undo speculation about the nature of their growing friendship.

It was a hot summer evening, but here in the middle of August, there were subtle changes that were signaling the coming transition into the next season. The sun made it's descent a little sooner, casting longer shadows and lending the warm air a hint of coolness, like a refreshing aftertaste. The smells were changing, musky overripe vegetation, the smudgy scent of fires the local landowners had set to burn weeds, and the pervasive spicy top note of acres and acres of green chile plants so loaded with shiny green pods they bent forward, praying to be picked.

Charlie's trailer was near the river and the western edge of the Vigils' property. Deeper into the bosque, it was more wooded. Towering ancient cottonwood trees, their thirsty roots satisfied with their easy access to the water table, their fluttering heart-shaped leaves cooled the air a few degrees. His trailer was parked under one. His small corral held Sweetwater who whinnied a greeting as they approached.

"He can smell those carrots in your sack from here," Charlie said.

She pulled one out, a good ten-incher that had grown too large in CeCe's out-of-control garden, a garden that had become a veritable jungle of ripe vegetables, that despite feeding them all on a daily basis and despite her canning and freezing long hours every day, somehow still looked like an overstocked produce market on steroids.

Sweetwater's shiny coat flashed as he trotted back and forth in anticipation of the approaching carrot. Abby held it out and stroked the flat warm bridge of his nose as his chunky teeth ground the carrot, his grateful dark eyes looking into hers with a profoundly personal expression. It was easy to see how humans fell so desperately in love with these creatures.

Charlie lit the charcoal, a beer in one hand. He soaked some mesquite chips to throw in once the coals were ready.

Abby always felt like she was in a real cowboy camp there. She sat in her favorite chair, an old wood-and-wicker woven sling-back, frayed around the edges. Charlie kept a cushion in it for her these days, one of his many unspoken, unacknowledged gestures of kindness. The kind of thing, when you're alone as much as she was, you always notice and appreciate with almost a little surprise to remember people do these things for each other.

"I've got iced tea," he said after catching her eyeing his beer.

"I was just thinking how good your beer looks." Bobby always had a beer in his hand when they grilled on their hibachi on the balcony. What was there about men and fire and beer?

"One sip won't hurt anything." He held the bottle out to her. When she hesitated he pulled it back and wiped the mouth off with a corner of his grimy T-shirt and handed it back with that teasing smile of his.

She took it and drank a swig and handed it back. It was a dark Mexican beer, its cold malty richness exploded in her dry mouth. "Ummm—good!"

"Sorry, that's all you get. Now my iced tea will taste even more pathetic."

He set the picnic table while the coals readied. She made the salad. Potatoes were baking in his trailer oven. Like some Arabian tent, his trailer seemed amazingly larger than expected once inside. The first time she had climbed the steps and taken the tour he had said, "Not bad for the cast-off ex-husband in exile."

"Are you really waiting?" she had asked him once, meaning for Rachel.

"What else can you do?" he'd said.

So, they both waited. Against each of their natures, the passive role chafed, for Rachel to open her closed heart, for Bobby to come home. Two mysteries, two tragedies, two people left behind too stupid or too stubborn or too strong to give up.

The steaks sizzled on the grill as Charlie spooned his secret marinade over them. Smoke engulfed him; he stepped back and then advanced for more. Men didn't so much cook with fire as they engaged in some prehistoric battle with it.

"See if the potatoes are done, they oughta be," he called.

She climbed into the trailer. It was neat as a pin as always. A canning jar held a bouquet of native flowers on the miniature table. She grabbed a towel and reached into the oven to find the two crusty yet tender potatoes, their slightly charred scent made her stomach rumble in hunger.

She came out, the potatoes wrapped in the towel, hot against her chest as she used her other hand to hold onto the door handle while she descended the three stairs. Charlie was placing the steaks on the two plates that not so surprisingly matched the set the Vigils always used.

Charlie dashed back into the trailer and brought out the flowers and a lit candle for their centerpiece.

The steaks were tender and perfectly cooked; she'd never served a more delectable steak in Abigail's on china plates and linen tablecloths for twenty-five dollars.

Here she was, on a splintery picnic table, the singing cicadas providing the music, the sun setting behind the wall of trees between them and the Rio Grande River, eating the best steak she had ever tasted.

"So Javier's working for you?"

"Yeah. I met with him this morning to give him some money and information, documents he needed."

"He's a good guy. He's worked a lot of high-profile cases, you know the kind that seem impossible. He comes through more times than not. Real tenacious character. I've played cards with him a few times and he always takes my money. I think it's the way he can read people."

"He's going to make me carry my cell phone every minute, so he can always reach me if he needs to."

"Sounds good. You should always have it with you anyway, with your time getting closer and all."

Abby smiled at the old-fashioned way he had of speaking about her pregnancy. It was his ever-present respectfulness. "CeCe is most pleased, we go to our first childbirth class tomorrow night. The other couples will probably think we're lesbians."

"She told me you had your sonogram the other day. Did you find out if it's a girl or a boy?"

"Mary offered to tell me but I don't want to know what Bobby can't know."

Charlie nodded, pausing with his fork in the air, taking that extra beat to make sure she realized he understood.

"Maybe it's the beer talking," she joked to ease her awkwardness, "but how can Rachel ignore how amazing you are? Most men would never ever listen to a woman like you always listen to me. That's like the greatest thing and it's not even your only redeeming quality. Why doesn't she get it?"

The candlelight created shadows around his eyes. He smiled and seemed to want to toss off one of his self-deprecating jokes. But he stopped himself and instead drew in a slow breath. "Rachel is complicated. I know she comes off as some ball-breaking bitch. But that's just her protection, her quills. She was hurt once, real bad. I've been underneath all that, when she could let herself be loved and be happy. She's like a wounded animal whose wounds are having trouble mending."

"But if she was able to be with you for a while, what changed? What set her back?"

"When you've been hurt so bad and you can't blame the one who's hurt you, I think you turn it against yourself. She got happy there for a minute with me, scared the holy hell out of her. There must be something terrible about me to want the likes of her."

"How do you change that?"

"I don't. She will. Healing is slow and doesn't take a steady course. You can see that in animals all the time and what else are we? Sometimes it's three steps closer and two steps back."

"In front of everyone, Hazel said Rachel used to have a crush on Bobby back when they were teenagers," Abby mentioned. "Rachel overheard, standing there in front of me and her mother and CeCe's friends. I thought she'd die of embarrassment. I felt sorry for her."

"Yeah, they were real thick. It's a sore spot with her."

Sweetwater began to prick his ears and make a low throaty sound, tossing his head. Squinting into the twilight, Abby could see someone on a horse approaching at a slow walk.

"Speak of the she-devil," Charlie said.

Sweetwater danced back and forth along his fence, whinnying to Rachel's horse, who whinnied in response.

"I feel like I should hide or something," Abby said.

Charlie stood as Rachel came up to them. "Just in time for dessert."

Rachel dismounted, led her horse over to the corral fence to tie him. She petted and cooed over Sweetwater before joining them.

It looked like she had just showered. Her dark curls were damp against her pale blue T-shirt. She sat on the stool made from a tree stump, wearing shorts, her long bare legs crossed and tucked close to her, her arms folded protectively across her chest. In the twilight, it was hard to read her expression. But something in the way she held herself, told Abby she was troubled.

"Having a nice dinner?" Rachel asked with a tentative smile.

"It was. Very. This guy really knows what to do with a steak," Abby said.

"Good enough for your restaurant?" Rachel asked.

"Too good for city folks," Abby replied.

"I've got cake," Charlie said quickly. "CeCe's chocolate cake and vanilla ice cream. Can I get you both some?"

"Sure," Rachel said. "You know how I like it."

"Abby? Would you like your piece warmed a little bit before I put on the ice cream, too?"

"Sounds good."

Rachel reached over and helped herself to Charlie's beer. "I hear you hired CeCe to be your labor coach."

"I'm grateful she's willing to do it."

"Should have asked Charlie. He's good at delivering kids. He's delivered most of mine."

Abby smiled. She thought she detected a little jealousy where Charlie was concerned and that had to be good for his cause. "I should have thought of that."

He emerged from the trailer carrying a tray with their three heaping plates of cake and ice cream.

They ate in silence. The candle flickered in the growing darkness, the barbecue embers glowed ashy red. The horses made gentle sounds that blended with the insect noise and a barn owl hooted in the distance. How perfect this night would have been if there had been four at this table instead of three. Without looking, Abby could feel the empty space on the bench next to her, its utter lack of life, a looming absence more palpable than what surrounded it, what was actually there. She looked up to see Rachel staring into the same void.

The next morning, Abby and CeCe were seated at the kitchen table when Rachel walked in to grab an apple from the fruit bowl full of apples and nectarines. Rachel and CeCe had planted the apple tree together when Rachel was about five. Her mother had told her one day the trees would bear fruit and all Rachel could envision at that age were bears dancing around with fruit necklaces, like her mother's decal of the Grateful Dead. That was the earliest memory she had of their countless misunderstandings. When the tree began to bloom, her mother never shut up about singing, "I'll be with you in apple blossom time," a song CeCe's mother had taught her. For some reason Rachel always felt an urge to sing along with her. She leaned against the counter, bit in and crunched loudly, the taut apple skin giving way with a snap under her straight white teeth.

"I'm glad you're here. Abby just started asking me about your goats," her mother said, "and I said maybe you could take her to the barn sometime. Do you have time now?"

Rachel looked at her watch. "I have to be somewhere in a little while," she said, crunching again into her apple and half hoping they could do it some other time.

"That's okay. It'll only take a second." CeCe smiled.

"It'll have to be a quick one," Rachel agreed. Besides, her mother would just corner her later and give her some kind of lecture about Karma if she didn't do it now.

"If it's not a good time—" Abby said.

"Oh, don't be silly. Right, sweetie?"

"Right. Let's go," Rachel said as she pushed herself off of the counter. She hoped Abby wouldn't be too disgusted by the scent of the cow manure that traveled in the breeze with a swarm of flies riding with it.

Abby held her stomach protectively as they walked to the goat barn. The sun shone through the fine blond hairs on her bare arms and created a golden haze around her. Her limbs were firm and lean, which only brought more attention to her potbelly of a baby, dredging up a molten envy in Rachel, while also drawing out an almost childlike curiosity. Does the baby flutter when it moved, or jerk like a Mexican jumping bean? Can Abby tell if the baby liked chile? Would it look like Roberto?

"I love goat cheese. I cooked with all different kinds at my restaurant," Abby said keeping up. "What kinds do you make?"

"Just plain and maybe once in a great while some fresh dill for Ma."

Up ahead she saw Santi in the pen where she kept her two wethered yearlings. She tried to give her young males away as pets rather than send them to the chopping block. She prayed for girls at kidding season, but boy goats were an inevitable part of breeding. Santi was in a head-butt with one of the younger ones. Neither one was moving. The kid's tail wagged happily during the standoff. Then it would rise on its hind legs to slam down another head-butt, and Santi would do the same. They'd lightly bonk heads and the standoff would start over.

"Hi, Santi," Abby yelled and gave him a wave. "I've wondered what he was up to when he wasn't with me," she said to Rachel.

"He spends a lot of time here, too. I worry about him. Living with those *cholos* . . ." She felt honestly relieved to hear he had been spending time with Abby. Funny, when it came to Santi, Rachel trusted Abby fully.

Abby nodded in agreement. "I wish we could steal him away from there."

"Abby!" Santi cheered and ran to the gate with the goats jumping, twisting, and hopping sideways after him. He caught up to them outside of the milking barn.

"Abby wants to see the goats and the milking barn. Want to show her?" Rachel asked.

"Sure!" Santi took their hands and, walking backward, pulled them into the barn. He took Abby over to a box stall. "This is where we milk the goats. They stand on this," he said pointing to the fifteen-inch stand. "They get their heads put in here. It's called a"—he looked to Rachel for help; she mouthed the word to him—"it's called a stanchion," he blurted proudly. Abby ruffled his hair and smiled over his head to Rachel, who smiled back. Abby's features were so feminine yet not girlish or obscured with a bunch of makeup. There was a freshness about her, an honesty Rachel had never noticed before.

"You put grain in here and they eat while they're getting milked so they don't mind as much," he said, pointing to the feeder Charlie had built onto the stand.

"Wow, do you do the milking, too?" Abby asked.

"No, Rachel does all the milking. Sometimes I help her clean udders with this special soap before she milks."

"I don't know what I'd do without him," Rachel said, giving him a side hug. He grinned with embarrassment. "He also helps me clean pens and holds goats while I shave udders and flanks. Not glamorous work."

"They hate being shaved. They try real hard to get away," Santi chimed in.

Abby laughed. "I bet they do!"

"Not an easy business, goats," Rachel said, rolling her eyes. She realized the conversation was happening easily. And not once had Abby looked down and grimaced at the multitude of dark, round goat droppings she had to walk on. And Santi obviously loved her.

"I admire you," said Abby. "A woman who can carry the physical burden of this kind of business, believe me, I know how much work is involved."

Rachel wanted to say that it was a lot easier when Charlie was around, but she didn't want it to sound like a jab. She had been pretty horrible to Abby at times. "I have Santi," she said instead.

"He's a big help around my place, too. Charlie has shown him how to do the mowing." She put her hair behind her ear. His name wedged an awkward silence in the conversation.

"Meh!" chorused a small group of goats that had come in from their pasture and now were looking at them over the stall divider. Their nostrils were tinged green from alfalfa, and their ears drooped about an inch past their muzzles. "Meh!" they all screamed again. A little louder this time with tongues.

"Nubians. The attention they demand is embarrassing," said Rachel.

"Well, of course they want attention. Hi, girls," Abby said to them as she walked over and started petting their eager snuffling noses and scratching their floppy ears. They were in a sniffing, nibbling, snorting frenzy for her. "They're adorable." She kissed the noses of the ones that stood up against the wooden divider to sniff at her better. A goat kisser.

Santi joined her standing on tiptoe on the two-by-four frame of the stall wall. He giggled as one of them nibbled at his extended palm. "See! They don't have any top teeth in front!" Several sneezed heartily sending a wet spray of green on them. "Salute!" he yelled over the wall. They laughed.

"Now you've done it, Abby. You've been nice to them. You'll never get rid of them now," Rachel said, smiling at the way they looked panicked for Abby's touch. Rachel hoped she had not looked like that when she and Roberto had met again at the funeral. Eager, panicked. It was what she had felt then.

"Niceness is all they need to feel happy," said Santi, stretching to his fullest to reach the ones in the back.

Rachel stayed up late that evening. She sat out on her small flagstone patio just beyond the French doors of her bedroom and she stargazed the way she and Roberto had done on blankets so many times. He had a way of seeing the constellations quickly and clearly. She had a harder time of it. Of visualizing a pattern out of trillions of stars. "There! Right there!" he would say, and point to the vast sky as if he were pointing to a bulletin board. She would squint and try so hard to see a pair of twins or even a ram. You'd think she'd be able to see a ram. She'd laugh then, but now wished she'd been better at it. This time around she would be better at everything. She remembered Abby from that afternoon in the goat pen. How strong she must be to be getting through this. To still be able to smile and laugh in the moment. And here she'd been throwing hand grenades in Abby's path on top of it. Roberto loved Abby enough to marry her. What would he say if he knew how she was treating her?

She padded off to the kitchen in her bare feet. The bricks felt cool. From the pantry she grabbed three jars of her goat cheese and arranged them in a basket she had lined with straw and a red gingham napkin. Nothing wrong with being kind for a change. She smiled as she realized her mother had had some kind of influence on her growing up after all. She picked a card from the CeCe's card drawer for all occasions. She chose it because it had a golden retriever puppy like Santi's on the front sitting in a basket. In it she drew simple petroglyph-style goats and wrote: TO ABBY, FROM THE GIRLS.

Chapter 16

When Abby found the gift basket on her porch, she thought Santiago had really outdone himself. Then she read the card, FROM THE GIRLS, and realized it must be from Rachel. She was so flabbergasted she had to sit down, the basket balanced on her knees due to her ever-diminishing lap.

After all of Rachel's sniping and barely contained resentment this was utterly amazing. She never thought she could get out from under the pall of being Roberto's gringa, the one who made him betray his family and culture, and then this, this lovely gesture, this peace offering.

She thought back over the last several months and realized that in her ordeal she could have been more understanding with Rachel. She felt her cheeks warm when she imagined how Bobby would feel about how she had been treating his best friend. True, a lot of it was in reaction to Rachel's outrageous rudeness, but still that was no excuse. She should have been able to see past her own grief and fear long enough to understand that Rachel was experiencing her own pain. They should be united in this, not adversaries. Bobby would want them to be a source of strength and comfort for each other through this hell.

Rachel was so wonderful with Santi, with her animals, like she possessed some sixth sense with gentle, helpless souls in her care. CeCe had the gift with people in general and Miguel, too, in his quiet way. Charlie said Rachel had been hurt and responded like a wounded animal. She needed the same kind of care she gave Santi and her animals and Abby would have to figure out how to give it without raising her defenses.

"Papa, what's wrong?" Rachel asked as they sat on their horses overlooking the chile fields. The crevices in his face and forehead had deepened during this growing season. He had not been as talkative as usual, and she sensed his distance. She had thought this horseback ride together might help.

"I may not get the yield I was hoping for. There was a split-set in this year's crop. See how the fruits on most of the plants are setting high? They're more susceptible to wind and sun damage that way." He took off his hat and wiped his forehead in a gesture that signified more than removing sweat. "I hope I get enough chiles to make my orders. The Frontier Restaurant alone uses eighty tons a year, easy. *San Ysidro!*" His eyes moved across the sky, appealing to his saint.

"Is there anything we can do?" she asked, steadying her horse from going to graze.

He looked at her for a moment before speaking, as if the words hadn't come to him yet. His horse snorted out a bug.

"What is it?" she urged. Her leather-gloved fingers tightened her hold on the reigns and saddle horn.

"This land we own is worth a fortune in today's market. This is the legacy we pass to our heirs, if you ever bless us with some. You know I don't believe in loans or mortgages, so we own everything we have outright. That is why we can live so simply, growing our own vegetables and meat, and with all of your mother's hard work our living expenses are modest for four adults."

"Why are you telling me this?"

"It would only take one or two bad crop years to change all of that. This year's crop is looking threatened. Our yearly cash flow, what we use to live on, veterinary bills, equipment maintenance, anything we have to pay for out of pocket, comes from our crops. Alfalfa prices are low, chile prices are good but if our crop fails . . ."

Rachel looked at him with worry. Her papa had never talked to her so intimately about these matters. Where was this leading? He looked at her so sternly.

"Mi'ja, it is time for you to grow up. The future of Sol y Sombra, this land, will be in your hands. You play at raising goats like they are your children instead of having grandchildren to carry on our way of life. You are thirty years old. If you are going to have a goat business then run it as one. You need to start making a profit, right now it is a financial drain that makes no sense. You need to sell off a good portion of your herd for the money their meat will bring and decrease your expenses. I want you to keep better books and I will review them periodically. Even at its most productive, you and Charlie were barely breaking even. You divorced your partner who had the business sense. I've been waiting to see how you would do on your own and all I see is you living in some dream world with your tía Maria, being rude to your mother and taking no responsibility for the life you enjoy. La familia, dear mi'ja, is a two-way street."

Her mind raced with his harsh words as tears began to form in her throat. Her papa whom she idolized was ashamed of her! And yet he was asking her to murder her goats!

"I'll market more. I know I can get more places to buy my cheese and soaps," she said, trying not to sound like a begging child. God! Did he realize what he was asking her to do?

"You wouldn't be able to keep up by yourself and it makes no sense to hire people when you are already so far in debt. Besides, even if you could, there's no guarantee you'll get more orders," he said. "At the very least, meat's a sure thing. Prices are very high right now. I need to see that you are growing up and making a real contribution."

He blinked and looked toward the fields. Row after row of green leafy plants possibly robbed of their potential.

"My dairy, my goats are everything to me, Papa. You know that. I need some time to think about this," she said, fear constricting her heart, whirling her thoughts. She wished she could tell him that Roberto would be here soon to help her. The dairy would thrive then. And that he will have grandchildren. Reflexively she blurted, "Is this Ma's idea?"

He stiffened. "Why are you are so quick to blame anything that makes your life difficult on your mother? Because Maria has filled your head with such nonsense you don't know how to think straight. She's poisoned your brain, and I blame myself for not trying to put a stop to it sooner," he said, jerking the reigns and turning his horse around to head back. He didn't seem to care if she were coming with him or not. He didn't look back.

She caught up to him. "Tía can be very wise," she defended. "How would you know? You never spend any time with her anymore."

"She's loco. She used to be a good woman, but that was a long time ago. Her age only makes it worse. I don't visit her because she doesn't watch her tongue about your mother."

"Maria wants what's best for me, just like you say you do. I don't think that's so crazy. She's the only other family I have besides you and Ma," she said. She felt so betrayed by him asking her to give up so much.

He rode on ahead as she deliberately lagged behind. Her breathing shallowed and huffed from her turned-down mouth until tears came. High clouds moved in, eventually blocking out the sun.

It rained that night as she lay in bed. Heavy drops hit tin roofs, gutters, and aluminum pails with strong plops that sounded like the Jamaican metal drums she had heard on the Brooklyn subway the one time CeCe and she visited CeCe's family. In the distance she heard restless goats crying their disapproval. She tried to imagine loading them into the trailer to take them to auction, their wagging tails as they tried to butt her in play, trusting her love. And how would it feel to see them go off with sour-smelling strangers who wouldn't talk nice to them? That was what her father expected from her. For the family. She tried to resist remembering his other words and the painful sense they made. About her living in a dream world, not growing up. She wasn't ready to think about that yet. She needed more time. She prayed Roberto would come back soon. He would help her with this and then everyone would see her dreams were justified.

To avoid the echo of her papa's words, she decided to go check on her goats. Make sure those two high producers with their sore udders were responding to treatment. She'd check their temperature. Put on some more balm.

She pulled on her jeans and T-shirt. When her left boot gave her a little trouble, she crumpled to the floor sobbing into her palms. She could survive closing the dairy and selling off the equipment. But don't ask her to sell her goats to slaughter. She couldn't murder her babies. There had to be another way. She would do anything.

"You've been avoiding me," Charlie said as Rachel gave her horse an after-ride rubdown and grooming. He sounded more amused than perturbed.

"I'm your ex-wife, it's my job," she said, not turning around. The barn had just been shoveled and raked out and old straw replaced with shiny new. He must have been working since dawn, about the time she saddled up for her long morning ride. She had even bumped milking to late morning so she could have the rare solitude of her ride and room to think. He probably knew what Papa had asked her to do.

"I mean more than usual," he said, coming in and giving her horse a firm pat.

The other horses came to their stall gates to get their love pats from him. Horses were charmed by Charlie the same as women. Actually, there were a few at the Caravan that were real horses. Cloddy on the dance floor and looking as if they needed a good grooming. You'd be hard pressed to find as handsome a man as he, even counting the ones in the movies, but it wasn't always just his looks that women reacted to. It was the way he made them feel. Like they were all beautiful creatures. Same with the horses. Pulled the same stuff in their marriage, like she was some queen when she knew she wasn't.

"I wanted to talk to you about the other night when I was with Abby," he said.

"You don't owe me an explanation. It's none of my business," she said, hoping he wouldn't listen to her. She stepped past him to the equipment room. She felt the way he inhaled her when she passed. "Where is that hoof pick?" she complained and rooted around. She knew he was looking at her butt.

He came in and reached to a fixture on the barn wall that held some tools, bits and bridles, plucked out the pick and handed it to her. "I'm offering an explanation, not owing you one. You must think I'm some kind of louse, Rache, to insinuate I'm moving in on a pregnant woman with a missing, maybe dead, husband. She needs support and a lot of help. Hell, she needs all the friends she can get right now."

His words made her feel guilty. More and more it seemed like Abby's pain was somehow her fault. Her horse resisted giving over its hoof so she could dig out the mud and pebbles wedged in around its frog. "You may need to get yourself another horse, cowboy. I don't think Sweetwater's high enough for you anymore." She continued to try and lift the horse's lower leg glued to the floor.

"The horse feels you tense up, it tenses up," he said, coming around to her side. He ran his hand over the horse as he rounded it, cooing over its muscled, curvaceous hip. You'd think he was going to sleep with it instead of dig out debris from its hoof. Her horse lifted its leg easily for him as he bent and rested its leg on his. She handed him the pick when he reached up. She never had to ask him for help, luckily; it was in his nature. He began picking and digging around the fleshy pad on the bottom of the hoof. "So what are you so tense about?" His voice was kind.

Part of her longed to seek his comfort, confide in him about her papa's devastating lecture, ask for his advice, his help. The love she knew he still held for her would come pouring out, he would wrap her in his arms and solve all of her problems. But that would be so unfair when her heart belonged to Roberto, who in that moment was struggling with his own problems, alone and lost, but on his way back to her. She couldn't take advantage of Charlie and then hurt him again when Roberto returned. So she turned her back on his love. "I've got a lot on my mind. I see my horse prefers the mindless type."

He smiled up at her. "I don't think Sweetwater is high enough for you," he mimicked in a falsetto voice. His muscles looked as chiseled as the horses as he put the hoof down and rubbed its lower leg. The horse gave a guttural moan, and he whispered something intimate in its ear. He moved to the back leg, same side, and she had to step out of his way. His scent was offensive only in its familiarity. He had on a shirt she had bought him right after they were married, now threadbare and faded. How long had it been? He looked weeks past a haircut as his waves and curls bounced when he dug.

She wondered if he'd move away when it was all over. Ma would sure miss him. Papa would have to hire help and in light of the chile situation, it would be terrible timing. She imagined, for a moment, him giving Abby's baby a horsey ride on his knee. What if he ended up with Abby? He'd be a good father. Charlie would get into bath time and telling bedtime stories and loud good-night kisses on cheeks and tummies. He'd be great at scaring off boogeymen and monsters under the bed. Abby knew a good thing when she saw one. Again.

There was a knock at her propped open door. "Come in!" Abby hollered over the noise of the swamp cooler fans, the bubbling of her pasta water, and the sizzling emanating from her sauté pan.

Rachel entered her kitchen. "Ma said you wanted to see me."

"Yeah, sit down. Want some iced tea? It's that herbal mix your mom makes since I'm off caffeine until after the baby comes."

"Sure." Rachel sat down, looking warily around the kitchen.

"Hang on, just a second here—" Abby tested the linguini and found it al dente. She drained it in the sink, a thick hot cloud of steam rising up to engulf her face and no doubt melt off her makeup. She tossed it into a bowl. "I hope you haven't eaten lunch yet."

"No, Ma said come here first. Did you want something?"

"Yeah." She turned to face her. "Please have lunch with me. I need the company, I'm going nuts here alone, waiting on word from Javier and he just left yesterday, so it's way too soon."

"Why me?" Rachel asked in such a soft voice Abby almost missed hearing it.

"Because I realized something." Abby picked up her tongs and placed a small mound of pasta on each of the two plates on the counter in front of her. She spooned her homemade sauce over the pasta and grated some fresh Parmesan cheese over the top and tossed a handful of toasted pine nuts to finish the dish. She set the two plates on the table and poured the iced tea.

Rachel was watching her like Abby had lost her mind and might attack her with her chopping knife that lay gleaming on her cutting board.

Abby took another moment to fan herself with her napkin and take a swig of tea. "I swear I'm addicted to this tea. When it's this hot, I go through gallons of it."

Rachel was staring into her plate, prodding her food gingerly with her fork. "You said you realized something."

"Right." Abby sat down and tried to seem natural, as if this were some casual girlfriend lunch. "First of all, thanks for the wonderful gift basket—"

"You didn't have to do this because of that. You don't owe me."

"No, that's not why I'm doing this. I mean, it did sort of wake me up to the fact that I've been remiss about something." Jesus! Remiss? "First, though, I want you taste what I've made for lunch, I want your opinion on it."

"What is it?" Rachel picked at it with her fork, "I see zucchini and mushrooms and onion."

"Right, and garlic and seasonings. The red slivers are sliced sun-dried tomatoes. But the body of the white sauce is your goat cheese. Taste it."

Rachel took a tentative bite and then another larger bite. "This is great. How did you do this?"

"One of my recipes from the restaurant. I used to get the best organic goat cheese I could find, I did all kinds of dishes with it: Italian, Greek, Arabian. I think most cultures use goat cheese in their cooking. So when you gave me the cheese, it sparked something in me—I realized how much I've missed creating dishes and cooking. I stopped cold turkey to move out here with Bobby and then, well . . . your gift helped me to do something that's very therapeutic for me. So thank you, I just wanted to share what I made and say thank you for that."

Rachel continued to eat. This time, Abby took her lack of response differently. When before she would have felt slighted by her silence, now she saw it was Rachel feeling ill at ease in the situation.

"Also, I wanted to say, I haven't been fully respectful of all that you and Bobby were to each other, are to each other."

Rachel jerked her head up, still chewing, a smidgen of sauce on the corner of her mouth, her eyes involuntarily wide.

"He did talk about you, you know. He told me how close you were growing up."

"He did?" Rachel took a gulp of tea, the look of shock still on her face.

"He'd go a long time without talking about his past and then sometimes he'd just open up, like just before he'd go to sleep he'd sort of ramble on, telling me this flood of memories. Like when you guys were kids and Miguel would make you both show him your math homework before you got to go out and play and how CeCe would mend your clothes for you. He loved you guys so much."

"Loves. Not loved."

"Right. Past tense because I was talking about when you were kids."

Rachel began to eat heartily. When she looked up to see Abby noticing she put down her fork. "This is excellent. I've never had goat cheese like this."

"It's good cheese." Abby smiled and started eating again. Like she had learned to do with Santi, she let there be long pauses in the conversation without nervously rushing in to fill them.

"What else did Roberto say?" Rachel asked after several minutes of nothing more than the ticking of the wall clock and the distant yet ever-present crowing of roosters from the Baca place.

"He said after his mother died, you and your family were his 'soul's sustenance.' Bobby is such a poet sometimes. Ricardo was so immersed in his own grief that Bobby felt invisible to him. It was so quiet and sad in his own home he felt like he was slowly dying. When he was with you and your family, he felt alive. Sometimes he felt so happy with CeCe he would feel guilty and pray to God to please not think he didn't miss his own mother."

Rachel smiled. "CeCe would get him laughing so hard he'd pee his pants or spray milk out of his nose. I knew even then she was doing it for Magdalena. She loved her Maggie like a sister."

"That's what Bobby said about you, when we first met. We were only eighteen and out on our first official date. I asked him if he had any girls back home and he said, 'Yes, but before you get all worried, let me explain. Her name is Rachel and she's my best friend. I love her as if she were my own sister and I always will.' I knew right then that any guy smart enough to have a girl as his best friend was worth getting to know."

Rachel stopped eating. She shoved the plate away in a tiny gesture that Abby would have missed if she hadn't been watching closely. She stared down for a moment and then took a gulp of tea.

"I'm sorry if I've upset you. There's times when I can't bear to even hear his name and other times I'm wallowing in memories and can't shut up about him. What I'm really trying to say to you is your feelings about all of this are as valid as mine. I finally get that now. And I know you had other feelings about him, too, when you were teenagers, which is fine. I'm just sorry that I've been insensitive, like this was only happening to me. We both can love him and miss him in our own way." Abby felt tears brimming in her eyes and held herself back from reaching to touch Rachel's forearm that twitched only inches from her fingertips.

Rachel finally looked up. Her eyes, her expression seemed saturated with some intense emotion that she was bursting to name but was determined not to articulate, to reveal. Her cheeks flushed, her eyes filled with tears as her ambivalence seemed to wage war within her. "What Roberto and I have been to each other and will be for each other after he returns is not so easily defined."

Abby listened to Rachel's carefully chosen and pronounced words. Then she nodded. "You're right. I didn't mean to trivialize it or imply that I have greater claim or status as his wife. We both have deep and powerful feelings for him. But there's room for both of us, isn't there? We could be more together on this, right? I mean, that's what I would wish. When Bobby comes back, won't he want the two most important women in his life to be friends?"

Abby's words found their mark. Rachel exhaled as if the breath were knocked from her chest by a blunt blow to her back. "Yeah. For Roberto, that's what we need to do. You're absolutely right."

Abby jumped up. "Hang on. There's something I wanted to give you!" She went into the bedroom, where she had been going through a photograph album of when she and Bobby first met. In it, she had come across an old black-and-white photo of Bobby and Rachel. She held it in her hand a moment. They were around seven or eight years old and wore matching striped T-shirts. Rachel had a skinny arm tightly around Bobby's neck; he was mugging a big grin and was missing a front tooth. He tilted his head toward her sidewise so that their dark heads looked conjoined.

She brought the photograph to where Rachel sat and placed it on the table in front of her. Rachel picked it up and grinned the same grin she wore in the picture. Her index finger slowly traced a circle around their faces. "My God, where did you find this?"

"Bobby is a total pack rat. He saves everything."

"Wow. I remember this day so well. We were playing pirates. That's what the shirts are for, red and white, we saw some pirates in a movie . . . Anyway, we pretended the hen house was a ship and we boarded it and stole all of the eggs—they were gold doubloons, you see. Ma went nuts because we broke half of them in the battle. So we got all cute on her and when she went to get the camera, we knew we weren't going to get it after all."

She started to hand the photograph back to her. Abby shook her head. "Keep it. If Bobby wants it back he can ask you himself."

"Thanks," Rachel said. "You know, you can have all the goat cheese you want. In fact, maybe you could give me some ideas about a problem and I know you're good with business stuff." She looked as surprised to hear her words as Abby was. "Papa has kind of lowered the boom on me about my goats. I have to start running the dairy like a real business and show a profit like right away or he'll make me sell off most of my herd for slaughter—"

"Oh, you can't! That would be terrible!" Abby could feel Rachel's agony and felt her own sadness when she pictured those innocent, playful creatures meeting such a fate.

"I'll do anything to prevent that," Rachel said.

Abby nodded, realizing what it must have taken for Rachel to ask for her help. This proud, guarded woman had swallowed her pride for the sake of her surrogate babies. "I think there are tons of possibilities to dramatically increase your market."

"Really?"

"Albuquerque has some excellent restaurants. Have you checked with any of them to see if they could use some high-quality organic goat cheese? I'll bet Scalo, Artichoke Café, Seasons, the French ones—there's a whole long list—would be interested in a local supplier. I read the local restaurant reviews and their menus sound like they could incorporate goat cheese in their cuisine, if they aren't already. I even know of some of the chefs, we all kind of hear about each other through the grapevine, write-ups in national magazines. I could make some inquiries, if you like."

"Yeah, sure. I mean if you want."

Abby rushed on. "And, there are also some nice natural food grocery stores and gourmet-food shops that might be more interested in your cheeses if we were to can them in pretty jars with fresh herbs and olive oil, ready to use over pasta or salads. I mean it's endless the combinations and recipes. Your mom grows all the herbs we would need, and to tell the truth I really need something to do, I need to feel productive."

Rachel leaned back in her chair and smiled. "Papa will be so impressed if we can pull this off."

"We can and we will. I won't let you lose one of those precious animals, not when they can not only earn their keep, but make money for you, too. I'm going crazy here waiting. Javier will be away at least four weeks and he's not one to call and reassure me—he's only going to call when he has something substantial. I've always worked and worked long and hard. I miss the focus and feelings you have being productive—so this helps me, too."

"What about the baby? Ma told me about your blood pressure and what the doctor said."

"Sitting around stressing out is harder on me than doing something useful. Food is therapy for me. This will be fun. Besides, my blood pressure was back down this week and I gained five pounds, so I'm off the doctor's bad list."

"Then, let's do it." Rachel put out her hand and Abby clasped it, surprised that it was as warm and sweaty as her own. Bobby grinned up at them from his picture on the table.

After doing the dishes side by side, Abby and Rachel walked over to the Vigil's to talk to CeCe about their plans and draft her and her herb garden into service.

They found her outside under the shade of a tree with Santiago sitting on a kitchen stool, a dish towel tied around his neck, while Miguel looked on, sitting against the gnarled trunk of the tree. She was trimming the long shaggy mop of Santi's hair. He scrunched his face, his dark lashes fluttered as fine dark splinters of hair sprinkled over him.

"She caught you," Rachel remarked.

CeCe's scissors moved deftly over his head. "I used to bribe Bobby the same way, remember, Miguel? They're both suckers for a big bowl of ice cream with chocolate sauce, right, Santi?"

Santi nodded and smiled, hair clinging to his lips. "You've got to take the bitter to get the sweet, no?"

"A philosopher! Put it there, mi amigo!" Miguel high-fived Santi, who laughed as he slapped his hand hard against Miguel's palm. Miguel's laugh was low and boisterous, a countermelody to Santi's higher notes.

Abby noticed Rachel's enthralled expression as she watched her father with Santiago. Her expression was bittersweet, equal portions of happiness and grief. Perhaps she was remembering Miguel with young Roberto, or perhaps imagining her father with a grandchild she may never give.

Just as the sunlight began to invade the cool sanctuary of the shade, CeCe whisked off the towel and used it to brush off Santiago's face, pronouncing him done.

"There, go get your ice cream!"

He took off, Miguel at his heels, prompting a raucous game of chase around the yard. Bésame woke from her nap, tripping over the tree roots to catch up to them, barking and jumping up to Santi, a blur of wagging yellow.

CeCe laughed. "God it's so good to see Miguel playful, forgetting his worries for a minute. Having that kid around is good for all of us."

"Ma, we have a proposition for you," Rachel said.

CeCe looked from her daughter's face to Abby who nodded and then back to Rachel. "We—did you say we? Oh, I gotta hear this, this oughta be good." She sat on the vacated stool, her chin resting on her hand in teasing, rapt attention.

After Rachel outlined their plans, CeCe nodded. "Count me in, I have more dill and basil and whatever else you can use, than I need. I've already dried enough for the entire year. I just bought four cases of these pretty half-pint jars that were on sale. And I have these cute labels we can put the name on—what are you calling this enterprise, anyway?"

"If you don't mind," Abby said turning to Rachel, "I really think we should call it Sol y Sombra, after your farm." Abby relished the look of surprise and happiness on Rachel's face.

Chapter 17

"Here hold this towel on it until the bleeding stops," Abby said, putting pressure on the knife wound Rachel had inflicted upon herself while chopping jalapeños.

"I've told her a million times she'll end up losing a finger if she keeps chopping that way," CeCe said, as if this had some negative reflection on CeCe.

"I'm afraid to look at it," Rachel whined. "I need my fingers for milking." She could feel the wound throb under Abby's tight grasp. The jalapeño juice was battery acid in her cut.

Abby said, peeking under the towel, "Successful businesses take sacrifices. Yep, the finger's gone."

Rachel pulled her hand away and looked at the small slice in her index finger. It had felt a whole lot bigger. They had been working all night on these orders and she was feeling a little punchy. She wanted to be pissed off at Abby for teasing her, but how could she be? Abby was saving her goats and her diary. And how will she show her gratitude? By taking her husband and ruining her life? The knife wound might as well have been through Abby's heart. The more she began to like Abby, the tougher it became to lie. Roberto better hurry up and get home. The sooner they could set Abby straight, the less guilty she would feel.

She managed to smile at Abby. Her mother peered over from her canning jars, even though she was trying her best not to be conspicuous.

"I'm sure with olive oil, goat cheese, and jalapeños, my finger will taste wonderful," Rachel said, sticking her cut under cold water.

"I have a great recipe for ladyfingers with chocolate and raspberry mousse," Abby offered.

"You girls are grossing me out," CeCe said as she put the olive oil, garlic cloves, and peppers in jars with the goat cheese. The directions on the labels CeCe had designed read that the cheese could be eaten as is, or the entire contents could be put in a food processor to make a spread or dip. The address of the website Hazel had created for Sol y Sombra cheese was also put on the label, directing customers to more recipes. Eventually, they expected orders coming in from the web, maybe from all over the world. They would need to expand quickly. Even with CeCe's girlfriends and Ramone generously helping out, this was requiring long hours. It scared her to think how big this could actually get. She would need to think about updating her milking equipment, more room, more help. But Papa was so happy, she would do whatever it took to reap big profits and keep that proud look on his face.

Abby was the one with all the business finesse. Rachel hadn't even been very successful marketing at local village fairs and farmers' markets. She tried to not get ahead of herself and focus on the orders from local restaurants and gourmet markets that had to go out the next day. As much as it unsettled her to need Abby, she'd have to depend on her to figure out the rest when the time came; and she would continue to do what she did best, raise great milk-producing goats.

"If it isn't all of my favorite women," Charlie said, coming in from making a delivery. "The chef at Casa Vieja is creating a special tonight using the sun-dried-tomato-and-basil flavor. He gave me ten bucks for bringing it out there to him last minute," said Charlie, holding it up, proud as a boy on his first paper route. He had been an angel and come to their rescue handling the deliveries, and not that it mattered, but Rachel couldn't help but wonder whom he was doing it more for, Abby or her. "Here, Abby," he said, as if in answer to her unspoken question. He tucked the bill in Abby's apron pocket that lay taut against her round stomach. "Put it toward the baby's college fund." He patted her roundness.

Rachel about dropped her knife, watching Charlie put his hand on Abby. It stirred something she didn't want to feel. Just an old territorial reflex left over from her marriage. Yeah, that was all it was.

"Rachel, why can't you thank Charlie for all his help, huh? Would it kill you?" CeCe scolded, screwing the lid on a jar of cheese that floated in the oil like a lava lamp.

"Ma, would it make your brain explode if you kept your opinions to yourself now and then?"

"There's not a Jewish mother in the world who could do that," CeCe said, pushing back an escaped wisp of hair with the back of her wrist. "And I'm imparting decent manners, not opinions." Her arms were a golden brown, but her hands were still light from the floral gloves she always wore while gardening. She held them palms-up when she said, "I'm just older and wiser. You should take advantage of it."

"My mother didn't impart anything but distance," Abby said, not looking up from dicing the sun-dried tomatoes. "We never had girl time in the kitchen. You two are very lucky and entertaining."

"Were you closer to your father?" Rachel asked, trying to ignore Charlie as he munched on a hot pepper. He liked to think eating hot peppers would make him a hot lover. He even used to call his hard-on his hot pepper. She suppressed a smile when she looked up and saw him throw her a wink as he left the room.

"No," Abby answered quietly, her knife chopping rhythmically. "No, my father was all about his business empire. No brothers and sisters, either. No wonder Bobby and food became my whole world."

Rachel's stomach dropped suddenly as if a cable had been cut. Roberto and the baby really were Abby's only family. No wonder Abby had glommed on to CeCe. No wonder she waited so faithfully for her husband to return. Rachel cast her a sympathetic look, feeling awash in guilt. She needed to see Maria to feel right about this again. Tía would snap her out of all this guilt, remind her that she and Roberto belonged together. Reassure her that Roberto was so unhappy with Abby that he had left and his return to Rachel would be his choice, not something she perpetrated against this poor woman. Her hands were clean, why did her soul feel tainted?

"By the way you're carrying, I think you're going to have a girl," her mother said. "I carried the same way with Rachel."

Abby stopped chopping and wrapped her arms around her mound of baby. "You think so? Are you a little girl in there?" she said, looking down as lovingly as an icon. "Sometimes I think I know for sure. Sometimes I haven't got a clue." She caressed her stomach, the ten-dollar bill still sticking half out of the apron pocket. "I wouldn't mind having a boy. Bobby would like a boy," Abby said quietly.

"Santiago reminds me of Roberto when he was little," CeCe said. "Roberto needed the same kind of attention after Maggie died. When he and Rachel were teenagers, would you believe he confided in me more than my own daughter?"

Rachel laughed nervously, too loud. Confided what? Certainly he wouldn't have confided about them being lovers. Her mother would have said something to her by now. Maybe CeCe had promised him she wouldn't in return for his total confidence. Suddenly the big kitchen felt too crowded with the three of them.

"Rachel, I've been wanting to ask you to tell me more about Bobby when he was younger. I was thinking you could come over some evening, we could hang out and talk." Abby looked at her hopefully.

"Sounds like my mother is the expert on him."

"I've heard her stories."

"Okay, then," Rachel agreed. She'd start at the beginning and go slowly. It could take weeks. By that time, the end of the story would have returned to speak for himself.

"Did you see their faces when you introduced yourself as 'my mother-in-law'?"

CeCe's belly laugh flew up and out of her Mustang convertible as they soared down I-25 toward Esperanza with the top down like a couple of teenagers. The setting sun cast ripples of magenta across the deepening turquoise sky, creating a wild tie-dyed T-shirt design.

"You could have warned me you were going to say that!" Abby laughed. The wind tore at her hair and she felt her own laugh blow back into her open mouth.

"I didn't know I was going to say that until I heard myself say it—I was as surprised as anybody!" CeCe revved the engine as she pulled out to pass the slower traffic.

"I don't know whether the women or the men looked more shocked at the idea of a mother-in-law being a labor coach."

"Oh, the men, hands down. I kept thinking what my mother or Miguel's would have said to that idea when I was pregnant—God! It makes me laugh to imagine their faces! The only thing our mothers have in common is to hate their kid's spouse."

Abby tasted her anger like a swig of soured milk and spat out her words just as quickly, "I just don't get how they can hate someone they haven't even bothered to get to know! Someone their own adult children love and want to spend their lives with! And then, they react by rejecting their own flesh and blood—who they claim to care so much about—it's insane!" She screamed to be heard over the wind, she screamed because it felt so good.

"They're the losers! Life is just too damn short."

Abby thought of Magdalena's untimely death somewhere along this very road. She started to think about Bobby, her right hand's fingers unconsciously twisting her wedding band, a pang of guilt echoing against her heart. Her growing pessimism felt disloyal. The way her thoughts involuntarily strayed from the path of hope, wandering into the stark, prickly briars of logic and reason.

CeCe slowed down as she turned off onto Highway 47. There were long rows of taillights ahead of them. Isleta Pueblo's casino was really packing them in tonight.

"Besides," CeCe said after darkness settled around them, the lights on her dashboard creating a kind of intimate campfire they could talk around, "that's what I feel I am, your mother-in-law. Bobby was mine to raise for most of his life, I love him not 'like a son' but as my son."

Abby reached over and lightly squeezed CeCe's hand that rested on the gear shift. There were no adequate words for this woman whose strength she clung to like a tether keeping her feet just above the burning flames of hell. CeCe's love had rescued little Bobby and now it was sustaining her and his unborn child.

Tears leaked from her eyes, blew to each side of her face and shunted into her scalp tracing cool paths before evaporating. Raging into the wind, crying private tears under a starry night sky at least made her feel alive.

The rest of the drive was in silence. As CeCe pulled up to Abby's house, she felt the long hours she had spent chopping herbs, canning goat cheese, writing out labels, dashing into Albuquerque for an evening of childbirth classes, siphon the energy from her all at once.

CeCe came in with her and put the kettle on. Abby sat wearily at the kitchen table. Nine p.m.

"Are you sure this goat cheese business isn't too much for you? We could skip tomorrow—"

"We have another order of twenty-five jars, that's a total of another hundred we need to get ready for Charlie to take up by Friday. I haven't even heard back from the Santa Fe shops yet." Abby yawned. "Besides, I need to do this. If I stop, these walls close in. And, it's helping Rachel. It's a relief to be on her good side. I think we're actually becoming friends."

"Well, this little operation is almost pure profit. Who knew we could get seven bucks a jar! It's taking a little stress off Miguel, too. Plus, his chile yield is looking better than he feared, and the prices are up due to the drought in the south."

CeCe stopped talking and scrutinized Abby's burning blinking eyes. She knew she must look like death warmed over.

"I'm just worried you're overdoing it, kiddo. Let's get you into bed. Tomorrow, we have to practice our breathing, too. We have to do our demonstration next class." CeCe handed her a cup of chamomile tea. "You got to save some energy for your little one who's going to be here before you know it."

"It seems so unreal. Everything does." *Unreal is as good as it will get,* the voice inside her said. *Hang on to unreal as long as you can. Because real is going to be here before you know it.*

Over the next several days, with Carmen's, Hazel's, and Bonnie's help, they prepared another one hundred jars of cheese. One shop in Santa Fe had ordered fifty of their green-chile flavored. Now, it was Friday. A day of rest while Charlie made deliveries, including his rounds at five different restaurants with plain cheese. Abby wondered if Rachel would go with him. She had tried to casually suggest it yesterday, under the guise that she should make personal contacts with her customers—it was just good business. Charlie had given her a sneaky look of gratitude when Rachel said she'd think about it.

Now, a day to rest. As if that were possible. Between the thoughts she was actively avoiding, there was her constant companion the dreaded cell phone lying silent and ominous, ready to go off like some hand grenade at any unexpected moment with news from Javier that could ruin her life. Javier had been away two weeks with no news. In this case, she no longer believed no news was good news.

Then there was Bobby's boyhood room. Every time she passed it she had to think about converting it to a nursery, buying a crib, boxing up his things. Today was September first. Her baby was coming in about eight weeks. Time was running out. Everything was riding on what Javier could find out, so many decisions depended on that. If Bobby wasn't coming back, would she even stay here or would she take Edward up on his offer and go back to San Diego? And if she might go back to San Diego, then why even set up a nursery here?

It was much easier to stay busy, stay distracted because there was nothing that could be decided until Javier had answers. But today she was trapped inside an exhausted body. This was how a beached whale must feel, all that power rendered helpless, motionless, inert. Only her beach was this sofa she rested on in the gray morning light, waiting for a promised rain shower.

Between her continuous heartburn (normal at this stage, according to Dr. Lark) and the need to pee every two minutes and the nearly constant movement of her baby, sleep for any length of time was impossible. In class, Nurse Kathy said they were supposed to be developing their skill of nap-taking. Naps were the key to survival after the baby is born, sleep when it sleeps. She had never been a napper, even as a young child. She remembered her eyes furtively darting around her darkened nursery, trying to fool her nanny so that she would get her reward of cookies and milk after napping like a good girl.

She heard a knocking at her back door. Tentative and apologetic. It must be Santiago.

She hoisted herself up, feeling like an overturned sea turtle trying to maneuver on land. His dark head was visible at the kitchen-door window, behind the filmy yellow of the curtain.

"Good morning," she yawned at him. He smiled and walked in, making a beeline for the sofa. His hair hadn't been combed. He was in yesterday's clothes. He carried his Harry Potter book; Bésame trotted behind him already up to his knees. They made themselves comfortable, Santi reclined on the sofa and opened his book. His shaggy yellow companion lay at his feet.

"Rough night?" Abby asked.

He nodded. "They brought all these people back to party."

"Hungry?"

"Not yet."

Abby settled into Bobby's recliner, pulled the afghan over her legs and opened her own book. It began to rain, a gentle but insistent patter against the window. Despite herself, Abby felt sleep overtake her like a spell cast from one of Harry Potter's wizards.

She woke to Bésame licking her toes, Santi giggling from the sofa, his hair standing up at goofy angles. His face was puffy from sleep but his eyes were bright and alert. Nap time was definitely over.

She made breakfast, blue-corn pancakes with some of CeCe's strawberry preserves and turkey sausage.

"Doesn't school start next week?"

Santi nodded, a milk mustache hovered over his smile. "They're going to be all surprised at how good I read now."

"*Well*, you read."

"Well, I do!" Santi teased and then his face became as clouded as the view from her window. "Is today September first?"

"Yes, Friday, September first."

"I'm supposed to register today at my school."

"Will your dad take you?" Abby asked, knowing the answer.

"If I wake him up he'll be mad."

"Then I'll take you. Go in and take a quick shower, I'll iron your shirt—it'll be fine."

Kids from Esperanza attended school in Bosque Farms for elementary school, a quick bus ride down the highway. Middle school and high school were farther, down in Los Lunas, Santiago had explained on the drive over. He would be ten on October eighth, so he would be starting fourth grade.

Abby walked with Santi up the sidewalk to the one-story beige brick building with the red terra-cotta roof. The rain had stopped but the sky was still dark and fast-moving clouds were reorganizing themselves for more. Parents, mostly mothers, herded children, waving and greeting each other in that small-community way. Abby noticed there was a pretty even balance of Hispanic and Anglo families. Kids broke free from their parents, running wildly in circles, giggling, jumping up to balance on the raised-flowerbed walls or stomping in puddles. Santi observed them, smiling, but did not join in, nor was he invited to. He seemed attracted to their joyful exuberance but separate from it.

Abby put a hand on his shoulder and guided him through the door.

A tall woman in a pressed blue suit with upswept blond hair that was more than halfway on its way to becoming white intercepted them. "I'm Mrs. Kirk, the principal." She smiled at Abby and extended her hand.

Abby shook it and caught a whiff of lily-of-the-valley perfume. "I'm Abby Silva, Santiago's neighbor and friend."

Mrs. Kirk smiled down at Santiago, who looked down at his grubby torn sneakers. "Santiago Baca. I hope your attendance and grades improve this year," she said so sternly Abby winced.

"Yes, Mrs. Kirk."

Abby squeezed his shoulder. "Is there somewhere we can talk privately for a moment, Mrs. Kirk?"

"Young Mr. Baca can stand over there in line to collect his forms while you and I step into my office."

Abby followed her into a large multiwindowed office with bulletin boards covered in fresh construction paper and posters. Large green-leafed plants with masses of trailing vines lined the sill, looking as if they had been there for decades.

Mrs. Kirk motioned for Abby to sit and positioned herself behind her tidy desk. "I was your husband's fifth-grade teacher. He was an intelligent child, though easily distracted. But a very well-liked boy. Have you had any word?"

Abby was momentarily startled to remember that everyone knew her business. "I hired a private detective, who is currently in Mexico exploring some leads. I wanted to talk to you about Santiago. His home life is—"

"Forgive me for interrupting, but I'm afraid I am well aware of Santiago's home life. I've called Human Services to express my concern but nothing is ever done."

"He has people to look after him now. He spent the entire summer with me and the Vigils. He's read probably fifteen chapter books—his reading skills have really improved."

"You care about this boy."

"Yes, I just want him to have a fresh start here. Between the Vigils and myself, we'll make sure he gets here and does his homework," Abby trailed off, unsure now what it was she wanted from this woman.

"Do you or the Vigils have any sort of agreement with Mr. Baca? Legal or otherwise?"

"No, according to Santi he doesn't approve of outsiders or even want us around his son. But he's oblivious most of the time, more so as time goes on, I think. He and his brother are either under the influence of something or they go away for days at a time. Can't we arrange something informal? Maybe you could communicate with us directly when you see Santiago needing anything or when there are school events we can participate in. Kids need that at this age and—"

"Mrs. Silva, we have to be very careful with this. Legally, Mr. Baca has all the rights and without his permission—"

"You and I both know that will never happen. It's not like Mr. Baca is going to show up and claim his parental rights. There's a void here and I'm going to fill it, with the Vigils. We're going to make sure that Santiago has adults who are involved with his education. Do you have a problem with that?"

Mrs. Kirk's thin coral-lipsticked lips pursed and then twitched at the corners. She smiled, her blue eyes nearly disappearing into the deep pockets of her wrinkled lids. "No, I don't have a problem with it. I was testing your resolve. The last thing Santiago needs is fair-weather do-gooders who are here today and gone tomorrow. This is a long-term commitment and frankly, God knows what Mr. Baca may or may not have to say about it."

"I don't believe he'll sober up long enough to ever even notice."

Abby helped Santiago complete his registration forms and then had to argue with the secretary about letting her sign in the box marked PARENT'S SIGNATURE. Mrs. Kirk overheard the argument and stepped over to whisper something in the secretary's ear that made the horse-faced woman flush red but hand the forms back to her for signature.

Santiago showed her his classroom, a cheerful, clean room decorated with Harry Potter characters on signs and posters. There would be a Hedwig the Owl reading contest where students read books and then write book reports. The student who read the most books by winter break would win a Harry Potter trivia game. "I'm going to win, easy," Santi said, holding the cellophane-wrapped game in his hands. "We'll play this with Rachel and Charlie and CeCe and Miguel."

"And you'll beat the pants off us because you're the only one who has read the whole Harry Potter series."

Santi giggled as he put the game back in its display. "I can just see you guys sitting there in your underwear!"

Abby copied down the dates for upcoming school events that were posted on the school calendar in the hallway. "Open house is September thirtieth. Parent teacher conferences are in early October. Does your dad ever go to these things?"

He gave her one of his "duh" looks.

"Well, this year, you'll have people there. Look, there's going to be a Halloween carnival and then a school play in November."

"Cool," he said, nearly dancing out of his skin.

On the way back, Santi read a few pages in his Harry Potter book and then closed it, looking over at her as she drove. "Abby?"

"Yeah?"

"You know how in Harry Potter he's taken to his mean aunt and uncle when he's just a little baby, and so he doesn't know he's special and a wizard? And then on his eleventh birthday Hagrid the big hairy guy comes and finds him and rescues him and tells him he doesn't have to live with those muggles anymore and he gets to go to Hogwarts Academy and learn how to do magic and stuff?"

"Yeah, that's about as far as I got before you started reading ahead all by yourself."

"It's cool how he gets away from those people who treat him so mean and finds out he has all these secret powers he didn't know he had and he gets a magic wand and a flying broom and he learns magic spells—"

"Yeah?" Abby interjected, wondering where this was going.

"Do you believe in magic?"

Abby glanced over at his hopeful face. "I'm not sure I believe it's the kind that has spells and magic wands . . . but I think there is magic in the world, sometimes."

"Me, too. But if I did have a magic wand, first I'd use it to bring back

Bobby. I'd wave my magic wand and he'd be home when we got there and we'd all live together. I'd help take care of the baby or if it's too crowded I could stay at Rachel's. She has a big house. That would be cool. But I'd come over every day and see you and Bobby and play with the baby and feed it bottles. And read him stories, I'd read to him about Harry Potter and tell him how my magic saved his daddy and brought us all together."

Abby was stunned into silence and it was all she could do to keep the car on the road. He was right; it would take a magic wand to bring Bobby back now. You'd have to believe in magic to think he'd ever be home again. Her heart contracted with such pain she wondered if she was having a heart attack. No, of course it wasn't. It was a reality attack.

Santi hummed as he read his book again. She looked at him, horrified. What the hell was she doing? Parent-teacher conferences? School plays? If Bobby wasn't coming back, she wouldn't even be here. Why should she stay? She was only making a life here for Bobby—this was his dream, his idea. If he wouldn't be there, she wouldn't be there. And then she saw it like a train wreck, each car piling into the next beginning with the conclusion that Bobby wasn't coming back.

No Bobby in Esperanza, Abby would go back to San Diego. And then the harm her absence would inflict on people she claimed to care about, people she had involved herself with, interfered in their lives. How would she extricate herself from this sticky web she found herself entangled in? What was she thinking starting up goat-cheese businesses and becoming vital to a fragile little boy? Giving him hope built on what, fantasies and dreams and magic? He didn't even think of using his magic wand to bring back his own mother or to turn his father into an attentive, caring parent. He chose her. And Bobby.

A long-term commitment, the woman had said. The last thing this child needs is some fair-weather do-gooder.

Here today, gone tomorrow.

Chapter 18

It was her secret. While Abby waited for Javier, she went about her business with the Vigils, Ramone, Charlie, the cheese business, spending time with Santi, and never said a word. In some ways she took every opportunity to prepare them for her possible departure. Subtly, she used the excuse of her advancing pregnancy to watch with her aching legs propped up on CeCe's kitchen chair while Rachel, CeCe, Hazel, Carmen, and Bonnie combined the herbs and oil with the cheese before putting it into the jars. They were learning her recipes and becoming more confident in their own experimentation.

She made sure Santi knew how to ask Charlie or Miguel for help with his homework as easily as he came to her. She felt a little like someone with a terminal illness beginning to prepare her loved ones for her absence.

It would be easier to retreat into the solitude of her home, withdraw from CeCe's hugs, avoid the comfort of close conversations with Charlie, not answer the door when Santi came calling. Each moment with them was becoming painful as she became aware that her feelings for them had grown unchecked. It was shocking to her that in these horrific months she had formed close connections with these complete strangers, no doubt stronger and more intimate owing to the trauma of Bobby's absence.

Even Rachel was a friend now. She was beginning to understand her complexities and appreciate what Charlie saw in her. It was so frustrating how clearly perfect Charlie was for Rachel and it confounded Abby why Rachel prickled under his worshipful gaze.

Abby was beginning to feel the strain of having to maintain a show of optimism. The only question in her mind was when it would be finally established once and for all that her husband was never coming back and everyone else would have to know what she already knew in her shattered heart.

"They said in childbirth class," CeCe was saying to Rachel when she thought Abby was far away enough to not overhear, "that in the last weeks, a pregnant woman sort of goes into herself more. I wouldn't make more out of it than that."

They were outside, escaping the heat of the kitchen. Another fifty jars of goat cheese sat cooling on the counter. The calendar might say it was September tenth, but it still felt like the dog days of August. Abby lifted her hair from the sticky wetness of her neck. She hadn't cut it since coming to Esperanza. It hadn't been this far past her shoulders since high school. She winced at a sudden visceral memory of Bobby's fingers threading through her hair as he kissed her, cradling her head as tenderly as he would have cradled their baby.

"Staying for supper? We have leftover turkey, thought I'd put together a pasta salad—," CeCe began, seeing she was within earshot.

"Thanks, but no. I think I just need to rest tonight. I've got stuff at home to eat," she said, trying to fend off a visit from one of them later with a care package in tow.

"I'll walk you," Rachel said.

Abby smiled, touched by the offer, and disguised her regret.

"Did you see the coffee shop is up for sale?" Rachel asked as they headed out.

"No, I haven't been by there lately," Abby said, and paused to look up as a flock of Canada geese flew noisily overhead on their way to the natural water reservoirs of Bosque del Apache. Migration. Was her thought of returning to San Diego something like that, an instinct to return to a familiar place? The place before this. The place where she and Bobby had spent their days as if they had their whole lives ahead of them.

"I have this idea," Rachel said, a smile gracing her face, softening her features, raising her tanned cheeks up under her sparkling blue eyes. Her smile fit her better these days, she wore it more frequently.

"Yeah?" Abby said, letting her mind wander. Charlie had taken Santiago fishing on Isleta Lakes. Thank God his dad didn't keep track of when he came home anymore, or even if he came home. One night recently he'd accidentally fallen asleep in the Vigils' den and no one had noticed until he missed the school bus the next morning and CeCe had to race him to Bosque Farms Elementary in her Mustang.

"I think we should buy it. It has a good-sized commercial kitchen for the cheese business and couldn't you just see CeCe serving guests her pies, cakes, and cookies with their coffee? Later on, after the baby, maybe you'd like to expand the menu, nothing fancy just casual lunch stuff. Or Ma could make enchiladas. What do you think?" Rachel stopped, cupped her hand over her brow to see Abby's face in the slant of sun as it began its descent.

Abby nodded. "I can just see you guys running that place. I think it would be a hit and you do need the room to expand with all the orders you're getting from the website and catalogue." She turned to walk on, aching for the solitude of her house.

Rachel caught up to her and touched her shoulder. Not a grab, exactly, but with enough purpose that Abby stopped in her tracks. "What about you?"

"What about me?"

"You see us doing it. But are you interested—do you want to go in on it?"

"It sounds fun but it's just hard for me to know what it will be like once the baby's here. Maybe you shouldn't count on it, but you and your family should go ahead. I really think it could be very successful. CeCe's an amazing cook. Her personality alone would bring people in." She stopped, seeing the smile fade from Rachel's face. "I could always join in later," she added, unable to completely disappoint her.

"It could make real money and supplement what we make on the farm. And I really do need the bigger, commercial kitchen, and eventually some part-time help," Rachel went on, apparently encouraged.

"I could at least help on the business side, more of a silent partner at first," Abby said, realizing it was the least she could do. She could even help with that from San Diego.

She went directly to her bath for a long soak. Candles burned, the only light except for the soft glow of twilight behind the pebbled-glass window.

The mound of her belly was like an island emerging from the foamy sea of bubbles. Her baby shifted and she could easily sense his or her feeling of confinement in the shrinking space. She slid her soapy hand over a sudden promontory point on the island—a foot, a knee? She pushed against it and felt it respond. She never imagined how thin the veil between her and her baby would become. There was no question of its separateness these days, of its fully formed unique self counting the days until it could break free of her body and wail in celebration of its first major move to eventual independence.

In the quiet, she thought she felt another presence, beyond her baby and herself. It was a thickening of the air, a wisp of light, a shifting of shadow. If she stared straight ahead, she could nearly see it from the corner of her eye. Was it this presence inciting the candle flame to flicker and dance, casting ghostly images against her wall?

The other morning she had awakened from a deep sleep hearing her name, "Abby!" She had sat up, and instead of her heart pounding, her lungs gasping in fright, she had felt a deep calmness settle through her.

Since she had begun to release the struggle of her illogical hope, these moments had repeated themselves. Was it the lingering echo of his love for her, reverberating across the dimensions? Was it Bobby floating free without his body, drawn to his boyhood house like some sentient homing pigeon? Or drawn to her, his soul trying to keep the promise the man had so earnestly made ten years before when slipping this golden band around her finger? When he had refused to say the line, "For as long as we both shall live," substituting, in his stubborn, dramatic way, "forever and ever no matter what."

As searing as her own pain was, it gave her no comfort to think wherever he was, if thought or feeling were even possible, he was feeling worse. Not only would he be suffering as much as she was, he would compound it by feeling responsible, guilty, that he had let her down. She knew him. And because she knew him so well, she knew she would never see him again in this life.

Or, was she some selfish, crazy woman who only wanted closure? Who would rather believe he was dead to just end the ambiguity? Hope had become too difficult to carry. She had cast it like a boulder from her shoulders, trading the vulnerability of hope for the finality of grief.

Was she too weak to keep hope alive or finally strong enough to let it go?

Charlie had said her heart would tell her when she was ready to listen.

"I hear you, Bobby," she whispered into the fullness of thin air.

That night, a thunderstorm rolled in from the south. Warm gulf moisture whirling up from Mexico collided with a cool air front slamming down from Colorado.

Physically relaxed by her bath, emotionally drained after a long racking cry, Abby fell asleep before eight p.m., before the first wave of bone-rattling thunder.

For a time, her dreams began to weave their plot line from the audible stimulation of the rumbling thunder. Bobby was there, it was the first night they had arrived, only the house looked as it did now. It was storming. They were arguing. Abby was screaming, "We have to leave here tonight or I'll never see you again!"

Bobby was furious. "I just signed on for a twenty-year hitch!"

She started to say something when she noticed water was sloshing against the windows, as if the house were sinking into the ocean. Suddenly, she was viewing the scene from above and the house became a submarine diving beneath the surface. "No! I'll go, I'll go, too! Don't leave without me!"

A loud crack of thunder woke her so suddenly the dream seemed to play on around her. "Bobby!" she screamed, fumbling for the light, and found the electricity was off. She had to stop him. She scrambled out of bed, a flash of lightning exploding like flashbulbs around her. "Bobby!" she screamed again and ran smack into a firm, muscular chest, arms that enveloped her.

"Abby!" his voice said.

She held onto him for dear life, her lips finding his cheek, his lips. She pressed into him, and it was still not nearly close enough.

"Abby, it's Charlie!" the voice said.

She was awake now, and in that split second when reality hit her all at once, unaware, like taking a sucker punch full in the nose, she had to hang onto Charlie just to keep from flying backward.

"I came to check on you. I know how hard storms are for you."

She sobbed into his shirt, wet from the rain. She gasped into his sweaty neck that smelled nothing like Bobby's. "I-I can't bear this!" she managed between sobs and breaths that gagged her.

"Can't bear what—the storm?" Charlie asked in a near frantic voice.

"Bobby's dead!" She pushed him away, and held on to the wall in the dark.

"You heard from Javier?" Charlie was holding her up from behind as her knees buckled. He picked her up and carried her to the bedroom. She hung on around his neck, feeling like a little girl, wishing she were a little girl.

He sat her on the bed and kneeled in front of her, clutching her arms above her elbows. His stricken face searching hers for answers in the strobing light.

"I don't have to hear from Javier. I just know." Her voice was small and apologetic, like a seven-year-old's confession before First Communion.

He got up and sat next to her, his arms around her. "I'm so sorry. Oh, Abby, I'm so sorry."

"I don't think I can do this—God! How do I do this? I can't!"

"Somehow you will. For this little one, you will."

She sobbed, only his arms kept her body in its proper molecular configuration. He contained her, just barely, from having her every atom separate, her every atom split in a blinding nuclear explosion, vaporizing everything in a fifty-mile radius, raining down nuclear winter for eons to come.

"You're not alone in this. You don't have to do it alone."

She had exhausted herself. It was like succumbing to a sedative as she gratefully fell into unconsciousness, but not before thinking: *Alone is exactly how I have to do it.*

She woke first, on her side, Charlie behind curled against her, his arm around her. A soft gray light suffused the room. She could see the thick ceiling of clouds from her window. She didn't move for a long while. Charlie's warm breaths puffed against her neck. His body felt so natural next to her, his intentions so pure that isolated in this moment with nothing else to consider, she let herself enjoy it. Just the simple comfort of another body next to hers.

It was Sunday. Everyone, even Santi, slept a little later on Sundays. Not that she cared if anyone found them like this. Charlie was fully clothed except for his boots. Rachel might make some big deal out of it if she managed to walk in right now. Santi might need a little explanation or reassurance. But in the scope of terrible things that really mattered, this could not matter less.

When her heartburn began to roil in her chest and her bladder felt as if it would pop, she reluctantly eased herself from Charlie's embrace and stood up. He was beautiful even as he slept. No slack-jawed snoring, no drool. A slight shadow of beard showed itself along his strong jawline. How could Rachel resist this perfect man? Maybe that was it; he was just too good to be true. Maybe it was impossible to believe she deserved him or it was too hard to be that vulnerable.

She remembered when Bobby first loved her, how frightening his intensity was, how every insecurity her childhood had imbued came to the surface and made it so difficult to trust. Not so much him—his sincerity was palpable—but to believe if she truly claimed this happiness as her own, the universe would let her keep it.

If she hadn't been able to trust, she would have missed out on twelve incredible years, a decade of married love, when some people miss out entirely. She wanted fifty or sixty more years; it wasn't fair. Still, to have those twelve. And to have his child.

As she turned to go, she clung onto that fragile feeling of gratitude and willed it to stay. She planted it like a seed to grow, to gestate inside her. She was going to need it.

Charlie found her in the kitchen, dressed in one of Bobby's long-sleeved faded denim work shirts and her maternity jeans for the cool weather front had decided stay. She had already showered, her auburn hair loosely wound up in a clip. She was making French toast and bacon.

He sat down and studied her, scratching his wavy hair into place. "You are amazing."

"I know," Abby smiled. "So are you. We are just too damn amazing for mere mortals."

He laughed. "You have a ton a fans to bear that out. I, on the other hand . . ."

She put his plate in front of him, some maple syrup and a cup of coffee.

"You have fans, don't give me that. CeCe and Miguel refuse to acknowledge their daughter divorced you. Santiago practically genuflects every time you show up. Even Rachel when you aren't looking casts a proprietary gaze your direction."

"Really? The part about Rachel?" His mouth was full in a boyish way.

Abby sat down and began to eat. "I think she can't help herself. I think she gets jealous of the two of us, even though she'd never admit it."

"Huh. So what would she say now that we're sleeping together?"

Abby smacked his arm. "She would say nothing because not only are we not sleeping together, we aren't telling her about last night. She's finally my friend and letting herself be softer and vulnerable. She'd never understand our friendship anyway."

"She probably wouldn't. She'd accuse me of trying to get into your pants."

"That's her jealousy. See, I told you she still has feelings for you." Abby chewed the crisp, smoky bacon and hoped it wouldn't give her heartburn later. "But, you know, Rachel should understand us because we're like I imagine she and Bobby were, like soul mate friends. Except for her schoolgirl-crush part."

Charlie gave her a look. "It was a tough act to follow—I'll tell you that much." He got quiet then, eating, sipping on his coffee.

"If you hadn't shown up last night, I don't know—"

"Sweetwater was going nuts so I rode him over to the big barn and bedded him in a stall for the night. He does better near the other horses. As twitchy as he was, I knew I had to get to you. I wanted to be with you."

"I'm grateful. There's a lot to get through. It's coming, you know? After all this waiting. I'm trying to get ready for it."

"When is Javier supposed to check in or be back?"

"He said it could be several more weeks."

"What will you do?" His hazel eyes connected with hers, his hand was over her hand.

"I'll have the baby here, it's too late and I'm in no shape to move right now. After that, as soon as we're both ready to travel, I think we'll go back to San Diego. But don't tell anyone else yet."

He squeezed her hand. "Whatever you need, I'm here."

She managed a small laugh even as tears brimmed in her eyes. "I do have a request. Pretty soon, in the next couple of weeks, could you scrounge me up a crib and help me set it up? I can't put off getting ready for this baby much longer. And now, there's no reason to wait."

When her forwarded mail arrived, Abby held the expensive cream envelope in her hand before opening it. Her mother's perfect, formal cursive, *Abigail* seemed out of some other century.

She dreaded reading the infinite number of ways her mother would find to say four simple words. *I told you so.* She hated that her personal tragedy was a victory for her parents. That Bobby had somehow unwittingly managed to do in death what he swore never to do in life, prove them right.

She ripped it open and forced herself to read.

Dear Abigail,

Recently, a very scruffy and rude Mexican man came to our home to interrogate us regarding the "disappearance" of your husband and his probable flight into Mexico.

While I have a certain degree of sympathy for your plight, I must point out if you had only listened to your father and me you would not be in this painful situation. We were trying to protect you from something precisely of this nature.

One can only hope this has opened your eyes. If this is the case, your father and I are amenable to extending our assistance in you coming home where you belong. You are still young enough to reposition yourself in respectable circumstances, though your pregnancy will not help matters. A mixed-race child will provide a challenge in attracting eligible men of quality.

Fortunately, with your restored family status and wealth, this might be overcome.

A second chance is a rare thing in life. Let us hope you have gained enough wisdom and maturity through the intervening years to make the right choice now.

Regards,
Your mother and father

Chapter 19

Maria didn't hear Rachel come in. But her hearing had started to go years before. Rachel found her sitting in her kitchen alone having a conversation. The sun shone in, brightly lighting up the contained jungle of plants and herbs vining and growing thick about the window and counters, the wide-eyed flowers of the Mexican tile peeking out wherever it could.

"Buenos días, tía," she said loud enough to be heard.

Maria turned around and reached out her hand. It shook a little and her fingers resembled the crooked roots she collected. "Ah, mi'ja, come in." She beckoned. A vessel had broken in her eye and the blood reached through the white part toward the washed-out brown center in tiny, spindly creeks. Rachel came in and sat down at the table with Maria, who smelled like she'd been drinking.

"Something is bothering you, mi'ja. I sensed it when you came in. I see it on your face," Maria said. "What is it?"

"I'm worried about Roberto. He's been gone way too long. I keep wondering if he's hurt or needs help."

Maria's eyes widened and for a second Rachel thought she might pop another vessel. Her eyes narrowed as if she had trouble seeing her at all. "That guera is putting those thoughts in your head. You don't trust your old tía anymore." Something foamy and foul bubbled up over the pot on the stove and hissed like a pissed-off snake. Maria got up, stirred it and turned it down.

"What am I supposed to believe?" Rachel asked. "You say he's coming back and still no Roberto. If you're so powerful, make him appear now!" She found herself standing.

Maria brought up something deep from her chest and spat it out on the brick floor. "I told you he's not ready! *Ayee!*"

"I don't care if he's ready or not, get him back here! Abby and I have become friends and I can't watch what this whole thing is doing to her!"

"*Qué lástima!* Serves her right for stealing him away in the first place!

"There's nothing evil in Abby, and she doesn't deserves this. I want to help her. Where has your heart gone, tía? There's got to be something you could do."

"I still say you do this out of guilt. Guilt is a weakness! You better pray that Roberto is not overcome with guilt," Maria said, growling like a nasty old pirate, the booze spiraling her eyeballs, "or he will choose the baby over you." With a dismissing wave of her hand she sent out a zephyr of body odor and turned back to the stove. Maria had never taken this long to give in before. Her head seemed to be getting harder and harder the older she got. The battle was really with the tequila she'd been drinking. "Of course, of course, what was I thinking? I have just the thing," Maria said, opening the door of the fifties-style refrigerator. She bent down and examined all the corked bottles. There must have been a hundred of them. Where was her food? "*Aquí, aquí,*" she said, pulling out a small bottle that could have, at one time, held horse elixir. "This is what she needs. *Mira.* Fix her right up. Give her *corazón duro,* a strong heart."

Maria handed Rachel the bottle. The cork resisted her pull at first. She put her nose to the bottle feeling a cold shiver as she sniffed. She looked at the label Maria had chicken scratched. Her anger boiled the tears welled in her eyes by the time she spoke. "This is what you gave me."

"I have given you so many potions and remedies, mi'ja . . ."

"I will never forget this smell. It permeated out of my skin long after it aborted Roberto's baby." She winced, remembering the terrible cramping. How she had fought to stay conscious after losing so much blood.

"You're confused!" Maria spat with a wave of her hand. "I don't know what you're talking about!"

"What the fuck do you think you're doing!" Rachel screamed.

Maria turned back around. The blue cast over her eyes made her look like something evil peering out from the dark. "As long as she has the baby, there's the chance Roberto may do right by her! I have to watch out for you! Without the baby, he has no tie with her. Now go," she said, "I'm too tired for your ingratitude."

"Have you lost your mind? I've never wanted that!"

Or had she? And had she ever in the slightest way let Maria think that was what she wanted? Did she imply to Maria to do whatever it took?

"I know. You are soft like your mother. I have to protect you, mi'ja. I'd do anything for you. I am old. What do I care what happens to me?"

"You're talking murder! And you tried to trick me into killing Abby's baby! For God's sake, I haven't gotten over killing my own! I will never forgive you!" Rachel cried, as she turned to leave.

"No, mi'ja! You don't understand! It was for you!"

Maria's words hit her like bullets in the back as she walked away.

Maria had lost her mind. That was all Rachel could think about since the day before at her house. What would have happened if she had not recognized the contents of the bottle? What if she had given Abby the potion in blind faith that Maria was actually doing her a favor? She hadn't been able to stop thinking about it. The pain in her stomach from the ulcer that must have developed overnight kept her in bed a little longer that morning. Her tía had gone over the line and Rachel didn't know what to do about it. Certainly she could never trust her again. She'd never been without the world of Maria and her magic. Everything was now changed forever. Nothing seemed important anymore. The milking could wait. Peeing could wait. She doubted she'd ever eat or sleep again. This secret she would carry inside of her for the rest of her life would be like a rotting fruit, touching and ruining everything around it. As if there were room for more dirty secrets.

She turned on her side, pulled up into a fetal position and prayed into her cold, shaking fists. An abdominal pain hit her like an electrical shock, curling her up tight as a pinworm. She deserved it.

A terse knock came at her bedroom door. She straightened and sat up. Her father entered, still damp and disheveled from working in the fields since dawn. He didn't smile, but he wasn't angry. He came and sat on the bed next to her. "Mi'ja, Luis Vargas just came out to the fields to get me. He had an appointment scheduled with Maria this morning. He found her unconscious on the floor. She's in the hospital." He put his hands on hers. They felt scratchy and warm like a favorite wool sweater. "We need to go. Hurry."

Rachel stared out of the truck window as her father drove them along the interstate toward Albuquerque. Nothing short of a coma would stop her mind. First, she had come close to being an accomplice in killing Abby's baby. Now she was killing Maria. She knew it was because of her and the argument they had had. Makeshift crosses stood along the roadside every mile or so, garnished with plastic flowers and faded, limp ribbons to let people know a loved one had crashed and died there. Patches of small sunflowers whipped past her with blank, accusing stares. Her tears came despite her attempts to stop them. Rachel couldn't quell her rage at Maria for changing her world overnight, and now for threatening to drop out of it.

Her father reached over and patted her leg. It felt so loving and yet so impotent. When had he lost his ability to comfort her? When had she grown beyond her father's safety?

"Papa, I had a big fight with tía yesterday. It was bad, Papa. I know I brought this on . . ." She wiped the tickling drip of snot from her nose.

"Mi'ja, Maria's around eighty. She's been sick with diabetes for a while now. Refused to listen to doctors, did that spitting thing on their floors. Your mother and I washed our hands at that point." He honked at some RV pulling off a ramp in front of them.

"Why didn't you tell me? I could have talked to her. Made her take better care of herself." And maybe have kept her sane. She blamed herself for not noticing Maria's decline in health—physically and mentally. She was the only one, besides Reyes, who ever spent much time with her, and he was no one to judge someone's mental health.

"She made us promise not to. Your mother wanted to. You know what she thinks about keeping secrets. No good ever comes of it. But Maria convinced her."

Like *The Wizard of Oz*, she guessed, Maria wanted to remain great and powerful to her. No peeking around the curtain.

The muscles in his jaw and forearm twitched as he held the wheel firmly in alignment. "Foolish old woman! She just kept on drinking and eating whatever she wanted. Didn't take the pills they gave her. I've been expecting this. She did this to herself. Don't for one second think you had anything to do with it. She was beyond help, mi'ja."

More than her Papa knew.

He took the Lomas exit toward the hospital where she was certain Maria lay dead from deep, wordy lacerations of the heart.

A weary-looking young male doctor in rumpled green scrubs came out of Maria's room and told them she was regaining consciousness. She seemed to be stabilizing. She had a good chance, but she would need to start taking care of herself. He and Miguel continued talking as they walked off down the hall. Reyes waited nearby looking bleary-eyed and a week past a good bath. Whether his eyes were bleary from worry or he was just hungover, Rachel couldn't tell. She guessed he had followed the ambulance over with a few of Maria's things.

As if she hadn't been through enough in the last twenty-four hours, she had to run into Reyes. She was not in the mood for his stares and slimy way. Rachel ducked into Maria's room to avoid him.

Maria looked so thin, wrapped mummy-like in the pink cotton blanket stamped with UNIVERSITY HOSPITAL across the top of her chest. Her breaths were shallow and ragged. A bag hung down on the side of the bed collecting her urine as yellow as dandelions. The room reeked of her ripeness.

Rachel came closer. Maria's round eyeballs moved behind her translucent lids. How was her magic being protected during this vulnerable time? According to Maria, powers could be snatched away by other brujas under these circumstances, weakening them further. She made a mental note to tell the nurses that no one, absolutely no one other than family was to visit Maria. Once this got out, the whole village would want to come and pay their respects to her. She rubbed a patch of Maria's forearm where they had not stuck a needle or taped on a monitor.

Maria opened her eyes. "Mi'jita," she said, her yellowish eyes now watering. She weakly reached up to take Rachel's hand, who took it and brought it to her cheek.

"It's me, tía." Maria's fingers were like a cluster of small icicles Rachel held delicately.

"Mi'jita. I was afraid I'd lost you. Let me look at you," she said, with obvious strain to see better. "Damn these eyes!" She coughed and choked as if she had swallowed too much water.

"I am furious with you, tía, but I still love you. Tell me what I need to do for you, what tinctures to mix to make you better," she said, smoothing Maria's hair until the coughing subsided, then wiped her mouth with a tissue.

Maria presented a small gap-toothed smile. "*Mi pobrecita*. There is nothing to be done." She tried to reach for the glass of water with the bent straw.

"I don't believe that, tía," Rachel said, holding the glass as Maria sucked thirstily. She had seen Maria's powers bring people back from the brink of death, even after their families began calling relatives and making funeral arrangements. But has she brought back Roberto? She had always believed in Maria's magic. All of her many satisfied customers believed, too. What did she mean, nothing could be done?

"I believe it, mi'ja. That makes all the difference. There is nothing to be done." Her bluish lips trembled. Maria tried to squeeze her hand. "I wanted to make it happen for you, mi'ja, but who knows what's in a man's heart? Your hope was my happiness. That, and my love for you." Maria fought to keep her eyes open.

"I have always believed in that," said Rachel. She might be doubtful now about her magic, but not of her tía's love.

Maria dropped into sleep saying, "I believed I could give you your dream."

Skipping the state fair sounded tempting to Rachel. She didn't have the energy after everything that had happened. At every fair, as far back as she could think, she had always helped her father tend to a couple of his prize bulls, and this time she brought a couple of cases of Sol y Sombra cheese to sell at the New Mexico shop in the Bolack Building. There was going to be a table set up with samples and recipes and business cards.

Rachel felt guilty and preoccupied, having left CeCe on her own canning cheese, Abby at home complaining of an upset stomach, and Maria lying in the hospital. And it was a real bitch trying to keep up with the milking during the fair time, constantly in the truck driving back and forth. On top of that, she had pulled a muscle in her forearm jerking a bale of straw. Milking was painful and aggravated it. She couldn't wait until the new automated milking equipment arrived that she ordered with her papa's blessing. Maybe Maria had some of her miracle-working liniments in her house somewhere. She would ask her tonight when she visited her at the hospital.

But when Papa asked for her help, she couldn't refuse. Well before dawn she had helped him load up his top bull and ridden silently in the truck beside him as he sipped his coffee and stared intently at the road. The absence of her mother and her prize winning produce, pies, and jellies left a sudden window of opportunity for her good-natured rivals that CeCe had beat out the previous years. Rachel wondered if CeCe thought about that at all. Probably not, since her mother had always urged others to get their egos out of the way.

After she helped her father settle in Ferdi, the young bull, she realized there were a couple of hours to spare before the bulls would be shown. A sudden urge to get lost in the crowd came on strong like a craving for chocolate. She cut through the midway heading toward the main street lined with her favorite buildings to peruse. The Indian and Spanish art buildings, the wildlife and forest conservation building, and the agriculture building with all the produce and canning entries, except for her mother's this year, as well as the new farming equipment and farm-gadget displays in the varied industries building.

"Hey, c'mere. You! c'mere," seduced a barker, with a wink, as if he was going to treat her special if she would try out his ring-toss game. The sharpshooting booths were lined with gangbangers showing off for their girlfriends. Children and adults screamed in flying and whirling circles around her and above her head. Clashing, loud music played all at once. Second upon second came other welcome distractions. Children threw exploding caps on the blacktop in a never-ending barrage, causing old women to jump as if snakes just shot up their skirts. She passed a screaming small boy holding a broken, empty plastic bag in one hand and a dead goldfish in the other while his mother yelled at him. A bungee jumper was about to take his plunge from a very tall crane above her. She fantasized about it for a moment, but bought a double-scoop chocolate-fudge ice cream cone and sat on a bench in a grassy area instead. People picnicked spontaneously around her on the grass, taking time to enjoy a barbequed turkey leg or powdered-sugared funnel cakes in paper cones with paisley-patterned blotches of grease.

She could not sit for long without her foot jiggling anxiously, trying to keep invading thoughts away like barn flies. Still they came at her, carrying a disease that left her feeling like she was allergic to her own blood and guts. That she was a stranger to herself. She thought of her unborn baby and wondered if its little spirit flitted around her sometimes. Did he forgive her? Would she ever forgive herself? Why hadn't Maria talked her out of it? Helped her think it through? Maria had said she was too young and Roberto ran off and married someone else, so what else was there to do? What would her mother have told her to do? Rachel realized now that with or without Roberto, the baby would have been loved. Rachel loved it still. He would have probably started middle school this year. She'd have been a soccer mom or something right now had Maria not pressured her.

She jumped up and headed for Indian Village, where practically everyone carried paper plates with either Indian tacos fragrant with green chile or plate-sized fry bread with honey. Small, fat-cheeked Indian children ran around in traditional garb waiting for their turn to dance in the big dirt circle in the middle of the village. The entire perimeter of the village was a winding snake of jewelry, art, and food booths with competitive BUFFALO BURGERS SOLD HERE and NAVAJO TACO signs. A group of third graders from Cesar Chavez Elementary, known by the tall signs on sticks some held up, stood and listened to their teacher at the horno oven describing the way in which oven bread was made. British tourists gawked around the Navajo hogan a few feet away with the look on their faces of people trying to imagine what it would be like to live with an entire family in this small, round wood-and-mud house with no electricity, no water, and no privacy.

The drums started and leather-skirted male dancers with little jingle bells on their calf-length moccasins began hopping and turning in the circle. Their magic pulled Rachel to them as they danced to thank unseen spirits for an abundant harvest, or so said the man on the microphone who introduced them. Despite everything, they managed to keep their culture alive through past centuries and into a new millennium. They seemed so grounded, their chanting so certain as they embodied their faith in swirls of color and motion, their sweating legs and moccasined feet stirring the dust in the arena, their faces reflecting the kind of peace she thought she might never again possess.

She asked one of many men wearing a baseball cap the time. Oh, thank God. In a couple of hours she could leave. She couldn't wait to get home, shower, and go to the hospital to see Maria. She needed to find some peace.

CeCe had Santi wiping dishes when Rachel walked in the back door, just as she had every man in her house do. One thing about CeCe, she was good at training men. Both her father and Charlie just couldn't seem to do enough to please her. And Roberto had been even worse.

Santi smiled at her and ran over so she could scruff up his hair. Rachel thought he might just give her a big hug this time, but he stopped short and waited for her to pet him first, and then Bésame, who was always by his side, her strawberry retriever fur starting to show signs of random cowlicks and waves. This time in Santi's smile she noticed another lost tooth. She hoped it had come out by the natural process of growth and not decay. It was hard keeping a mental road map of his little boy bumps and bruises, but she tried. It helped to know Abby, her parents, and even Charlie were as vigilant as she was.

"I'm just going to have a quick cup of very strong coffee and then get ready and go to the hospital," she told her mother. "Ferdi took top prizes, Papa is bursting his buttons."

"I'll make it for you," offered CeCe as she put a plate of strudel down on the table in front of Santi and Rachel. He helped himself to a napkin out of the holder on the table and a square of apple strudel. CeCe plopped down a big glass of milk next to him. He drank goat's milk by the gallon, which was good because the higher fat content helped put some weight on his bones. But she would rather have had him too thin than like some of the boys in his class. Boys whose bodies already looked like their thick-waisted fathers' who also sat and watched too much TV or played too many video games gorging on fast food. Her mother had already filled his head, as she had Rachel's years ago, about the evils of fast food establishments and their effect on the human psyche and the planet, not to mention the toxicity they created in the intestines and colon, or *kishkes*, as she referred to them.

The phone rang. "I hope that's not Prairie Star calling back about their order. They wanted it yesterday, but they keep changing it. Enough to drive me nuts," CeCe hissed, snatching the receiver off the wall.

"What have you been doing with yourself today?" Rachel asked Santi. She watched his cute face chew round and round and swallow before he spoke.

"I helped Abby. She's still sick. I let her lie on the couch and I got her everything and pulled weeds while she slept. I think she's feeling better now."

"You're such a good boy," she said, tweaking his chin. "I'm sure she can't help but feel better when you're around." They all did.

Her mother walked slowly back to the table and put her hand on Rachel's shoulder. "Santi, go get Charlie and tell him to find Miguel," she said.

"Papa's in the pasture getting Ferdi settled in," Rachel supplied.

"Santi—tell him to come here quick!"

"Ma?"

"That was the hospital. Maria just died."

Rachel set out on foot. Ended up walking the irrigation ditch. *Maria's dead?* She wanted to make it a question. That way it didn't sound so final. A part of her felt cast adrift to fly aimlessly like a helium-filled balloon. How much more could she stand to have happen? Could she be cursed? Did she even believe in spells and curses anymore? What was real and what wasn't? Where once the lines had been clearly drawn, everything now spun together in contradictory confusion. Maria couldn't leave her. Not now! Damn her! No, she didn't mean that. What did she mean? What did any of this mean? She stopped and steadied herself a second against a tree. *Roberto. Then what's happened to Roberto?*

She headed back in a daze. By the time Charlie found her, she was in the goat barn sitting in the straw as three goats sniffed, nuzzled, and tasted her. He saw her crying, and she didn't try to hide it. Tears that she could not put feelings or thought to, but tears of blinding devastation. A bomb had exploded and she felt strewn in a million pieces.

He came to her quickly. "Babe, Rache," he said as soft as a whispering angel. "I'm here, it's okay," he said, inviting her into his arms. The sound of his familiar voice lured her to his chest where she collapsed, no strength left for pretense. As to a mast in a hurricane, she held on to him for dear life.

Abby sat in her lawn chair, a pillow behind her back, one under her seat, her legs propped up on another lawn chair. She was recovering from a minor stomach virus, a few days of nausea and no appetite. The shade of her huge cottonwood tree made the late-morning heat tolerable. Besides, she couldn't take the quiet of her home one more minute. At least out here she could hear birds, the Bacas' roosters, dogs barking in the distance, the sound of farm machinery harvesting the last of late summer's crops.

She wasn't sure if she was still recovering from her virus or if she was just plain exhausted from launching the cheese business. Or maybe this is just what the last month of pregnancy was going to feel like. She automatically sent up another prayer of gratitude and held on to her big belly. Having this baby without any complications had become her single-minded focus. Everything else became peripheral. Even thoughts of Bobby were immediately transformed into bringing his child safely into the world; her purpose, her reason for being. He would want that. And Javier could stay gone as long as he wanted.

She didn't want one more thing to deal with right now, not one distraction, trauma, decision, crisis, news, detail, anything that would interfere with her job as a human incubator. She was like a great surly chicken hunkered down on her nest, ready to peck the eyes out of anyone who came near.

She looked up to see Rachel coming, carrying something. She hadn't seen much of the Vigils in recent days since Maria had passed away. She had avoided the funeral. Charlie and CeCe had been by to check on her a few times. Ramone called or stopped by every day. Hazel was checking her blood pressure every few days and Carmen brought over a stack of women's magazines for her to relax with. Bonnie helped her with her crocheting and Santiago entertained her with stories about his new school friends, "the smart kids," he proudly called them. She was not lacking for attention.

Rachel seemed to be carrying a pot of something. "Hi," she said as she drew near. "Ma sent me, said you hadn't been feeling well. Chicken soup with matzo balls, Jewish penicillin." She looked as if she needed some. Her face was gaunt except for some dark puffiness around her eyes.

"Stay and have some with me," Abby said.

Rachel stood over the pot on the stove. Abby sat at her kitchen table.

"I'm really sorry about Maria. I know you were close."

Rachel shrugged, avoided eye contact. She turned away, but not before Abby could see tears spilling onto her cheeks. Her hair was loose around her like a blanket or cape to mourn under.

"Sit down, Rachel. Cry with me."

She peeked past her hair, her hand that was furiously wiping her face, let out a sigh and sat down. "I'm sorry."

"You don't need—"

"No, I do. I feel terrible. I've been so mean to you, from the moment you got here. I never gave you chance."

"That's ancient history. You're a good friend to me, now. Bobby would be really proud of us."

She sniffed back her tears. "You get the credit for that. I'm having to face the fact I've made a lot of mistakes. With you, with my mom. I've shut her out my whole life when the truth is, I admire her, you know? It sounds stupid, but when I was little, it bothered me that she didn't look like Papa and me or the mothers of the kids I wanted to impress. She was different and I talked myself into being ashamed of her."

More tears momentarily strangled her. She shook her head. "I made Maria my mother. She encouraged it, bad-mouthed CeCe the whole time, and I ate it up. When I was really little, it was like I had to make a choice, Jewish or Hispanic. Jewish was too different here, I was too chicken to take any part of it. Nobody told me how you can be both."

"Being both looks pretty good to me. Not only did the genetics make you beautiful—you have two of the best people I've ever known as your parents. My parents, on the other hand, well, don't get me started—just know how lucky you are for both of them." Abby got up and ladled some of the simmering golden broth into two bowls, then a tennis-ball-sized fluffy matzo ball to sit in the center of each. The delicious smell alone was enough to restore her appetite. She felt the first actual hunger she'd felt in days.

She set the soup bowls on the table. "All I have is filtered water. I'm off the tea now. Dr. Lark said to stay away from it in case I had developed some kind of allergy to one of the herbs and that's what made me sick."

Rachel stared down into her bowl. "You had bad parents and you turned out to be great. I have great parents and I turned out terrible."

Abby put down her spoon. "What?"

Rachel began to cry again, her hands went up to her face. "I don't know, since Maria died, there's just so much hitting me. I feel really bad about so many things. I trusted her, I believed in her. But it was wrong, so much was wrong and it's tearing me up."

Abby didn't know what to say. She knew from her own grief it was better not to say anything.

"All my life she was there for me with the answer, the cure. I told her what I wanted and she made it happen, she worshipped me. CeCe, you know, she'd tell me no. She'd punish me when I made mistakes. So who is a little girl going to choose?" She sobbed harder. "Then, I got into real trouble. I . . . I got pregnant and the boy didn't want me. I was so hurt and angry, I went to Maria and asked her to get rid of it. God help me! Before I knew what was happening, she gave me foul-tasting stuff to drink. I'll never forget the stench of it! There was so much pain and God, the blood! And my baby was gone." Her crying was angrier now and filled with anguish.

Abby sat in stunned silence. Her own baby stirred. She reached out to touch Rachel, who was shaking all over.

"You were young and afraid. You didn't know what else to do."

"Maria should have talked me out of it. She should have seen I'd regret it. She should have made me tell my parents. She killed my baby! I killed my baby!"

"Nobody knows? You've been carrying this around? Not even Charlie knows?"

"Don't tell him, don't you dare tell him—" Rachel snapped out of her crying to look her in the eye, pleading with her. "Don't tell anyone!"

"No, of course not. That's up to you. You have to stop blaming yourself—you did the only thing you thought you could do at the time, you were a young girl, alone, and that son of a bitch who deserted you—"

"He fell in love with someone else. I don't blame him. Not anymore." She took a long drink of water and blew her nose into her paper napkin.

Abby sat back, realizing her pregnancy was yet another reason for Rachel to resent her. Without even knowing, from the day she arrived she had been Rachel's painful reminder. And yet, Rachel had chosen her to tell. "Have you ever thought about having more children. I mean, you're young—"

"That's all I used to think about. But now"—she looked away and hesitated—"I just don't know anymore."

Abby wavered but then spoke. "Maybe this isn't my place but I have to say this. Charlie loves you so much—"

"He's very fond of you these days, too," Rachel said. "Charlie just likes to win, that's all. He stays just because he knows I wanted him gone."

"I don't believe that for a second. Look, it's no skin off my teeth if you two ever get back together or not, but you should at least face the truth about him. He talks about you all the time, all he wants in this world is to be with you. From where I'm sitting, it's a terrible waste."

Rachel pushed her soup away. Abby rinsed her bowl. The meal infused her with strength and comfort. CeCe had put all of herself into it and the soup had become her proxy. She marveled at the power of it. She looked at Rachel and felt such compassion and sadness. Here was a woman surrounded by love, yet starving, unable to take it in.

She sat back down. Rachel's expression was caught somewhere in her private pain. "It's hard to be angry with someone who is dead. But it's okay, you know. It's part of it. I know you loved Maria, but she also took something precious away from you."

Rachel nodded, twisting her napkin with such intensity her knuckles were white. "I'd give my soul to have it back."

The kitchen door thumped and swung open so suddenly they both jumped. Charlie stuck his head around the door, a big grin on his face, pulling some big wooden strapped-together object behind him. "Somebody order a baby crib?"

Rachel looked at him with abject horror and nearly knocked him down on her way out the open door.

Chapter 20

"What's with her?" Charlie asked, watching Rachel run in the direction of home.

"She was crying about Maria and embarrassed to have you see her," Abby said quickly. "Where did you find the crib?"

"I was just driving by and there it was at a garage sale, leaning up against a tree. The woman said she'd used it for only one baby. See, it looks brand-new and she said the rails are the right space apart so the baby's head doesn't get stuck."

"It's . . . fine. Thanks, Charlie," Abby looked down at his leather boots, aged and worn in a way that advertised his hard work ethic. She couldn't meet his proud eyes, his excited smile.

"I'll just get my tools and put her together. Unless this is a bad time."

She looked up. "I'm just one bad time after another. You saw me happy one time, at a funeral for Godsakes, how pathetic is that? And I didn't even know how grateful to be."

Charlie looked into her face and then at the crib leaning against the wall. "You were counting on Bobby putting this together for your baby. I'm a real dumb shit."

"No—no, you're exactly right, it's one more hurdle to get over without Bobby. So let's do it."

"I'll just go get my tool box out of the truck."

He worked for a while in silence except for the occasional moments of talking out loud to himself about which piece connects to what and where the hell was his smaller Phillips screwdriver.

Abby held together whatever two pieces he was joining and tried not to imagine how this event would have played out if Bobby were there. Intrusive flashes of his beaming smile, his muttering in Spanish, wiping sweat from his brow. They had talked about it, constructing the scene ahead of time in great detail. It was one of those predictable things, a cliché to most people, but a ritual they counted on to make their impending parenthood more tangible. But that was to have been a crib they picked out together, extravagantly expensive, only the best for their baby. Not some garage sale castoff.

Charlie lifted the mattress and placed it onto the spring-metal support platform. "The lady said this is adjustable 'cause you want it higher at first for a newborn, saves your back from bending over so far. Then as the baby gets older and can pull up on things, we need to lower it down so it's safer."

"It's a nice crib, Charlie. Thanks." She didn't remind him she wouldn't be there that long. This was only temporary, for the first few months until they were ready to move.

"You never said why Rachel was so upset to see me. I don't buy that stuff about her being embarrassed for crying."

"It wasn't you. We were talking about some upsetting stuff. She's opening up to me, trusting me more."

Charlie started throwing tools back into the old red chipped tool box. "I'm glad. She needs that."

Abby noticed the sharpness to his tone, the way the tools were clanking against each other with a little more force than necessary. "What is it, Charlie? I really do appreciate your help in this—"

He righted himself, loose washers and screws jingling in his cupped hand like spare change. "It's nothing."

She put her hand over his and looked up into his eyes.

He blew out his breath and met her gaze. "I don't blame you for a second for wishing I were Bobby putting together that crib. There's just times, what with Rachel tearing out of here like I'm the last guy on earth she wants to see—you just get sick and tired of always being the wrong man, that's all."

"You get a lot of that around here. I never thought about it from your end. It's just 'good old Charlie, he'll do it,' whatever it is, putting together cribs, delivering cheese. Everyone depends on you for everything. It's a crime a man as wonderful as you has to feel like a cheap substitute."

"Maybe you have the right idea about leaving. Maybe Rachel was right, maybe I should have left after she divorced me. I'm starting to feel like I'm wasting my life here, pushing thirty-four. I don't know, putting together that crib stirred up the fact that I still have a dream of having a family, putting together a crib for a woman who loves me, who's having my baby."

Abby put her arms around his neck and leaned into him as much as her big belly would allow, her head against his shoulder. She felt his arms tighten around her in a gesture of relief. The washers and screws fell to the wood floor, clinking together like a miniature wind chime.

Rachel's heart pounded in her ears as she ran. The distance she put between herself and Abby's house did nothing to dilute her panic. She stopped along the ditch under the shade of some mature mulberry trees near her father's chile fields.

She thrust her hands into her damp hair and held it back tightly until it tugged at her face and eyes. She and Maria had killed her baby. She had said it out loud and to someone else, not realizing the life sound and air would give her words. Give her baby. She steadied herself against a tree and cried for the child she lost so long before. Her arms now ached, having held only emptiness all these years. Her sobs were so deep she swore she could feel a tearing down in her uterus as she held herself tightly. It was happening all over again. She remembered the never-ending blood after she aborted, getting it on her hands as a guilty recrimination. The horrible cramping as if the angry fists of the unborn spirit raged within her. She had never admitted to herself that she could have been wrong, or that Maria could have ever been wrong about anything; but having witnessed the perfection of Abby's roundness progress, and the strength she drew from her baby, even in the middle of all this—my God. What had she done? Just whose shame had she been carrying all these years? Maria's dismissing hand of good riddance was buried with her.

If it had been up to Maria, Abby would have lost her precious baby and she would have been the unwitting instrument of death. Abby was already sick—the potion might have killed her, too. Thank God she remembered the stench of the potion, or she would have slipped some to Abby, blindly trusting Maria, believing she was helping Abby to feel less pain about Roberto. Out of all the endless guilt she carried, losing Abby or her baby would have been completely beyond redemption, in this life or the next.

And Charlie. He had seen the look on her face when he brought in the crib, a tearful look of all the jealousy and remorse she had held silently inside. She had felt shamefully naked as he stared.

A piñon jay squawked at her from a limb above her head. She moved along the path, watching the rushing river water in the ditch. Toads leapt out of her way. She thought about their ability to lay their eggs in the mud and forget about them.

"Rachel!" she heard Santi yell as he and Bésame ran to meet her at the old wooden gate to their property.

The latch was splintered and stuck and she tried hard not to cry as she struggled with it. A large sliver of wood imbedded under her nail just as her minuscule patience was spent.

"Goddamn it!" she yelled just as Santi got there. She plopped down in some crisp, sun-baked weeds, holding her finger and bawling unabashedly.

Santi climbed through the fence slats and took her hand to look at her finger. "That's a bad one," he said. "I'd probably cry, too. I can pull it out. The end is sticking out, see?"

She nodded even though her vision was impaired by the pool of tears in her eyes, refracting light and Santi into a kaleidoscopic image. She quickly wiped them away.

Santi's eyes begged her to let him take care of her. Where had she seen that look before?

"Do your stuff, kiddo." She relinquished her finger to him and he smiled.

"Ready? I'll count to three. One. Two . . ." He pulled on the count of two, catching her by surprise, and held the splinter up proudly like a caught fish. "Charlie fooled me like that when I got a tack stuck in my foot."

Her finger still throbbed as he kissed it. CeCe had showed him that one. He looked like one of the angels painted on the old church ceiling tending to the baby Jesus.

"All better now?" he asked.

"Like new," she said, feeling a similar throbbing in her heart. She could not love Santi more if he had been her own child. She reached for his hands, and he leaned back on his heels as he helped pull her to her feet. He must have grown two inches over the summer with the help of CeCe's cooking. Her mother seemed excited to have a child around the house and couldn't wait for Abby's baby to come, even more than she let on to Abby. A lot of her free time was spent in her sewing room working on something for, no doubt, one of them.

Bésame wanted to join in and jumped at their sides, barking in excitement. Her legs had grown and she no longer had the roundness of early puppyhood. Her ears flapped up and down as she jumped like the wings of a golden bird, her once puppy-pink nose now half brown and freckled.

"I better get home," Rachel said. "I promised Ma I'd be home in time to help with an order before she does the whole thing herself."

"She sent me out to see if you were on your way," Santi said, working the latch open and letting her through first.

"Thank you, sir," she said as he whistled Bésame through and shut the gate behind them. "You are my gallant knight." She ruffled his dark hair and embraced his head to her. What mother on earth could ever have abandoned this child?

She had been standing silently next to her mother for a half hour preparing a cheese order when her panic started to infiltrate her body again without her even thinking. The thoughts started popping in like unwelcome guests. What if Abby decided to tell CeCe about the abortion? She never made Abby cross her heart and hope to die not to. Did that need to be said? Shit, she didn't know how this worked. She'd never had girlfriends in school. Didn't know how to talk to one. The chopped jalapeños made her sneeze. CeCe would say she had sneezed on the truth, but Rachel was having trouble figuring out what the truth really was. She was venturing into territories blindly.

Her mother, thankfully ignorant for the moment, canned cheese at the kitchen counter across from her in a mother-daughter silence Rachel had worked years on developing. She knew if she had told her mother about her pregnancy and abortion, CeCe would have held it over her head throughout eternity. Or, if Rachel had trusted her mother when she found out she was pregnant, would CeCe have convinced her to keep the baby, saving her from this torture, saving her and Roberto's baby's life?

What if Abby told Charlie? God, how could she ever face him again? And he was the worst when it came to keeping secrets. Soon everyone would know! Even her papa who would have embraced a grandchild, even out of wedlock, especially a flesh and blood link to his best friends, Magdalena and Ricardo. She couldn't bear the shame of her papa's disgust.

She had always tried to avoid personal pillow-talk stuff with Charlie, for the same reason she wanted the lights out when he made love to her. Too intimate. As much as he wanted to look at her while they made love, it had always felt like she would have revealed too much of herself. If her dirty secrets had spilled out, he would have divorced her first. The threat their growing closeness had presented was what made her pull away from him, divorce him. She had been protecting them both.

She put the knife down, realizing she had been gripping it like a weapon. Abby would figure out who the father was. Even though Roberto was never mentioned, it was obvious. Abby would hate her now.

"You feeling okay?" her mother asked, looking up from her labeling.

Rachel nodded. "Strong peppers," she said, as if they were life-threatening. Certainly a good excuse for her tears.

"Go outside for a while, sweetie, air out," her mother suggested. "We have enough chopped jalapeño."

She darted out the screen door onto the back porch. The door squeaked and slammed shut causing the goats to give a throaty response in the distance, even in their hypnotic, afternoon sleep. The chickens came at her like children after an ice cream truck on a hot summer day and black bugs swirled in funnels in front of her. She looked up the road and imagined Roberto walking toward her house, as he had thousands of times. Dark from the sun; he swore it was from drinking too much coffee. She used to sneak her father's cowboy coffee when she was little, in hopes of darkening up her too-fair-to-be-Hispanic skin. She'd run out to meet Roberto in the road, and throw herself into his arms. He'd swing her around a couple of times, then put her down pretending to be exhausted and say she was getting too fat. He was not dead to her. Not when she could still imagine him so clearly. The image faded from her hopeful mind's eye as if God were striking her blind. It was all so believable when Maria had said it.

The giant sunflower heads drooped next to the wooden fence along part of the road, accepting their fate to the pecking birds. She wished she could surrender like that. There were no more potions, no more incantations and smudgings that allowed her to believe she had any control over anything. And if Maria was a fake, did that make Abby right? What if something horrible had happened to Roberto? She let herself go there in that moment. Just for a moment. That place we're afraid to look; under beds, inside closets, in front of our faces.

She had to sit down on the porch step as her knees gave out. She would have to make sure Abby never found out she had been pregnant with her husband's baby. And if Abby guessed, she would deny it. She would say it was some rebound boyfriend or one-night stand. It couldn't be proven. One more secret to keep.

"Push! Push! Push! Come on, you can do it! Push!" CeCe's voice commanded in Abby's ear. "Okay, take a cleansing breath. Very good."

Abby let go of her knees and leaned back against CeCe who sat behind her on the rug in front of the sofa. "I can't believe in a few weeks we'll be doing this for real."

"You're ready. You know this stuff inside and out. I don't suppose you heard anything from Javier?"

"I talked to him a few nights ago. He's in Juarez, having trouble finding Hector Casteneda. So you're stuck being my coach."

"I love doing this with you! So show me the crib. Let's work on the nursery." CeCe helped her up from the floor. "You and Rachel sure have been spending a lot of time together here lately."

"We're really getting closer. It's great." She stopped as CeCe stood in the doorway of Bobby's childhood room, unchanged except for the crib standing where his twin bed used to be.

"This is all wrong. We need to pack up all these model ships and books and stuff and put them in the storage shed, Bobby won't mind. We need to paint or wallpaper and get a changing table—I better make a list."

"Wait, CeCe. I wasn't going to do all of that. Maybe just clear out the top couple of drawers on the dresser for the baby's clothes and blankets."

"Why? It'll be fun, I'll do all the work. You just pick out colors and stuff." CeCe's eyes were flashing with anticipation. A big smile on her lovely face made her look a lot younger than Abby felt. She couldn't tell her she was going back to San Diego, not yet. It would change everything. She'd have to go along with this, it was the least she could do.

"All right, but I want to keep it real simple."

"I can do simple. Let's talk about it over lunch."

CeCe had brought a picnic basket with chicken salad and homemade bread and a big wedge of watermelon. They sat outside at Abby's table in the dappled light under the golden leaves of the cottonwood tree. Late September brought burnished hues to the fields, slightly cooler temperatures, but the bright sun and expanse of blue sky gave no hint that summer was yielding to autumn.

"My favorite time of year here," CeCe said. "I'll drive you over to Fourth of July Canyon. Gorgeous red maples, gold aspens. The kids, Rachel and Bobby, used to love to go and collect the leaves. We'd press them into books."

Abby smiled. Another little snippet of Bobby's past to store away for his child to hear about one day.

"So many memories!" CeCe said, clearing her throat and dabbing at her eye with her napkin.

Abby could feel everyone around her begin to know that Bobby wasn't coming home. The truth of it hung between every spoken word and in a way allowed for a calmer atmosphere. The palpable anxiety had diminished over time and they were left with a unifying sense of loss.

"I notice you aren't wearing your wedding ring."

Abby pulled a chain out from under the front of her shirt. "My fingers got too swollen, so I wear it on this."

"Bobby's dog tags? Good idea. I never heard about your wedding, tell me about it."

Abby finished chewing and took a drink of water. "We eloped. It was spring break for me, Bobby had a week off before his first sub rotation. We'd had the big blowout with my parents the week before so we got a license in San Diego and took off for San Francisco right after my last midterm exam. Got married at city hall, it had just been renovated after the earthquake. It has this huge dome, bigger than the U.S. Capitol and the inside, the rotunda, is designed after St. Peter's Basilica in Rome. We stood in front of the marble steps, glass lanterns glowing, all this ornate plasterwork, looking up four stories. It was the most beautiful place either of us had ever been. God it was exciting, two twenty-year-olds madly in love, mad as hell at my parents. I took over three thousand dollars and we blew it all at the best restaurants, staying at the old Palace Hotel. We went back for our anniversary every year, even if it didn't hit the exact day or even month because of our schedules. It's our magical place."

"Sounds lovely. You were only twenty? That's about the time Bobby's letters stopped, but there hadn't been more than a couple that last year. It was tough seeing Rachel rush to the mailbox every day."

"He should have stayed in better touch. If I'd had any idea about his connections to you guys I would have made him. I'm afraid we kind of made up our own little selfish universe."

"As it should be! I'm so glad Bobby found such happiness with you. Let me see his tags."

Abby lifted the long chain from around her neck, trying not to tangle it in her hair. She watched as CeCe read the tags, running her fingers against the bumps behind the letters.

"I still have my brother's tags. Sammy. They found them in Vietnam but never found him. Missing in action. It's so damn hard not getting to know what happened. Sometimes, you just don't get to know." She raised the rectangular pieces of metal to her lips and slowly kissed Bobby's name.

Then, she reached over and held the chain over Abby's head, guiding it down over her hair. Abby slipped it under her shirt until her wedding ring and the tags rested against her heart like an amulet.

Chapter 21

"How are you doing in the reading contest?" Abby asked as Santiago carried a box of Bobby's childhood belongings to the closet in the front bedroom. She was nearly finished clearing out the nursery to CeCe's satisfaction.

"There's this girl named Holly and she's a real fast reader. I'm only two books ahead of her right now." He shifted the box to his other arm as Abby opened the door to the closet.

"Just put it there on the floor and shove it back under the coats. I still think you'll win, but even if you don't you can still be proud of all the books you've read and hopefully you won't get out of the habit."

"I'm addicted already. I'm a bookaholic." He pretended to stagger back to Bobby's room, bumping into the walls. "I can't get enough!" He grabbed a book from Bobby's bookcase and smashed it open against his face, sniffing loudly.

Even as Abby laughed she realized part of his impersonation was inspired by his substance-abusing father or uncle. It frightened her a little how good he was at it, how funny he thought it was. "Drugs and alcohol take your smarts and your imagination away. Books make them grow."

"Duh. I'd never be that stupid."

"I just had to be sure you knew where I stand on the subject. Thanks for helping, CeCe's been on my case lately and gave me a deadline so she can paint in here." She reached over and tousled his hair.

"I want to help paint!"

"You've got books to read and a science project to work on and that's just the stuff I know about. Open house is in a few days, remember?"

"Yeah, everyone will freak out. Usually I never got to go because my dad would never go. Who's all coming?"

"Everybody," Abby said. "Miguel and CeCe, Charlie, Rachel, all of us. So many we'll probably embarrass you."

"Holly's only bringing two." He smiled and puffed his skinny chest out.

"It's after five. Is your dad going to be looking for you tonight?"

"Eeeyikes!" He started to zoom out of the room.

"Wait! I want to give you this. Bobby would want you to have it for helping me so much." She held out the model battle ship she had noticed him eyeing every time he was in the room.

His face lit up only to darken just as quickly. "I better not. My dad would probably just break it."

"Why would he do that?"

"He doesn't want me to even be over here or be getting stuff. He hates Bésame—she keeps bothering his roosters but they always start it."

"Well then, it's still yours but you can keep it over here. How's that?"

He nodded, running his hand over the sleekly painted gray side. "Are you sure Bobby wouldn't mind? Maybe he wants his own kid to have it."

"There's a lot more. Like I said, Bobby would be so grateful for all the help you give me. You're a real lifesaver."

Santi jerked his hand away from the ship and left Abby holding it while he tore out of there. "I have to go," he called over his shoulder as the whack of the screen door punctuated his exit.

Abby sat cross-legged on the floor in front of Bobby's dresser. She carefully folded his high school–era sweaters and shirts and placed them into the open cardboard box. Funny how his father kept everything just as Bobby had left it, as if he might slip back into it and his old life someday. But, these were the clothes of a slightly built adolescent, not the muscular man that age and the Navy had created.

At first she buried her nose into them, searching for his scent. But she could only smell the particular scent of this house and the musty wood of the drawer. She didn't weep as she thought she might. Her sadness was deeper than tears could reach. Her grief was pervasive; it was the mortar in the walls of every cell in her body. Without her sadness she would evaporate into a tiny sprinkle of dust so light, so inconsequential as to be invisible to the naked eye. The merest movement of air would scatter her into oblivion.

Without his models, his posters, his books, the room was barren and generic. A room his father could never force himself to confront. It was so understandable, suddenly, how comforting his wild clutter must have been. The chaos of random objects, no discernible pattern, nothing to identify with, completely free of any attachment or memory. The house, left the way it had been when his son and wife had been there, had become unbearable. Emptying it of their history would have been even worse. Disguising it, burying it under a mountain of debris, was his pathetic attempt to find peace.

She pulled open the last drawer. Her legs threatened to cramp, her back was killing her but she had only one more to go and then tomorrow CeCe could knock herself out transforming this blank slate into a room fit to welcome new life. It would please Bobby.

If it would please Bobby, somehow she found the strength to do it. Imagining his smiling face, his expression of approval, made the difference between eking out one more moment without him and collapsing on the floor to give up and die.

The last drawer would be easy, just some dehydrated tennis balls, a tangle of old wrinkled neckties, and a shoe box. Her tired muscles eagerly anticipated the soothing warmth of her bubble bath. With a loud sigh that reverberated in the empty room, she tossed the ties and tennis balls into the trash bag and pulled out the shoebox. Converse All-stars, size ten. Black. The lid was held down by a rotting red rubber band that came apart in her fingers. The box was heavier than she expected.

Inside were letters. Letters filed upright, still in their open envelopes crammed so tightly, that to pull out one brought several more.

Rachel Vigil, Esperanza, New Mexico, to Roberto Silva, U.S. Navy, San Diego, California. The postmarks began in October of 1988, right after he left when he was only eighteen. Abby smiled. How like Bobby to save everything. Wouldn't Rachel be touched? He must have brought them home to store on one of his early visits.

Should she give them to Rachel untouched? She hesitated, the first few letters in her hand. Would it be an invasion of privacy to read a few? She took out the next handful and saw that the dates proceeded in order chronologically. Now that there was more room, she could flip past them like recipe cards, glancing at the dates. She was curious when the letters stopped.

1988, 1989, 1990 . . . She and Bobby had met in 1989 and married in 1990. At the back of the box, there was a separate bundle tightly bound with a black cord. She lifted them out. Under the cord was a scrawled note:

Here are your own filthy lying words, you bastard!

By the time you hold these in your hands your baby will be gone—let that be on your conscience!

She ripped off the black cord. It was the much smaller collection of letters from Bobby to Rachel covering the same years. The last one was postmarked the month they eloped to San Francisco. *Your baby . . .*

Screw privacy! She would read every damn letter, all of Rachel's and Bobby's, from the beginning, if it took her all night. She grabbed the loose ones she had taken out and piled them on top of the box, her heart pounded, the clear white light of rage energized her as she managed to get up from the floor and take the letters into the living room to read more comfortably on the sofa. She went to the bathroom, poured a tall glass of cold water from the refrigerator, took a couple of cheese sticks for her overdue supper and set the cell phone next to her.

Rachel's letters were written in her tight, feminine script. She poured out her anguish, how could he leave her? She filled pages with detailed erotic memories and fantasies, begging him to leave the Navy and come home to her. Abby grabbed one of Bobby's from the first few months. He described the barracks, his new friends, his C.C., daily activities of boot camp, how terrible the food was, how tired he was, ending it simply, *I love you, too.*

The pattern continued, ten or twenty letters from Rachel to Bobby's one. Hers complained about CeCe, how boring life was without him, when was he coming home?

His were matter-of-fact, except to say how much he loved San Diego, learning communications, computers, dreaming about submarine duty someday.

It was clear young Rachel's heart was breaking as she refused to accept the obvious; her Roberto was moving on without her, he even began to sign his name Bobby. Abby could almost feel sorry for her if she hadn't been so angry. She skimmed through most of them, getting to the last of them as quickly as possible. Bobby began to try to let Rachel down easy, encouraging her to get out more, make new friends and she wouldn't be so lonely. *You need to make a life for yourself like I am.*

You are my life, she had replied. Then a short letter from Bobby dated September 1989, he was coming home for a quick visit with his father at Thanksgiving. He needed to talk to her. Abby put down the letter. She and Bobby had met in September and were already falling in love; he was going home to break it to her.

Then two more letters in December, after his trip home. Rachel was giddy with happiness:

> *I know you said you met someone else, that you don't love me anymore, but your body said something else. Words lie, I felt the truth in your arms.*

Bobby's response was apologetic:

That never should have happened, I was weak. Please, you're beautiful and smart; you can meet someone new like I did. I'll always care about you and love you as my best friend but that is all. My life is with Abby. We are telling her parents soon. We're getting engaged New Year's Eve.

Rachel's response came in early January 1990.

I'm pregnant with your child. Come home, Roberto. Don't you see this is God's will? We are soul mates and are meant to be together. I forgive you for being unfaithful. We can start fresh. Isn't it wonderful, my love? A baby of ours grows inside of me. Maria said it will be born in August. I can't wait to hold it in my arms. Our families will be so happy to be joined. Your father will be so happy that you are coming home where you belong. I know this is a shock, but trust me, mi amor, it will be wonderful.

Roberto wrote back quickly.

You did this on purpose! I will not let you ruin my life! I am a man of honor and I will stand by my child if you decide to go through with it but I will never be your husband. I love Abby. Why can't you get it through your thick skull? I never wanted to hurt you. I care about you. But, I don't love you the way you imagine or want me to. I'm sorry these are painful words but you don't seem to be able to get it any other way. Let me know what you decide about the baby. My heart is Abby's and always will be.

Last, the note from Rachel returning his letters. Abby looked at the pile of letters in front of her on the sofa and picked up the phone. "Rachel, I know it's late. Can you please come over? We need to talk."

"What's going on—are you all right? Did you hear something about Roberto?" Rachel burst into the back door where Abby stood waiting, mustering her courage for this confrontation. She wanted to stay calm, hoped to be reasonable and understanding.

Instead she let out a sarcastic laugh. "Oh, you could say that."

Rachel stood looking at her, hands on the hips of her faded navy blue thermal long-sleeved T-shirt and pants that probably served as her pajamas. She was showered, damp hair forming ringlets. "Well, what?"

Abby led her into the living room where the pile of letters covered the coffee table, a few stray envelopes had slid to the floor.

"What's this?"

"Take a closer look," Abby sat down on the sofa, feeling her throat constrict against her rising dread. Maybe this was crazy.

Rachel leaned over and picked up one. It took only a moment for her to process what this meant. "Where did you get these?"

"Bobby's a pack rat. Never give him anything you don't want him to save forever."

"How dare you read them! They're none of your business!" She began to gather them up, frantically scooping them into her arms, dropping most of them.

"You should have told me!"

"Why should I tell you when your own husband hid it from you?"

Abby took in a sharp breath. "He should have told me. When we were moving back here, he should have. I'm pissed that he didn't."

"What does that tell you, huh?" Rachel tilted her chin in her old defiant gesture Abby hadn't seen in months.

She stared at Rachel, feeling her jaw drop in amazement. "You actually think he was leaving me for you. You've been thinking you had a chance to get him back, admit it. That's what this whole summer has been about."

"He loved me! We had plans to be together before you came along and ruined everything. When he got back here for the funeral and saw me again, Maria said—"

"Maria? She was at the bar with him that night, what does she have to do with this? What else haven't you told me?"

"She told me how angry he was, how lost he looked without me. She knew he was struggling, trying to find his way back to me—"

Abby shook her head in frustration. "You are so wrong. She was a crazy old woman telling you what you wanted to hear, maybe trying to make it up to you for the baby she helped you lose. Face it, Rachel! Has Bobby contacted you one time in ten years since his last letter? Did he ever call or come see you when he came home to see his father? Go ahead, I can take it! Were the two of you illicit lovers behind my back or only in your dreams?"

"Shut up!" Rachel cried, dropping the letters and sagging into the chair. "Just shut up, okay?"

Abby watched her bitter, angry tears. Her tone was softer now. "I'm sorry, I'm sorry about your pain when Bobby left you and if you need to blame me, fine. But he'd already moved on. It's obvious in his letters. I'm sorry you felt so alone you ended your pregnancy when you really didn't want to. It's terrible what happened."

"I don't want your pity." Rachel wiped her face, recovering her composure, staring off to the side, unwilling to meet her eyes.

"This isn't pity. There just isn't any reason to be fighting."

"You sit there so high and mighty and pregnant. So cocky you won't think for a second that Roberto might want me instead of you—that I'm even worthy of him."

"Worthy? There's only one man I've ever known who's even in the same league as Bobby and he's desperately in love with you. I wish like hell you'd wake up and realize how worthy you are! You're chasing after a phantom and losing what is real."

Rachel gave her a startled look. "What about Charlie?"

"It's what sank your marriage, isn't it? He could never live up to your Roberto fantasies. You have Roberto so idealized I don't think even he could have measured up! How long do you think Charlie can live like this? The pain of not having you but seeing you every day is ripping him apart. I don't know how much longer he can last before he has to leave. He told me he's thinking about it. I've lost the man who loves me the way Charlie loves you. Don't do this to yourself!"

Rachel finally looked her in the eye. "If you love Roberto so much how can you believe he's never coming back?"

"Trust. If I'm wrong about him now, then I've never been right and you deserve him more than I do. He comes marching through that door—you can have him!"

Rachel looked incredulous and then horrified. "For you to say that, you must have no doubt, no hope . . ."

Abby shook her head, feeling the first tears in a very long time sting her weary eyes. She shrugged helplessly.

In the silence, Abby could feel something change between them, something like a current that had switched directions, an energy that instead of colliding from opposite poles now was in alignment. Before either could speak, a low rumbling came from the distance, slowly building like approaching thunder.

"Do you hear that? Sounds like Charlie's truck," Rachel said, going to the kitchen to look out of the open door. "Abby—come here!"

Abby walked as quickly as her aching legs and back would allow and peered into the darkness where she saw a pickup truck drawing nearer.

Its headlight beams bounced as it made its way slowly over the rutted road. Abby let herself out of the screen door, switching off the porch light to see better under the generous light of a full moon. She shivered in the cold breeze and squinted toward the slow-moving vehicle. This was not Charlie's larger, white, newer-model truck.

Rachel gripped her arm, "That's Ricardo's truck! It's Roberto!"

The truck pulled to a stop in the driveway. Quality plumbing since 1932 flashed like a mirage before Abby's eyes as the driver-side door swung open with an audible creak.

Rachel ran over the grass like a little girl welcoming her daddy home. Abby watched, unable to move, caught somewhere between a glorious dream and her worst nightmare.

Rachel stopped abruptly five feet from the man who emerged from the truck.

"Mrs. Silva?" he called. Javier Tapia.

Javier walked past Rachel who seemed frozen in place. "Let's go inside," he said to Abby, who felt incapable of such logic.

He put a hand on her back to guide her when she noticed Rachel still hadn't turned around. "Go ahead, we'll be right there."

"I'll just quick use your baño."

The wind kicked up a few early fallen leaves that scuttled around her feet. Her daytime flip-flops seemed ridiculous now that the temperatures had suddenly plummeted after nightfall. She stopped and looked up at the moon, so perfectly full it seemed somehow sacred, so swollen and round like a pregnant belly. A powerful feminine presence traveled through its moonbeams. She sent up a spontaneous prayer to whatever goddess might be looking down upon them, a prayer for the particular kind of strength women have needed since the beginning of time.

"Rachel?"

Her back sagged slightly but still she didn't turn around.

"Come inside with me to hear Javier."

"I can't."

"I need you." She put her hand on Rachel's shoulder.

"I'll go get my mom for you, I can't do this."

"It's you I need. Please."

Rachel turned, a gust of wind pressed Abby from behind. Instinctively her arms opened up and Rachel stepped into them. As they hugged, Abby could feel a surge of strength flowing between them, a giving and receiving in equal measures. And though the wind was cold, the moonlight began to warm her as well as any sun.

Abby squeezed her hand as they parted. "Let's go inside."

Chapter 22

Javier stood at the sink drinking water in a way that reminded Abby of old western movies when a stranger stops at a ranch house needing water and grub after a long ride.

She took out a plate of leftover enchiladas from the refrigerator and put it into the microwave.

"I tried to call you earlier. Is your cell phone dead or what?"

"Is my husband dead or what?" Abby blurted. The microwave dinged and she set the plate officiously on the table in front of an empty chair. He eyed her and sat down.

Rachel and Abby sat too, their chairs loudly raking the linoleum.

Javier wolfed down as many bites as their stares would allow. "Thanks, I'm starving."

"Talk with your mouth full," Abby said.

"In the month or so I've been gone, I went to San Diego and talked to Navy buddies, your restaurant friends, your parents. Nada. I went up and down the Mexican coast, all over the Baja. Nada. I took the most direct and sensible route from the Baja to Juarez, no one remembers a guy on a purple motorcycle and believe me in some of those sleepy villages that would have made an impression. I checked Mexican prisons, hospitals, and death records. Nada. So, I decided my initial hunch was correct, the story was bogus and went back to Juarez to find Hector Casteneda."

He gulped down a few more bites and swigged his water like he wished it was beer. "No longer in Colonia Anapra. Nobody knew anything there. Transient place, no? People come and go. I staked out Pericos Bar. Guy there said Hector wasn't a regular anymore. So I went to the maquiladoras—the foreign owned manufacturing plants. Good old NAFTA: Fortune 500 companies moved their factories for the tax breaks and cheap labor. Five or ten bucks a day those people make so they come by the hundreds of thousands and there's no place to live so they set up shanty towns and live in squalor. What a mess! Anyway, I went to their personnel offices and went over lists of employees. Keep in mind there are more than three hundred maquiladoras around Juarez. I got lucky, found him listed at about the fiftieth place I checked."

He pushed back his now-empty plate and rubbed his eyes with his palms. He hadn't shaved in days and was in the same shirt Abby had last seen him in.

"I followed him for a few days to see his routine. He lives in Juarez now, sharing a dump with ten other men. He's working two jobs. Days at the factory on an assembly line making staplers and evenings he's a part-time janitor at a motel. He never goes to bars, so it's hard to buddy up to him. He does go to church, spends long hours on his knees. I see this and figure I've found a man who feels real bad about something. So there's my angle."

He scraped his chair backward, got up and refilled his water glass, looked at it and yawned. "You have any coffee?"

Abby noticed it was nearly midnight and except for it being dark, it might have been approaching noon. She should be exhausted but felt completely awake and wired as if she had already downed an entire pot of coffee. "I'm not sure. I don't drink it anymore. Wait, I think CeCe keeps some in the freezer."

"I'll do it," he said, taking the bag from her. "Do you want some, Miss?"

Rachel nodded. "If you can talk at the same time."

"So, I hang out at the chapel for a few days when I know he's going to be there. Sit and pretend to pray in a pew near him. One night as he's leaving, I ask him if we can talk. I tell him I'm looking for my brother who I love and miss so much. He begins to weep. He is haunted by my brother's spirit who torments him for his lies. He sold his soul to the devil for a truck and some money. This Mexican-American stranger came to him when he was drunk and bribed him to tell some stories about a dead man. He wrote down and made him memorize what to say if anyone came looking, which was doubtful since it happened so far away, but just in case. Like insurance. Everything was fine until the policeman and the two beautiful women showed up. He wanted to tell the truth but the American had told him if he didn't say what had been arranged, he would know about it and kill his parents. He thought probably the cop had also been bought so he couldn't risk it though it broke his heart to lie to the widow. His parents were so afraid and ashamed of him they moved back to their village where the man could never find them. He wept and begged my forgiveness. Said he doesn't care if the American stranger comes and kills him, it would only free him from this nightmare and satisfy the dead man's ghost. He had two requests. One, don't send the police for him because he doesn't know any more than he told me. And two, give the widow this and tell her how sorry he is."

Javier dug into his frayed jeans pocket and reached for Abby's hand. He placed something in her palm, keeping his hand over hers to look into her eyes for a long moment. "I'm sorry, too."

She looked down to see Bobby's wedding band. "Oh, my God," she heard her voice sound so strangled, so disembodied from the pain coursing through her chest, knocking the wind out of her. As prepared as she thought she was, to have his wedding band burning a hole in her palm brought a crushing certainty beyond anything she could ever have imagined.

Javier caught her by her elbows and sat her in her chair.

"How do you know Casteneda's not lying now? Maybe Roberto left the ring before he left for the Baja!" Rachel sprang at Javier, pleading and crying.

Javier calmly faced her. "Hector Casteneda never met Roberto Silva. Whoever did this to him made a bad mistake. He trusted his dirty secret to a man with too much integrity and too much of a conscience to lie sober. For all the trouble he took to cover his tracks, he bribed the wrong man. Amazing when you consider the odds."

"I want to know who did this and why," Abby said, putting Bobby's ring on her swollen finger. Still too big. "I want to see my husband's body and give him a proper burial. What are you going to do now?"

Javier poured himself a cup of coffee, took some quick sips and sat back down.

Rachel sat back down next to Abby. She could still feel her resistance, her struggle to accept that Bobby was lost to them both. Abby reached over, touched her arm, "Are you all right?"

Her eyes flickered. "There has to be another explanation. We just have to think of it."

"We owe it to him to find out who did this and not let them get away with it," Abby said sternly.

Javier nodded. "Hector begged me to take the truck, he was sickened by the sight of it. He never pawned the ring no matter how bad he needed the money. I had to force him to take some money for his honesty. He'll probably give it to the church or send it to his parents. I tried to tell him Roberto Silva is happy with him now and he will have peace. Whatever happened to your husband happened here in Esperanza on the night he disappeared. I'm sure of that. He knew personal things about him to get Hector to repeat. I think it's someone who knew him. I think the guy

Hector met could have just been hired to do the job, not the actual killer, but it could have been. What I can't figure out is, why go to such trouble, why not just put his body in the truck and set it on fire out on the West Mesa like everyone else, or send it off a cliff in the mountains?"

Abby said, "It sounds so hopeless. Like we're at the end of the road."

Javier drained his coffee cup, got up and poured another. "No, no, we're just getting started. Now we know we have a murder investigation. I'm taking the truck up to Albuquerque tonight. I have a buddy in the FBI field station there. I'm not trusting it to Bowman. The Feds will go over it for evidence. Bowman will reopen the investigation. Repost the reward money, after over four months somebody might be ready to talk. I'll start with who was at his father's funeral, who was around the bar, who knew he was coming home, who Bobby might have gone out looking for that night. Anybody who for any reason wouldn't have been happy to see him. Who stood to lose something or wanted something from him he wouldn't give. It starts with everyone closest to him and spreads out from there. I have to know every little family secret to find motives. No one is above suspicion. We're so close now, I can taste it. After this miraculous break, we'll solve this case."

Rachel left Abby's as soon as Javier fired up Ricardo's truck and headed for Albuquerque. She stumbled around under the stars and full moon feeling betrayed by everything that was holy, everything her parents said was up there, watching over all of them, keeping them safe. Javier called Roberto "the body"! *This can't be!* It tore at her, ruthless talons ripping into those places already shredded by Maria's lies and death. How could she contain all of this pain, all of this dreadful bullshit that just wouldn't go away, one thing after the next, each more terrible than the preceding. Her precious Roberto—her brother, her lover, her friend—was dead. How ridiculous her claim on him had been, how pathetically inconsequential all of that was now.

She ran in circles like a mad woman, crying and wailing at the heavens until in her exhaustion, she sought refuge in the goat barn, curling up like a mortally wounded animal waiting to die. She stayed there all night with Buster, her weathered male, who that morning had snuffled her and tasted her collar as she sat in his stall. He never failed to love her. Feeling completely unworthy yet undeniably starved for this comfort, she scratched his long sloping brown ears and convex nuzzle, on up to where his horns would be had he not been de-budded as a baby. Her sleepless night, her hysterical rage and grief left her calmer for the moment.

Abby had believed Roberto dead weeks ago but had still been devastated by Javier's confirmation. Even though reason said too much time had passed for Roberto to be safe, even though Maria's promises turned into lies, Rachel had still been praying for the day of Roberto's return to her. Like a scene from a classic movie, it had played over and over again in her head. Now what? Just stare at a blank screen? How could she grieve the loss of him? She had only begun to grieve for his unborn child. Now him? Whose God do you have to believe in anyway to protect you from this hell? Her father's and the community's Catholicism? They all feared God and his retribution for every little sin, which was everything and anything, it seemed. Her ex-flower-child mother's benevolent supreme being? That one-with-everything crap? What the hell did that mean, anyway? Who knew how her Jewish God would explain any of this. With Maria's sorcery thrown into the mix, Rachel didn't know what to believe. Her life had been a lie, so how could she reach within for any truth?

But today. Right now. She needed a God. A God to confront. A God to blame. Try as she might, the blame kept landing back on herself.

She closed her eyes, and tried to remember Roberto's face. The one she had seen when he had come home for his father's funeral. He had changed a lot. She had been surprised. There, in his suit and salon-cut hair. Obviously well-fed and happy. His face had changed from when he was a young man. He called himself "Bobby." Had she known that that was going to be her last time to be with him, she would have been more observant, pressed the memory indelibly into her soul. She should have seen him for the man he had become, not the fantasy she wanted him to be. Were her tears for the loss of him or the dream? Without Maria around, she stood without the smoke and mirrors and without the belief that you can always do something about a situation to change it, enhance it, or kill it. No more abracadabra. Damn her! Maria should have told her that sometimes you just have to come out with your hands up, and that letting go was far easier than hanging on. Instead, they had interacted as if they were playing dolls. Everything made up and with happy endings. The rug had been pulled out from under her fantasy world. She had fallen hard and was still falling. She resisted the idea of surrender with every fiber of her being and yet in her exhausted, defeated state it beckoned with loving open arms.

Buster's two stomachs rumbled and belched up a jowl-full of cud that he chewed lazily. The sweet, mother's milk scent of alfalfa lingered and his rhythmic chewing lulled her to sleep.

"I thought I'd find you here," she heard her mother's voice say. "Abby called. I know about Bobby."

She opened her eyes and saw CeCe standing at the stall wearing an old calico dress with her hair loosely braided and over one shoulder. Buster got up and went to her wagging his tail. "Thought I might check on you before I went over to finish the nursery. Wanted to see if you needed help with anything . . ."

Humiliated in front of her mother, Rachel wondered how tear-streaked her face looked, how exposed her wounds. She felt like there must be huge pools of drying blood saturating the straw around her. But instead of worrying about what her mother might be seeing, she instead looked more closely at her mother. She saw sleep-deprived, swollen, reddened eyes. She saw deep lines of heartbreaking grief for CeCe's surrogate son. She saw concern for her, her daughter. She saw love. Rachel stumbled to stand in the straw, her arms outstretched, "Oh, Mom!"

CeCe caught her and they sobbed in each other's hair, arms wrapped so tightly around heaving backs it was hard to tell where one ended and the other began.

"CeCe's demanding I stay here this afternoon while she's painting and if the fumes are still strong, I may have to spend the night," Abby said.

Rachel nodded. The black circles under her eyes were even more prominent today. Abby doubted she'd slept at all after Javier finally left long after midnight. She almost felt guilty for having slept so soundly. The sleep of the dead, Bobby used to say.

"Don't feel like you have to baby-sit me. I know where everything is. You could go rest or something."

"No, it's okay." Rachel walked with her into the living room. They both sat on the oversize Southwest-patterned sofa. It was so quiet in the room, the ticking of the antique grandfather clock reverberated over the shiny brick floors. The afternoon light was diffuse as it found its way through the tangle of honeysuckle vines at the window, casting faint shadows on the creamy plaster of the adobe walls.

The silence was companionable. The silence held their sorrow and united their hurting hearts.

"I just keep asking myself who would do this to Roberto, everyone loved him," Rachel said. "Who do you think Javier will interview?"

"All of us, like he said. The fact that everyone loved him doesn't mean anything in a murder investigation. People kill people they love all the time. I could be the jealous wife who resented him for dragging me out here so that he could be near his lover. You could be the jealous lover who killed him when he wouldn't come back to you. Charlie could have killed him because he threatened his plans to reunite with you. Either one of your parents could have done it to protect Charlie's interests and protect you from yourself."

"That's crazy! Javier doesn't believe any of that, does he?"

"He's got to consider anyone and everyone at this point."

"When I couldn't sleep, I tried to think if there was anyone from high school who had a grudge against him or someone from the community." Rachel shook her head. "I was the hothead who constantly got into it with people. He was voted best-liked in the class."

"I put out the press release this morning, reactivating the reward. Javier got the truck up to the FBI and is meeting with Sheriff Bowman as we speak. We'll just have to let them do their jobs."

"How can you be so calm, so resigned? I'm so angry—so pissed! How dare anyone do this to him, to us!" Rachel yelled against the ages-old adobe walls, her words echoing against them before being swallowed by the wooden-beam *latillas* overhead in the ceiling.

Abby hesitated. There was no explaining, no words that could convey to Rachel all she had already gone through since the night Bobby disappeared. She had been accused of wanting him dead rather than holding out hope, when all the while his soul had been whispering to hers that he was gone and it wasn't his fault. The shock of it that Rachel was now feeling, and the bitter all-consuming rage, well, she had been there and done that. She had struggled and wrestled with it and fought against it in some private hellish battle all summer, until forced to surrender, powerless to achieve any other outcome. Surrender. And like her, eventually Rachel will be forced to feel the bottomless pit, the cavernous depths of resigned grief. The vast emptiness of immeasurable sadness that somehow fills you until there is no room for anything else. But it was impossible to explain all of that. So she merely shrugged. "It doesn't bring him back and it's not good for the baby."

Rachel tugged nervously at the fringe on the pillow she was holding. "What Javier said about family secrets . . . How much are you going to tell him?"

Abby felt the weight of Bobby's wedding band against her heart, next to hers on the dog-tag chain. Her baby shifted in the tight space of her womb. "I burned all the letters in the fireplace after you left. There was nothing in them of any use, wouldn't you agree?"

Rachel looked at her with relief. She exhaled and hugged the pillow tightly to her chest.

"Whatever else he hears is up to you or whoever else knows something around here," Abby said. "I've already told him everything I know."

"Anybody Javier wants to ask in Esperanza knows about Roberto and me being tight in high school. Maria took the rest of it with her to her grave."

"So did Bobby."

"And so will I," Rachel said, pressing the pillow to her eyes.

Abby felt herself drift into a light sleep shortly after Rachel began to doze on the opposite end of the sofa. The grandfather clock was ticking off the moments until her baby was born, ticking off the time that she was surviving Bobby's death. She stopped herself from considering how far those seconds stretched out before her, like some endless road she was sentenced to travel without him by her side. She could think only as far ahead as the birth of their baby and leaving this place that had taken him from her.

She woke to see Charlie sitting in the big brown leather chair next to the sofa. He sipped a cup of coffee. He was dressed like he'd been to town: clean white shirt, newer jeans. The window behind him revealed October was arriving and September was taking the last remnants of summer with it. Leaves flew and rustled against the flagstone patio, as if an invisible witch stirred them with her broom. The sky was brooding.

Abby met Charlie's eyes over the rim of his coffee mug. She started to get up. He set his mug down and was there to assist her. As she stood he put his arms around her in consolation. Her face pressed into his sweet-smelling neck and she cried silent warm tears, so grateful for his constantly accurate sense of her, his ability to know without words.

He held her, a gentle sway made it feel like a dance suspending time and all that came before and all that lay ahead fell away and there was only this safe moment of comfort.

When she did register the ticking of the clock once more as it crowded out the softer rhythm of Charlie's heart and quiet breaths, she had no idea how long they had stood like this. Without moving her head from his chest, she saw Rachel's wide-eyed stare. As she met her gaze, she didn't release Charlie right away. She shut her own eyes and hugged him tighter, treasuring his boundless worth, the sheer wonder of him. Then she let him go.

Charlie smoothed her hair and then stopped when he noticed Rachel watching. "Rachel."

"Charlie."

"I'm sorry about the news. I was just over at the sheriff's with Javier. He's taking statements."

Miguel joined them, carrying his own tall mug of coffee, also dressed for town. "You should see what that woman is doing in your nursery! It's a work of art! Hello, mi'ja," he leaned down to kiss his daughter's head.

"Hi, Papa." Rachel managed a brief smile.

"Abby, I'm so sorry for your loss. We will all miss him terribly. He was a good man."

Abby nodded and accepted his formal hug.

When Miguel sat on the other brown leather chair, they all sat as if he were the minister of their flock. "Before I forget, CeCe said we are having dinner in about an hour and a half. It's a matter of heating up the green chile chicken stew and making some fresh tortillas. I invited Javier but he said he'll be working late, interviewing people before they have a chance to think too long about what they should say or talk too much among themselves. Ramone is assisting him."

"Did he say how it's going?" Abby asked.

"He hasn't said. He's just taking command. It's funny to see old Bowman looking as useless as teats on a bull. He's been shamed you know, for how wrong he's been."

Abby nodded. Small satisfaction.

"Any hint to how he's going about this?" Rachel asked.

"He's gathering every detail from the moment Abby and Bobby first arrived, the funeral, everything until he left the bar around nine-thirty that night. It happened sometime between then and when the guy drove the truck over the border, which the tape clocked at four a.m. So figuring around four to five hours down there, probably closer to five with how old the truck is, that leaves a window of opportunity of maybe an hour and a half."

"Who all was at the bar again?" Charlie asked.

"Pablo, his nephew Milo, Sammy West, and Maria," Miguel said, his fingers counting against the side of his coffee mug. "But he's not limiting himself to them. There were forty-some at the funeral and twenty of those came back here afterward. He's compiling lists. Everyone will have to account for themselves between nine-thirty and eleven p.m. that night. The only one who left the bar before closing was Maria. She followed Bobby out."

"Mi Dios!" Rachel blurted.

"What is it?" Miguel asked as Rachel got up and ran from the room.

Rachel walked in frantic circles in the kitchen. Had Maria done it? She could have! She had tried to kill Abby's baby and maybe even Abby, so she knew Maria might be capable of such a thing. But why would she want to kill Roberto? That didn't make sense. But the diabetes had gotten the best of her thinking, which had become pretty twisted. Maybe that night at the bar she had confronted him, told him to go back to Rachel and he had refused, told her how much he loved his wife. Would that drive Maria into a murderous rage? Knowing her potions and magic would be useless, had she chosen another weapon?

She clanked around the dishes, pots, and pans in the cabinet to start dinner and to let the others know where she was, so nobody would come looking for her. Her mother's hot green chile chicken stew was never served without fresh flour tortillas drenched in honey butter and brewed-that-day iced tea. It gave her an escape from the others and their questioning eyes.

Maria had probably followed Roberto to the bar. But what happened after he stepped outside, angry, drunk, and vulnerable? Maria knew. Rachel knew her own selfish obsession with Roberto had fueled the fires in Maria's twisted mind. More guilt surged through her veins, turning her blood black and thick.

She carried the pot of tea water to the burner that sometimes needed a little help with a match to light. This time it didn't. Lucky for it. She wouldn't have been able to contain any more anger. She was so angry with Maria. For being dead, for being such a liar and a fraud, and for letting herself get so sick and so screwed up that murder could become just another option.

She practically collapsed into the large glass bowl of flour she held in her hands to make tortillas, and then slid down the counter and lower cabinets like spilled pancake batter. She sat and cried into her knees and prayed to God that Maria had not killed Roberto, because if she had, how could she survive it?

Chapter 23

Abby pulled up the quilt she had kicked off sometime in the night. The chill of the morning kept her in bed. Yet there was nowhere she felt more alone. She closed her eyes against the growing light of the intruding day. The ghost of Bobby pulled her to him, welcomed her icicle toes against his ever-warm flesh, and strongly massaged that place in her low back that constantly ached. Bobby's ghost insisted she transcend boundaries of reason and so-called reality, because if she was lonely, what the hell was he? Bobby's ghost convinced her it was selfish to deny him. She must be brave enough to reach for him across the dimensions, he told her. They had crossed boundaries before for their love and after all, flesh is the illusion. Flesh gives rise to the lines we draw deciding who to love, who to hate, who is inferior, who is privileged. It traps us in circumstance. She must learn how to let her soul lead the way to him. It might take practice, but he wasn't going anywhere.

The phone rang and Abby felt herself jerk as if she were landing with a thud back into the housing of her own body. "Hello?"

"Are you sleeping, girlfriend?"

"No, I was traveling out of my body to be with Bobby."

Edward's sigh was loud in her ear. "We got to get you home, no doubt about it."

"Don't worry. It's a round trip ticket. Bobby knows I have a job to do here, having his baby, living on earth another sixty or seventy years. He just wants his fair share."

"I wish I could find a man that loyal, that persistent. I can't get my boyfriend to even drive down from La Jolla—"

Abby laughed. "Stay with the living—definite advantages. God, I can't believe I can laugh. It feels so weirdly good."

"I have news, girlfriend, news that proves San Diego is where you belong. It's like the universe is building big neon signs for you. Margaret is moving out!"

"Get out of here! Madam Margaret is finally leaving?" Abby could instantly smell the dusty dankness of the antique shop that had been ensconced next to her restaurant forever. The obstacle that had long prevented Abigail's from expanding.

"She told Paul she's going to get rid of everything and move to Portugal. A psychic told her to do it. Paul said if he knew it was that easy he would have paid off some psychic years ago."

"So you can finally have her space."

"We can finally have her space! You can have her space—she's selling the condo, too, and the timing is perfect. She's leaving after the holidays, in January. You'll live next to Paul and Sandy and the babies can play together—I think I'm going to cry!"

Abby let herself imagine it. Back above the restaurant. Her friends nearby.

"Abby—did you ever answer Mommy Dearest's letter?"

"No."

"How much would you come into? Come on, tell me. Is it like tens of millions?"

"I'm not selling out for any amount. I don't need their money."

"Hundreds of millions?"

"Something like that, but that's not the point—"

"Abby! Think of your baby! Think of your friend Edward! Don't let your feud stand in the way of what is rightfully yours. Grow up already. You don't have to sell your soul to claim your trust fund. Think about all the good you could do with that kind of money. You could really piss them off! You could put money into college funds for Hispanics—a culinary arts school for kids from the barrio—or HIV research—"

"Bobby would have a fit if I took their money."

"Abby, I'm sorry, but this isn't about Bobby anymore. It's about you and your future and your baby's future and generations beyond that. What better way to correct the sins of your parents than to take their money and put it toward good? They're going to die someday—you want all that money going into the hands of their evil lawyers to spend the way they decide in their twisted wills? God forbid it go to the Republican Party! Mommy opened the door—if you pretend to make nice, you get to control what happens. You have a responsibility, like it or not. And that's more important than your silly pride."

"It's not that simple," Abby said, imagining the "making nice" part. Even if she never said it or meant it, taking her mother up on her second chance was tantamount to saying her parents had been right. Was that silly pride or respect for Bobby's memory? Would reclaiming her trust fund and inheritance be a betrayal or the smartest way to take care of herself and her baby? "I'll think about it. I have to go—CeCe's on her way over to unveil the nursery and I'm still in bed."

"I'm going to say this and then I'll shut up. Think about how Bobby's biggest concern now would be for you and his baby to live in comfort without the stress or separation of you having to work too hard. He would never want to stand in the way of whatever would give you that freedom. Okay—I'm done saying my piece."

"That'll be the day," Abby said as she hung up.

"Okay now, no peeking, I'll lead you from here." CeCe held her hand as Abby took tiny steps behind her, her eyes squeezed shut. The walk from the kitchen to the nursery seemed endless.

"Ta-da!" CeCe let go of her hand.

Abby stood in the doorway, stunned by the transformation. CeCe had hand-painted murals that wrapped seamlessly around all four walls. New Mexico scenery in all of its enchantment: purple-hued mountains, turquoise skies, the salmon tones of the earth dotted with green shrubs and patches of colorful wildflowers, a jackrabbit here, a herd of wild horses in a distant canyon, a red-tailed hawk soaring high, a pair of hummingbirds hovering low over the flower tops, all in the soft natural tones of watercolors.

"This is incredible," Abby breathed. "How did you do this so fast, only two days? And a quilt and curtains. CeCe, this is too much!"

CeCe beamed. "You like it, right? I've had it sketched out for weeks now. God it felt good to get into my painting again, to have the excuse, you know? There weren't really any fumes, I just needed the time. You like the colors?"

"They're perfect. I can't stand all those pink-and-blue cutesy nurseries." She walked over to the dresser and found it stocked with baby undershirts, disposable diapers, and nightgowns. A stack of receiving blankets were neatly folded at the head of the crib, now graced with a patchwork quilt that pulled the soft turquoise, beige and salmon tones from the walls. Matching curtains, a soft beige oval area rug, a rocking chair Abby remembered CeCe picking up at an antique store in Albuquerque months before, now with an overstuffed cushion seat.

"Sit down. It's really comfortable. Just what your sore bottom will need."

Abby sat, stunned. "You're just too wonderful. My own mother never would have . . ."

"That's what you got me for, kid. I had a blast! This is all my latent grandma frustration coming out. And it was practice, too. I needed to see what I could do after all this time. I want to do one in our new coffee shop. We finally closed on the place. Did Rachel tell you? We got the place for a song so the cheese-business profits will cover the payments and we don't even have to worry about making money the first year on the coffee shop."

"That's great. Rachel said she was going to be interviewing for some help with the cheese business."

"What a great thing for her, and all your idea. And that idea led to taking the coffee shop—I'm already planning the start-up menu. I've always dreamed of having a little place like that. I want it to be a real community hangout, local musicians, poetry readings, a place where teenagers can go after school. I got all kinds of ideas. Rachel can run her cheese business in the back kitchens and office, you and little Whosit can drop in—I already have a playpen. Later on, if you get in the mood, you can add some specials to the menu."

Abby let herself go with it and could even envision herself in the middle of CeCe's vividly painted dream, until she remembered that someone in the community CeCe longed to nurture had killed her husband.

"CeCe, it's just so hard to think about bringing a new life into all of this . . . death. I live every second with this terrible thing!"

CeCe dropped to the rug in front of her, leaned up to what was left of Abby's ever-shrinking lap to squeeze her hand. "I know you do. We're going to find who did this, I can feel it. But life does this, you know? We get the worst of times and the best of times, sometimes right on top of each other. The thing is, you're not alone. This baby has a whole crowd waiting for it. That's what this room is all about. I could see you just couldn't deal with it. I was thrilled to do it. We're all here for each other and it's not a burden or a favor. It's just love, that's all."

Abby wiped her face, trying to get herself back together. "Don't forget, Santi's open house starts at seven tonight. He's so excited we're all going to be there, even if we're not his real family."

"We're as real as it gets, sweetie."

There was a loud knocking at the back door and voices calling.

CeCe laughed. "Here's your surprise baby shower."

Hazel, Carmen, Bonnie, and Rachel were carrying trays of food and bundles of wrapped presents, all talking at once.

"Oh my God, this is lovely!" Abby grinned. In light of everything, she hadn't even thought about this simple female tradition and yet now that it was happening, it felt so right. She loved them for knowing how important it was to do this, no matter what.

"My white layer cake is a little lopsided and I'm sure it isn't as good as CeCe can make, but she had her hands full with the nursery," Carmen said, her little sparrow eyes twinkling.

"It's perfect!" Abby assured her, noticing the real flowers Carmen had used to decorate the top.

"Don't worry. I made her put chocolate fudge between the layers," Bonnie said, starting to reach a long fingernail toward it for a taste, but getting smacked away by Carmen.

Hazel uncovered a large bowl. "Before we raise your blood sugar to new heights, we'll have some of this healthy chef salad I made for brunch. You need your protein and vegetables!"

They sat around the table, laughing and eating. Even Rachel participated, emanating a gentle energy. Her hair was in a beautiful French braid that she gave her mother credit for and she wore a lovely floral-print skirt with a white sweater set.

"Come on, let's get to the gifts," Carmen said, starting to clear the dishes.

"Oh leave those, we can open the gifts in the living room," Abby said.

They ignored her, of course. The three older women buzzed about her kitchen while she and Rachel carried the gifts into the living room.

"Come see the nursery," Abby said to her.

Rachel nodded and followed.

"Wow," she exclaimed, seeing the mural. She stood back and silently let her eyes take it all in, turning in a slow circle. "This is absolutely amazing," she breathed.

"Your mom is absolutely amazing," Abby said.

Rachel smiled. "I'm starting to realize that."

Their gifts were each unique and a part of themselves. Hazel gave her an entire carved Noah's Ark set, each animal smoothly sanded and polished with nontoxic vegetable oil, so it would safe for a toddler to play with. Carmen had cross-stitched a baby pillow and sheet set with baby ducks and chicks. Bonnie had crocheted a matching baby sweater, hat, and booties with her rainbow yarn. And Rachel presented her with some children's books by New Mexico author Rudolfo Anaya. *Maya's Children: The Story of La Llorona* and *The Farolitos of Christmas,* both gorgeously illustrated.

"I love these!" Abby breathed, flipping through the pages. She turned to the back and looked at the author's picture. A very handsome older Hispanic man, with wisdom and light emanating from his eyes. He could have been Bobby thirty years from now. She sighed as her heart felt the knowledge she would never see him in his later life. He would stay forever young as she aged over the coming decades.

She closed the books and held them against her chest, her eyes welling with tears. "Thank you Rachel, these will be perfect for Bobby's child. All of these gifts are so wonderful . . ." She trailed off as her trembling smile lost the battle against her coming tears.

The books slid from her arms as she was enveloped into the embrace of strong women's arms, soft female scents and loving voices whispering in her ears like angels.

Santiago showed up just as Abby stepped out of her back door to look for him. He darted over the field as if someone had sicced the hounds on him, but not even Bésame was at his heels.

His slicked-down hair reminded Abby to remind CeCe he would need a haircut soon. He was wearing a pair of jeans she had found for him at the thrift store, gently worn but not so new that his father would catch on, and an oversized red University of New Mexico Lobos T-shirt that Charlie had given him. Where his father thought his clothes came from or why his hair never seemed to need to be cut was beyond her. Maybe he just didn't care anymore.

"You look like a million bucks! Ready to go?" She opened the car doors.

"Yeah, my dad and uncle aren't even home so it was easy to get away. Where's everybody else?" he asked, climbing in and buckling his seat belt.

"We're meeting them at the school. Don't worry, they won't forget."

The school parking lot was so full that cars and pickups were starting to park along the highway in the grass. They met up with the Vigils and Charlie just outside the cafeteria where there was a short program hosted by Mrs. Kirk. Abby felt the stares in her direction had shifted, changed in quality. Previously, she was the pitiful city woman who couldn't keep her husband from roaming. Now she was one of them, the designated village widow, and the looks were etched with sympathy and respect.

Mrs. Kirk was wrapping up her presentation. "You will have an hour to visit your child's classroom and then you are invited back here where the PTA will serve refreshments. Thank you all for supporting your students and this school with your attendance here this evening. I'm sure this will be a very successful school year here at Bosque Farms Elementary, and remember, my door is always open and I'm listed in the phone book if you have any questions or concerns."

Santiago was like an excited puppy who didn't know which way to turn. He gravitated first to Rachel, then to CeCe, looking back at Abby all the while. Then he stepped up to keep pace with Charlie and Miguel as they made their way down the hallway to his classroom. Finally he settled on walking between the two men, but kept his eye on Abby, CeCe, and Rachel as they trailed behind.

Miss Archuletta, his impossibly young teacher, greeted them at the door. "Santiago told me you were all coming! I'm so happy to meet you! He's such a wonderful student and so well behaved. Santiago, show them to your desk. He has a folder of all of his work so far this year."

His desk was in the front row by the windows. They gathered around as Santi opened the blue construction paper folder that he had decorated with gold and silver stick-on stars. "Look at all these papers! I can't believe how hard I worked already this year and it's only the first month. This is more than all the papers I did last year!"

Rachel leaned down and kissed him on top of his head. "We're so proud of you, mi'jo!"

"You said 'my son.'" Santi grinned.

"So? You want to make something out of it?" she teased.

"Whatever!" He blushed and grinned so wide Abby could see he'd finally lost that loose bicuspid he wouldn't let her near. "I can't stop you!"

Abby watched as Rachel hugged him against his fake protests, while Charlie looked on with unabashed worship.

"Take it like a man, Santi," Miguel advised. "It's easier that way. That's what I do when they start all that mushy stuff, just pretend you like it."

"Pretend, huh?" CeCe laughed. "I'm nominating you for the academy award."

The room was full of parents and grandparents of the students, all talking at once or laughing as younger siblings or cousins chased each other around the room. Abby looked on, letting herself imagine her own child here in this atmosphere of unrestrained enthusiasm. It was in stark contrast to the formal proceedings held at her private San Diego grade school, associated not with celebration but with critical scrutiny. She remembered the panicked thumping in her thin chest as her parents compared her work with her fellow students, her teachers who equated a stern and stiff demeanor with optimal student performance and the all-important approval of the parents whose large tuition checks paid their bloated salaries.

San Diego must have something like this somewhere, she would just have to do some research when she returned, that was all.

"What the hell is going on here!" a loud male voice boomed over the din, which quickly silenced the room. "What do you think you're doing with my son?"

"Oh no," Santi said, shrinking back behind Miguel. "It's my dad!"

"Get over here, you little shit! What I tell you about sneaking off when my back is turned? I been looking all over for you!"

"Señior Baca, Miguel Vigil." He put out his hand, which Baca ignored. "Why don't we step out into the hall to sort out this misunderstanding—"

"I don't need to step nowhere! My son is coming with me!" Baca weaved where he stood, the strong smell of alcohol and cigarettes wafted around him. His hair was shaved close to his sweating scalp. Poorly done amateur tattoos lined his gesticulating arms. Sunglasses hid his eyes, though it was well after sunset.

Miguel spoke so softly to him that Abby could barely hear what he was saying. "We meant no disrespect to you as his father. We simply wanted to show our support as his friends, that's all."

His responses were still too loud but somewhat less agitated. "We don't need no support. Santiago, your goddammed dog was at it with my roosters again. What did I tell you?"

"Sorry, Papa." Santi's head was hung and he assumed the posture and expression he had when Abby first met him.

"Mr. Baca, I'm Miss Archuletta, Santiago's teacher. I'm so happy you could join us tonight." She smiled as warmly as if he were the president of the United States gracing her classroom with an impromptu visit. "Come over here, I'd like to show you privately, in my grade book, how Santiago is doing so far this year."

He looked her up and down a moment and then smoothed his index finger across the stubble above his upper lip. "Yeah, sure. Santi didn't tell me his teacher was so pretty or I'd have been around here sooner." He followed her to her desk, his strut so like any of his roosters. The room resumed its previous noise level.

"What are we going to do? We can't let him drive Santi home in that condition," CeCe said.

Miguel nodded. "I think all of you should go on ahead, take Santi. Leave me the pickup. I'll tell him Santi wanted to go home to tie up his dog or something. It'll be okay. I can handle him."

After they managed to slip out into the hallway, Abby put her arm around a dazed Santi and tipped his face up so that she could look into his eyes. "Don't let him take this away from you. We're all so proud of you. Hold your head up high and walk tall, you're the star pupil around here. He can't ruin that."

Santiago's eyes began to well with tears. "He made a fool out of me."

"He made a fool out of himself, not you. Everyone can see that."

CeCe and Rachel stood by. Rachel seethed with anger. "You are not him, mi'jo, and you will never become him because we won't let you! Now I'm not leaving this place until I have some of those damn cookies and punch—what about you?"

Santi nodded and a tentative smile formed. "Damn cookies are my favorite."

Rachel could tell by the knock it was her father at her bedroom door. She was lying on her side on her bed looking at old photos she took of Roberto years ago with an Instamatic camera she had gotten for her fourteenth birthday. She remembered what a willing subject Roberto had been and together they instamatically became obnoxious and obsessive with picture taking. "Come in," she called out, seeing Roberto's silly poses and smiles disappear as she shuffled them under the bedclothes.

Papa looked tired. Talking and thinking tired. He perched himself on the edge of the bed. "They have a warrant to go through Maria's house. They say it's routine under these circumstances. Thought you'd want to come with me."

As they rode in silence to Maria's, Rachel finally thought of Reyes and how Maria's death would affect him. She knew how unstable he was. Maybe he would go on some kind of rampage. She couldn't even remember for sure if he had been at the funeral, so many people had appeared out of the woodwork to pay their respects.

"Papa, what about Reyes? I mean, do you think he'll be there?"

"I didn't even think about it. I forget he's even there. Do you think Maria would want for him to stay on and live there? Is he even capable of taking care of himself?"

She felt such guilt and responsibility for everything, now there was something else for her to add to the list. As much as Maria had refrained from treating him like a son, he was her dependent and he deserved something for his years of hard work and loyalty. But Rachel would be happy and feel safer if he wasn't around, especially now that Maria wasn't there to structure his time. "You're her real heir, Papa. I think you should decide."

Miguel jiggled the key into the lock on Maria's front door. Probably first time he'd ever used it in all those years. Rachel never remembered Maria locking her door.

He allowed Sheriff Bowman, Javier, and Rachel in first as he pushed the door, which opened like a wide, lazy yawn. There were no candles lit in the foyer. Jesus was in the dark. The house smelled from years of smudgings and boiled herbs. The aroma caught Rachel by surprise and jerked her to tears she swallowed back. She had hoped her anger would ward off any feelings of nostalgia. Through the kitchen window she noticed the marigolds still standing bright and proud around the spent tomato plant cemetery.

"Don't touch anything," the sheriff said, snapping on a pair of latex gloves. "This could be a crime scene." She almost passed out when he said that, but instead hooked her arm into her father's and he gave it a reassuring squeeze.

"We'll be careful," said Javier, giving them a wink. "Thought you might need some answers along the way, you being Anglo and her being a bruja and all. Gives a big cultural slant on what we consider normal household items. Besides, without the body, we don't even know what we're looking for."

"He had a name, for Christ's sake! It's Bobby!" she cried, confirming the man he'd become for the first time, respecting the name he had chosen for himself. The silence hung there a moment like a dead body on a rope, and the three of them stared at her.

"Look! Someone's been here," the skinny sheriff said. His yellow hair was more yellowed by all the nicotine, and he looked like a pesky dandelion. He pointed in the old enamel sink at a saucepan filled with soapy water.

"Her ward, Reyes Saavedra, lives here," her father supplied.

"Where's this guy's room?" Javier asked.

"He lives in the converted garage," Rachel said.

The men went first. She stood for a moment feeling a cool gust of air move past her legs, and thought she saw a shadow move from the corner of her eye. "Maria?" she couldn't help but whisper, so strong was her presence in the room. If anyone could defy the boundaries of death it would be her. But there was such stillness in the half-light, it was like a photograph, devoid of all life. She fled the room before her tears could come.

The three men were staring slack-mouthed at the walls of Reyes's room when she got there. There were pictures tacked everywhere. Pictures of her. Pictures of her and Roberto, only Roberto had been intricately cut out with a small penknife in some, and ferociously ripped out in others. What the hell?

"Do these belong to you?" asked Sheriff Bowman, holding out a handful of her panties, some new, some that she hadn't seen in years. She thought those had become casualties of her divorce. Just missing in action.

"He has my panties?" she asked, suddenly feeling strangely detached and faint. This wasn't happening.

"Mi Dios," her father said, so calmly it sent a shiver from the end of her tailbone up to a tingling in her scalp. He fondled a crocheted baby hat of hers she could not remember having. It hung there, innocent and white next to a pornographic drawing of a female with a photo of Rachel's head attached. Newspaper articles about Bobby being missing hung all over the wall like streamers.

Bile and puke rose in her throat as she couldn't help staring at the collage in disbelief. All this time he'd been having these thoughts about her? That explained his lascivious behavior and jealousy toward Bobby. "He might have killed Bobby!" she blurted, her trembling hand covering her mouth, holding back a scream that threatened to rise from her throbbing throat. "To get him out of the way—because of me!"

The sheriff slipped his finger in the drawer pull of the pine nightstand and pulled out the drawer. A thirty-eight revolver lay there sleeping like a vampire. Could that be the weapon that killed Bobby?

"What's going on?" Reyes shouted from the doorway, scaring the shit out of all of them, especially Rachel who inched closer to her father. He was carrying a case of beer to put into the small refrigerator Rachel had bought for him at a garage sale.

"Sir, you're going to need to come with us," the sheriff said, walking toward him, hand readied for his handcuffs and billy club. "We need to ask you a few questions."

Reyes threw the case of beer at him and took off running. They all scuffled after him and stood on the front porch as he hauled it across the property, Javier in fast pursuit. There were garblings back and forth on the sheriff's walkie-talkie as he gave specific directions and descriptions to his officers. "He may be dangerous," Sheriff Bowman warned, "may be armed."

"Ten-four," said the officers over their walkies.

Sheriff Bowman brought the bulky black walkie-talkie close to his mouth. In light of the recent bad publicity surrounding local authorities' overzealous shootings of suspects he added, "And for Pete's sake, try not to shoot this one dead!"

Chapter 24

Abby sat in her rocking chair. Her eyes drifted over the mural, finding little details she had missed before, like the blue tail lizard sunning itself on a boulder.

This was a room for a child who loves the outdoors. Rugged beauty, delicate nature brought inside to soothe, to inspire. A child like Bobby.

How a man like him could have spent so much of his life in a confined space, submerged in the depths of the ocean was a mystery. But once he broke surface, he surfed its waves, scaled mountains, slept under the stars. Earth was his playground.

There was so much he would miss. If he had some kind of consciousness that survived his death, she could only pray he was somehow spared the intensity of his human attachment. The torture of losing her and the chance to raise his child, everything ripped from his grasp against his will, down to his very last breath. A man so full of life had so much more to lose.

If her own grief weren't enough, she felt his, too. And the grief for their child, an innocent incapable of knowing all that he or she had lost. She carried the sadness for all three of them.

The future that lurked just beyond the perfection of the world CeCe had created on these walls paralyzed her. Alone, she must make every decision that would also affect her child. She would have to provide not only her own portion of nurturance and guidance, but Bobby's as well. The weight of it kept her in her chair.

At least in San Diego she would be back in her element. Her business contacts gave her so many more lucrative options, and as the sole breadwinner she had to be practical. She was still going back and forth about her parent's offer. Her head agreed with Edward's argument, but her gut still rejected the charade it would entail. Maybe Edward was right. Maybe the statement she and Bobby had made was moot now. Should her pride or some wish to avenge Bobby's mistreatment by them still be the determining factor? Or was that unfair to her unborn child and the countless, nameless people who could be helped by that much money? What would he want her to do?

"Abby!" Rachel's voice, from the kitchen.

"In here," Abby yelled back, still unwilling to move.

Rachel appeared in the nursery doorway, a disheveled tear-stained mess.

"Jesus, now what?" Abby didn't want to know.

"It's all my fault! He killed Bobby because he knew I wanted him!"

"Charlie wouldn't—"

"Not Charlie! Reyes! That's how he knew—he heard Maria and me! They just arrested him. God, he had pictures of me with Bobby—with Bobby crossed out and pornography with my face on it! And newspaper clippings about Bobby being missing and my underwear in his bed!"

As shocking as this was, Abby stopped to notice Rachel was not referring to Bobby as Roberto. "Did he confess?"

She paced back and forth in the small room, her chest heaving, wiping at her tears with a clenched fist. "No, he denies it. They found a gun."

Abby sat quietly. Her feelings were somewhere else, beyond the mountains and mesas spread out in front of her.

"How can I live with this! He spied on us—Maria and I were talking and scheming about getting him back—if I hadn't wanted him so much—he'd still be alive! I'm so sorry, Abby! Bobby—I'm so sorry!"

Abby stood up then and caught Rachel by the shoulders, "Stop it! Just stop it! It's not your fault. You can't be responsible for what some deranged man did! I know you loved Bobby and never wanted him harmed—he knows that!"

Rachel's hot breaths puffed into her face, fresh tears flowed from the brilliant blue depths of her eyes. Abby saw the measure of her own agony reflected there, the stabbing guilt, the relentless hellfires of impotent rage and the eviscerating physical pain of inconsolable grief. She embraced her tightly, this other half of herself, as if to reclaim some sense of wholeness, put pressure on the wound, stop the hemorrhage.

Rachel held on for dear life and Abby realized the sobs she was trying to hush were her own.

Abby was surprised at how little the arrest of her husband's alleged killer affected how she felt. The relief it provided was inconsequential compared to the damage done. The media circus started up again as the arrest of Reyes Saavedra was made public. Abby declined all interviews, letting Javier or Ramone be her spokesperson. Sheriff Bowman had no such reluctance, especially with the fall elections drawing near.

Abby decided it was time to talk to the Vigils about her plans to leave and the perfect opportunity came when CeCe invited her over for dinner following her latest prenatal visit with Dr. Lark.

"So, the doctor said the baby is getting big and starting to drop a little. Everything looks on schedule for an October twenty-seventh delivery," CeCe said. "Two weeks! I'm so excited!"

Abby felt her stomach churn and it wasn't exactly excitement. More like cold fear and dread. Partly of the rigors of childbirth, but also of the task at hand. She looked around the table. Miguel giving CeCe a quick kiss, smiling at her enthusiasm. Rachel sitting next to Charlie. Charlie, giving her a silent nod of encouragement to just come out and say it.

She put down her fork and stared into her half-eaten slice of roast beef and baked potato. CeCe's buttered peas, frozen early this summer, tasted as fresh as the day they had picked them. "I've been doing some thinking."

Suddenly the small sounds of silverware and chewing seemed loud as everyone looked at her. "I think it would be best, a few months after the baby is born and we're ready to travel, if we go back to San Diego."

"You mean like a visit, maybe try to mend things with your parents—?" CeCe began.

"I still have my restaurant there, and my friends. I have to be practical. I have to think of the baby and the future."

There was a stunned, awkward silence.

Charlie cleared his throat. "Well, Abby, we'll sure miss you but you have to do what you think is right—"

"No!" Rachel came alive. "That's nuts! What will you do, work twenty hours a day in your restaurant, ship the baby off to day care?"

"No, of course not. I have friends, I have Edward—"

"He's a chef, too, how's he going to have time and no offense he's gay. What does he know about babies?" Rachel said.

"Rachel, it's not our place—" Miguel began.

"You guys are so wonderful, I couldn't have gotten through any of this without you—it's not about that. I can't even explain it. It's just home, you know? I need to go back to where Bobby and I were happy and together. It makes sense financially, I could just act as a consultant, name my own hours, have my baby with me even. Edward and Paul want me back at Abigail's. Or I can work from home on a restaurant guide or a food column for the newspaper or that cookbook I've been planning."

"You're just running away from Esperanza," Rachel said. "Bobby isn't in San Diego anymore, either. Esperanza was his dream for his child, don't take that away from him."

"Nothing went the way Bobby dreamed it would. None of this is what he wanted."

CeCe bit her lip, strangely quiet in all of this. She looked at Abby and sighed. "Bobby is dead. Everyone at this table who knew him, loved him. He was part of our family and you've become part of our family. Families support each other. If you have to leave, we don't love you any less. But families also tell each other the truth. Abby, I think it's too soon to make such a difficult and important decision. I urge you to take into consideration what Rachel said and give it more time."

Rachel was looking at her mother in shock at her endorsement. Abby took advantage of the moment of silence. "I need you guys to trust me. This is so hard to do on my own, but that's how I have to do everything from now on. I am alone. Thinking about it is all I've done for weeks now. I just wanted you to start to get used to the idea. It isn't happening tomorrow—it'll be months from now. At least January or February. And I'll stay in close touch and we'll visit—"

"First we lose Bobby and then his baby! We've been believing all this time that you would be here—that we'd get to see his child grow up, be a part of its life and now you're taking that away and we're supposed to trust you?" Rachel got up as her tears came. "I don't know how much more I can take!" She left the table, nearly knocking over her chair in the process.

Charlie gave Abby's shoulder a squeeze as he rose to follow Rachel.

CeCe began clearing the table, snuffling her own tears into her wadded paper napkin.

Miguel frowned as CeCe grabbed his plate out from under his poised fork. Then he smiled and winked at Abby as he stage whispered, "Couldn't you have waited until after dessert? She made pie!"

She smiled weakly. "Actually that went better than I was expecting."

Rachel could tell fall was fast approaching by the way her fingers and toes were feeling after a cold October morning of milking. But after the sun was out and high, it still warmed her back in spite of any briskness, as Charlie had when he had slept bent-spoon behind her, his warmth in the cold winter room. She thought more about things like that lately.

Her goats were dropping a pound or more of milk production a day and she attributed it to all the commotion that was happening. She tried to hide the panic she felt about Abby leaving and not have it surge through her cold, milking fingers. But as she milked, she'd find herself wondering if the business would survive without Abby. And thinking that losing her would be like losing another piece of herself. Of Bobby. She wanted to confide in her goats, put sound and syllable to what she was feeling, but raising goats for milk was a very codependent operation.

Her biceps tightened and she still felt the tendonitis in her right forearm while carrying two full pails of milk. Over by the horse barn Charlie and Santi were head to head about something. "Can I borrow your ranch hand a minute?" she called out. Both heads snapped in her direction and Bésame came running toward her, lips flying and bouncing like birds skimming water. Santi hopped down from the corral fence and he and Charlie followed. They both hurried over, their cowboy boots scuffling in the dirt, Santi seeming especially proud in his. Charlie had picked them up for him at a yard sale. Charlie figured Santi would be better off learning to be a cowboy than a cholo dismantling cars somewhere with a gang. CeCe had told her he had said that. He always said it took a great soul to be good with horses, and that they were the best judges of people. Santi had the touch. And not just with horses. No wonder Charlie could not help but want to nurture that kind of boy.

She shielded her eyes from the sun as they approached. Behind them, hundreds of hot-air balloons speckled the sky and hung motionless, like a poster for that year's balloon fiesta that was in full swing. The balloons followed the river and a couple were so close you could hear the whooshing of their burners overhead. It spooked some of her goats.

Charlie moved quickly toward her as Santi and Bésame veered off to watch balloons. "Are you okay?" He made a couple of clumsy moves toward her like he wanted to take her hand or hold her, and the warmth of his gaze competed with the sun. Shaded by his hat, his eyes were the color of burnt sugar with flecks of gold like chopped peanuts on caramel apples.

"I still can't get over it," she said. "He'd turned into a sexual pervert, but I never would have thought he'd be capable of murder. Just shows you how wrong I've been—about a lot of things." She met his eyes.

"Do you think he was the one that did it?" Santi asked wide-eyed. They hadn't realized he had wandered up at the last second.

"When people have a sickness in their head, Santi, they could be capable of things like that." Rachel explained the best she could. "They say he'd been drinking which just makes things worse."

Santi's face paled. "I gotta go," he said, and took off running toward the direction of his house. Bésame followed in the dust.

"Wonder what got into him? He's been awfully quiet around me lately," said Rachel.

His sleeves were rolled up exposing the sun-bleached hair on his bulky forearm where she saw two deep healing gashes. She wanted to ask him how it happened and if he put something on it, but couldn't. Now it was shame that kept her from showing him she cared.

"Santi's getting older. He's been asking about men and women and babies. Probably from stuff he's seen at home. So, we had a little talk, you know, in general about it. I didn't get too detailed. But he had serious questions and I thought he deserved some answers. He could never talk to his own dad about it. Besides, I may never have a son of my own to get to do that with. I'm not getting any younger. Chances look pretty slim around here. Time for me to move on." He shook his head and then looked straight into her unprepared eyes. "I deserve more."

She walked away quickly and fiddled with the knot on the rope that held a bird feeder from a low branch. "I don't know a woman in this village who wouldn't love to have you and your baby." She flinched hearing her own flip words, words that came so easily before now felt cheap and dishonest. But what were the right words now? How can she find them before it is too late?

She could feel his eyes bore into her back.

"I do."

Miguel worked at his desk in his den while Rachel kept an eye on him as she cleaned and tidied around the living room. The afternoon sun was breaking in behind him through the cathedral-style window, in the center of which hung a stained-glass window of Our Lady of Guadalupe that had come from an old church in Mexico. His den was a room directly off the living room lined with carved, dark wooden shelves and cabinets filled with his books and personal mementos. His large wooden desk was covered with paperwork, a computer, small printer, and phone. His reading glasses sat on the end of his nose as he studied his mail.

She stopped the vacuum outside his door. "Papa, do you mind if I run the vacuum in there for a minute?"

"No, mi'ja, but I'm afraid I tromped in some mud yesterday. See, there, it's all over the bricks and on this rug behind my desk." He pushed his chair back for her to get a look.

She shut off the vacuum, took a deep breath and proceeded to do what she came in there to do. "Papa, did Charlie tell you he was thinking of moving away?"

He looked up from his brochure and over his rectangular glasses. "What's that?"

"Has Charlie talked to you about moving away?"

"He's made some noise to that effect," he said, going right back to the brochure.

"What exactly has he said?"

"Said he's planning on moving away."

"And what did you say? Did you try and talk him out of it?" She strangled the hose of the vacuum.

"Why would I do that? The man needs to move on. Get himself a life." Back to the brochure.

How could he be so cavalier about this? "He'll listen to you, Papa! Tell him he has to stay!" The vacuum attachments came undone from her shaking, the small brush head hitting the floor.

He got up from the desk, walked around it and sat in front of her. "What for, mi'ja? Huh? What for? So you can treat him badly? All he did was love you. It shames me how you treated him. A woman who will not love. I don't know, mi'ja, where you get it. Maybe it's my fault. A father's love can be crippling. You are just now beginning to see what a loving woman your own mother is, and what a wonderful partner she is to me. But you wouldn't show your love for her. You couldn't see it. And now with Charlie."

His words speared her to the floor. What did he mean, a woman who will not love?

"But Papa . . ."

"No, mi'ja. Let me finish. I can't watch it anymore, the way you treat him. If you're going to love him, then love him like a woman and not a spoiled girl. But, if you're going to treat him like the mud on this floor, then let him go, mi'ja. For his sake, and for mine. If you want him to stay, you ask him yourself."

You can't be in love with somebody who doesn't give it back. CeCe had said it was a metaphysical impossibility, and Roberto had proven that to her. She also said love was an intertwining spiritual dance. A flood of give and take without expectation.

A woman who will not love. That was what her father had said.

Rachel could hear them there in Abby's kitchen before she knocked on the back screen door. She stood for a moment listening, her knuckles still readied inches from the wood.

They were laughing hard about something. She peered in. The

morning light shone brightly through the window against them as if they were on stage. She could see them holding fast onto counters and sinks and finally each other, as if neither one was able to sustain enough air to remain upright.

Rachel knocked at this point. What if they were laughing at her?

"Oh, hi! C'mon in," Abby said from around Charlie. They distanced themselves a little bit from each other. Charlie scratched at the back of his head.

"I'm interrupting something?" asked Rachel.

"Oh no. We were just . . . You know how it is when you're tired and something hits you and you just lose it?" Abby began, but when her eyes met Charlie's, they burst into sputters and laughs again. Abby held her roundness like jolly old St. Nick. "I think the baby is laughing too. What a kicker!"

Charlie reached out and spread his thick fingers around her stomach. She positioned his hand over the kick. "He's kickin' up his heels all right."

The broadness of his smile as he felt the baby coaxed Rachel to interrupt them. "I brought this over," she said, offering Abby a rectangular plastic container. Abby reached for it, separating from Charlie.

"It's leftover carrot cake I made for Papa's birthday."

Abby brushed lightly against him as she received the cake. As innocent as a breeze, yet for some reason much more disturbing than when a dancing partner melted against him like hot wax. "Thank you," Abby smiled.

Reflexively, Rachel started to tell Abby that Charlie shouldn't get to have any of her carrot cake, the old rule since their divorce now seemed so childish and mean. She still felt a desperate urge to engage him, but not by pushing his buttons anymore. But what was it she wanted? Was she only playing a game of come here, go away? Maybe her father was right about her.

"*Yummee!* Rachel's carrot cake," Charlie said, winking at Rachel and trying to get her going. He was so conditioned to the tug of war between them. It had never felt honest. She resisted the knee-jerk response that would have normally sent them in a barrage of cutthroat jabs and accusations. Words she used that kept them attached and yet distanced. But without them now, in her silence, emotions floated upward to surface in her like flotsam. Sadness, regret. Hopefulness. Fear. Finally, something she named as love emerged, gasping for air like the last remaining survivor. Was it really something she had resisted?

She made herself look at what came up. Look hard at all of it. Even peek behind the curtain and see for a moment what she wanted most, but feared like hell having. She had never let herself get to the point where she wanted love enough to deal with being scared to death of it. Of its all-consuming nature. With her mother. With Charlie. Could she survive it? Would it be there if she let herself need it? Did she deserve it?

Loving Roberto had been so easy. He didn't love her back. He wasn't even who she thought he was. There was nothing to risk. There was nothing at all. Just a place to run and hide when her marriage to Charlie had started to bring up her fear-of-intimacy crap. A place where the guilt over killing her baby didn't hurt so bad. Her misplaced love and devotion to Roberto had been like falling into quicksand. She flushed with humiliation at how clear it was now. She loved Charlie.

Charlie maneuvered around Abby in the small kitchen to get to the coffeepot, his hand protectively guarding her stomach as he went. Was that gesture as simple as inherent male behavior just protecting offspring? A beautiful gesture, nonetheless. That was plain to see. Charlie was a decent and good man. A loving man.

"I'll just get three forks," Abby said, pulling out the flatware drawer. "These puny dessert forks or something more heavy-duty?" she offered, holding up one of each. She mimed two-fisted eating. "This works."

"Fork?" asked Charlie.

Charlie rarely used utensils if he could help it, especially when it came to her carrot cake. He would usually cut a big square and jam the whole thing in, one or two bites tops. Rachel's smile lingered to the point that she probably looked like an idiot by now. She felt like one. Especially since Charlie was watching. But she couldn't help it.

Abby plowed aside a pile of mail and newspapers to one end of the table with her elbow, while Charlie peeled back the top of the cake container and licked off the cream-cheese icing that had stuck to it. *"Mmmmm,"* he groaned as Abby cut pieces and doled them out.

"My God, Rachel, this is delicious," said Abby, not knowing a *blop* of frosting clung above her lip as she popped in another bite. "Fantastic," she mumbled. "You should sell this at the coffee shop."

But all Rachel could wonder was if Charlie had the urge to let Abby know about the frosting on her lip. He probably would have, had she not been there. But how? With a word? A fingertip? A kiss? Have there been kisses? Passionate kisses?

Suddenly Rachel stood up. It was like a bolt of something shot up her ass, but she wasn't sure what. Flustered, she didn't know what to say. She only knew she wanted to get out of there as if the place were on fire.

Charlie and Abby stared at her, waiting for her to say something.

"I think I forgot to close the gate to the goat pen," she finally said, feeling like she was in a dream she always had where she was halfway through the school day, usually fifth-period biology, before she noticed she was totally naked from the waist up. No one but her ever seemed to be bothered by that fact. "I need to go."

Rachel hadn't been showing up for lunch at the house lately, growing accustomed to grabbing a fried burrito at Benny's, a roadside takeout nearby, or a chicken bowl from the Teriyaki Express, a place that never looked busy. But after leaving Charlie and Abby that morning, she found herself in her mother's kitchen.

Her father sat in his usual place at the table. She preferred to stand against the counter and observe as she sipped a glass of water. Juan and Pedro, two of Papa's usual crew that traveled up this time of year for work, sat across from him. It was strange not seeing Charlie there, too, smiling, joking, and shoving his lunch in between the lines and laughs.

"Just leave everything where it's at," her mother announced at the door, "I'll be back within the hour to clean up." A basket hung on the crook of her tanned arm that held fresh eggs, a jar of strawberry jam and a loaf of her bread, the top glistening brown like her arm. She was probably making a charitable trip to old Mr. Herrera's house, whose wife was laid up with the shingles, but she didn't bother to say.

Juan and Pedro finished up. Their sweat-stained hats seemed to jump into their hands as they reached for them, like old, well-trained dogs. They bowed slightly at her father in thanks and headed back out to the field.

Her father hung back, as usual, to savor his coffee, a piece of apple pie and some silence. Rachel made up a plate from what was left on the stove and scooted to sit down with him at the table. She had never felt so alone in this world. Especially after seeing Charlie that morning with Abby.

"Mi'ja, this is a nice surprise," he said. He sounded like he actually meant it. She had not met his eyes yet.

"I hope I'm not interrupting anything," she said. She just wanted to be near him. Wanted to feel loved, despite her ugly shortcomings.

"You think something could be more important than time with my daughter? Mi'ja." His face gave a disappointed twitch, as if she should have known better; then he sipped at his coffee with both hands, which were worn and beaten up, like old football leather. A striking contrast next to his youthful face that was still victorious over its battle with the sun. "Tractor's acting up again. You haven't seen Charlie lately, have you?"

Hearing his name took her by surprise. "He's over at Abby's," she said. "I think he's going to fix something or other."

"He's damn good at that. That time we busted down in the middle of nowhere . . . I think we only had a screwdriver, a wrench, and two pocketknives between us, but he got that old truck going. Don't know how long we would have been stuck out there."

"Papa, remember the time I sprained my ankle real bad, a couple of years ago, and Charlie saw me trying to use those damn crutches and he started carrying me everywhere? Even out to the barn so I could visit my goats while he did all the work?" Her father stared at her as tears began to stream down her cheeks. "He put me up on Sweetwater and got on behind so we could go riding. Bareback, which I never do, but he held me and I felt safe. It was one of those beautiful days, you know? No wind, not too hot."

"Yes, mi'ja." His expression softened and his eyes connected with hers in a way they hadn't in far too long. He reached for her hand. He smiled and reached over to wipe a tear from her cheek. Another quickly replaced it.

"Remember when I put off doing my term paper for history and Ma stayed up all night typing it for me and never once complained."

He nodded and squeezed her hand.

"I want to be different, Papa," she realized, feeling that she could finally name it.

"Then you will be, mi'ja. You will be." He rose to leave but turned back to kiss the top of her head.

Chapter 25

The coffee shop was an adobe that looked like it had grown there many years ago, like an old tree, more majestic with age, probably used for a small home at first and a store of some kind in its second or third incarnation. It had a small porch on the front they planned to make into a screened patio. Hollyhocks grew all around the house in total disregard of anything, but CeCe planned to groom and transplant some of them in the spring.

With Abby backing out of the cheese business, Rachel was glad her mother took on so many things with her endless talent. And the cabal came in to help regularly. She had enough to think about with the dairy and goats. The new milking equipment would speed up production and save her weary hands and arms. She'd still oversee the cheese making for now, no sense risking the quality decreasing while they were trying to get the coffee shop off the ground. The cabal also was going to help CeCe with the baking and cafe activities, if they behaved themselves.

Her mother sat at a table by a window costing out recipes for the menu. The sun shone brightly in the thick adobe window, the wood trim, painted years ago royal blue, faded to cornflower. A huge blood-red geranium plant, too big for the previous owners to move, inhabited the corner. Food bills and recipes lay in a patchwork design on the table in front of her. Granny-style reading glasses stopped close to the end of her nose as she added and divided things down to cost per plate on a calculator. Down, down, down to smallest piece of garnish. Her mother took on responsibility without flinching. More and more her mother rapidly transformed before her eyes, like a bad guy in one of Maria's Spanish TV novellas into the hero. But it wasn't her mother who was changing.

Rachel had been unloading boxes of supplies in the large commercial kitchen that had been added on in the back in the adobe's life as a restaurant. The refrigerator, the stove and ovens, everything came with the purchase at a killer price.

Why was it some things happened so perfectly and others didn't? She and her mother had scrubbed all of it whistling clean with a heavy-duty degreaser discussing that very topic. Ma had said that a lot of perfect things don't always feel that way. We don't always see the big picture. And our pain keeps us from seeing it.

"Honey, what did Feinstein's quote you on corned beef?" her mother yelled back to her.

Having no clue, she stayed silent, hoping it would turn into one of Ma's rhetorical questions.

"Because I'm just going to make my own. I'm not going to pay these prices," Ma said, determined to carry what she called back-east deli items on the menu. Some with yummy twists, like green chile Reuben sandwiches, or green chile chicken soup with matzo balls.

Rachel came walking in from the kitchen. "It'll be ten times better if you do make it yourself," she said, massaging the stiffness out of her hands from opening boxes.

"I'm no chef," Ma said, "not like Abby."

Rachel made herself examine her mother's sadness, forcing her jealousy aside. She'd had so many losses, with more on the way. They all had. All so deeply connected and yet coming apart at the seams. When Rachel looked at her mother's shadowed expression, she felt stirred with a longing to journey closer to her and now the path was visible.

"I still can't believe they are leaving. This is a hard one for me, let me tell you," Ma said, starting to tear up.

"I know, Ma," she said. "Me, too. Abby and I have come a long way. Now I don't want to lose her." It wouldn't be for months yet, as if delaying the loss would help. It would only give them time to get attached to the baby, only to have it taken away.

"But we can do this, Rache, I know we can. We just need to keep all the plates spinning at once." She was referring to the man they'd seen once at the circus who ran up and down a long line of plates spinning on sticks and kept them going. Even when one was dangerously close to tipping and falling off the stick, he'd always managed to get there in time. Nothing ever came crashing down. Ma was like that.

It'd just be the two of them now. She didn't know if she could fill her own shoes, let alone try to fill a void as big as the one that loomed in front of them. But then she realized that wasn't right, either. Some holes just weren't fillable. Bobby, Abby, the baby, Charlie, Maria, no one could take their places. You can only be who you were, warts and all, and love who is in front of you, warts and all. Familia. She understood now nothing held family together but love. And not as some word you say. Love was behavior. Blood had nothing to do with it.

"Hey, I didn't even know you knew how to make corned beef." She went over to the small stage to tinkle a couple of the keys on the fat-legged piano in desperate need of tuning. Even she could hear that.

"Darling, I'm from Brooklyn," CeCe said looking over her glasses. "I can turn even an old pair of galoshes into great corned beef. Think what I can do with actual beef." Her face held the light tan from summer gardening, as she continued to look young despite the sun-blaring southwestern desert. Good genes, Ma claimed. All the bubbes on her mother's side of the family had never grayed or sweated and all had the skin of a woman twenty years younger. Rachel had her mother's skin. And Ma her mother's skin. For centuries. A line of strong women, beautifully pale in winter.

She started playing a *boom-de-yadah, boom-de-yadah* over and over on the piano, remembering when CeCe had tried to teach her to play, a little girl who would have nothing to do with sitting still or staying indoors.

Ma smiled at her, pushed herself to a standing position and ran over, scooting her over on the bench with a push of her hips. She began playing the upper part. The part she was good at. The heart and soul part.

That night, Rachel found CeCe at her sewing machine working on some quilt squares. She recognized the fabric in each patch as an old dress or blouse of hers from the past, and other odds and ends that felt familiar.

Rachel snuck up from behind and tapped her shoulder, startling her. "Jesus! Oh, it's you, honey. You half scared me to death!"

"Sorry. Are you making Abby a quilt?" she asked, trying not to sound jealous.

"These are all patches from your life. Why on earth would I make Abby a quilt with your history in it? Mothers do this sort of thing for daughters," Ma said, whirring the fabric through the machine. "I wanted it to be a surprise."

It was. A nice surprise. She closed her eyes, and inhaled the faint fragrance of honeysuckle emanating from the waves in her mother's hair. It took her back to a time she allowed herself to be mothered by CeCe. A safe time. Honeysuckle time.

"It's going to be beautiful," she said.

"Look, remember this?" CeCe held up piece of cloth, purple-and-green jungle print with little long-tailed monkeys. "This was your favorite little short set. I had to bribe you to give it up. The seat of the pants were worn away. People began to talk!"

"I remember," Rachel smiled. "You promised to get Papa to make me a tire swing."

Ma laughed, "You were always such a determined little cuss. A handful for your Papa and me to handle at first," she said, laughing again. "Still are, but that's what makes you Rachel."

She wanted to tell her mother how sorry she was, how she was going to be different from now on, not perfect, but better. Her pain was changing her. She kept her words, knowing they would be too easily spent. In her wish to make things better, her impatience to wipe the slate clean, she couldn't be off the hook so fast. Time was part of her penance due.

"God, don't use that piece of horrible dress Aunt Matilda sent me for my thirteenth birthday."

"It deserves its place in the story," Ma said, placing it under the needle of the machine. "If a quilt is like a life, some patches are harder to take than others."

She watched her deftness on the sewing machine for a minute. She felt a rush of giddiness, a lightness that spread through the battered center of her being, not taking away her pain but expanding her beyond it. As if something long closed had been flung open and there was all this recovered space for new possibilities and choices.

She felt awkward but determined when she leaned over and wrapped her arms around her mother like packing twine. Her mother reached behind and felt her face with searching fingers. "Okay whoever you are—what have you done with my daughter Rachel?"

Dr. Lark had told Abby that much of her weight gain was increased blood volume and fluid retention. As she took her daily walk, she felt exactly like an enormous water balloon. Though she had only gained twenty-five pounds with her pregnancy and Dr. Lark felt that was on the lean side of healthy, it felt like twenty-five hundred pounds. Even her usually thin face with its delicate bone structure looked strangely round to her in the mirror. CeCe blamed it on hormones. "Kid, you have too much and I got too little, maybe you could give me a donation."

She would miss them all so much, but she didn't let those feelings do more than wave from a distance before shooing them away. She had enough to deal with. Now was not the time to load that on top of everything else.

Her light jacket became too warm, despite temperatures in the fifties. Clouds flitted by, casting sudden shadows followed by quick blasts of sunshine. An unexpected gust of wind was followed by dead air. One extreme into the next, like two warring weather gods were battling for the controls.

Indian summer into autumn. Transitions were never smooth; the lines were never clear. As she reached the village, she tried to walk with a little more dignity, which was difficult since the mental image she had of her gait was that of a waddling duck. To think last June she was jogging like a young colt down that road.

"Mrs. Silva!"

Abby turned to see Javier walking up to her.

"I've been meaning to call you for the last few days now. Do you have a minute?"

"Yeah, I'm just getting my walk done for the day. The coffee shop is closed for remodeling but we can grab something to drink in the junk shop and sit out on Barbara's porch."

Barbara met them at the door, "Help yourselves—it's on the house. I just need to dash over to the post office. Be right back!"

"I'll get it," Javier said, pulling out a patio chair from the set on the porch that had been for sale all summer. "What would you like?"

"Bottled water," Abby sat down, watching Barbara scurry across the street, neighbors greeting neighbors, a dog whose path took him straight down the center.

Javier returned with a soft drink for himself and Abby's water, which he opened before handing it to her. He carried a package of potato chips with his teeth. "Lunch or breakfast, I'm not sure."

He tore the bag open and stuffed a few into his mouth. "Salt and grease—my favorite food groups."

"So what's new?" Abby asked.

"I have my expense account log and reports done along with the final bill back in my car."

She took a long swig of water. "This case never would have been broken if I hadn't hired you. At least we got the guy. But isn't there some way of getting him to tell us what he did with Bobby's . . . remains?"

"There's nothing in it for him to tell. No body, weak case. A motive, opportunity, no alibi, but no hard evidence. Just circumstantial. No priors, his lawyer doesn't even have to be smart to tell him to keep his mouth shut. I don't know if the DA will even try him and if he does it'll be because of public pressure. The chances of a conviction are slim unless new evidence comes to light."

"So he gets away with it."

Javier shrugged. "If he did it."

Abby set down her bottle. "What? You don't think he's the one?"

"He might be. He's a sick dude. I'm just not sure he's the right sick dude."

"But everyone is saying he did it."

"Everyone wants it to be him. Hell, I want it to be him. But let's face it, could he mastermind all of this? The truck didn't come up with any of his DNA, nothing to link him to that. He matches the very generic description of the man who drove it across the border. Even with the electronic enhancement, the video tape is inconclusive. I could try to take his mug shot down to Hector in Juarez to see if he can ID him; I mentioned the idea to Bowman but he's satisfied he's got the right perp, even claiming Reyes almost admitted as much before his lawyer showed up and stopped the interrogation. The community wants to believe we got the son of a bitch so they can sleep better at night. Who am I to cast doubt on it?"

"But wouldn't the case be stronger with Hector as a witness?"

"Hector took money, a gold wedding ring, and a truck to lie. The defense would have a field day with him, especially since he was also an admitted drunk at the time. I doubt if I could ever convince him to cooperate and as a Mexican citizen, the subpoena process could take forever."

"I have to know we have the right man. I'll pay you to go down and see Hector."

"It's better I stay here another week or so, keep an eye on Bowman, help with whatever evidence we might still dig up. We're still going through Maria's house, bagging and sorting a pile of evidence for the lab, all those herbs and potions. God knows what else we'll find. She was mixed up in this somehow, even if it was just aiding and abetting, or harboring the guy after the fact. We have some time before any trial. I don't have any other jobs pending, so if nothing else turns up, I'll go see my bro Hector."

Abby was waking from an afternoon nap when Ramone appeared at her door. He carried a bouquet of pink roses.

"How beautiful! What's the occasion?"

"I saw them and thought of you. And then I thought they'd be a great excuse to come see you." He smiled and sat down at the kitchen table. The silver streaks in his wavy hair shone in the sunlight. His shirt was freshly pressed as always.

"You never need an excuse to come see me. How's your dad?" Abby carefully snipped the ends off of the roses' stems.

"He's fine. In fact he's come so far after that small stroke he had, I'm thinking about taking Bowman on, running against him for sheriff."

"You should! You need to save Esperanza from his incompetence," Abby said, arranging the roses in a tall clear vase of water. She deeply inhaled their scent, thinking of Bobby and all of the roses he had given her in their time together.

"Would it change your mind about leaving?"

She turned to him. "Wow. News travels fast around here."

"Why didn't you tell me you were thinking about it?" Ramone asked, not unfairly.

They had become very close over these five months. She loved him like the father she had never had. "I'm weak. I'm sorry. I was just trying to avoid anything else hard. And leaving, even if it is right, is hard."

He nodded. "You said, 'if it is right.' Do you have some doubts about it?"

Abby smiled as she placed the roses on the table and sat down. "See, only a great sheriff would have caught that 'if.' I have doubts about anything and everything—you name it. I'm torn, I admit it. There's pros and cons about here and there. I'm leaning toward leaving because of my restaurant and fond memories of living there with Bobby. We didn't have a chance to try to make a home here together and even if we had, I'm not positive we would have stayed. Remember, we were going to give it a year and see how we liked it? That's why I hung onto the restaurant as a co-owner."

Ramone nodded, his sadness evident.

"And then after he disappeared, I was stuck here while we searched for him. Now that I'm free to go, I have to consider all my options."

Ramone chewed his lip a moment. "I guess you have friends back there in San Diego, but you told me how it is with your family. We've all come to love you and think of you as our own. It won't be easy to let you go."

Abby reached over and squeezed his large, balled-up hands. His fingers relaxed under her touch. "Like I told the Vigils, even if I do go, I'll come back and visit. I wouldn't sell Bobby's house, it's his child's to inherit. I'll keep my ties here, for me and my baby."

Chapter 26

Rachel found herself walking through the thick-trunked cottonwoods down by the river near Charlie's trailer. The leaves on the trees were in various stages of surrender to the late October air. Some bright golden and still hanging on, some already brown and plummeting to the ground for next spring's mulch. Lately her walks had become longer; as she became so absorbed in her thoughts she would be shocked to see how much time had passed.

She ended up in this spot in the trees frequently, hiding and hoping to get a glimpse of him. Not too long ago she had been telling herself she was sick of the sight of him. With the clarity she now possessed, it seemed unbelievable that she could have so successfully hid her love for him from herself.

It was quiet except for the neighbor's peacock and peahen calling for each other in the background. *Help, help, help,* the female seemed to cry.

As she neared the trailer's clearing, she could see movement. She stayed hidden behind a tree and watched as Charlie carried boxes to the back of his already-loaded truck. Her lungs seemed to shrink, unable to contain air, as her heart imploded in her chest. He was leaving.

She fought the impulse to charge out of the woods and demand that he stay. Not so very long ago she would have done some such thing. Or dramatically pleaded, or slyly manipulated. But the kind of love she was learning knew better. The weight of the responsibility for this kept her rooted.

Maybe she owed it to him to admit it and apologize, instead of hiding and spying on him. It felt like the kind of thing the person she wanted to be would do, so she mustered up her courage and walked out of the shadow, into the sunlight.

Charlie noticed her at once, gave a nod, but kept on with his loading while she drew nearer. "Well, hello Miss Vigil, what brings you to this neck of the woods?"

She saw his banter as his defense and it saddened her he'd needed to go against his forthright nature to manufacture it. "I just have some stuff I needed to say before you go. I don't blame you for leaving, even though I wish you'd stay."

"Why, because Roberto is dead? What am I, first runner-up?" Charlie's tone seemed to surprise them both. He looked down, biting his lip in that way that he did when he was ashamed.

"I'm sure it looks like that. You don't have to believe me, but the regret I feel has nothing to do with Roberto except I used him to kill what we had, or stop it from ever becoming what it might have been. I ruined us. You did everything you could to try to stop me. So I'm sorry. You do deserve better. If that's Abby, then I'm happy for both of you."

"I'm not leaving with Abby—"

"Well, wherever you go, I hope you stay in touch." She desperately needed to end this before she cracked wide open and the old Rachel would step over her limp, discarded wrapper to engage him in battle. She looked down now, knowing she couldn't take the gentle connection of his gaze.

He was digging in his pockets as the breeze picked up, ruffling his hair. He pulled out a piece of folded paper and put it into her hand, closing his hand over hers. "This is where I'll be." He leaned over and kissed her softly on her forehead. "Bye, darlin'."

He got into his truck, waved out of the open window once and without turning around drove away slow enough so as not to kick up any dust in her face. A gentlemen to the end.

Tears choked her, her chest felt the searing pain of genuine loss, not the fantasy kind. But she was proud of herself. Her love was true enough to set him free. Maybe they would stay in touch, anything could happen.

She opened her fist and unfolded the paper with shaking fingers. It was a flyer.

October 25th is flea market day at Our Lady of Fatima Church. Donations of all kinds welcome, with a special need for household items. Come support our work with our community's needy.

Her laughter exploded out of her, sending a flock of doves peeping heavenward.

A week before her due date, Abby decided it was time to pack her bag for the hospital. She looked over the recommended list and began selecting items to tuck into Bobby's smaller duffel bag. She had a nicer, newer overnight case but there was no question that she would take Bobby's. He had picked it up one day in the condo after learning she was pregnant and pronounced it perfect for the job. She pulled open the top drawer on his side of the dresser and found the miniature stuffed bear he had bought in Sea Harbor Village nestled in with his meticulously folded boxers she had carefully removed from his suitcase just the way he had packed them.

When she realized she would not box up his clothes and donate them to charity, she realized part of her was still in denial. If she got rid of all of his things, what could she possibly say to him when he returned?

Was she really so concrete operational that she would never accept his death without seeing his body?

One minute it seemed she had a handle on this, was working through her stages of grief just like the books described, and the next minute she caught herself believing he would burst through the door with one hell of a story to tell.

Now Javier had to let it slip that he wasn't totally convinced they had even arrested the right man. What minuscule shred of comfort she had taken in that was now tainted. Now her mind began to gnaw at it, find less and less sense in it, as if any sense could ever be found in her husband's murder. As if frying even a beyond-the-shadow-of-a-doubt right man could ever provide her with any semblance of peace. That was the real lie in all of this, that there could ever be "closure," that anything could ever happen that would somehow balance the scales, ease her mind, put it to rest. One thing, the only thing she could be sure of, was that this would have no end.

After putting everything she could think of in the bag for herself, she took it into the nursery to pack for her baby. Packing for two. Suddenly, on some visceral level, she realized her baby would soon be this separate individual, with its own wants and needs. Birth began its leaving. The incremental steps that divide and eventually separate. As time flowed irretrievably forward, no matter how important her role, how great her love, this soul was embarking on its own journey.

As she placed a pale turquoise gown and receiving blanket into the bag, she heard knocking at her kitchen door. She cradled the dark blue duffel bag with its faded white letters, U.S. NAVY—ROBERTO SILVA, before laying it in the crib.

As she walked to the kitchen she noticed she rested her hand in the small of her back as if she were a little old lady. It felt like a balancing maneuver to compensate for the sway of her belly. When she looked down, the wide circle of her faded denim jumper obscured her feet. Bobby would have found that hilarious.

She swung open the door, closed against the invading cold front that had moved in and overstayed its welcome. Rachel's smiling face, hair flying in the wind, her worn pale brown leather jacket hugged tightly against herself. Rachel smiling. It was like catching a double rainbow.

"Hi, Abby." She was always careful to wipe her boots on the rug before coming all the way inside.

"Would you like some hot tea? I made chocolate-pecan brownies last night when I got the worst craving—I even had to run out and get ice cream to go with them."

"Pig-out time! Let's ruin our suppers." She took off her jacket, pulling a black folder out of where it had been tucked against her chest. She laid it on the table. Still with the smile.

"What's that?" Abby asked as she set the vanilla ice cream on the table with the plate of thick fudgy brownies.

"First I want to apologize. I was a real bitch when you talked about leaving." She hesitated, trying out a series of silent words, as she seemed to be carefully choosing what to say next. "If I promise not to browbeat you, could we talk some more about it?"

Abby nodded, taking two dips of ice cream instead of the one she had been planning on. This was definitely going to be a two-dip conversation. The ice cream began to slide and melt against the warm brownie. When had her sweet tooth gotten so out of control?

"I don't blame you for wanting to get this nightmare behind you. It's obvious you've really given San Diego a lot of thought, imagined a life there with your baby. I guess I just want to give equal time to Esperanza. I mean, you want to make sure you've given this a real balanced and fair consideration, right?"

"Okay," Abby said cautiously. Why did this remind her of talking to venders who used to come into her restaurant with the latest line of cooking supplies? She got back up and poured Rachel's tea and a glass of milk for herself. She must be working on those last five pounds Dr. Lark wanted her to gain.

"The first reason I want you to stay is selfish, big surprise, right? So let's just get that one out on the table right off." She took a bite and rolled her eyes with pleasure. "I'd miss your brownies too much, no I'm kidding. God, this is hard." She took a sip of tea and became serious. "I've been wrong about, well, everything, for a long time. It's weird, it's like I'm coming out of some zombie state and everything has shifted. If I can trust it, things are getting better for me and you're a huge part of that. If you hadn't come here . . . Well, I can't say that because if you hadn't come here Bobby would still be alive."

Abby could feel her struggle with this. "It's easier to think that. If only we hadn't come here . . . But who knows for sure? Maybe it's true about 'when it's your time' . . . I'm not sure what to believe but it doesn't do any good to blame everything on this place, on this choice."

Rachel looked relieved. "I feel so guilty . . . See, my life is getting better. It's like this terrible nuclear bomb went off and I'm the cockroach that survives the fallout. Not just survives, but thrives . . . I think."

"Are you and Charlie . . . ?"

Rachel nodded. "I'm going to give it a try. Hopefully, he'll eventually forgive me and start to trust me. I need to earn his love, earn this second chance. It's scary as hell. But that's not all—you affected everything in my life, how I see my mother, myself, everything." She hesitated, wincing at her own realization. "How can I ever repay you or thank you enough? I've never had a friend like you. The only person I was ever this close to was Roberto, Bobby. I don't want to lose you, too."

Abby felt her eyes threaten to well up as Rachel's had. "If some kind of good can come out this, that's great. Bobby would want that. He wouldn't want his death to devastate us and ruin everything. You deserve to be happy, Rachel, you've always deserved the kind of love Charlie wants to give you. Stop feeling so guilty or you'll never let it work out, you'll push him away again."

Rachel rolled her eyes. "Yeah, I have the Jewish-guilt thing and the Catholic-guilt thing."

"We have to give ourselves permission to get on with our lives, that's all I'm trying to do. His life brought us all so much, his death should have some kind of positive meaning, too. Isn't that the best kind of tribute?"

Rachel nodded. "I can't tell you what to do, how your life can be a tribute. None of us can. But all of us think you are wrong. Can you stop and consider why we think you should stay? Aside from the fact that we want you here and want to share in the life of your baby. If it were just our own selfish trip, we'd get over it. We'd say, how sad for us, but look at all she's going to gain if she leaves. We love you enough to want what's best for you—for your baby—at least give us that much credit."

"You're right. I can trust that you guys aren't being selfish. You are some of the most generous people I've ever known."

"So Ma and I were talking about why it's better for you to stay. All you really know about Esperanza is it took your husband away, so who can blame you for wanting to get a thousand miles away. Then Ma remembered something from a long time ago and she managed to unearth this.

Says it all right here." She opened the folder. "'Esperanza, by Roberto Silva. Mr. Lamson's eighth-grade English.'" Rachel took a sip of tea before continuing to read.

"'Esperanza is a place where everyone knows you and even if you don't like them you know they will help you if you need it. My mom died when I was little and if I only had my dad I would be lonely. But in Esperanza, la familia doesn't end at your own fence. CeCe and Miguel Vigil and their daughter Rachel are la familia to me now. Because of their caring, I can be strong. Everyone in the village will do anything for you and it doesn't matter if you are white or Spanish or Indian or Jewish like CeCe, Esperanza can be your home. When I turn eighteen, I can't wait to leave this place. What?—you are asking. Why would I want to leave a place I think is so great? Because, this place gave me so much it got me ready for the world. It filled me up with dreams and makes me believe I can achieve them. Can you think of a better place to grow up? I will go out and see the world and someday when I want to have a family, I will come back to Esperanza. Esperanza means hope but to me it means la familia.'" Rachel handed her the folder. "Look at the picture he glued into it."

Abby held the folder. Her eyes skimmed his too-perfect cursive script. The red A+ at the top of the page. The picture was an old blackand-white photograph that Ricardo must have taken because he wasn't in the shot. It was taken by the picnic table outside her door under the giant cottonwood tree. The table was laden with food. A younger CeCe beamed at the camera, Miguel had his arm slung around her shoulder. Rachel's smile was not for the camera, her thirteen-year-old attention was fully on Bobby, who was grinning, his arms outstretched like he was trying to embrace it all at once, a gesture of pride and celebration, his sharp dark eyes daring the camera lens to try to take this away from him.

"Bobby gave it to her for Mother's Day that year."

Abby smiled and began to reread his essay.

"Bobby knew both worlds and he chose this one. He didn't come back to Esperanza for me. Or even for himself. It was his gift to his child."

Abby closed the folder. A crowd of arguments jostled her thoughts.

"Back in San Diego you can make a lot of money, have success, pay for nannies and fancy private schools, but you aren't even speaking to your parents. And if you did make up with them, how could they ever really love your child when they could never accept the race of its father? Don't you think your child would feel their disapproval? So, you could do it alone—but why? You have family here who loves you, both of you. La familia."

She thought of Bobby's plea, the one that talked her into leaving San Diego. She had forgotten with everything that had happened, how there was more to it than just wanting to appease him. There was something tantalizing about the idea of home, of la familia. An idea she had never felt except in his arms.

Too many conflicting thoughts slammed against her weary brain. Then, Charlie's words came back to her. *The heart can know what the head can't. It speaks with something other than words. Softer. You got to be still and listen for it.*

"Well, I'll get out of your face." Rachel got up to leave. "Thanks for giving me my say. That's the last I'll hassle you about it. Come over later, Charlie's promised to grill up that mess of trout he and Santi caught."

As Rachel opened the door they heard a wild, high-pitched cry carried on the wind. Abby thought it might be a flock of migrating sandhill cranes heading for the bosque. "It's Santi—something's wrong! He has Bésame!"

Abby came to the door as Rachel held it open. Santi burst past them, Bésame in his arms, limp and bleeding.

"Help me!" Santi was screaming. "He shot her! You have to save her!"

Chapter 27

Rachel took the heavy dog from Santiago's collapsing embrace. Abby shoved their dishes out of the way and spread out some kitchen towels. Rachel laid Bésame on them, putting her head down to the animal's chest. "She's breathing—I can hear her heart beating."

"He shot her! Just like he shot Bobby! He came over to kick us out!"

Abby stopped cold. Rachel was examining the wound in Bésame's side.

Santi sobbed hysterically, his voice high and strangled, "Bobby told my dad he knew we never bought the house from his dad and we had to leave! He had papers. He was going to go to the sheriff! My dad told him no fucking way, got his gun and took him out to the rooster house!"

Abby grabbed Rachel's arm. "Are you listening to this?"

Rachel gave a quick nod. "Stay with Santi, he's in no shape to go—take care of him—I've got to get her to the vet or she'll die. I'll call CeCe from the vet and tell her what's going on."

"I want to go with her!" Santi cried, reaching for Rachel as she ran from the house with Bésame in her arms.

Abby pulled him back. "Stay with me, Santi. Tell me what happened to Bobby!"

Santi fell into her, sobbing and shaking. "I'm not supposed to tell you or he'll have to kill you, too!"

"It's okay now! We'll get help! My cell phone is right there—" Before she could move, the door flung back open and there stood Baca. Santi started to run for the phone.

"Mi'jo! Stop right there!" Baca staggered into the kitchen, stared at the blood-soaked towels on the table. Pointed at them with the gun in his hand. "Where's the dog?"

"Rachel took her to the vet," Santi said meekly, standing close to Abby.

"Why do you betray me, mi'jo, after all I've done for you? You break my heart."

"I'm sorry, Papa." Santi began to cry. "I'll do better to keep Bésame away from your roosters."

Baca looked at Abby with his drunken gaze, his eyes narrowing as he tried to read her expression. She looked away, terrified he would see what she knew.

"You can't look at me," he said quietly. "He told you."

"He told me you shot the dog," Abby tried, hoping it wasn't too late.

"Don't lie to me! See how he betrays his own father? I killed for him! You think I wanted to shoot your husband, huh? I'm not some cold-blooded killer! He stuck his nose in where it didn't belong! His father and I had an arrangement! But no! He didn't want our kind around his precious wife and baby! Like my boy don't count? Like I was going to let him make us homeless? I had a son to think about!" He waved the gun.

"Tell me what happened. Please." Abby said, Santi whimpering under her arm.

"Santiago! What did I tell you I would have to do if you told? Huh? Now you are making me have to kill a pregnant woman! Look at the sins you are making me put on my mortal soul! It's your fault your own papa will have to burn in hell."

"You don't have to kill me—I'm leaving town. I won't tell—it won't bring back my husband. No one has to know! They already arrested a guy, they aren't even looking for you!"

"Bullshit! I tried to tell you to leave town when you had the chance, remember? You didn't listen to me!" he screamed, wiping his own drunken tears and sweat from his eyes. He pointed the gun at her.

Santi moved in front of her. "You'll have to shoot me, too! I won't let you hurt her!"

Abby tried to shove him away, "No Santi! I don't want you to get hurt!" But he was immovable, he had even stopped crying. When had he become so tall, so strong?

"Just tell me about Bobby before I die, please! You owe me that much!"

Baca heaved a sigh. "He pleaded for his life. He had a wife he loved and a baby to raise. He said we could work something out. But I knew he was lying. He knew I didn't buy it. So he made a final request. He would take it like a man if I promised to never harm his family. I told him I respected a man who put his family first. I felt bad, but what choice did I have? Just like now. Get out of the way, Santiago!"

"Where did you put him?"

"I buried him under the ground in the rooster house. I said a prayer for his soul."

"What about the truck and Juarez, Hector Casteneda?" Abby asked quickly, trying to keep him talking. Rachel had probably already called the sheriff, she just needed to buy time.

"My brother drove the truck to Juarez, met Hector at a bar, paid him to tell the story if anyone came looking. See, I went to a lot of trouble to keep my promise to your husband. I had to keep you off track to save you and it worked, then you stay too long and my boy fucks it all up."

"It can still work! I swear if you let me and my baby live, we'll leave right now—"

"I wish I could believe you, it sickens my heart to do this. Santi, I'm not telling you again. Get the fuck out of the way or you could get hurt. I'll forgive you if you start minding me now!"

"I hate you! I'd rather be dead than be your son! Abby is my family and Rachel and CeCe and Miguel and Charlie! What are you going to do—kill us all?"

Baca looked devastated and weakened. He blinked like he'd been sucker punched and wiped at his face, shaking his head. He actually started to cry some sloppy, angry tears, his voice pleading. "How can you say that to me, mi'jo? I'm your papa! Why do you hurt me so? You think I want to kill this nice lady and her baby? This is all your fault, not mine. And Roberto—with his hot head and too much to drink, ordering me to leave my own home . . . stupid *vato*!"

Just as Abby thought he might put down the gun, the sound of sirens began to howl in the distance. Getting louder quickly. Swallowing the space between them.

He raised the gun again and pointed it straight at them. "Last chance, mi'jo."

Santiago gripped a struggling Abby tighter from behind his firm stance. "You will have to look me in the eye, Papa, as you pull the trigger. Let her go!"

Car doors slamming, voices shouting outside. Another siren wailing closer . . .

"I can't kill you, mi'jo!"

Sheriff Bowman yelled through his megaphone, "Come out with your hands up, Baca, and no one gets hurt!"

Baca hesitated, still aiming the gun at Abby and Santiago.

"There's no way out, Baca, the place is surrounded. Put down your weapon and come out with your hands up!" Bowman repeated.

"I'm not going to no prison like some stupid pendejo!" Baca yelled. "Adios, mi'jo!" Baca raised the gun higher and in one quick motion, turned it on himself. Abby tried to put her hands over Santi's eyes as she pulled them both backward, falling to the floor, the single gunshot so loud, so shattering. The last sound Bobby ever heard.

One Year Later

Dear Edward,

Your birthday package arrived. I thought you were nuts sending a little Prada bag to a one-year-old, but Magdalena loves it. She's wearing it as a hat, as we speak. Did you get those last pictures I sent? Can you believe how much she looks like Bobby?

I guess I'll never find the right combination of words to help you understand why I am staying here. I look back on who I was in San Diego and I admire that woman, I am proud of her, how hard she worked. How singular was her purpose. The way her heart throbbed with adrenaline to begin another twenty-hour day, seeing her own face on the side of a bus, sitting in a television studio makeup chair discussing the latest skin-care products. Her mind whirred, processing a million vital details from wine pairings for the night's special to whether or not to force her husband into a tux for the mayor's charity ball on the night he came in from sub tour.

She loved it. She was in her element. I am not her. Not anymore, not ever again. Bobby was so right. We loved each other fiercely in the slots of time we had. That world we lived in, the way we lived, was such a compromise and I never even knew it. Staying here is not about my grief. It is not something to get over. I miss Bobby with a pain that has sometimes been so sharp, it nearly knocks me off my feet. More and more, the pain is quiet and wide and deep, more like a river flowing through me than a sudden burst of searing flames.

There is room for so much joy. And time. Time is what I notice the most these days. Long luxurious moments to watch the mountains change color with the light, watch my daughter learn how to balance herself on this earth and plant her two tiny feet, one after the other, until she is walking on its spinning surface.

Santiago comes home from school, bursting with stories about his friends, and we sit for long, unhurried moments at the table talking, listening, figuring out his math homework. He is blossoming again, after the terrible trauma last year. As hard as it was when they unearthed his mother's remains next to Bobby's, at least he knows she didn't leave him on purpose, a particular comfort tucked inside the greater loss. Something I know so well. After the long process of foster care and counseling, my adoption of him became final last week. The Vigils threw us a big bash, live music, dancing, barbecue—I think all of Esperanza came to celebrate. Santiago's happiness is intoxicating to me and the word "adoption" doesn't even begin to name what we are to each other.

From your world, which used to be mine, I know it doesn't sound like much to work part time alongside CeCe and Rachel at our small cafe with Maggie playing at our feet. The cheese business flourishes, the cafe is attracting more and more people from farther away. We are careful not to become too flashy, too successful. We keep it simple. It is not our lives.

Rachel and Charlie are soon to be remarried. CeCe is sewing her dress, a challenge given the bride-to-be is in her sixth month of pregnancy. Their new house is going to be ready just in time. It sits on a hill overlooking the river, not far from where Charlie's old trailer used to be. Witnessing them finding their way back to each other fills me with a kind of hope. Love doesn't protect us from loss, but it is the only way to have anything worth losing. The courage to embrace it despite the risk, that, to me, is what makes life worth having. Bobby taught me that and so much more. He rests in peace next to his parents. We bring flowers to his grave, but I know he isn't there. His adventures continue, of that I am certain. I feel him check in on us, I feel his love.

He brought me here to this new extended family that I feel I've known forever, and for that I am grateful. In this place called Esperanza, I am home.

Love you! Come visit us!
Abby